IMMINENT HOSTILITY

Innate Hostility Sequel A Kevin and Cole Novel

BRIAN DAVID SIMMONS

Imminent Hostility by Brian David Simmons

Published by Bright Crescent Sky. Bright Crescent Sky can be emailed at brightcrescentsky@pmt.org or brian@brightcrescentsky.com. Follow us on Facebook or visit our website for events, information, reviews, and new releases. Our website is brightcrescentsky.com. To contact Brian Simmons, email us at brightcrescentsky@pmt.org or brian@brightcrescentsky.com.

Library of Congress Control Number: 2023902180
Library of Congress Cataloging-in-Publication Data is available upon request.

International Standard Book Number (ISBN):
979-8-9859323-2-4 (print)
979-8-9859323-3-1 (ebook)

Cover by Melissa Thomas, Luminare Press

International Trade and Arms Regulation (ITAR) Statement: Any reference to weapons systems, rocket manufacturing or missile performance is readily available from internet sources or has been intentionally presented incorrectly in this work of fiction.

Printed in United States of America

Acclaim for Imminent Hostility

Great action adventure and a picture of what could actually happen. The story ended so quick it left me wanting more. Dominique was perfect for Cole, but I was disappointed when she…

Rex Riley, Godley Texas

Awesome. I really liked Dominique.

Kelly Hess, Ennis Montana

This book was a great follow on to Innate Hostility. Cole and Kevin still have a bit of an unsteady partnership, not quite trusting each other yet, but getting there. Dominique was a great addition. And who knew that Jack the pilot had that in him! Good story, plenty of action. Looking forward to the next book.

Joni Endicott, Mendon Utah

I love the story line and all the characters. Joe and Sylvia are very special. Interaction between Kevin and Cole is way cool. But I feel bad for Cole who can never live a normal life. Dominique was awesome. She and Cole would have been an unstoppable couple.

Patty Ault-Mota, Rupert Idaho

It's good. I really liked it. The only thing I didn't like was that Dominique…I was really getting to like her.

Mike Weatherwax, Twin Falls Idaho

*Dedicated to all the readers that
support unknown and emerging authors.*

Chapter 1

WASHINGTON POST

MIKE ARMENTA FINALLY GOT HIS INTERVIEW WITH General Whitten. The Washington Post was digging into arms buildup by the Argentine government, which was somehow linked to exports orchestrated by Chris Beech. Mike knew this was his chance for a really big story. Mike's investigative senses told him something was horribly amiss but he just couldn't pull it all together. Beech was an aerospace consultant specializing in ballistic missile technology and strangely exporting food processing equipment, industrial smoke stack scrubbers, and amusement park equipment to Argentina. Argentina had short range defensive missiles and had been trying to acquire upgrades from the French for years and then suddenly quit. Out in Utah, there were multiple homicide investigations. A ballistic missile expert, and known associate of Chris Beech, was murdered on the shores of the Great Salt Lake. A second rocket engineer had just vanished. Four other men died in a bizarre desert shootout. Adding to the confusion, Beech was somehow receiving huge sums of money through an Arkansas real estate escrow account. Collectively, it all just smelled.

Argentine missiles had to be the focus. Mike hoped he could get an official statement on the government's position related to short range missiles in Argentina. Maybe he could learn something that would help pull all the other pieces of the puzzle together.

Mike arrived early at the Pentagon and waited in line at the Defense Protective Service, DPS, office to get his clearance. He glanced at his watch and then studied the activities ahead. *This circus is just for looks,* he thought to himself. *If I was a foreign national spy of some kind, the cursory ID check ahead would be no challenge. I could probably get a visitor's badge with my sister's driver's license. Why do they even waste their time?*

Finally the line advanced to the lady in front of him. She was there for a visit with some procurement officer and negotiation for a lead pencil refills contract. *Why couldn't they just buy their pencil refills at Walmart like the rest of us?* After having answered all the questions correctly, she was granted her visitor's badge, directed through the metal detector, and given an escort that would take her to the procurement officer within the Pentagon maze. The short, heavy set, female guard barked, "Next," in a vulgar tone and Mike stepped up to counter. "I need a picture ID. Fill out your name, purpose of visit, citizenship status, point of contact and date of visit on the visitor sign-in sheet," she demanded in a caustic cackle.

Mike complied and then the questioning began, "Do you have any of the Covid symptoms listed on the sign? Cough, fever, headache, et cetera?" The et cetera came with emphasis as she shoved a personal certification in front of him to sign. Mike lied - just a little; he hadn't really felt fully up to par and had been downing throat lozenges by the hand full and seriously drinking cough suppressant. After he signed the form, she barked again, "Firearms, explosives, cameras, recording devices are not allowed. Do you have any of these devices?"

"No, I left my camera and recorder at home along with my bombs," he said with a chuckle followed by a slight cough.

"Just answer yes or no, unless you want to be arrested!"

Mike knew better and forced out an insincere apology, "Sorry. No, I do not have any of those devices." He studied the security patch on her uniform and concluded to himself, Yep DPS for dips.

"Do you have an appointment with General Whitten?" she snapped.

"Yes."

"I'll verify," she said as she dialed the phone. "Step to the front of the metal detector and I'll have your badge in thirty seconds."

She got her verification, handed him his visitor's badge, waved him through the metal detector and then barked at the people standing in line, "Next."

He'd arrived early, but he was now late and General Whitten's office was at least a mile hike. His escort greeted him and assured him they would make it in time. She was young, in a lieutenant's uniform and very unattractive. She was probably a jock of some type because her shoulders were wider than his and she was missing the visible features normally included on a woman. Mike wasn't going let any opportunity escape, especially since he'd waited nearly two months for this appointment. As they shook hands Mike asked, "Have you ever met a Chris Beech?"

She curtly replied, "Sir, I'm not at liberty to discuss any Pentagon business with reporters."

Mike studied her face for indications of recognition and asked, "Well, I didn't really mean Pentagon business. Just anytime, anywhere do you recall the name Chris Beech?"

Mike saw no tell-tale signs that the name, Chris Beech, triggered any sign of recognition. She insisted they get on their way. The Pentagon is a massive complex with five pentagonal concentric buildings connected by ten spoke connecting corridors sitting on thirty four acres. Mike and his escort needed to reach "4E8306," which meant fourth floor, "E-ring, eighth corridor, office six; they headed off at a rapid pace. Upon reaching the D-ring, Mike stopped; something was wrong. He broke into a sweat and began an uncontrollable cough; the more he hacked the greater the urge to cough. Mike had been to the doctor, who told him that it was residual symptoms of Covid or a bad cold and he would just have to work the congestion out of his lungs, but the doctor's assurances were no consolation at the

    Brian David Simmons

moment. His escort asked if he was alright and Mike was forced to gather his composure to respond, "Yes, just out of breath. Must be getting old."

They continued to the E-ring. Mike continued clearing his throat and struggling for the strength to hold back his cough. In-spite of what the doctor told him about working the congestion out of his lungs, Mike took a swig of a liquid suppressant; it helped. Finally they made it to the Air Force Corridor and moved quickly past several display cases and portraits. The last portrait was that of General Hap Arnold; it caught his attention because the man was smiling, almost to the point of laughing. And laughing was the last thing Mike wanted to do; it would aggravate his cough and end his chance for the interview.

Then Mike stopped and his escort turned to stare at him. Her mouth moved but he heard no words. He stooped over, hacking and gasping for air. Mike temporarily regained his composure and stood upright. His escort was saying something but words failed to register. His field of vision narrowed; the darkness started at the fringes of his peripheral vision and then closed down to a pinpoint of light. Mike stumbled and then extended his arms with his last conscious thought as he fell face forward to the floor.

His escort summoned on-site EMS and then began CPR. EMS arrived and hit him with the defibrillator. The third attempt with the defibrillator managed to restart his heart briefly, but Mike Armenta was already dead.

Chapter Two

Mr. Slow

Hamilton Cole Davis sat on the steps of his defunct camp trailer. Cole had purchased the trailer and an aging Chevrolet pickup for the sole purpose of blending in with the near homeless, along with the affluent snowbirds, that flocked to the Arizona desert in the winter months. Dry camping in the desert meant you survived on food and water brought in and managed waste needs with a biweekly trip hauling the camper to the holding tank dump station. In the desert, the elite with million dollar motor homes mingled with the poor surviving in tents or antiquated campers; it was really an amazing abandonment of dichotomy, with station in life secondary to the camaraderie of desert living.

The stove top in Cole's trailer worked but not much else. Refrigerator marginally cooled but most perishable food and beer had to be kept in a cool chest, which was becoming increasing more difficult as March was slipping away and daytime temperatures were on the rise. Cole had to make an increasing number of trips to the town of Quartzsite just for ice. Sometimes he'd treat himself to some of the best pizza he had ever eaten at Crazy's or a red beer at Bottoms Up, but always in isolation, minimizing interpersonal contact, always on high alert, and, most importantly, avoiding being captured on someone's cell phone or one of the twenty-eight surveillance cameras in town. There were those in the world that thought he was dead and it needed to stay that way. Truth was that the desert was the only place Cole didn't have to be on constant alert.

Some of the snowbirds had already fled back north with their motor homes and trailers, leaving his nearest neighbor five hundred feet from his front door. And they were unknowingly his best entertainment. From Cole's camper step he could monitor their comings and goings from their million dollar motor home. They were camped in an area known as the Magic Circle and played naked in the desert like children set free. They rode bicycles naked. They went on long walks naked. They visited their neighbors naked. They went to the community happy hours naked. They went to the community bonfire naked. They drove their Jeep through the desert naked – and drunk. Their lives were one continuous party and they were enjoying every minute of it. It was astounding to watch, having sagging body parts yet dancing through the end of life without a care in the world. Cole wished someday he could end up so lucky.

Cole studied the landscape's mix of volcanic and quartz rocks and the amazing vegetation that ekes out life in the absence of moisture and soil nutrients. Yellow Paloverde and Iron Wood trees flourished in a nearby wash that had been vacant of water for at least six months. Saguaro and Cholla cactus survived in the open spaces covered by volcanic gravel with no moisture other than a few hundredths of inch rain that had fallen over the last couple of months. Cole had been there nearly two months and it had only parsimoniously attempted to rain twice, leaving moisture that evaporated almost as fast as it hit the ground. His life was not that much different from the desert flora; surviving on the bare minimums of life. Where was the joy? Where was the companionship? Where was the nourishment that comes from the sense of community? Where was the freedom that normalcy offered? Was he going to hide from the world his entire life? Was this really life or just an avoidance of death?

Any hope of achieving normalcy meant controlling his 'sickness,' as his friend Kevin had phrased it. His thoughts wandered back to his childhood. Hate, assault, injury, and killing were embedded deep in his very soul by his upbringing. Much of the hate he had been able to purge, but the violence was always there, just beneath the surface. It was crazy by normal standards that parents would teach a three year old to inflict pain on another three year old and encourage slug fest contests to see who came out a winner. It was crazy by any standards that parents would teach a five year old martial arts skills intended to maim or kill. Even more insane that parents would encourage an eight year old to practice the skills on dummies made up to look like black children. Would a normal

     Brian David Simmons

mother beam with pride when her twelve year old son demonstrated long-range, high power rifle assassination skills on dummies made up to look like FBI agents? No! But such was the Patriot Rebirth Society compound of his youth.

He wished his parents could have enjoyed a different life, perhaps one as fun and carefree as his entertainment nudists. Cole's life would have been so much different then, as well. But, if this, if that, really didn't matter. It is what it is.

Circumstances in the past had required him to exercise his 'sickness.' It wasn't the act of killing that bothered him; it was the lack of remorse. Why didn't he feel anything? A normal person would feel something, wouldn't they? Did it mean he was a psychopath? He had loved his mother dearly and was saddened by her death, so he could feel. He loved his grandmother and was saddened by the memory of her death. He had once known and loved a wonderful southern bell that could have someday been his wife, so he had yearnings of the heart. Why then was killing such an easy thing? Cole usually found his answers with isolation and desert living. But even after months of soul searching, he had none.

Movement fifty feet out brought Cole back to the present. A rattle snake was slowly making its way towards Cole's trailer. He had seen them before. For the most part, they were harmless if left alone. But this one was on the advance. Off in the distance, the nudists had guests. They were having an early morning cocktail hour and were talking, laughing and drinking while sunning themselves in the Arizona sun. It still struck Cole odd that geriatrics would shed all inhibitions and literally just let it all hang out. It was even odder that he had become their number one clandestine fan over the last two months.

Cole reached into the cool chest and retrieved a morning beer; it was still cold, but the ice was nearly gone. He would have to make another trip to town. The rattle snake continued its advance. It was a four-foot Mojave Green clearly identifiable by its greenish olive color and a chain of black diamonds down its back. Interesting, thought Cole. Actually it seemed too early in the year for snakes to be on the move. And the Mojave Green usually hides in the brush: waiting for its prey, waiting to unleash its toxic venom, waiting to strike from the shadows, seldom showing itself unless tempted by gain or revenge. This one came right out in the open as if it wanted something; just slowly plotting its course across gravelly volcanic rock. Cole drew his fist to his mouth and blew as he considered the snake's fate and his options. What would bring a snake out in the open? He took another swig of beer.

Cole heard a buzz overhead and glanced up. One of his distant neighbors was playing with their toy again. Some people ran through the desert naked; others flew kites while they read a book; and others played with elaborate toys. The drone made a pass off

     Brian David Simmons

in the distance and then circled back directly overhead. Cole watched as it passed overhead and then made its path back to the west.

The Mojave Green made its way to within ten feet of where Cole was sitting. Cole got up and walked over to the back of the pickup truck. The snake strangely changed course and advanced in Cole's direction. Cole picked up the shovel in the back of the truck and met the snake on its path. The snake began to curl and prepare for its strike. His mother had routinely used a shovel to sever heads from snakes. Cole raised the shovel and then thrust it downward.

The shovel stabbed the ground directly in front of the snake; the Mojave Green stuck with lightning speed, striking the shovel before it ever hit the ground. It rebounded, shook it's head as if to say "what the hell" and then quickly recoiled only to strike again. Cole withdrew the shovel and thrust it downward again. The snake repeated its two strike attack and then, still stunned from its attacks, slowly recoiled.

"Slow learner aren't you," commented Cole.

Cole left the shovel in place and stepped back. Giving the snake a wide berth, he circled around to the camper door and went inside. Chicken in the fridge had probably already gone bad given the marginal performance of the fridge. He retrieved a breast and rejoined the snake still positioned at the shovel. Cole dropped the breast directly in front of the snake and it responded, swallowing the breast whole. The snake extended its body and the breast slowly began moving downward with subtle contractions and relaxations of its body. Cole watched as the snake's digestive processes slowly began consuming the chicken breast. "I think I'll name you Mister Slow: slow crawler, slow learner and slow eater."

Chapter Three

GUARDIANS

CHRIS BEECH BEGAN MAKING HIS PRESENTATION TO State Department Undersecretary Wilfred Woods and an assemblage of civil service analysts. The government didn't usually work on Saturday, but this came as an unusual request from the highest of sources. The undersecretary and his committee were entrusted with evaluating and recommending exclusions to the Technology Export Act of 1991. The Act specifically disallows export of technology that could result in damage to the United States, financial or other. Within the body of the legislation, an elaborate description of rocket motors, subsystems and their components is thoroughly laid out, all of which are subject to export restrictions. Simply interpreted, no U.S. citizen can sell for export, or export for sale, any high technology rocket system, rocket subsystem, rocket system or subsystem design, or any high performance rocket materials. But, Beech needed to stretch the rules.

Beech's presentation started with a semi-technical description of Argentine's POGO rocket and a basic comparison to U.S. ballistic rockets. His intent was to partially bore the panel, but also to impress upon them the antiquated technology of the Argentine system.

"The propellant formulation is a low grade perchlorate oxidizer in an aluminized polybutediene binder. The formulation is essentially ammonium nitrate fertilizer suspended in tire rubber. The propellant's performance is only 142 lb.-seconds/lb. as compared to the 1st stage Trident E-6 248 lb.-seconds/lb. In terms of payload and range, the POGO can only lift a sixth the load and achieve forty-five percent of the velocity at burnout as the 1st stage Trident. And, remember the Trident is a three-stage bird; the POGO is only a one. In other words, it would simply be impossible to use the POGO as an intercontinental ballistic missile. Even if they tried to multi-staged it, the tire rubber propellant doesn't have the performance to lift even a single upper stage."

Beech knew exactly what arguments the State Department needed to grant his license and delineated each critical point. He backed up his claims with calculations and graphs and then went on to elaborate on the current strategic uses of the POGO. With background laid, he made his proposal, only he left out the truth; he had been milking the Argentinians for years, extracting millions of dollars, and had already given them a complete upgrade design package.

"Gentlemen, my company proposes to retrofit the POGOs with a guidance system to better control their missile. We have already designed, built, and tested prototypes at considerable expense to my company, and we are requesting permission to enter into tech-

     Brian David Simmons

nical discussions with the Argentine government and eventually sell up to fifty-two guidance systems. To summarize, let me reiterate my key points. First, the POGO has no intercontinental capability and is, in no way, a threat to the United States. Second, my retrofit proposal does not increase performance of the missile; it only improves controllability of the missile. Third, the Argentine government is stable and for more than two decades has continually striven for peace within its own country as well as with other peaceful nations of the world. And finally, even in the unlikely event of a military dispute with Argentina, the POGOs could readily be defeated with superior anti-ballistic missile technology."

Beech went on, "Gentlemen, this is good business for our country and good business for you." He meant that in more ways than one. The only reason Beech had gotten this far in the bureaucratic maze was because he knew what it took. It had started with select campaign contributions and check presentation ceremonies clear up through Vice-President Cluttle. Beech had even met the president and had a private five-minute conversation with him; all because of a little contributed campaign money.

It was the president himself who had requested the State Department review the Beech's proposal. Undersecretary Woods and the panel understood the importance of political back scratching and the power of connections on the Hill.

"Mr. Beech," started the undersecretary. "If you will allow us a short caucus to consider your proposal, I think we can wrap this up this morning. Would you please excuse us for a few moments? Have Melissa at the desk out front get you a cup of coffee and a delicatessen roll. They're especially good today: powdered and puffed with pomegranate jelly on the side."

Chris stepped out of the conference room and helped himself to a cup of coffee. He felt confident about his presentation and knew he could count on a positive decision from the committee. He had only one concern: how to collect the most from the Argentinians. Truth was that he had already provided a missile guidance system based on motion simulator amusement park rides, but it only had an accuracy of a square mile. He'd promised a square foot. And if he didn't deliver, he would miss out on millions of fees.

"Well, Chris, the jury's in. Come on back in here," invited the undersecretary. When they all settled in at the conference table he continued, "You know we have a hard time granting exclusions for some things. Now, you say the Argentinians have upgraded their movable nozzle and that isn't a problem, assuming you didn't provide them with any upgrades in materials. But your electronics and guidance technology is a problem. A quick look at your design indicates targeting is probably better than ten feet; and that is a huge problem. You see, we have the highest regard for your integrity and intentions. However, if the guidance technology

     Brian David Simmons

you provide to the Argentinians is misused, adapted, or sold to someone who would do the same, then it's conceivable that this technology could be improperly used against us or a friend of ours. What can we do to back off on the level of technology for your system?"

Chris was caught completely off guard by the decision of the committee. Hadn't he paid enough? Over five million in bribes and political contributions, and these oafs weren't going to grant him his license. Inside he wanted to pound that fat double-crosser. Chris knew he had to conceal his emotion and come up with the right angle. "Yes, sir, I see your point; but I am truly disappointed. Especially since I have so much invested in this, both personally and financially. Would you reconsider?"

"We might be able to stretch the guidelines a little, but a full guidance package, no."

The line had been drawn and Chris could tell it wasn't going to move; Chris was going to have to compromise and work the angle another way. "Would you consider electronic controls for the nozzle, exclusive of the guidance package, as being acceptable for export?"

"Well, I'm not sure that our people could tell the difference. We would have to have the Air Force Ballistic Missile Office look over the design and perform the actual hardware inspections. But, I don't think that would do. It's not their function to monitor commercial rocket activities. Whatever we authorize will have to be verified by DTRA. They will require a Technology Transfer Control Plan and have responsibility for monitoring all design and information transfer."

Beech saw the bureaucratic meddling that was coming his way and searched for an out, "Would all that really be necessary if I limited the scope of my export request?"

"If we did grant a partial license, we would have to rely somewhat on your personal integrity to limit the electronic packages."

"That would be fine, sir," interrupted Chris. "I'll authorize production of the movable nozzle control boxes to start next Monday."

The undersecretary strained at the thought of doing something he knew was pushing the limits, but he agreed. His word was his promise and he would have the executive exclusion order signed by Vice-President Cluttle. Beech could pick up the documentation two weeks from Friday. There was little chance Cluttle would go against the recommendation of the State Department; in fact, he very seldom went against the recommendation of anybody that was willing to make a decision and take responsibility for it.

In reality, Beech had already provided the Argentinians much of what was needed, legal or not. Failure on his part to deliver the missile guidance boxes would cost him thirteen million dollars and he was pissed. The Argentinians weren't happy with the missile guidance boxes based on amusement park virtual motion ride electronics; they wanted the square foot

     Brian David Simmons

accuracy he'd promised. He was going to end up leaving millions on the table. But then maybe he could disguise the guidance package as "nozzle electronics." How would the bureaucratic meddling undersecretary know?

As far as everything else, he had delivered on all his other commitments. He had already pressed ahead with fabrication per the design his team had provided Haipler Aerotech Products. Haipler fabricated almost all nozzles for small ICBMs during the cold war days. They had fabricated Minutemans, Poseidon C-3s, Trident C-4s and D-5s, and SICBMs. When the wall came down and the world became a friendlier place, the demand for ICBMs had diminished and Haipler had gone out of business. All of the equipment still existed, mothballed, at their Compton warehouse. At least it was thought to be a warehouse; it was really put back in production running balls-to-walls turning out nozzles and rocket components. Haipler had agreed to turn the lights back on and fabricate Beech's nozzles, but only at an outlandish price of four million each. Fifty-two nozzles disguised as choke point constrictors for industrial smoke stack filtering systems had already been shipped.

As soon as Chris Beech departed, Undersecretary Woods started to get cold feet. Woods was a man of his word and he wasn't about to reverse his partial agreement with Beech, even if it caused him personal strife. This was one of Wilfred Woods' weaknesses. He was a mild-mannered, agreeable, easy-going guy who sometimes caved in to things he knew were wrong. On this one, he figured he'd let it happen and agreed to too much. What bothered him, perhaps more than anything else, was the way the conversation had ended with him being outmaneuvered by a simple used-car-salesman's closing technique: Beech interrupting at a moment of conciliation with "that will be fine, sir. I'll start tomorrow." The words just seemed to hang with him like indigestion.

The more Woods thought about the salesman's closing, the madder he got. That maneuvering weasel is probably lying through his teeth, thought Woods. I'll support his export license exemption, but, if he steps out of line just a little, I'll pull the carpet out from under him. Woods picked up the phone and called Jeff Monson at the CIA. Jeff was the deputy director and Woods had known him for years. He also knew that Jeff was about as dedicated as they come and worked every Saturday and most holidays. Jeff was all business and no play.

"This is Wilfred. Glad to see I'm not the only fool working Saturdays. How are things?"

"Things are fine. You still kissing Cluttle's lily-white for a living? Or do you want to come over here and do some real work?"

"You guys just put up a front. As for real work, nobody knows what you really do. Besides, if I went to work for you, I would probably have people calling me on Saturdays asking for favors."

"What do you need, Wilfred? The neighbor kids bothering you and you think I'm a policeman?"

"Kind of. We are going to grant, or I should say Cluttle is going to grant, an exclusion to the Technology Export Act for export of rocket nozzle control electronics to Argentina. But I have an uneasy feeling about it and I'm not sure I trust the guy running the show for the Argentinians. I'd like you to get involved and do some checking up on this guy and his operation. His name is Chris Beech and his company's name is Space Sciences Corporation."

As Jeff scribbled a note, he reviewed his simplified summation of the situation, "Let's see, Beech, Space Sciences, technology export, Argentina, nozzles, electronics, and rockets. I'll flow this down to the high-tech guys and have somebody contact you on Monday for all the details. Anything else?"

The phone conversation ended and Wilfred Woods felt better. It might also earn him a little atta-boy from Cluttle. He could tell the vice-president that the exclusion was very limited and to be checked on by the CIA. In truth, he could tell him that the CIA was already investigating.

Chapter Four

GAME

Kevin McKuel stared at his monitor. Nothing —it just wasn't the same. He actually missed his job at Omage creating secure cloud based platforms that were a complex interaction of hardwired servers, computational computers and software. The "game" that had once consumed every moment of his non-work related life had lost its appeal. Tid-bits of misinformation placed within the tentacles of the web, intrusion into individuals' social media and email accounts along with clever postings, erroneous reports filed in law enforcement databases, half-truth stories posted to the API news website, and other web transgressions could destroy an individual. He had once prided himself as a master of illusion and cyber-assassination going after public and corporate figures that violated his sense of right and wrong. But the allure was now gone.

He thought of his precision tuned Porsche. He missed the acceleration and paddle shifting up through the gears that had once been so exhilarating. The Porsche was the only thing, other than his "game," that had given satisfaction to his life. But that was all in the past. Now his life seemed isolated and empty. Isolation had once been his solace and allowed him to focus all his energy on the cyber world. Hamilton

Cole Davis had changed all that and turned his focus to the criminal money laundering world. He had been an enthusiastic participant at the time but now questioned the sanity of it all. Isolation had now become a survival requirement instead of a choice.

Money laundering through the commodity futures market is simple in concept with managed losses of dirty money replaced with managed gains coming out as clean and reportable money. Teanzo Vincelli would lose short on oil and corn but win long on pork and oranges; Alfonz Winfree would lose short on pork and oranges but win long on oil and corn. The complexity was in management of the futures contracts to make it all work out in the end and that's where Kevin had hurt them. Their broker and master of artificial intelligence orchestrated trades had millions of illicit dollars riding the ups and downs of the commodity futures market. Kevin had attacked their broker's complex computer system and algorithms and used a multiplicity of five-to-one leveraging to turn dozens of accounts ripe with dirty money into enormous client deficit margin calls. The managed clean money side of the ledger had left Cole and him with all the gains. Losses weren't the only thing to raise their ire. Kevin also ensured that the financial crimes arm of the United States Treasury had their broker's client list and trade history.

How long would he live if anyone of the broker's clients found out he was responsible? Had he and

Cole sufficiently hid their actions? Kevin continued to ponder. If the domestic cartels, U.S. government, or foreign elements discovered what they had done, would he survive past noon? Incarceration at first, maybe, but in the end the criminal elements would ensure he died.

Kevin continued to stare at his monitor. The screen was blank and the computer had gone into sleep mode. How many days had it been since he'd seen the sunlight, he questioned? Soon Sylvia would be bringing lunch down to his self-imposed dungeon; she was such a sweet woman. Then she and Joe would be off for a walk down the beach. If they found him, what would happen to Joe and Sylvia? Would they become "collateral" damage? Even worse, if they found out one of the winning futures accounts was in Joe and Sylvia Atkins names, their fate would surely be the same as his. Could they trace Joe and Sylvia's futures market successes back to the broker? If they did, finding them here on Tobago, Robinson Caruso's island, would be an easy feat.

The blank computer monitor glared back at him and transcendentally scolded him for what he was about to do. Not just wrong, but really wrong. Over the past several months he had put together banks of servers and cloned elements of Japan's Fugaku supercomputer to give him storage and computational capability exceeding most third world countries. His version of the Fugaku paled in comparison to the real Fugaku, but still had 2,566 teraFLOPs of processing power. It also paled in comparison to Huey, Dewey and Lewey, the three Hewlett Packard supercomputers used by the Department of the Treasury's FinCEN (Financial Crimes Enforcement Network) organization. And that's where Kevin was headed.

Blaine Higgins, director of the CIA's Strategic Resource department, had once been a target of Kevin's game. Higgins had been diverting funds from congressionally authorized programs to investigate politicians not of his liking and Kevin had discovered enough circumstantial data to at least raise questions. Kevin had accessed Higgins's home computer and sent incriminating email's, texts, and Facebook posts to hopefully generate an investigation. An investigation had never materialized but Kevin still had access to his personal computer. Along with other embedded routines, Kevin had implanted a change to the operating system that left the system powered even after the computer had been properly shut down. Essentially, the "Shut Down" command just put the personal computer into a sleep mode accessible only by Kevin.

Kevin stared at his monitor and planned his attack. Every step had to be with extreme caution to avoid detection and would take every bit of his skill. His concentration on the blank monitor screen was intense and he heard something from behind. It didn't deter his planning. Then he felt a hand on his shoulder as he began to emerge from his trance.

"Kevin, I swear you're going to go blind if you keep looking at that thing," said Sylvia Atkins. "And you didn't even eat the lunch I brought down earlier."

"Huh," replied Kevin as he struggled to return to the here and now.

"You have to eat sometime and a little sunshine wouldn't do you any harm either."

"What time is it?"

"It's dinner time and I'm not bringing it down to you. You're going to have to leave that chair, come upstairs and eat with Joe and me. It's just not right that you should stay down here with all these computer things and their little blinking lights," pleaded Sylvia gently.

"I'm sorry. I'm just getting ready to do something that takes a lot of concentration."

"So that's what you call it. Kevin, please come up stairs. It's just not healthy for a young man to spend all his hours down here in the dark. You have to eat and get some exercise. Please, just do it for me."

Kevin's heart melted at the request and he relinquished, "Okay, but I really do have work to do tonight."

"It can just wait. Now come take my arm and help me up the stairs."

Kevin did as Sylvia requested and was soon seated at the table staring across at Joe Atkins. Joe's stare was strong yet somehow still kind. He was a big man, more than six feet and still had the muscular build of a man half his age. They were an odd couple thought Kevin:

Joe, a burly black man in excellent shape for a man approaching seventy, and Sylvia, a delicate Hispanic flower. But they were no doubt in love and that's what mattered most.

"Sylvia's meatloaf is amazing. Glad you decided not to miss out," stated Joe.

Kevin glanced out the window. The sun was still shining bright and reflected off the pure white beach sand. The ocean waves gently lapped up onto the sand and a beauty he not noticed before warmed his inner being. For a moment, he felt content. And with the first bite of meatloaf, he felt cared for and loved. It was a strange feeling. This was truly an amazing couple living in truly an amazing place. He ate slowly and savored every bite.

"I know better than to ask because I know you boys are up to super-secret stuff. But how is Cole?" asked Joe.

Kevin took another bite of meatloaf and then replied, "I really don't know but I need to call him soon."

"That would be good. Want to go put your toes in the ocean with Sylvia and I after dinner?"

"No, I really need to work."

"All work and no play make Johnny a dull boy."

"I know but it's important."

Kevin finished his dinner and little more was said. He helped Sylvia clear the table and load the dishwasher as Joe read a few pages of the Atlanta

Times he'd gotten in the mail. Kevin departed towards the basement stairs but promised to be back up for breakfast.

Back in front of his monitor, he stared and waited until it felt just right. He swirled the mouse and the screen came to life. He checked his list of routines in his tool box and then entered his passport. The passport allowed him to emulate IP addresses and he chose Margret Brenner from Whitman, Arizona, who was seventy-eight and currently a resident of an assisted living home. It was just an additional line of defense and if anyone ever tracked it back to her, no one would believe her guilty of the transgressions that were about to occur. Higgin's PC was his second fixed IP address and hopefully he would get the blame for what was about to happen.

If detection traced back through Higgins's PC and through Margret Brenner's PC, detection would be faced with a passported IP address changing randomly at an average rate of fourteen times per second. And the majority of random IP addresses would be of Russian origin. Who better to blame? That was Kevin's primary line of defense.

Margret Brenner's PC sent a short string of code fed through the random web server IP addresses to enter the dream state of Blaine Higgins's PC. Her computer copied all of Higgins's files and then downloaded four programs from Kevin's tool box. Blaine Higgins's PC then dialed up the FinCEN fax number

     Brian David Simmons

to give Kevin access to the telephone multiplexer system. From there he initiated an iterative password search for each phone number listed in the directory and got four positives before the system locked out the search routine, which Kevin expected. He backed out and then repeated the process, gaining four more positives. He repeated the process until he had a total of one-hundred-twenty-eight confirmed telephone message system passwords. He was betting that the phone passwords would be variations of computer passwords and that's where he was headed next.

Blaine Higgins's PC then accessed an open portal of the FinCEN computer network. Kevin readied his Fugaku clone. The clone first hit each user account with a short string of register expanding code and then bombarded the portal with thousands of instantaneous variations of the associated password from the telephone directory. Normally a user is given four password tries before a system locks the user out. But the speed of Fugaku clone, along with temporary register expansion, expanded the number of iterative tries before locking out future attempts. The Fugaku yielded seventeen successful user names with associated passwords.

Kevin quickly accessed each of the user login-ins and checked the level of security clearance allotted each. Most were restricted as Confidential. But Sally Stromberg, with a telephone message system password of LOVETOSKI69! and a computer system password of LOVETOSKI69+, had Secret clearance.

Sally Stromberg logged in. Kevin explored the FinCEN computer system computational elements and data storage servers. He'd been there before, but never with Secret clearance. His first violation of the FinCEN computer system had been in search of money laundering data, but this trip was personal and much different. Kevin found his acquaintances Huey, Dewey and Lewey, FinCEN's three super computers.

Kevin's mind metamorphosed from the human world to become one with the ebbs and flows of electron pathways in and out of microchips, following the ones and zeros of code, and swirling down the fiber optic pathways. He probed and searched being ever watchful for signs of his nemesis, the Gatekeeper, whose mission was to identify unusual activity and send a spike through to the source and leave it open so its human masters could identify and capture the offender. The Gatekeeper was ever watchful with tentacles of exploratory code, always searching and challenging user activity to identify suspicious activity and those who went outside need-to-know parameters.

Kevin found what he was looking for. In the age of interdepartmental cooperation, federal agencies had provided for computerized data sharing between systems. Kevin's metamorphosed mind commanded his fingers on the keyboard at lighting speed and his hand to swirl and click the mouse with the ferocity of a tornado. Kevin accessed the FBI system and began exploring: more banks of super computers and a mas-

     Brian David Simmons

sive reservoir of data storage. He found active investigations and queried his name. Nothing, he wasn't there. He queried closed investigations. Again, nothing, he wasn't there. His mind momentarily returned to the human world and he breathed a sigh of relief.

Kevin queried Cole Davis and was befuddled. Cole Jefferson Davis, now deceased, had been a white supremacist leader in an organization called the Patriot Rebirth Society. The Patriot Rebirth Society had been classified as terrorist organization and was known for hate crimes against African Americans and Hispanics. Cole Jefferson Davis had been wounded during a FBI led raid on their compound in Kootenai County, Idaho. He later died while in custody of the local officials. His wife had been killed during the assault on the compound and his twelve-year-old son, Hamilton Cole Davis, had been sent to live with his grandmother in Boston. Kevin instantly did the math on the year of the compound assault and the age of his friend; it was him; Hamilton Cole Davis was the son of a white supremacists leader. "That deceitful jackass," mumbled Kevin. What else hadn't Cole told him?

Kevin read on. The investigation was closed except for one aspect. The sheriff who had made the activities of the Patriot Rebirth Society known to the FBI had been brutally killed in his own front yard one year after the assault on the compound. It was suspected that elements of the Patriot Rebirth Society were responsible for the sheriff's death and were still at large.

Kevin searched on Hamilton Davis and came up with his friend. Hamilton Cole Davis was a person of interest at one time associated with the death of an aerospace engineer in Utah. The murder of the engineer was yet unsolved and still an active FBI investigation. Hamilton Cole Davis, himself an aerospace engineer working at the same firm, had gone missing and at one time was wanted for questioning. But the summary also classified Hamilton Cole Davis as deceased. There was no mention of money laundering or the killings Cole had committed in Atlanta. Cole, as well as himself, could potentially re-enter society without facing legal consequences.

Kevin next went to the FBI's Facial Analysis, Comparison, and Evaluation (FACE) data base. He searched on himself and found nothing. He searched on Hamilton Cole Davis and found a depiction. The database also had links to fingerprint data and other captured personal data. Kevin went exploring. Hamilton Cole Davis had graduated from MIT with a master in aerospace engineering, had been granted a Confidential security clearance as part of employment with the SDRC aerospace firm, had an abandoned checking account and four unused credit cards. Status identified no spending activity and no known criminal acquaintances. Throughout his search, he found the repeated theme: deceased with terminated inquires.

Kevin went back to FACE and searched for the update routine. He copied a picture of an Asian male about Cole's age and inserted it into the update routine for Hamilton Cole Davis. At the instant the mouse clicked update, Kevin's metamorphosed world exploded in a brilliant flash of light and Kevin was hurled uncontrollably back through the fiber optics. He never saw it coming, but the signs were all there. The FBI had their own version of a Gatekeeper and it was pursuing him. Kevin fired one of his downloaded programs called Enslaver, designed to turn a Gatekeeper into a time keeper. The code attempted to attach itself to the advancing Gatekeeper tentacle but was instantly rejected and Kevin was in a forced retreat flying back through Stromberg's login, Higgins's PC, Brenner's PC, and on towards a Russian IP address. In a fraction of a second, the FBI Gatekeeper would spike his Fugaku clone and Kevin would be captured. The Passport blinked to a new IP address and Kevin terminated with only milliseconds to spare.

Chapter Five

POTATO-ROTI AND PIZZA

KEVIN SLEPT THROUGH MOST OF THE DAYLIGHT HOURS and awoke hungry. He could smell a fragrant cooking aroma of potato-roti in the house, even with his bedroom window open to the ocean breeze. He glanced out the window at the setting sun and watched the ocean waves gently lap up onto pure white beach sand. How awesome, he thought.

Sylvia had prepared fish tacos made from red snapper that Joe had caught earlier in the morning and a local specialty, potato-roti, as a side dish. She was excited about a scarlet ibis they had seen on their walk and that was the conversation that overtook all others at the dinner table. They had first seen it as a brilliant streak of red in the sky and then watched it settle into an inland swamp area.

After dinner, the subject changed to Cole; Sylvia insisted on talking to him. Kevin retrieved his satellite phone and dialed twelve numbers. The encrypted satellite phone triggered a signal transfer box hidden in the wall of a Days Inn motel in Atlanta and Kevin entered ten more numbers. The phone buzzed six times before being answered.

"Yes dear," came Cole's response.

"You ass. I'm here with Joe and Sylvia and they want to talk to you."

"Oh, how are they doing?"

"You ask them yourself," replied Kevin as he handed the phone to Sylvia.

Sylvia took the large unusual looking device from Kevin and held it awkwardly. "Cole, is that you?" she asked. And that started a phone call reminiscent of a mother-son conversation. Sylvia wanted to make sure he was doing okay and getting enough to eat. She went on to recount sightings of scarlet ibis and then on to describe other strange creatures they had seen, including chachalacas, leatherback turtles, horned screamers, and more. Cole talked about living in the desert and some of the walks he'd taken.

When she was done, she handed the phone to Joe. "Hi Cole. I can't add much more than Sylvia hasn't already told you. But Kevin did tell me a little bit about some of your adventures. I now understand more than I think I want to. So, I just want to say be damn careful. When you get a chance, come visit. I'll take you fishing."

Joe handed the phone back to Kevin. "I need to talk to Cole about some technical stuff," stated Kevin. "But I gotta go downstairs."

"Tell Cole he needs to come visit," commanded Sylvia. "Tell him I miss him."

"I will," finished Kevin as he headed for the security and privacy of the basement.

As Kevin started down the stairs, he asked Cole, "What the hell is the Patriot Rebirth Society?"

"Why do you ask?"

"Because you ass hole, you never told me a damn thing about being a white supremacist."

"I'm not a white supremacist. You've been prying into things again, haven't you?"

"I saw the FBI records on your Patriot Rebirth club. Or should I say KKK. Hang anybody lately? Maybe that's why you're such a psycho nut-case."

"Kevin!" shouted Cole. "I'll fill you in sometime, but not now. So just focus. I want to talk to you about something else. I've had just about enough of this damn hiding. It's time to do something different and I've been doing a lot of thinking."

"Oh yeah, I was going to tell you," meekly replied Kevin. "I did some checking. You can probably quit hiding from the cops. You're only flagged as a once-upon-a-time person of interest in the FBI database. You're deceased and they don't care about you."

"That's good to know," replied Cole, "because I've been captured on camera several times."

"Who got you?"

"Maybe it won't matter. But, I've been going down to Los Algodones Mexico with my Cody Calhoon passport. What I didn't realize is that the Border Patrol takes your picture at the ID check station when you re-enter the United States. Then, they get me again half way between Yuma and Quartzsite at a roadway check station, which means they got a picture of me as well as my truck."

"Why'd you go to Mexico?"

"Because I needed to feel normal. You know - go to the bar, go sight-seeing, chase a senorita, and do it all without having to hide from every video camera they have in this country."

"Oh, now I understand. You just wanted to get laid – didn't you? Cha-cha-cha style, I'll bet."

"Knock it off, Kevin. Stay on task. What about the Border Patrol capturing my picture?"

"You made multiple trips and they didn't stop you or anything?"

"Nope."

Kevin pondered a moment and then concluded, "I think they just use facial recognition to verify the picture on the ID is the person coming through. I'll check."

"Then maybe I shouldn't worry about it. Besides, I've had enough of not living life. I need to get out.

"It's still risky. Keep using Cody Calhoon and don't leave fingerprints anywhere."

"I'm not sure I care anymore. I'm going crazy out here."

"Going. You're already crazy. We already established that fact."

"Shut up, Kevin. Anything else?"

"Just because the Federal Government has software to filter out the dead, it doesn't mean anyone else will. So you still need to stay off video. Maybe state or local cops won't have the Fed software. Or maybe even some commercial facial recognition programs could ID you. You'll never be totally free and clear in today's world."

"Well, at least Cody Calhoon is going to live a little."

Cole slept in the following morning and woke with a slight hangover. He managed a bowl of cold cereal with canned milk and then stepped out into the sunshine. The temperature was already at least eighty; it was going to be hot one. And another boring day watching the theatrics of the geriatric nudists; Cole didn't know if he could stand another day of not living. Maybe he could take the truck and go explore more of the remnants left by George Patton's army when they were training for World War II, but he'd already been out there a dozen times. He'd also visited all the mines and deteriorating structures strewn across the desert at least twice. Another trip to Mexico was an option.

Movement from above caught his eye; it was the geriatrics again playing with their drone. Then Mister Slow appeared from the wash and began making his way towards Cole. Cole retreated to the fridge and pulled two chicken legs from a package. When he returned to the front door of the camper, it seemed as if Mister Slow's speed increased in anticipation of the chicken. Cole sat on the step and waited. Mister Slow arrived and paused at a distance of about five feet. Cole threw the first of the chicken legs out and Mister Slow took it whole. The chicken leg began its

     Brian David Simmons

path down through the snake. Cole didn't wait; he tossed the second leg in the snake's direction and it too was consumed. The two lumps slowly moved down the snake's body with contractions and relaxations. This is nuts thought Cole. There has to be more to life than hiding in the desert with a lethal snake as your only companion.

Chapter Six

SATURDAY NIGHT POKER

THIS WEEK'S GAME WAS BEING HOSTED BY JACOB McCarry who had prepared a fine feast of lasagna, pork wieners, cheese, crackers and apples. Apples were odd for the poker feast but they were Jake's favorite. Players were all either CIA or FBI. Gardner shuffled the deck and then back-shuffled with a whirling sound only he could produce. Each shuffle of the cards was done with precision, just like his investigative work for the FBI. Frank Wallace worked with Gardner in the D.C. office of the FBI and Jake figured him for tonight's real challenge.

After hours of play, there was no clear winner or loser. Frank got up and stretched as poker night neared its last hand. Frank retrieved his third plate of lasagna and pork wieners. Jake didn't know how he could eat so much.

Betting began for the last hand. "The bet's two dollars," said Jake in a western yelp. Norman threw his two dollars in, clapped his hands and then smiled as if to say: "I'm going to screw you." David, also FBI, slid his cards across the table face down. Frank tossed in four dollars letting everyone know he had something. To his surprise, they all, except for David who had folded, followed sequentially adding two more dollars.

Gardner pulled three cards one at a time off the top of the deck and laid them face up on the table: Jack of Hearts, Three of Hearts, and Six of Spades. Hanley folded his cards. Norman threw in five dollars; Frank hesitated for just an instant before adding his five to the pot. Jake commented, "Looks like that little pair ain't enough."

"Is two bullets little enough?" replied Frank before Gardner called.

"Still just a little pair. You ought to know better."

"Are you trying to bait me? I'm going to kick your ass, Jake," replied Frank and then pointed at Gardner, "Let's have it."

Gardner slid another card off the top of the deck and turned it over next to the other three. It was an Ace of Spades. The bet was now back to Frank "Check," said Frank coolly.

"I'll check along," followed Gardner.

"I always knew you FBI boys were pussys. Let's go max bet," smarted Jake as he tossed in a folded five dollar bill.

"How's five and five more from this pussy," said Norman in a cocky tone.

"Make it fifteen," said Frank.

Gardner quietly added fifteen to Frank's surprise and Jake didn't hesitate either. "Pot's right," said Jake as he added a ten. "Let's see the last card," Jake added in a momentary sign of weakness.

Gardner peeled off another card from the top of the deck and dramatically laid it down with the others. It was a Nine of Hearts. Jake thought he saw a hint of smile from Frank. The bet was now around to Gardner who added a five without hesitation. Jake finished the beer on the table next to him, took a bite from an apple to further the delay, and then emotionlessly said, "Make it ten."

Norman reluctantly slid his cards to the center of the table and commented that he didn't think he could beat trips. Frank looked at his face down cards, as if he'd forgotten what he had. "Let's go up another five," he said in a whimper.

"Three raise max, right?" asked Gardner before adding fifteen. "That's ten more to you Jake."

Jake added ten more and Frank followed with another five to even the pot. "Let's see em cowboy," demanded Frank.

"I say I got you beat," replied Jake. "Didn't you say something about kicking my ass? What'd you say to little side bet? I still got sixty-two dollars here in front of me that says you don't kick my ass."

Gardner interrupted, "No way. We all agreed to the poker rules up front. This is just a friendly little game and nobody gets hurt."

"No, it's alright Gardner. And this is last hand for the night, anyway. The cowboy and I'll just have a little side bet," said Frank as he contemplated the outcome. Jake knew the wheels were turning in Frank's head: best hand Jake could have was trips but he didn't play that way. The possible flush didn't appear until the last

     Brian David Simmons

card. He got strong in the middle which means he's only got two pair and that won't beat my three nines.

"You're on cowboy. Let's see'em," Frank said.

Jake flipped his cards right side up and tossed them to the center of the table; he'd been holding a six and queen of hearts. The cards landed next to the three, nine, and jack of hearts already face up in the middle of the table.

"Damn. You got balls boy," exclaimed Frank and threw his cards to the center of the table.

Chapter Seven

Woo-Zoo

Cole could take no more. This morning would be just like the last: get up, eat a crappy breakfast, feed the snake, and go to town for ice and beer. Then this afternoon, sit here all day watching the geriatrics. He decided today would be different.

Cole had breakfast and threw a chicken thigh out the door for Mister Slow. Cole retrieved his cell phone and, with a cup of coffee in hand, took his place on the camper step. Mister Slow was on the advance and the annoyance of the drone returned. Mister Slow arrived at his breakfast delight and began the swallowing and digestive process. "What are you going to do when I'm gone?" Cole asked the snake.

Cole finished his coffee and then dialed Kevin. It took twenty-two numbers in all, including going through a signal transfer relay in Houston. The phone rang and rang; Cole was about ready to disconnect.

"What?"

"Kevin?"

"What? I'm sleeping."

"Well then get up. We got shit to talk about," insisted Cole

"You ignoramus. Maybe I don't want to talk to you."

"Oh come on. You love me and you know it."

"The hell I do!"

"Now you're hurting my feelings."

"You don't have any feelings, remember. You're the psychopathic lunatic. So what the hell do you want?"

"I just wanted to let you know what I'm going to do. I'm going to walk back into the world under my Cody Calhoon name. I'm going to town this afternoon; I'm going to use a credit card; I'm not going to hide from the security cameras; I'm going to drink more than usual; and then in the morning, I'm going to haul this piece of shit camp trailer to the RV dealer and give it to him. How about that?"

"That's stupid. That's what that is. You know if the local cops haven't canceled the Person of Interest then it's just like an All-Points Bulletin and they will arrest you."

"I'm clean. I'm just a free spirit that decided not to work anymore and wondered off in search of enlightenment. You said they didn't have anything on me. I'll just have to endure some bullshit questioning and then ask for a lawyer. What are they going to hold me on?"

"They'll find something. How about your fake passports, drivers' licenses and such?"

"I'll burn them in a liberation celebration."

"Now that just shows how stupid you are. At least hide them somewhere out in the desert. I had to work real hard to get all that made and put into all the required data bases."

"Maybe just for you then. Anyway, just thought you should know. I'm pulling the plug on this hiding-out insanity."

"Well at least you used the right word, even though it's in the wrong context. Good luck," concluded Kevin and disconnected.

Cole cleaned up the trailer and organized his personal belongings. The truck and trailer both had to go. Maybe he could trade both truck and trailer for an upgrade: maybe a Tesla. Cole started the water heater in the trailer and laid out go-to-the-bar attire. With the temperature already at eighty plus, it didn't take the water heater long.

Showered and with clean clothes, Cole made the five mile drive through a twisted array of desert roads to the highway and then drove another five miles to Quartzsite. Crazy Pizza's parking lot was nearly full and Cole had to wedge his pickup in between two side-by-side 4-wheelers. As Cole entered, he intentionally looked directly at the overhead video surveillance camera. The restaurant and bar were bustling with activity. The majority of the patrons were thirty or more years his senior and having a great time; laughing, drinking and eating pizza. Cole was seated with full view of the bar area at a small table intended for two along the wall. Cole was definitely a stand-out among all the senior citizens, but he felt good; it was an opportunity to be and feel normal.

Cole ordered a full pitcher of beer, just for him-self, and a Crazy's Woo-Zoo pizza. He didn't just feel good; he felt great. And then she walked in. "Oh my God," he mumbled to himself. She would have been a standout in any place, at any time. In this place, among all the gray-hairs, she was a preeminent goddess. She had facial features reminiscent of a young and well-tanned Sandra Bullock, but far more fantastic. Her face was trimmed with shoulder length dark brown hair, which settled on the shoulders of a perfect body. Every curve, every inch of exposed skin, every wiggle of her hips, every movement of her arms, and every stride of her legs all screamed beauty. She was adorned by a sunflower decorated summer dress showing just a little cleavage and terminating just above her knees. Cole hardly realized his pitcher of beer and glass had arrived as his secret desires exploded.

Every man's eyes in the pizza tavern followed her to the bar area where she took her seat; Cole's eyes were no exception. She delicately sat on a stool at the bar and subtlety wiggled to attain just the right position. She ordered a mixed drink of some kind and perched her lips around the little swizzle straw to seductively nurse a first taste.

Then it happened: an incidental glance in Cole's direction. Cole felt subconscious with his constant star-ing and quickly turned his head away, but then turned back to meet her eyes and smile. She glanced back and then returned to the swizzle straw of her mixed drink.

Cole poured himself a glass from the pitcher and consumed it in one tilt of the glass. He poured another and consumed it as well. He filled his glass a third time and she turned again to meet his eyes – and this time it came with a smile. Her lips, mouth and teeth were another compliment to her beauty. As she turned back to her drink, Cole began to contemplate his actions; he made a fist and blew through it. She'd probably heard every pick-up line ever conceived. With her looks, she could probably acquire the attention of any man she wanted. Who knows, maybe she's married and just waiting for her companion. Cole decided to just be placatory: eye contact, smile back when smiled at, maybe a wink, but no other action. If she was interested in him, she could make the move.

Cole poured another glass of beer. Cole's pizza arrived and he pulled a slice from the metal pan and nibbled at it. And then took a full bite. He inspected the toppings; it was truly amazing; maybe the best pizza he'd ever eaten. He caught her approach out of the corner of his eye.

She stopped directly in front of his table with her drink in hand and inquired, "Pardon me, but that pizza looks very tasty. If you don't mind me asking, what kind is it?"

Cole smiled at her and inwardly said to himself, "Alrighty then."

"It's Crazy's Woo-Zoo. Would you like a sample? There's more here than I'm going to eat. Please help yourself to a slice. More if you like."

She set her drink on the table and said, "I'll be right back." She retrieved a small handbag from the bar top before returning to take a seat. "My name's Dominique," she said as she settled into the chair directly opposite Cole. "What's your name?"

"Cole, actually Hamilton Cole Davis, but I go by Cole," Cole managed to get out, as he was awestruck by the beauty of this woman and the momentary confusion of using his real name. She was more beautiful up close than he'd imagined.

"Are you sure you don't mind sharing your pizza. It looks absolutely fabulous."

"Please," replied Cole as he raised his hand and beckoned the server to bring another plate and another glass. "Can't have pizza without beer, you know."

"I'm not much of a beer drinker," commented Dominique. "I'll have just a little. Say half glass."

Cole complied and re-filled his glass to the brim. They ate pizza, drank beer, talked and laughed and eventually ordered mixed drinks: Dominique a vodka tonic with a splash of cranberry juice and Cole a Montana Mule. Dominique was a travel agent and had traveled extensively. She knew all the tourist destinations in the country, as well as many places around the world. Cole was mesmerized by her knowledge, intelligence, softness of her spoken word, humor and sparks of excitement in her personality. She was on a reconnaissance quest to learn about Quartzsite and the surrounding territory. Cole told her about

George Patton's desert training ground, Apache Cabin, Spanish Cabin, Arizona Trail, Desert Resort, Native American petroglyphs and Beer Hill. The travel discussion evolved to subtle flirting and then more, not so subtle, flirting. At one point, Dominique reached over and rubbed Cole's cheek with the back of her hand. Her touch was amazingly soft and it sent a feeling of extreme excitation flooding throughout his body. Cole continued ordering Montana Mules and Vodka Tonics as day drinking turned into evening hours.

As the state of inebriation increased, Dominique revealed more and more about herself and Cole loved it: "All my foster dad wanted was for my mom to put another log on the fire and cook him up some bacon and beans. Then he wondered why she was leaving him. Ha, I can sing that song, you know. Want me to? No, I'm going to." And Dominique started singing, "Wash me up some socks. And fetch my beer. Come on baby tell me why you're leaving me - Okay, now I'm thirsty. Get me another Vodka. Please. I haven't had this much fun in forever."

Cole waved his hand at the bartender, held up two fingers, and mouthed, "Two more."

"Want me sing another song?" continued Dominique. "Oops, not good grammar, huh. 'To sing,' it should be. You know, I sang Karaoke when I went to college. I could have majored in Karaoke instead of criminal law, you know."

"Know any country western? What's your favorite song?"

     Brian David Simmons

"Not much. Oh, 'honey bees, whiskey and wine.'"

"That would be Blake Shelton. Wait here," said Cole as he got up and went over to the Touch Tunes. Cole inserted a five and selected three songs. He glanced back at Dominique as she studied something from her little hand bag.

Returning to the table as Blake Shelton's "Honey Bee" started, Cole took Dominique's hand. "Let's dance," said Cole as he gave her little choice pulling her from her chair.

"I can't do that. I mean Two-Step and all that twisting and spinning."

"I got you, don't worry."

Dominique was a fast learner and by the end of "Honey Bee" she had the rhythm. By the end of the second song, she knew spin and cuddle moves. Cole loved holding her and, by the third song, had her pulled close feeling the warmth of her body and igniting the desire within.

Evening hours flew by with dancing and the consumption of way too much alcohol. The announced last-call for the bar surprised them both.

Dominique was noticeably disturbed by the announcement and Cole questioned, "Is something wrong?"

"Not really. I mean. Oh well. I just didn't expect to stay so long. I didn't make a reservation for a motel assuming I could just, you know, pick one up on the fly and it's a little, oops, late for that. Besides, I'm a little drunk." She giggled, "Did you do that?"

Cole giggled back, "Yep."

"I don't know what I'm going to do. There's two of you, you know. Which one are you? She laughed. "I can't drive fifty-five. Oh, that's another song. I mean I, me, can't drive."

"I'm not in much better shape than you are, but I can just run the truck down the wash and then take the desert trails back to my place."

"Can you take me with you? No, wait. I really like you but I don't know you. You don't have a shovel or something like that in your truck, do you? You're not going to bury me out in the desert are you?"

"You never know," responded Cole and laughed. Dominique giggled and then joined in with full laughter.

When the giggling and laughing subsided, Dominique confessed, "I like you a lot but I don't know. You live in the desert? No, I can't go. Wait, okay, never mind. I decided. Take me to the desert."

"Tyson Wash here we come."

Cole left four hundred dollar bills on the table and drained the remainder of his Montana Mule. As they made their way toward the door, Cole noticed two Arabic looking men at a table in the far corner. Dominique and he were out of place in Crazy's because of age; those two were really out of place, but whatever.

The four-wheel drive Chevy clawed its way through miles of sandy wash until an obscure trail to the east gave the truck relief. They followed the trail and then another and another, talking and laughing all the way.

Eventually the myriad of desert trails delivered Cole and Dominique to his travel trailer and his heart rate accelerated.

As the headlights flashed on the trailer, Dominique's eyes squinted and she frowned. "Maybe you should have left me out in the desert." She laughed and so did Cole. "You don't really think I'm going in there? You might, up oh, do something, you know."

They hadn't reached the trailer door when natural forces took over and they embraced with uncontrollable kissing, feeling, touching, and wanting. They barely made it through the door before the sunflower patterned sun dress hit the floor. Cole's jeans and T-shirt weren't far behind. Underneath the sundress were only panties and they too found the floor as Dominique and Cole crashed onto the bed in passionate enjoyment of each other. Love making continued through the early morning hours until nearly dawn when exhaustion overwhelmed both of them and they fell into exhausted sleep.

Dominique woke first, or so she thought, and went about making percolator coffee. Cole secretly watched her through his near closed eyes. She was as beautiful as ever. Wearing only her panties, Cole studied every inch of her body as she toiled at the stove: perfectly shaped hips, breasts that perked just right, skin smoother than silk, and the panties that cradled that all too special feature. Cole was absolutely spellbound by her beauty and entirely captured by her personality.

He watched as she checked the pot, waiting for it to boil. Then when percolation started, she turned to check the time on the wall clock. What perfect shape, his mind registered again. As the coffee perked, she readied two cups; one was a simple cup with an SDRMC logo, the other was an irregular shaped cup with a fishing saying. When the coffee had perked long enough, she carefully filled both cups. He watched the steam rise up past her perfect breasts.

With coffee ready, she paused and studied something inside her little handbag. She pulled something out, hesitated, and then, as if she'd changed her mind, quickly replaced it.

Dominique just delivered his coffee to the bedroom. It was then that Dominique saw the mass of scar tissue on his right side. She just stared. Cole instinctively dismissed it as an old accident.

After coffee, Dominique was insistent on getting back to town and her car. She had several appointments that just couldn't wait. Cole delivered her back to Quartzsite and her car. Then it was over. She closed her eyes, kissed him softly on the lips, provided him with a phone number and then drove away.

Chapter Eight

BEECH

Jacob McCarry arrived early for work on Monday, as he did every day, at the CIA offices in Langley. He scanned the cubicles for signs of life; he was the only one in at this early hour. Jacob and his section, Space Technology, were part of the Clandestine Information and Technology Office, which was part of the Directorate of Science and Technology. Buried deep in the high tech think-tank, their function was to gather and analyze technical information from around the world and make assessments on weapons, communications, and intelligence capabilities. Jake was the junior member of the section having only been on the job two years and only holding a Master's Degree from Wyoming State in Electrical Engineering. Other members of his section had Ph.Ds. from prestigious schools such as MIT and Purdue. But what he lacked in experience and prestigious paper, he made up for in enthusiasm, dedication, and a unique out-reaching approach to gathering data. Someday he hoped to transition into fieldwork and fulfill his dream being a CIA operative. But, the guys that did the real intelligence work weren't even part of his directorate and Jake's repeated transfer requests had been turned down. All of which was a frustration, but it didn't deter his enthusiasm and determination.

Today was a little different because he'd been given the worthless title of acting supervisor while his real supervisor was on PTO. Roger Sims rotated his delegation among his staff when he was on TDY or PTO. This week, it was Jake's turn in the rotation, which really meant nothing. Nobody in the section needed a supervisor; they all knew their job. In fact, nobody ever took the acting title seriously.

JEFF MONSON, DEPUTY DIRECTOR OF THE CIA, finished his Monday morning coordination meetings. He got caught up on key domestic and foreign activities and then prepared his summary report that would be passed upward through the director and cabinet members to the president before noon. Everybody was expected to know everything so that if the president had a question, they could provide an answer. He expected several calls before the report was submitted to the president to educate those above him. That way, they could portray the image of being in command, which was more important than actually being in command. Monson was only the deputy director but he, as well as others that worked for him, knew that he was really in command of the CIA.

It was the same routine every day except that Mondays were always harder than the rest of the week. Just one day away from the office distanced things and it took extra concentration to catch up. Jeff went about refreshing in his mind all the ongoing activities of the previous week and identifying new activities. He reviewed his notes from Saturday while waiting for the first of several calls about his daily report. He scribbled down some additional information between the notes to clarify his cryptic chicken scratch before he called out the door for his secretary. Dell's job was to maximize the efficiency of her boss and she dropped all else when he beckoned. He handed her the scribbled notes and she was off to compose several memos, filling in missing information and putting the right connotations to them. One of the memos she was to prepare was direction to initiate data collection and analysis on Space Sciences Corporation and the potential illegal export of rocket motor technology to Argentina.

Monson picked up the telephone and called down five levels of management to the supervisor of the Space Technology section, something that always irritated mid-level CIA management. Monson had never learned how to step back and let his management team do their job. He took a direct, hands-on approach that yielded instant responses and always gave him unfiltered feedback. The secretary five levels down answered the phone.

"CIA Space Technology. How may I direct your call?"

"This is Jeff Monson. Let me speak to Roger."

"I'm sorry, sir. Mr. Sims is on PTO this week. Jacob McCarry is acting supervisor while he's away. Would you like me to connect you?"

"Certainly."

A few moments passed and the unsuspecting junior analyst answered, "Yo, this is Jake."

"This is Deputy Director Monson. I need you to do a quick study on an outfit called Space Sciences and their technology export to Argentina. Dell will e-mail you the request as soon as she gets it typed. I want a preliminary report by COB today. Let's say six o'clock. Any questions?"

"No, sir. The e-mail will have all the information I need?"

"Contact Wilford Woods over at State. He'll fill you in on any additional details."

"Undersecretary Woods, sir?"

"Tell him I sent you and he'll see you."

"Yes, sir."

The phone call was brisk, to the point, and just the first of several dozens to follow. But for Jake McCarry, the assignment from mount high was the biggest assignment of his life. He had only been out of school two years and was still classified as a junior analyst. And he had just been given an assignment directly by the deputy director. This was his opportunity to take command and do something really important. Jake quickly typed up and sent out an e-mail message for an emergency section meeting. He then picked up the phone to make a call that ordinarily he would have never considered.

"State Department. Undersecretary Woods' office. May I help you?"

"Yes, ma'am. My name is Jake McCarry. Deputy CIA Director Jeff Monson said I needed to talk to Mr. Woods about Space Sciences Corporation."

"One moment please. I'll see if he can take your call."

A few moments later Jake was talking to the undersecretary of the State Department. At first, he was so nervous that his voice broke as he struggled to breathe and talk at the same time. But after a while, Jake relaxed and the conversation progressed normally. Woods explained the proposal presented by Beech and the State Department's intent to issue an executive exclusion order to the Technology Export Act. He expressed his concerns about ensuring that only limited aspects of what Beech proposed were to be allowed, and if there was anything that wasn't right about this export exclusion then he intended to cancel it. Woods promised to have an expediter hand carry a copy of Beech's presentation package over to him and requested status reports on their investigation. The phone call fueled Jake's enthusiasm for his new assignment.

Ordinary, Jake's supervisor would have just added the Beech investigation to their list of ongoing analyses. Jake's section, buried deep within the Clandestine Information and Technology Office, only gathered information electronically and never from the field. Jake was so far down on the management food chain that his conversations with Monson and Woods were like a bottom feeder surfacing to see sunshine for the first time. He was ecstatic. In his mind, this required no-holds-barred action, and he and his section were going to work this assignment night and day until they got all the answers.

Jake held an emergency section meeting and commanded his resources like a fire boss directing battle on a high-rise blaze. His section normally didn't investigate people, domestic companies, or conduct any form of espionage, but that didn't matter to Jake. This was the CIA and intelligence was intelligence, technology or other. Jake initiated the development of a complete history on Beech, his company, and his associates. He ordered broadband identification of potential co-conspirators within the defense industry, review of satellite surveillance photos for the South American region, database queries on Argentine missile programs and capabilities, queries on U.S. Custom's export records, and summary profiles on ongoing Argentine intelligence operations.

It overwhelmed the eight-man team but they accepted their assignments and went to work. Jake received the e-mail from Monson's secretary and the presentation package from Woods. Jake had copies run for everybody in the section, which inculcated and reinforced his commanded direction.

Jake and his eight-man team of technocrats worked feverishly throughout the day, skipping lunch and foregoing other bodily needs to amass a compilation of data on Chris Beech. The computers ran database searches and correlation studies with outputs being sent to hard copy. They commandeered the conference room and used it to lay out computer printouts and organize different elements of the analysis. They made hundreds of calls and had hundreds of people responding to a "CIA inquiry." The team that ordinarily never talked to anybody was surprised at how eager everyone they contacted was to respond and help out the CIA. The CIA doesn't normally do things the direct way and it was so unique to have the CIA call them directly that scores of helpful people within the government, defense contractors, private companies, law enforcement agencies, and even the FBI, all scrambled to get the requested information.

Incoming phone calls with responses soon overwhelmed their secretary, and she called for help from the department secretary to help manage and direct the calls. Responses coming in from earlier inquiries were categorized and typed into the computer for later recall. Hard copies were printed and accumulated with the rest of the information in the conference room. As the piles of documentation in the conference room grew, Jake started selecting pieces of information to compose his report. At five o'clock, Jake broke off the intense flurry of information gathering and asked the secretaries to momentarily hold the calls while he reviewed his summation with the team. It was a brief three-page report enunciating very concisely what they knew and what actions they were still working. With some minor comments and corrections, he was ready to go see the man in charge.

With the team turned loose to resume taking calls and crunching data, Jake headed for the elevator with six copies of his report. It was a fifteen-minute walk through the maze of buildings over to the headquarters building. The CIA complex consists of twenty-one office buildings sitting on two hundred and fifty-eight acres. Jake's office was located about as far away from the headquarters building as possible. It wasn't very often that anybody from his office visited headquarters and so his section had been relegated to the far extremity of the complex.

The main headquarters building is connected to the original headquarters building, which was built in the fifties and still houses some of the administrative staff. An office in either building was considered prestigious by the nearly twenty thousand CIA employees. Jake entered the side entrance of the original headquarters building and then swiftly proceeded down the hall to the central lobby and then on to the corridor linking old and new headquarters buildings. He turned left at the central lobby and passed the inscription carved in the stone wall that is intended to characterize the purpose of the CIA, *"And ye shall know the truth and the truth shall make you free."* Glancing at his watch, he hurried his pace down the corridor toward the main headquarters building. He wasn't late, at least not yet; he just wanted to make sure he wasn't.

 Brian David Simmons

He exited the corridor into the new headquarters building, passed the elevators servicing the east tower, and continued on to the atrium in the center of the building. He glanced at the suspended spy plane replicas of the U2 and SR71 in the four-story glass enclosed atrium as he passed through. Finally, Jake reached the elevator for the west tower. Floor selection was easy; big guys always sit in high places. Jake hit six. He was on time but with only two minutes to spare.

He quickly found the office of the deputy director and entered through the oak door to an empty secretary station. It was after quitting time and she had obviously gone home. Her desk was neat and tidy and ready for the following day. Past her station through an open door he could see a thin gray-haired man sitting behind a large desk. He was reading something from the stack of papers on his desk. Jake nervously approached, gaining the attention of the man sitting behind the desk.

"Can I help you, son?"

"Yes, sir. I have the Beech report you requested."

"I thought a Jacob McCarry was going to come by and brief me. Not just send his report over."

With a broken voice, Jake replied. "Yes, sir. I'm Jake McCarry."

Jake got a cold stare and a quirt-stinging response from Monson. "You are. Where's your supervisor?"

"He's on PTO, sir."

"All right then. Let's have it," said Jeff as he leaned back in his chair.

Jake approached with trepidation and handed Monson his report. Monson grunted and didn't even give him a second look. Jake took a seat in the padded chair directly in front of Monson's oversize desk and waited for a response. Monson glanced up once at Jake as he read the report. Jake was startled when Monson quickly flipped from page one to page two. It seemed like an eternity waiting for Monson to finish reading. At least Jake was prepared when Monson abruptly flipped to page three.

"Interesting. How long have you been with the CIA?" said Monson as he turned back to the first page.

"Two years, sir."

"Hum. All right. What do you mean here about Beech soliciting designs from aerospace contractors?"

"Beech requested design concepts for movable nozzles from two propulsion contractors and guidance package designs from three system integrators. In each case, he got the contractor to use their proposal funds to prepare preliminary design concepts. They expected to be awarded a contract for fabrication and delivery of components for up to fifty-two systems. This was predicated on obtaining State Department approval for technology export. Beech, in turn, charged the Argentine government for the preliminary designs, even though it cost him nothing. We believe he's already turned over the designs without the proper approval. Fees paid by the Argentine government for Beech's services to represent them total over forty-

    Brian David Simmons

seven million and we don't believe they would pay that if they didn't get something in return."

"Has he sent them any hardware?"

"No, sir. We don't believe so. But we are still cross-checking exports against any of Beech's business activities."

"What are the Argentinians going to do with these components?"

"They are going to retrofit them to reloaded POGOs. We do know from satellite surveillance photos that they have been washing aging propellant grains out of their POGO rockets. The satellite photos clearly show propellant washout and evaporation ponds that are burned once they evaporate. If they just reload them with original propellant formulations, that results in no international violations."

"On page three here, you say you initiated a broad spectrum search to identify individuals that may have given information to Beech. Explain that."

"Yes, sir. We have accumulated a list of all guidance, control, and propulsion engineers that are in a position to have information Beech may need. We got the information from defense contractors for current employees. We are still adding to the list for past employees. The names are being run against financial records to identify any irregularities and cross-checked against Beech's past business dealings and associations."

"You realize you're bordering on a violation of Executive Order 12333 prohibiting accumulation of surveillance data on U.S. citizens without probable cause of espionage."

"Yes, sir. But if they're giving, or have given, information illegally to Beech, then there is no violation to the executive order."

"How many people are we talking about?"

"About fifteen hundred, sir."

"Ha! Fifteen hundred suspected of espionage! Nobody would believe that." Monson smiled and then continued, "You're going to get us both fired."

"Yes, sir. That's always a possibility."

"All right then. Come see me Wednesday with an update. I think we have enough in this report to make a recommendation to the State not to grant Beech's exclusion. And with your final report, we'll make a decision whether or not we should go after this guy."

"Yes, sir. I'll have that report for you first thing Wednesday. Anything else?"

"Call tomorrow and have Dell set up an appointment."

"Yes, sir."

Monson smiled and extended his hand as Jake got up and the two parted with a warm handshake.

Chapter Nine

RABBITS

THE FOUR-LANE STREET IN LITTLE ROCK WAS QUIET in the early hours of the morning. A woman stood motionless against the front of the Winsyon Real-Estate office building and studied an approaching pickup truck. She hunched over and pulled her shoulders forward to maximize portrayal of an elderly woman in a baggy cleaning uniform. The truck was an aging Chevrolet with one headlight out; peeling and deteriorating yellow paint was giving way to encroaching patches of rust and its defunct muffler broadcast the miss-tuned sound of its engine. The driver's eyes focused forward from beneath a ball cap and never gave the woman more than a glance.

As the truck passed, the woman inserted her key into the lock, turned it, opened the door and slipped inside. She paused, peered through the front window and felt comfortable that she had entered undetected. Elastic surgical gloves snapped as she pulled them on. With a dim light coming through the front window from the street, she quickly moved to the corner office. The placard on the door read: "Nathan Monahay, CEO, Winsyon Real-Estate Incorporated." Again she used her key to gain entrance. Once inside, she pulled a pin light from her waist-pack and searched out the coffee maker. The exterior was clean but upon swinging open its basket and inspecting beneath its filter, she confirmed her suspicions. It hadn't been cleaned since her last visit. She smiled and thought: one less irritation and another two-hundred K. How long will it be? A day? Can't be another week?

She pulled a small bottle and tiny brush from her pack. Carefully, she opened the container and the thought of what was inside made her hold her breath and extend the bottle away from her face. At arm's distance, she dipped the brush in the bottle and began painting the bottom of the filter basket with the vile, opaque liquid. As she painted the second coat of the liquid, she recalled what Chang had told her. The liquid was a blend of human albumin and a white puss extracted from the liver of diseased rabbits. Twenty-five rabbits had been raised in captivity and intentionally infected with the liver disease. The animals were slaughtered and then the puss was scrapped from their livers and put into concentrated form. Nathan Monahay's coffee maker had already been treated with almost a quarter ounce of Chang's noxious liquid; it should have already done its job. The thought of it made her shiver. She still had half an ounce left and it had an indefinite self-life. That would provide for another victim and another two hundred K, she contemplated.

The mixture produced symptoms similar to botulism yet more deadly and completely undetectable.

The human albumin was a natural substance and overshadowed any signs of the liver puss in laboratory analyses. Besides, who would ever believe Nate Monahay would ingest rabbit liver puss. One dose should have been enough, but Monahay had survived a surprising week after the first coffee maker painting; this final exposure would surely kill him. She continued painting as her mind wondered and calculated her profit. The ounce of lethal fluid had cost her fifty thousand, which meant that the cost for Monahay's two dosses was twenty-five grand. After travel and other miscellaneous costs, total expenses would approach thirty-five-thousand. With a contract value of two-hundred-thousand, that made this venture a six-hundred percent return on investment.

She placed the lid back on the bottle and slipped it into her waist pack. Then, having finished her work, she carefully replaced the filter with its used coffee grounds, which returned the coffee maker to its original appearance. She looked around to be sure everything was in its place and then left, locking the door behind her. The sun, still hidden behind the horizon, was just starting to lighten the Arkansas sky. Traffic was beginning to pick up as she crept from the entrance, hoping that no one had noticed her exit.

She hurried around the corner and slipped into her rental car. With fluid motion, she quickly shed wig, glasses, cleaning service uniform and packed them in a small bag. She accelerated away from the curb and set her course for the airport; she had a ten o'clock flight to Dulles International.

Contracts were coming all too quick and it was taking everything she had to keep up. The next contract would have ordinarily taken weeks to plan and prepare. She had had to compress it all into 36 hours. But the payoff was well worth it. The client had readily agreed to triple her normal fee plus outlandish expenses for payoffs, which made the job worth a cool million.

Chapter Ten

COFFEE

THE SUN WAS JUST COMING UP AS KEVIN EMERGED from the basement. Joe was already up making coffee and turned to greet Kevin, "Morning son. You look like you had hard night."

Kevin yawned and replied, "That's an understatement. Almost fucked up big time."

"Almost implies you didn't do so well in the super spook world. Give me a minute and I'll have a cup of coffee for you."

"Well, it might not be alright if I make a mistake. I mean who knows who could come here to find me. And it's not safe for you and Sylvia."

"Look Kevin. I'm no dummy. When Cole asked me to set this place up as a safe house, I knew there could always be a flip side to safe. Sylvia and I talked about it and we knew the risk we were taking. And Sylvia loves that boy. She loves you too, you know."

"So what if it was the United States government that came looking for me? What if it was the FBI or CIA? What would you say about that?"

"Coffee's ready, that's what I'd say." Joe poured two cups of coffee and then continued, "In my days driving truck, I saw lots of shit. Faced off hijackers and thieves more than once. My tire iron against their knives and guns. Never lost a fight, except for one. Two cops pulled me over out west in New Mexico. They didn't like the color of my skin. I knew better than to fight back and let them beat the shit out of me. Better than being shot and left for dead. So I'm no fan of the police or anything that smells like them. And today, if they ever showed up at my door, I think I'd go after them with my tire iron or whatever I could get my hands on."

"How much did Cole tell you about what we did in Atlanta?"

"Not much but I figured it out. You and Cole stole a bunch of money from that drug dealing son-of-bitch Bartrum and then killed him. And I figure you're still at it, somehow."

"We did more than that. We bankrupted lots of people just like Isaac Bartrum. I mean lots and they're still out there."

"Good for you."

"If they ever find out it was us, it would be bad."

"So be it. Right now Sylvia and I are living our dream. I never imagined we could finish out our lives in a place as beautiful and serene as Tobago. The opportunity Cole gave us is the most awesome retirement we could ever wish for."

Kevin paused as thoughts twisted in his mind and then he asked, "Well you're invested in our collective future. Want to know more?"

"I guess I'm curious. I'm also a little nervous. Knowledge can be a bad thing sometimes."

"Your decision."

"If I'm invested, I guess I should know."

"I hacked a futures broker who was doing money laundering for a whole bunch of people like Isaac Bartrum. After three days of trades intended to clean their dirty money, their downside leveraged trades were compounded ten-to-one losses. All told, we took more than two hundred sixty million from a lot of very, very bad people. What do you think they would do to get their money back? And after they recovered their finances, what do you think they would do to anyone involved? At the very least, they'd just kill us; maybe our families and anyone we ever knew, as well."

"You know, the thing with hornets is, that given enough time, they settle down."

"Hornets don't hold a grudge and jump at the chance to carry out a vendetta."

Joe scratched his head and noticeably struggled with the thought. "Maybe," he said.

Kevin continued, "Then it gets worse. What would the Department of the Treasury, FBI, or Federal Reserve do if they found out what we did?"

"I worry about you boys. Maybe I shouldn't have asked. But now I understand Sylvia and my role."

"Last night I hacked my way into the FBI databases and did some exploring. I'm clean; no references at all. But Cole's in the facial recognition database."

"Does Cole know?"

"Yes. But Cole is usually the most paranoid person I have ever known. Except right now he's going through some kind of emotional trauma. I'm so tired I can hardly hold my head up. But after I get some sleep, I'll call him to talk about it."

"Do me a favor. When you do call him, make sure Sylvia gets to talk to that boy."

"Sure," replied Kevin as he turned to head towards his bedroom.

Joe called after him, "Sylvia's going to be disappointed you missed another meal, you know."

In the Arizona desert, Cole finished his second cup of Coffee, fed Mister Slow, and his thoughts went to Dominique. Cole studied his phone and contemplated what he would say. Meeting Dominique was the best thing that had happened to him in a long time. There was the sex, which was awesome. But it was more than that; he relished every spoken word and just loved being near her. He looked at the scrap of paper with her number on it and dialed.

"Hello," came Dominique's cheery response.

"Hey, this is Cole." Cole still couldn't believe he'd given her his full name on their first encounter. If Kevin knew, he'd have to put up with at least a half hour of tongue lashing.

"I was just thinking about you, you know."

"Well, I've been thinking about you for several days," confided Cole.

"And what have you been thinking?" seductively replied Dominique.

"Just how much I enjoy your company and how much I'd like to see you again. I could catch a flight out of Phoenix and be there in a few hours. Where are you at, anyway?"

"Oh, I'm traveling. Doing the travel agent thing, you know."

"We could meet somewhere. I can come to you. And, by the way, I don't even know your full name."

"Ooh. I'm a mystery woman then. Maybe I'll just keep you in suspense."

"That's not fair. You know my name. You know where I live. You know I'm a free spirit ex-aerospace engineer. At least tell me your last name."

"Suspense versus fair: that's an interesting trade. I think I'll take suspense, intrigue, and keep our romance mystifying. It's more exciting that way. Don't you think?"

Cole was elated just hearing her voice and the conversation continued for nearly an hour. Dominique talked about the challenges of setting up travel arrangements for elite customers. They laughed about dancing at Crazy's Pizza. Dominique was thinking about taking country western dance lessons; she wanted to learn the pretzel. Cole said he could teach her. The chit-chat went on and on, sometimes bordering on flirtation and absolutely delightful. Cole's heart swelled with every sound of her voice and a chasm of emptiness emerged in his very being when the call ended.

Thirteen hundred miles away in Arkansas, Nate Monahay managed the pains of his failing body and convinced his wife that he would be fine for a few hours at work. He feared the reaction of his special customers to the thought that he was so debilitated that he couldn't even make it to work. Even worse, his personal secretary had told him that the FBI had come with warrant in-hand and confiscated records and his personal computers. He had to see for himself. Real-Estate escrow funds were discretely used to transfer funds for his special customers and now the FBI had his records. Would they figure it out?

Doctors had been unable to diagnose his condition; the best they could do was suggest that his nervous system was being attacked by a toxin similar to that produced by botulism, which was absolutely absurd. He just advised everyone that it was a severe case of the flu, but that story was losing its believability after a week-long bout. He just had to get better.

His wife inched the Lincoln curbside in front of Winsyon Real-Estate. She inquired for at least the tenth time, "Are you sure you feel well enough? You are awful pale and you know you haven't been able to hold down any real food for days. The doctor told you to just rest until the tests come back."

     Brian David Simmons

"They don't have a clue what I need. Besides, I'm feeling pretty good today."

"You're a terrible liar, but I love you none-the-less. You call me when you want a ride. Just call."

She leaned over and gave him a little peck on the check which earned her an affectionate smile. He struggled to get out of the car and the muscles in his arm flexed spasmodically when he pushed the door closed; shooting fire spread throughout his torso with the jolt of the door's impact against its jamb. He forced a smile at his wife through the windshield and then crept towards the entrance to the office complex, each step bringing more horrific pains to his stomach. He tugged at the door; it wouldn't open. He realized his mind wasn't really functioning and pulled the door key from his pocket.

The real estate office was now empty. The FBI had made sure of that. Normally, agents, loan processors, and secretaries all talking on the phone, hammering on the computer keyboards or face to face with clients would have made it a beehive of activity. But the office was now silent and entirely different. He paused when he felt a violent spasm shoot through his body. He remembered what his personal secretary had told him with detestation: "I stayed to watch the vermin snoop and crawl through everybody's files. They downloaded files from everybody's PC, trashed, tossed and stole paper files. When they got to your office, they took everything, including your computers. I let the vermin have a piece of my mind as they cleaned out your office and then they took my things too - just out of spite."

Nate surveyed his office; it was immaculately clean. His huge fine oak desk took center stage in the middle of the office with matching credenza against the back wall. The four chairs lined up facing his desk brought back memories of forceful deals he had negotiated, giving partial credit for his success to the layout and organization of his office. Pictures, awards, licenses and other memorabilia made the office a showplace. A new PC occupied the computer station in the corner and the decanter in his coffee maker glistened on the credenza behind his chair. He loved his coffee and he had missed it terribly. Nate swung open the filter basket and reloaded it with a new filter and his fresh ground Kona coffee.

As the coffee percolated, he mindlessly watched in a daze. The aroma woke him from his torpor before it finished. He poured himself a cup. It had a delight-ful taste. He glanced out the window to see the rising sun but the light slowly faded as a burst of nausea overwhelmed his body. He went forward as vomit flew uncontrollably from his mouth. He momentarily fell face forward into the pool of vomit, lifted his head, and then regurgitated again and again until there was nothing left. Breathing became a challenge as dry-heaves continued. Then breathing stopped, his head fell back into the pool of vomit, and life ended.

     Brian David Simmons

Chapter Eleven

Organizational Squash

Jake arrived early for work as usual even though he'd worked late into night the day before. He turned on his computer and waited for it to come to life. He closed his eyes and half dozed. He was woken by Roger Sims. Without coffee, Jake briefed his supervisor on the previous three days of investigation, leaving out the violations of standard operating procedures. After briefing Roger, Jake found coffee and headed to his early morning meeting with Deputy Director Monson. Roger declined the "opportunity" to accompany Jake; his supervisor knew what was about to happen.

Jake's report included an extensive background summary on Chris Beech, a complete history of Beech's business dealings, an analysis of all exports to Argentina within the last six months, an analysis of satellite surveillance photos, an assessment of strategic and foreign policy needs for upgraded weapons systems, a review of CIA field operations, and a screening of defense contractor personnel with potential links to Beech.

As before, Jake made the long trek through the CIA complex to the sixth floor of the headquarters building. He was a few minutes early and the secretary held him back until the appointed time. Two other men showed up while he waited and were granted immediate entrance to the conference room. Dell, the secretary, made the announcement to Monson that "they're all here" and he emerged from his office.

"Hello, Jake. You ready?"

"Yes, sir. Ready for what?"

"I'm assuming you've got this thing figured out for us."

"Partially, sir."

"Then let's go in and talk about it."

Jake followed Jeff Monson into the conference room where four senior looking men huddled at the end of a conference table sized for twenty. The chair at the end of the table was empty, obviously reserved for the man in charge. Monson took his place at the head of the table and Jake sat down next to a balding man thirty years his senior. Introductions were short. Jake recognized the names but couldn't exactly place them in the CIA's extensive organization. The name he did recognize was that of the balding man sitting next to him. It was Blaine Higgins, head of his directorate, who now had a face to go with the name.

Jake handed out copies of his report and started the briefing, "Chris Beech is a forty-nine-year-old consultant with a B.S. degree in mechanical engineering from Texas A&M. He began his consulting business, Space Sciences Corporation, eight years ago, following a divorce." Jake continued while the men at the table quickly scanned to the end of the report, looking for the conclusion and foregoing the detail.

"His business struggled for two of the eight years until he began representing the Argentine government. Since that time, he has received twenty-seven million dollars of reportable income from the Argentinians. The work performed is nondescript, other than to say it's compensation for representing them in identifying technology for potential export, coordinating its acquisition, and negotiating the necessary licenses. Recently—"

"What evidence do you have that he has violated any U.S. laws?" interrupted one of the men.

"None specifically. But we believe that—"

"And who is we?" interrupted another man at the table.

"My section and I, sir. We have—"

Interrupting again, "Your section is not qualified to make such judgments. I expect that you coordinated your conclusion with the appropriate directorates?"

"No, sir. We have been working to accumulate, condense, and analyze the data."

"If you haven't involved the right people, then you don't have any basis to draw conclusions."

"I am here to share our conclusions with you today. I hope you find them credible."

A feeding frenzy began, like sharks after a wounded comrade, with each randomly striking before the previous attacker had finished.

"On page sixteen, you base links to potential co-conspirators on a computer analysis. What's that about?"

"A massive list of defense contractor personnel was trimmed through a process of scoring and screening to yield a streamlined list of sixteen possible candidates. Candidates were scored based on income, vacation, drug and family problems, arrest records, and any other inconsistency or anomaly. We further reduced the list through interviews with DCMC personnel who conducted a discreet investigation of their own. The list has been reduced to twelve, and we believe that—"

"You have no basis to investigate these people. Don't you understand?" stated a man with oversized eyebrows and nose hair.

"No, sir. I mean that if they are involved with Beech, then there is reasonable suspicion to believe they are involved in espionage."

"You don't have one single piece of evidence to conclude Beech is in violation of export laws, much less any information to suggest these people are engaged in espionage."

"Yes, sir, but—"

"No buts about it! Don't you understand? You have blatantly violated Executive Order 12333, and I order you to immediately discontinue all investigations of these people and destroy any associated records." ordered Higgins with a blast of bad breath.

Each successive question escalated, as if the inquisitors were trying to outdo one another. Jake maintained his cool and responded the best he could but he was increasingly dejected by the feeding frenzy. Jake thought they would never stop.

He concentrated on the facts as his defense, "We have potential illegal export of amusement park ride electronics and movable rocket nozzle designs that we believe warrants investigation of probable involvement of U.S. citizens."

Only to be battered with continued interruptions, "Probable involvement requires evidence of collaboration to conspire against the United States."

"How do you relate these characteristic anomalies, as you call them, to espionage?" interjected another. "There is nothing here but weak, unsubstantiated supposition, and I won't have this agency involved in such a feckless investigation."

The balding man next to Jake turned to the deputy director and said, "Jeff, I think it's pretty obvious that we need to terminate this investigation before the press or some subcommittee gets wind of it. It's wrong, it's in violation of the law, and it's completely fraudulent."

The message was clear to Jake. Their interpretation of his work was one of repugnance and all Jake had left was a sinking feeling of inadequacy. The past few days of sleepless nights had dishonored the organization and it was his fault.

When Monson started his concluding remarks, it compounded Jake's feelings of distress.

"Well, I don't see value in continuing to investigate the issue further, at least domestically. It seems pretty clear that we are skirting legal issues and need to terminate all domestic investigation. I want the file closed with no further action." Monson paused briefly and then continued. "I do believe there is something here and Jake just hasn't hit upon it. I believe it has to do with the Argentinians and we need to put some effort into it. I'd like Askew's directorate to commence a field investigation and follow up on Jake's findings related to solid rocket motor reloading and upgrading. I'd like a report back in no more than sixty days. Fair enough?"

A couple of the men nodded and another grunted. Jake got some comfort from Monson's final words but it wasn't much.

JEFF MONSON FELT GUILTY FOR HAVING FED JAKE to the wolves. The young man was too naive to recognize the political and territorial battles being waged at the table, but Jeff had seen it hundreds of times before. Jake had done an outstanding piece of work. However, Jeff knew better than to side with Jake against his trusted management staff. In the long run, it was the right decision. Besides, the work was outside the scope of Jake's directorate, and he could get the answers he needed from the organization with the appropriate charter. Everybody would win, except Jake. Monson considered transferring him, but that had its potential downside as well. The new kid on the block might

     Brian David Simmons

naively make the old guard look bad and they would squash him for sure. Jake was a promising member of the CIA and would someday do very well in the organization, but first he needed to learn the etiquette and he could do that better in his current position. Monson concluded the meeting and everybody went on their way.

THROUGH POOR TIMING ON BLAINE HIGGINS'S PART, he ended up on the elevator with Jake. Higgins glared at him and Jake glared back. Swallowing became difficult for Higgins as the intensity grew, making the elevator ride seem like an eternity. He had never seen Jake before and would probably never see him again; he really didn't care that Jake had been demeaned and humiliated, but the stare and silence were almost more than he could take. He broke the eye-lock with Jake and glanced at the elevator button; three was lit. Finally, he got his relief when the elevator sounded its dainty bell upon arrival at the first floor. Jake departed swiftly and so did he.

Higgins clutched Jake's report in his hand as he hurried to his office. It was only seconds after returning to his office that he made a call. Politics and the world of favors are avenues to personal advancement in higher ranks of government. Higgins wasn't about to let an opportunity pass. Positions at the higher levels are vacated by death, retirement, or by order of a new president, and opportunities didn't come along very often. Higgins needed an edge if he ever hoped to advance beyond his current position, and it didn't matter whether it was in the CIA, FBI, NSA, ATF, or even the FDA. He just wanted to advance. He called FBI Director Evert Hooster and once past the secretary, made a self-serving disclosure.

"Hey Ev, I think I've got something that you FBI boys can use. It came out of an extensive investigation on illegal technology export. The investigation was conducted under my directorate. Because of the potential implications, I took a personal interest in this investigation. We identified a group of engineers and scientists that are candidates for prosecution for violation of the Technology Export Act. I'll forward the report to you."

"Blaine, I don't know whether we are involved in that investigation or not, but give me what you got and I'll pass it along."

Evert Hooster was no ignoramus. He interpreted Higgins's offering as an attempt at nasal sodomy and was repulsed by it. As it turned out, some of the names provided by Higgins were already in the FBI data base. However, information was information and worthy of consideration, regardless of its source.

Chapter Twelve

TESTS

COLE AND DOMINIQUE WERE TALKING EVERY DAY. Cole thought about her continually and anticipated every call with eagerness. And yet, she was still elusive. He still didn't know her last name, even though they were becoming more than just acquaintances. He felt a desire and attraction to this strange woman like he'd never known. He thought she felt the same way about him, or at least he hoped so.

Cole sat on the camper steps and watched the sun crest the horizon. Anticipating the call, he made a fist, raised it to his mouth and slowly blew as he formulated the correct approach: ultimatum – no, simple request – always elusive so no, involve Kevin and bring his skills to bear – no way, or a test – maybe if phrased right.

Cole tapped the number on his cell phone and waited: two rings, six rings, eight rings and then voice mail. Cole disconnected. Maybe it was too early. Then his phone rang.

"Hey Cole. I missed your call; I was just getting out of the shower."

"Wish I was there."

"I'll bet you do."

"And you know, I've kind of figured out where you are."

"Oh, I doubt that. I'm the mystery woman, remember."

"Seven o'clock here and nine o'clock there. I know where you're at," lied Cole. All he really knew was that she was always up and about before the sun rose in Arizona.

"So you've been playing detective?"

"You know cell phones triangulate off cell towers."

"Some do. So tell me mister detective, exactly where am I?"

"You're at home."

"Yes and exactly where is that?"

Cole had already done the mental speculation. Biggest travel centers in the Eastern Time zone were Orlando, D.C., New York, Philadelphia, and Boston. He continued the charade, "Where the travel agent action is, of course. I mean with all the historical monuments, statues, parks and such."

"Ha, you're just fantasizing my love. I fantasize about you, you know." teased Dominique. "It's just part of the mystery and intrigue that makes it exciting, you know."

Cole's subtle test wasn't going anywhere and he let the conversation move on to dance moves and then to the beginning of baseball season. Surprisingly, Dominique was a fan and could talk Mets, Yankees, and Nationals details with ease. Her warmth and personality filled his heart and made him feel normal; he absolutely relished her every spoken word. But the emptiness returned the moment she said good-bye.

 Brian David Simmons

His test hadn't baited her into revealing her location. But based on her familiarity with baseball teams, he speculated she probably lived in either the New York or Washington D.C. area. Cole contemplated getting Kevin involved to trace the next call, but she strangely had this thing about remaining a mystery woman and maybe he would just let it go. She would confide in him eventually; the time, though, had to be of her choosing, he concluded.

ACROSS SIX STATES IN LANGLEY VIRGINIA, JAKE FELT like a wounded animal and motivation was going to be a challenge. Yesterday's meeting was terrible. He sat back in front of his computer, logged on, and then quickly went to his e-mail; his in-box was empty. "Crap," he mumbled to himself.

Roger Sims, Jake's supervisor, put his hand on Jake's shoulder from behind and interrupted, "Sorry Jake. Looks like you made the list."

Jake swiveled around in his chair. "What?"

"You made the list. You have to report to the infirmary within the hour to piss in the cup."

"You gotta be kidding."

"Not a chance. I got the computer alert at seven forty-five, which means you have until eight-forty-five to report. Failure to report buys you three days off without pay – and then you'll still have to take the drug test. Sorry."

"So why me?"

"Could be the random drawing. Could be something you did outside of work. Maybe you were seen in the wrong place at the wrong time and somebody reported you. Who knows? I wouldn't think too much about it. Just placate them; Go pee in the cup and let them do their thing."

"You know, Roger, this is stupid, really stupid!"

"Yea, we all know it's stupid, but we all gotta comply. Now get the hell out of here. Don't be late."

Jake switched off his computer, grabbed his jacket and headed for the infirmary. It was unusually cold; the April air had a bone chilling wet cold to it and his wind breaker was little defense. It wasn't at all like the dry cold of the mountains of Wyoming where he had grown up.

Days like today made him think of the small town of Pinedale and his Father's feed store. Instead of engineering and the CIA, he could have chosen a career in business; maybe helped his father grow the family store into a grain packaging and distribution company serving the entire Nation and expanding well beyond the ranchers of the Pinedale area. Horse saddles, bridles, tackle, and other animal husbandry supplies, in addition to the livestock feed products, could have carried the name "McCarry and Son." Instead, Jake was battling the Virginia wind and cold on his way to piss in the cup. He pulled the collar of his wind breaker up over his ears and ducked his head into the wind.

     Brian David Simmons

The cowboy attitude doesn't tolerate drugs, gangs, or anything else that detracts from the purest of values. If anyone had ever asked his Dad to piss in the cup, the insult would have gotten them a good old fashioned ass whooping. There were no illegal drugs in Pinedale, much less drug tests. This was not only stupid; it was a down right insult!

Jake arrived at the infirmary, shook off the cold and made the purpose of his visit known to the receptionist who promptly entered his arrival time into the computer data base. He took a seat and began filling out the questionnaire. Filling out the form just added to the irritation; he was taking no prescription drugs, had no physical or mental ailments and this was just more waste of time. Jake was in excellent health, just over six feet and one hundred eighty pounds. Blue eyes, blond hair – certainly they have all this information, thought Jake.

With the questionnaire completed, Jake was invited back to the examination room where a nurse gave him the cup. He did his duty in the bathroom and returned to the waiting nurse who promptly did pH, temperature, and blood count tests on the urine sample. She did an initial test for drugs, smiled, and jotted something down on a piece of paper. "Looks good but we still have to send it off for confirmation," she said.

She then sealed the container and had Jake sign his name across the container seal. He then had to verify this, read that, initial here and seal the container in a bag. The ritualistic ceremony was accompanied with lots of instruction and assurance about the careful and controlled handling of his sample. His sample would be sealed and controlled until received at the off-center testing lab where equally as protective procedures would ensure accurate analysis of his urine. They would check for common prescription medications, as well as street drugs such as marijuana, cocaine, heroin, and crack. If Jake didn't hear from them within three days, he could assume everything was okay. Jake had to restrain himself from lambasting the nurse with what he was thinking: what a bunch of bull, meant only for the inane.

When finished, Jake quickly exited the infirmary. He took a deep breath of the cold air and exhaled to cleanse his lungs of the clinical smell of the infirmary. This time, with the wind at his back, the trek back to his office complex wasn't quite so unbearable, but it was still a long walk. It was almost eleven o'clock before Jake got back to his office.

When he entered the office building, a secretary knowingly smiled at him. He passed someone he didn't know by name in the hall who smiled and inquired, "Did they hold it for you?" When he entered the office area of his eight man section, the entire section stood to peer over their cubicle walls and applauded in an obviously planned attempt to humiliate. Jake laughed and responded, "Yea, they did that too over at the infirmary. The nurse had to put the cup on the floor and get a stool for me to stand on. You guys are just envious."

With the joking over, it was time to go back to work. Jake sat down at his computer, logged on, and checked again for e-mails. It was a huge let down after the flurry of the last few days. The day lagged on.

It was lunch time and Jake's thoughts drifted to Katie. Whenever possible he had lunch with her; today he was to meet her over in the headquarters building atrium. It meant another long walk, but her company was always the highlight of the day. He had been dating her for six months and wondered if differing career paths would someday interfere with their relationship. She had managed to get into the field operations training program. Much to his chagrin, he failed to gain acceptance into the same program. If she made it through the program, she could very easily get assigned anywhere in the world and then what would happen to their relationship? For today, it would just have be enough to have the pleasure of her company. He grabbed his jacket and sack lunch and then headed for the door. Today it was his turn and he had packed a lunch for both he and Katie. As he exited the building and started the hike, a large smile grew on his face; all he could think about was her girlish laugh.

It was a fifteen minute walk through the maze of buildings over to the headquarters building. Jake entered the side entrance of the original headquarters building and then swiftly preceded down the hall to the central lobby and then on to the corridor linking old and new headquarters buildings. He turned left at the central lobby and again passed the inscription carved in the stone wall: *"And ye shall know the truth and the truth shall make you free."*

Glancing at his watch, he hurried his pace down the corridor towards the atrium and Katie. He exited the corridor into the new headquarters building and passed the elevators servicing the east tower and then continued on to the atrium in the center of the building. Katie was sitting on a bench reading. She spotted Jake approaching, stood, removed her glasses and waited for Jake's arrival. Jake quickened his pace. As he neared, both scanned the atrium to see who might be watching. There were a few people in the atrium but no one was paying any particular attention; Jake grabbed her in his arms and the two embraced.

Fear of being observed shortened their embrace and they both glanced around. Katie slipped her glasses back on, smiled and then let out a girlish little laugh. Jake was mesmerized. She broke his trance with an inquiry, "I've got a strange craving for grapefruit. What did you pack?"

Jake delayed his response; holding her at arms distance with his hands on her shoulders, he just cherished her with his eyes. She smiled at the warmth of his affection and he replied, "You're a silly girl. Grapefruit ain't in season. You'll have to settle for an apple and one of my western hoagies."

They ate Jake's specialty hoagie sandwiches and filled the remaining lunch hour with chit-chat. Katie talked about the morning's class room training activities: impromptu weapons while in the field. She talked about cutting ragged ends on a soda pop can, then smashing and rolling it for a two ended weapon. Wheeled back and forth, it could easily keep an attacker at bay or inflict horrendous wounds in an offensive encounter. Then there was the home-made garrote, weighted sap gloves, Kelly Come-Along and a few others. Jake couldn't imagine her being the least bit hostile enough to use any of the weapons she talked about.

Then she turned the discussion to company trips. She was excited that the CIA was again going to send her out west for specialized training. Jake quizzed her about it, but it was a classified trip and all he learned was that "it was going to be warm in the desert". He decided not to tell her about his drug test. It was really no big deal, anyway.

Chapter Thirteen

IT WAS A BIG DEAL

IT WAS UNUSUAL FOR ANYBODY TO BE AT WORK BEFORE Jake, even his section supervisor. This morning, however, Roger Sims was already there, but closed the door to his office when he saw Jake. As unusual as it was, it was even more unusual that he closed his door; Roger truly practiced an open-door policy. Jake turned on his computer and waited for the logon screen. It seemed unusually slow this morning. Finally, the logon screen came up and Jake input his user ID and password; the screen flashed and then came back with an error message: "Logon Incorrect." Jake clicked "cancel" and then tried again, but the result was the same. He tried a third and fourth time, but still failed to get logged on.

He picked up the phone to dial the Computer Help Line, but his phone had no dial tone. He smiled and thought to himself: who ever would believe Ph.Ds. could be such pranksters? I wonder how many of them are in on it? Which ones? They'll pay for it - that's for sure. I won't just get even, I'll get ahead. Jake inspected his phone and then followed the cord all the way to the wall. He snapped it out of its socket and inspected for taped or glued contacts; the contacts were clean. He had a left over phone cord in his desk drawer, but his desk was locked. He smiled again: just wait till those guys get in.

Roger Sims opened his door, stuck his head out and called for Jake to come to his office. He watched Jake all the way to his door before withdrawing back inside. Roger moved around his desk and then settled into his chair. He spoke slow and deliberately, "Close the door, Jake."

"There's nobody here."

"Close the damn door and sit down!" snapped Roger. "Don't make this any harder than it is."

Jake did as instructed and inquired, "What's going on, Roger?"

Roger couldn't look him in the eyes and meekly replied, "Your drug test results came back."

Jake studied Roger's face for a twitch of a smile, a wink, or anything other than seriousness. There wasn't any, but Jake asked anyway, "This is a joke, right?"

"Fraid not."

"Come on. This is bullshit. There is no way they found any drugs."

"Sorry, Jake. I truly am."

Jake bolted to standing attention with a puffed chest, "No way."

"Sit down, Jake." Jake didn't sit, but Roger continued anyway as he read from a paper on his desk, "They found some things called N,N-dimethyltryptamine, psilocybin and methedrine amphetamine. These are common compounds used in semisynthetic designer drug variations of DMT. The individual will experience hallucinogenic effects similar to the more commonly recognized LSD. Because of the complexity of this substance, paranoia, mental disorientation, and physical aggressiveness are common behavioral indicators. Large doses will cause the heart rate to increase uncontrollably leading to severe heart failure. If drug use is expected, approach individual with extreme - ”

“Come on, Roger,” interrupted Jake. “Damn it! I am not a druggy. You know me. I've never in my life touched any of that crap. I don't even take stuff the doctor prescribes. Remember when I broke my collar bone over the fourth of July. I tossed the prescription and came to work the very next day. Never missed a beat. There is no way. They screwed up the test! They had to.”

“I'm sorry, Jake. They do several re-tests when they find a positive. It's as close to one-hundred percent accurate as you can get.”

“Then let me take another test.”

“I tried Jake. I went clear to the top, Higgins himself. It's no dice. You know the policy. The best I could do is thirty day suspension without pay after which you can retest and appeal. Security will be here anytime to retrieve your ID and let you take personal items out of your desk. Sorry Jake. You have to be out of here by nine.”

“I don't believe it. This is insane.”

A knock echoed through the closed door and Roger yelled, “Go away!”

"Security," came the response.

"Sorry Jake."

Jake turned and opened the door to face two security officers. Both had holstered guns; one was short and fat. The other one asked, "Are you Jacob McCarry?"

"Yes," he meekly replied.

They escorted him to his desk, unlocked it, and watched as he packed his personal belongings. The rest of Jake's section began arriving, each studying the events taking place. Jake saw the disgust in their faces and he felt humiliation like never before. He hurriedly finished gathering his things, none of which really mattered at the moment. As the two security officers escorted him to the door, Jake could feel all the eyes upon him and just wanted to disappear. They escorted him all the way to the parking lot and his front row, early bird parking space. They continued to watch until he exited the employee parking lot and drove out of sight.

Jake pulled up to the curb in a no parking zone and just let his truck idle. He just looked straight ahead in a daze of disbelief. Now what? Now I'm an unemployed druggy. This is the nightmare of all nightmares. What will my Dad say? What will Katie say? Oh shit, I can't tell her. But what am I going to say? Nothing, just go home. Just go home.

He accelerated away from the curb still in his daze and soon found himself heading down Dolly Madison Highway. Traffic was heavy but he still managed an easy forty-five in his oversize four wheel drive truck.

At least he had satisfaction in his truck. Although it was out of place on the streets of the D.C. area, he found contentment in the height advantage that allowed him to watch traffic far in advance; traffic was moving extremely well as far as he could see. He glanced down into the car next to him in the fast lane and couldn't help noticing the pair of legs. Her skirt was short and the legs had a light tone of brown, but it didn't matter. Jake made the transition to Interstate Sixty-Six and was soon in Centerville. He exited the freeway, drove past the supermarket and followed the side streets around behind to his apartment parking complex.

He pulled his truck around back to the carport, but somebody had taken his parking space. That was definitely against apartment complex rules; everybody had their assigned parking spaces and, if he saw that person, they would hear about it, especially today. He backed out of the parking lot and drove down the street, finding a space more than a half a block away. When he returned on foot, he was now even madder. Jake noted the license number and would call the building superintendent.

Intent on avoiding his neighbors, he entered the stair well of his four-story apartment building and dashed upward, skipping every other step. Looking down at his feet as they attacked the stair-way, he almost ran into an old woman coming down the stairs. "Sorry Ma'am," he apologetically offered. But she was stooped over, looking away and didn't even acknowledge his presence. Kind of rude, he thought but people here in the East were different than back home in Wyoming; not that they were intentionally rude, just that they weren't as outwardly friendly. Besides, she was wearing some kind of uniform and maybe she was having a bad workday, kind of like his.

He entered his apartment and locked the door behind him. It was immaculately clean with everything in its place, which was the way he always kept it. First he paced, then sat, but soon resumed the pacing. He turned on the TV, sat again and then insatiably punched the remote to flip through the channels. Nothing distracted his thoughts; the worst of it was the intolerable feeling of embarrassment. He jumped up and paced into the kitchen with the thought that maybe food would fulfill an elusive need. From the fridge, he grabbed the aging container of left over lasagna from the poker game. When he popped the container top, it didn't look so appealing. The lasagna had fury looking little white spots intermittently across the top. Jake dumped the Lasagna in the trash and threw the container in the sink. He pulled the container of little sausage wieners from the fridge and found the same result. The more he inspected the fridge contents, the more confused he became. Everything seemed to have grown mold overnight.

One apple sat in the bowl on the counter; it would just have to do. But then earlier this morning, before he'd gone to work, he thought he had four apples. Jake grabbed the apple and returned to the easy chair and the soap opera drivel on the TV. The apple tasted good but it didn't make him feel any better. How could he have failed the drug test? There was just no way. Maybe a shot of whiskey, he thought. Should he call his Dad? What would he do?

Then the soap opera drama got his attention; a young beautiful woman slapped an older woman – he giggled. The soap broke off to commercial; it wasn't laundry soap, but it was close, shampoo. Then it was a Chevrolet truck commercial followed by previews of the evening's programming. When the soap returned, the background music turned dramatic as the older woman lambasted the younger one. The younger woman screamed back. Jake laughed outright and yelled, "Belt the old bat again. Yee ha. Let her have it." He took the last bite of the apple and tossed the core over his shoulder.

"Partee," he said as he jumped up and turned on the stereo. Country Western just wouldn't do; he tuned in Radical Rock and cranked it up. He turned back to the TV with a proposition, "Hey, sweet young thing. I'd like to have you. Oowooy." He began to dance and follow frantic lyrics blasting from the stereo:

Dead babies in the street need no heat cause
their momma's got lovin for me. Da da da da
da di du you too. Dead babies need no feet

 Brian David Simmons

cause their momma's got the street heat beat. Lovin me, doing me, eating me makes me fine. Momma needs no babies in the seat. All she needs is me. Eating me, doing me, making me fine. Da da da…

Insistent pounding at the door interrupted his singing and he sprang to open it. He flung it open and rejoiced with, "Hallaluya." He shouted at top of his lungs, "Come on in, Katie. Let's Partee." He grabbed her hand and pulled her inside before slamming the door. "God damn, I love your tits. Let me see 'em, now. Come on. Let me see 'em."

She slapped him hard across the face but it didn't faze him in the slightest. He reached out and pinched her breast and she slapped him again, only this time with a closed fist and then yelled above the level of the music, "What is the matter with you? I left work as soon as I heard. This means it's true, doesn't it?"

"Hey, let's partee. Come on, let's go somewhere. I feel like going ninety-five."

"I would have never believed it," she sighed as she studied his behavior. He went back to dancing. "I'm leaving Jake. Don't call me – you jerk!" she yelled. Katie turned for the door, but Jake grabbed her from behind and spun her around; as she turned, her knee came up and impacted his groin. It didn't hurt; he pulled her towards him, opened his mouth and stuck out his tongue to kiss her. Drool ran down the side of his mouth as he pulled her closer. She screamed, "You ass-hole," then ducked and spun sideways bringing his arm with her. She ratcheted it up behind his back and then used it to push herself away. He fell to the floor.

"Hey, Katie. Now you got me where you want me." He grabbed his groin and added, "I'm here baby."

"You're sick. Stay away from me!" she screamed before marching out the door.

Jake rolled over to thoughtlessly watch her leave and then stared at the open door. His mind wandered off to visualize himself in command of a supersonic jet screaming towards the heavens. Finally, he realized she was gone and jumped up in confusion. "Katie, where'd you go?" he yelled. Jake charged down the stair well, falling once, and then burst outside to find her nowhere in sight. He yelled, "Katie," looked left and right and then ran to the carport. He called, "Katie." The thought "where's my truck?" crossed his mind but quickly vanished. He cried out again, "Katie." His heart accelerated further into an extreme state of tachycardia. He took off in a full run down the street in search of her, but she had disappeared. When he reached the corner, he could see people in the super-market parking lot and concluded that's where Katie had to be.

He was sweating profusely and shed his shirt as he ran towards the parking lot. He saw what he thought was his truck and darted out into traffic to catch it; his momentum carried him into the bed side panel of the passing truck and he rebounded to roll on the asphalt. An oncoming car screeched to a stop and sounded its horn; another car slammed into it from behind. Jake jumped to his feet and charged toward the supermarket as he repeatedly screamed, "Katie. Katie." The center of his chest ached and his left arm had a tingling sensation, but it didn't matter. He charged on.

The parking lot was full of cars with people coming and going. Why am I here, he wondered? Whowzer that guy's got a big nose with green weenie boogers. Grandma's Cookies, that's what I want. Yeah, Grandma's Cookies. He dashed towards the supermarket entrance, running into a woman and overturning her cart, but it didn't slow down his race for cookies. His heart began ventricular fibrillation and this time he felt a sharp pain in his chest. He flew through the supermarket entrance and blasted into a bakery display, sending donuts, muffins, and pies flying; Jake went head over heels at impact and the world went dark.

Chapter Fourteen

Quaraysh Unity

In the south wing of the Saud ibn-Wahhab palace in the holy city of Medina, Hafez supervised attendants packing his luggage. His wife, Ashel, sat silently in the corner. One of the attendants dropped a shirt and Hafez lambasted him for incompetence. Hafez picked up the shirt and carefully placed it in the suitcase himself. He dismissed the attendants with a wave of his hand and then turned to his wife to take his good-bye.

He approached her in the corner, but she pushed him away and pleaded, "Hafez, why can't you confide in me? I have been your faithful wife for six years, bore you three children, and yet you still treat me as though I am a stranger. Can you please just tell me why you must leave again?"

"All will become obvious in due time. Now come to the bed with me," he said as he pulled her from the chair and tugged her to the foot of the bed.

"No, please, Hafez. Tell me why you must leave."

"You will find out soon enough. Do not make me mad. I wish to make our parting a pleasant one. So embrace me."

"I cannot, Hafez," she said as she broke into tears. "My sanity is going. I am nothing but a servant trapped in your father's house with no companionship, no affection, no trust, and no escape. I can't take it any longer. I think of suicide each day, searching for painless ways to leave this world. How can I embrace you when my thoughts are so confused?"

"You should not think such horrible things. You are my wife and will always be my wife," consoled Hafez while callously weighing his primeval desires against the pleadings of his wife. Hafez took her hand and caressed it. "What about your children? They need your kindred love, as do I. We need you."

She pulled her hand back and pleaded for answers, "Then tell me, Hafez, why do your father's pedagogues undertake the raising of our children while excluding me? The children aren't even part of my existence. They don't need me, Hafez, and neither do you. You leave for months at a time with no word, no messages, no phone calls, no anything. You can not do this again. You can not leave me alone again or I will surely go insane."

She wrapped her arms around him and pressed her body against his. Hafez languished with mixed feelings of sympathy, love, and desire; she could not know the whole truth. He had taken a sworn oath of secrecy, yet she needed something.

Hafez held her away with his hands on her shoulders and relented. "This pain you now endure is only temporary. I will tell you things guarded by a sworn oath of death. Even an uttered word to the children or my father will result in our death. Do you understand?"

She nodded and he continued, "Soon things will be different and you will celebrate in a coming of a new Quaraysh Unity, creating a great Arabic nation like the world has never seen before. This is what I do for you and for all Muslims. My father has guided my whole life to prepare me for the leadership role I now play in this battle. My childhood, my British education, our life here in my father's house, everything has been by plan, and everything has been to resurrect the Quaraysh Unity. You must give me time to complete the great task I now undertake. Do you understand?"

She didn't speak; she just nodded and then began to disrobe. Hafez admired her, but his eyes avoided hers; love, affection, and companionship were not what he desired most. He spun her around and thrust her face first onto the bed. He flipped up the back of her robe, unzipped his pants and minutes later, he had satisfied his primeval desire. Without another word to his wife, he bolted from his quarters barking commands at attendants to retrieve his luggage.

Two Mercedes with open doors were parked at the base of the palace steps. Two men stood watch with machine guns while three others smoked cigarettes and chatted. With his good-bye completed, Hafez ibn-Wahhab emerged from the palace doors, quickly pattered down the steps, and slid into the car in the rear. Two attendants followed with his luggage and then they were off.

     Brian David Simmons

The Mercedes accelerated as they reached the open road leading south from Medina. Hafez opened his briefcase and began studying his notes and preparing for the meeting in Mecca. It seemed that somebody was always trying to get more than their fair share of his father's money, especially his fellow Arabs. He was determined not to let that happen and had to be prepared to negotiate a premium for import and shipping fees. His father would expect nothing less in the family business. He would demand an outlandish price and then settle for a percentage of oil field royalties from his fellow Saudi delegates and representatives from other Arabic nations. It was a six-hour trip and he used every minute of it to study oil field production quantities, export projections, import needs and prepare his strategy.

The Mercedes pulled up in front of the modernistic three-story Coalition of Arabic Nations building in Mecca. The security force deployed and then Hafez and his most trusted guard made their way to front entrance. He was met at the entrance by a security guard who escorted him to the third floor conference room. Hafez's personal guard remained outside while Hafez took his place at the table inside the conference room. In secret acknowledgment, he received a subtle nod from an Iranian delegate across the table and then made acknowledging eye contact with another delegate further down the table.

Hafez was one of four Saudi representatives in attendance. Topics covered imports of grain and cotton from the United States, computers from Japan and machinery from Brazil. Hafez negotiated his position with fervor, at one point standing and pounding on the table to yell at his fellow Arabs. As a Saudi representative of the Coalition of Arabic Nations, Hafez assured the conference that Saudi Arabia and the Wahhab family would fulfill their commitment, but only if their best interests were served. The meeting continued late into the night.

Then, in response to a minor objection from the Iranian delegate, Hafez unexpectedly blew up. "What do you mean you don't have enough oil production to pay a royalty? You negotiated your own production rates with OPEC. If you cut yourself short, it's not my fault." Hafez pounded the table and then pointed at the Iranian. "Listen, you fundamentalist donkey's ass. If you don't agree to my terms for shipping, just try and get your goods shipped by somebody else. I can't believe this incompetence. I'm done with this meeting." And with that, Hafez slammed his briefcase shut and marched from the conference room.

He quickly exited the Coalition of Arabic Nations building and went immediately to his Mercedes. They left in a roar of engines and a swirl of dust. In a few minutes they pulled up in front of a westernized hotel far from the religious center of Mecca. The security man had secured adjacent rooms for all six and they each disappeared into their respective rooms.

After only a couple of hours' sleep, Hafez's alarm rang, signifying 4:00 a.m. He quickly dressed in old, tattered garments, unbecoming for a man of his prominence. When he emerged from his room, his most trusted security guard met him in the hall and they sneaked down the stairs and exited the hotel through a rear door. They made their way on foot toward the city center through the increasingly narrow streets until they reached a high wooden gate. They opened the gate and climbed into an aging one-ton truck, started it, and pulled out into the narrow street.

The street was quiet, city inhabitants were still sleeping, and they maneuvered through the city unobserved. They drove west from Mecca toward the Red Sea. Their destination was a meeting; one of many that had been planned years in advance. Its location had been secretly prepared and then guarded by the Hesimite Saudis.

The shores of the Red Sea abound with phosphates, manganese and other minerals. Small mining operations exist on the desolate southeastern shore. Small factories, workshops, and mines are scattered along the shoreline to exploit the resources of the Red Sea. Inside a shallow mine, a small room had been specially constructed with miles of electrical wire enveloping the room.

Hafez was first to arrive. As he approached alone, he studied for signs of life. There were none. A diesel generator outside the mine loped at low rpm to provide power for the electrical cage. He entered the mine. As current flowed through the miles of wire, a magnetic field was generated, disrupting all forms of electronic communication or any possibility of eavesdropping. This super charged Faraday cage was the location of Hafez's meeting.

Representatives at the meeting arrived one by one, each wearing unpretentious Arabic garb and inconspicuously entering the mine. The second to arrive was the Iranian delegate. Hafez watched as he paced the dirt floor of the cage, back and forth, building his anger in anticipation of the meeting. The Iranian said nothing at the arrival of each delegate; he just paced.

The Iranian delegate was ready when the sixth and final representative of the meeting arrived and entered the room guarded by the Faraday cage. He immediately assaulted Hafez with screaming accompanied by a stiff jab to the chest with a finger. "What do you mean 'fundamentalist donkey's ass'? What gives you the right to say such things and disrupt Coalition meetings? I do not make my life of Quaraysh sacrifice to be insulted by the likes of you! You are wealthy beyond all reason, yet you bicker for more at the expense of us all. I demand a quorum to slice your throat and end your miserable life!"

"You fool!" screamed Hafez. "These things are not for you. They are for them; those who spy on us day and night with electronic and parabolic listening devices. They see us, hear us, and are always there

    Brian David Simmons

with never a moment's rest. This show I do for them, not for you. They must believe we cannot agree. They must believe we cannot act as one. They must believe we are not capable of a Quaraysh Unity. If you were not so stupid, you would see this!"

The Iranian delegate snorted and then refocused his verbal attack, "It matters little. You have still failed the Quaraysh Unity. I say you shame me and all those we represent. The *Shir Ali Kahn* is still at dry dock. It has been there for a year and you have not prepared it for the greatness we have planned. Your incompetence will be the downfall of us all."

"When, when will it be ready?" voiced another delegate.

Hafez paused, took a deep breath, and then calmly replied, "Do not despair. I employed an American to provide the necessary parts. I have released inordinate sums of American dollars from Bank Islam as compensation for this Anglo roach. You know this greed to be the true motivation of the West. So do not fear. Necessary parts have already been delivered and installed. The *Shir Ali Kahn* will be put to sea before week's end. This will be done as surely as the other ships were put to sea."

"Then I still say you have betrayed us!" stated the Iranian. "The CIA will surely detect your American dollars, trace them and then discover us all. I say you are the fool!"

"I am no fool. I do not make transactions; I would not implicate myself or the Unity. I would leave no trail, no track, no sign that we even exist. You are a fool to believe otherwise. The transactions are filtered through the scourge of degenerate greedy dogs. It is the business of these Americans to cheat, hide, steal, and covet money for their own rancid desires. They hide from detection, just as we do, and with an opportunity to line their own filthy pockets, they gladly make the necessary transactions. Trust me. Our anonymity is protected. The *Shir Ali Kahn* will be at sea. These things you can count on, as surely as you can count on the Satan's greed!"

With a snort followed by a sniffle, the Iranian conceded, "Do not disappoint, then."

"We have pressing matters of greater consequence to discuss," went on Hafez and questioned the Egyptian, Aysut, "How goes training?"

"The crews have been selected and will soon be relocated to Siwa. They do not know the fate that awaits them, but know their mission is great. They will be relocated soon. Their training will start with a test to demonstrate their willingness and commitment. Those who fail will be executed."

"It must be so, I suppose."

"Practice articles are in place. I have personally attempted the assembly operations. It does not seem that difficult, but the two instructors from Novosibrisk have already received partial payment and are ready to begin training. Following the training, they too will be executed."

The Iranian chuckled, "It will be their final payment."

Hafez ignored the Iranian comment and responded to Aysut, "So be it, then."

Hafez then turned to the Iraqi, "Kermar, you and the great nation of Iraq must re-ignite the anger of the West. It has been long and their mindfulness has been diverted by the Russians, Koreans and Chinese. Strike to retake the country. Do it under the guise of an Isis front. Suggest that you secretly and single-handedly possess the weapons of mass destruction. Distract them with financial demands, such as have been given to the Iranians. Use your agents to fuel the disagreement between the Palestinians and the Israelites. This is your mission. You and the Palestinians must be the focal point of anger from the West."

"My country has suffered many long and hard years of oppression to give you freedom to act. I do not know how much longer my country can endure such pain. Our leader grows impatient. He will not wait; we must strike the heart of the Great Satan now."

"In your suffering, you achieve greatness. When all is told, Iraq will be hailed and its greatness celebrated. But you must again anger the Great Satan and endure its wrath to achieve your destiny. Do not fail us and all will be rewarded."

"I will carry the message home. All is well with the Argentinians? Is the final moment upon us? Can I report these things?" The Iraqi representative pleaded as he focused momentarily on each of the other delegates.

Silence filled the Faraday cage as each evaluated the finality of what they were about to do.

The Syrian representative nodded and then broke the silence, "Satan's Destructors are ready and awaiting delivery. My country has fulfilled its obligation and has the Russian components in storage at Batum on the Black Sea. When you say the word, Hafez, they will be transported across Turkey to the Mediterranean."

The Iranian added, "The Swords of Allah from my country are also ready. Our best engineers have completed fabrication and conducted simulation testing. We will eliminate all inhabitants yet preserve the holy ground. It will be a joyous day."

"I do not see the joy in killing Muslims," replied Hafez solemnly. "Do not view it as a joyous day, my friends. Many Muslims will also die in the extermination of Jewish stench. View it only as necessary for our collective survival and the coming of the Quaraysh Unity. Do not make it more."

The Iranian again snorted and then replied, "Necessity, yes—necessity for our greatness, and I find joy in greatness. But it is now up to the Argentinians and Saudis. We have all fulfilled our obligations. Now you too must fulfill your obligation, Hafez. We wait for the Argentinians to complete their work and the *Shir Ali Kahn* to be put to sea. Our greatness waits for you to make these preparations complete."

Enthusiastically, the Jordanian delegate chimed in, "These things too shall be complete. The Qua-

          Brian David Simmons

raysh Unity will happen; this we are confident." He pointed at the Iraqi and then continued, "Report this to your leader: the Great Satan will be struck down and smashed like a roach, just as we have planned."

Except for Hafez, the delegates cheered at the Jordanian's words. Syria was announced as the next and final meeting place and the secret rendezvous concluded. Nothing was said outside the Faraday cage as the delegates left as they had arrived, one by one.

Chapter Fifteen

FRIENDS AND ENEMIES

BLACK AT THE CENTER FADED TO BRILLIANT RED AND orange at the fringes as Jake struggled to open his eyes. His throat was incredibly dry and swallowing was next to impossible and his upper lip twitched at the tube in his nose; he could hear it hissing as it delivered oxygen, drying out his nose and everything else. A crack of light snuck beneath a heavy brow and entered his eye. Then came feelings of nausea and soreness throughout his entire body. Slowly his eyelids reached midpoint and let in a blinding light, driving the eyelids back closed. With repeated attempts, he finally managed to open his eyes and focus on the ceiling light panel.

He cleared his throat and his vision was quickly filled with a familiar face. She didn't speak; she just smiled. Tears formed and ran down her cheeks stimulating his emotions as well. He managed to get out a single word over the lump in his throat, "Mom."

She took his hand and gently stroked it. The warmth of her love gave him strength and soon he mustered a question, "What happened?"

"You had a heart attack, son."

"A what? I don't remember." His mind went backwards in time searching for what he did remember.

CIA, positive drug test, fired, home, and then nothing. Wait - the TV soap. Oh crap - Katie. What did I say?

"Has Katie been here?" he asked.

"No, but you've had lots of friends. I think one of them has been here continuously, at least since I flew in. They're all such fine gentlemen."

"How long have I been here?"

"Five days."

"Seems like years ago. Did Dad come with you?"

"He did."

"Where is he?"

"He's at the hotel."

"When's he coming to the hospital?

"He's, ah, not coming," she replied and looked away.

"What?"

"He won't come with me, Jacob. When we arrived yesterday, he talked to the doctor and he's not coming."

"Mom, why not?" he pleaded.

"He thinks you're a, ah, user."

"A what?"

"The doctor told your Father that the heart attack was brought on by some kind of illegal drug. Your Father says you're a druggie. He doesn't want to see you. Oh Jacob, I'm so sorry."

"It's okay, Mom. I understand. This is something that has to be cleared-up with Dad on his level. Tell him that I'm disappointed he would believe such a line of crap. In fact, I'm down right pissed that he would even think such a thing. Remind him that no son of his could ever be a druggie and he knows it. Don't tell him once; tell him at least three times and be forceful, Mom. He'll come."

"You're probably right. You and your Father are a lot alike."

He saw movement out of the corner of his eye and then another figure appeared at his bedside; it was Norman Holbrook.

"Back from the dead," Norm commented. "You almost died several times."

"What do you want?" snapped Jake. The world was confused; he didn't mean to bark at Norman. He was FBI but he might as well have been CIA and their drug test.

"Punchy. That's good."

"I'm tired. I want to sleep," stated Jake and then closed his eyes. He pondered Norman's appearance. What's he doing? Is he waiting to see if I freak out so he can report back? No, not harmless, clumsy Norman. He's such a goofball and really a good friend. I'm sorry was his last thought before slipping into sleep.

Kate Mantis, the Washington Regional Hospital administrator, was compelled to do something she resented but had no choice. Hospital staffing had been kept lean partly for cost reasons but also because of the challenge of getting good nursing help. Now she was shorthanded and in trouble. All but one of the nurses in Recovery had come down with some kind of flu bug. She needed to limit rotation of some of her better staff from the ER and surgery, which left the ICU and recovery with a critical skill shortage. She would have to go with at least one temp, which was both expensive and risky with an unknown. She made the call. The temp organization reviewed qualifications and work history of several candidates with Kate and then made several recommendations. In the end, Kate selected Sandra Robertson. A fifty eight year old semi-retired nurse with lengthy and impressive credentials whom had chosen to spend more time with her three grandchildren rather than work full time. Kate was also fifty-eight and had three grandchildren, which was somewhat coincidental and struck a real emotional synergy with her own desires; the burgeoning need to spend more time with her own grandchildren blossomed to a climax that brought tears to her eyes.

The temp agency emailed Sandra Robertson's certifications and fee structure to Kate and all was in order. What was even better was that Robertson had no restrictions on shift and Kate could use her on grave where she needed her most. Kate followed up with a short phone call interview and Sandra would start tonight at eleven. Kate thought that maybe she would come in early in the morning and they could compare grandchildren stories and photos. But maybe that was too personal; better keep it all professional.

Sandra Roberts arrived at Washington Regional shortly before ten; she watched the mandatory employee safety and procedures video and then was given a uniform. The uniform was too large for her and she was promised one two sizes smaller if she worked tomorrow as well. She arrived at her station on the fifth floor shortly after the shift change had occurred and it was only Kora, the regular on duty nurse, that met her. Duties were explained and patients briefly reviewed. Grave was usually a very mundane shift, especially in recovery where all patients were stable. The hospital just needed somebody to check IVs, administer any doctor specified medications or other special orders, assist with restroom needs when required, and document it all on the patient's computerized record, which usually took more time than the actual duty itself.

With introductions out of the way, Kora and Sandra made the first round together: checking blood pressure on one patient, administering Percocet to another, but mostly just peeking in on each patient. Back at the nurses' station, Kora put in a call for pizza delivery, which was pretty much standard procedure for the late shift. They chatted briefly but Sandra quickly immersed herself in review of patients' medical records and volunteered for each round at increasing frequency. Kora had gained confidence in Sandra and soon occupied herself with Sudoku, television, and pizza.

Sandra concentrated on the medical records for one of the patients. It was a young man, twenty-six, recovering from heart attack. Blood tests identified an amphetamine, some kind of designer drug, along with LSD, heroin, mescaline and other unknown drugs; all of which had been attributed as the cause for his heart attack. He had undergone a battery of tests to ascertain the extent of damage to his heart. The thallium exercise test had been the most revealing and his condition had been classified as stunned myocardium; actually a recoverable condition with time, limited exercise and proper medical monitoring. The doctor had put him on an aspirin regimen, with authorized use of nitroglycerin if the patient displayed signs of chest pain or other indications of another heart attack. A special note was made relative to stimulus; he was not allowed stimulants of any kind, including caffeine, and his level of excitement and exertion needed to be minimized. His projected release date was today, only hours away after a doctor's final assessment.

At mid shift, Sandra entered the young man's room. His features caught her attention, he was extremely handsome, but that was a distraction. A woman much her senior was sleeping in a chair next to the bed and another dark haired young man was half dozing and reading in the corner. In the partial light, she made a mental note of both their faces and then slid the light switch to further dim light. She quietly went about routine duties and the young man in the bed stirred.

She checked his blood pressure and pulse before providing him a tiny aspirin and a small cup of water; all of which was efficiently entered into the patient's record on the computer in the corner. She further dimmed the light upon leaving the room and returning to the nurses' station. Kora's head partially hung forward with her hands motionless on the computer key board; she let a subtle snore and her head shifted slightly.

Sandra continued her study of medical records. Mike Armenta had been admitted unconscious and temporarily had been in the ER. He had been diagnosed with severe pneumonia accompanied with a flu variant. After assessment in the ER, Mike Armenta was officially pronounced DOA. Cause of death had not yet been entered but there was nothing to indicate other than death by natural causes; she smiled. Of particular interest to her as she perused the hospital's data base were patients that had died and the doctor's entries leading up to their death. It was a wealth of knowledge that somewhere she might be able to utilize and it engulfed her in thought.

She broke from the study session occasionally to check the time and keep her eye on Kora who was now fully asleep. At five-thirty, a half hour before shift change, Sandra re-entered Jacob McCarry's room and began repeating duties as she had done earlier. The dark-haired man in the corner had ventured off somewhere, which elevated her senses. The unknown is always a threat, she thought. He didn't pass the nurses' station, did he? Then movement from behind the closed bathroom door caught her attention and she relaxed. When he emerged, he greeted her with wide eyes and a smile, which put her back on alert. She continued with the routine: first taking his blood pressure with the associated computer entry, then taking his temperature with the same computer routine. The dark-haired young man tried to start a conversation with her, but she shushed him with a finger to her lips and then pointed at Jacob's mother in the chair. Sandra recognized him from her research and had to be careful; his name was Frank Wallace and he was FBI. Just part of the challenge, but caution and a little play acting to get him out of the room was needed. She checked the computer screen and muttered, "Oh," for effect. "This could be a little embarrassing," she whispered to Frank. "Why don't you go for coffee or something?"

Sandra pulled back the sheets and took a quick peek at Jacob's genitals and then asked Jacob, "Is everything alright down there?" She looked at Frank, frowned and shook her head slightly.

Frank brushed past the bottom of the bed, smiled at Jake and said, "I'll wait outside until you're done," and then exited the room.

Jacob responded to the nurse's inquiry, "Just fine. I've been to the little boy's room this morning and it all works."

"Good. Almost finished. The doctor will be in to see you around nine. If all is well, you'll be home by ten," she said with grin. She returned to the computer and rattled in a few lines of text. She pulled a small Dansi bottle of water from her smock, twisted the top and handed it to Jacob along with two large capsules.

Jake took the caplets from her and popped them in his mouth receiving an approving grin. He smiled back at her before taking a drink from the bottle. The caplets were drugs and they would have to go.

"Keeping your fluids up is important; all of it now." She assured as he emptied the contents of the bottle and put it back in her waiting hand, but the capsules were still between his gum and cheek. He had almost swallowed the capsules, but there was something strange about her; elderly and friendly, yet commanding, probably alright but what were the capsules for? He didn't need them; he was feeling much better. The water now too seemed a little strange; it had a slightly bitter stale taste as it trickled around his tongue and down past the sides of his uvula. He watched out of the corner of his eye as she re-caped the bottle and then discretely slid it into her side pocket. With another few clicks on the computer, she signed off, gave him a departing grin and exited. Frank entered the room as nurse Sandra left.

Hands, they weren't right, he realized and spit out the capsules, which were now on the verge of dissolving. The soft touch, yet muscular snap on the cusp, as she'd taken his blood pressure weren't the hands of someone his mother's age. Her touch was soft and delicate, yet strong, as she handled his arm and took his pulse; even the back of her hand was soft as she checked his forehead for fever or dampness.

Frank started to speak but Jake interrupted him, "Did you see her hands?" He swallowed and then with more thought added, "They were the hands of a twenty year old. Fifty year old hands have age spots and wrinkles. No way were her hands as old as her face."

"Well, maybe she uses a lot of lotion. I didn't notice."

"I'm telling you, Frank; something was unusual about that woman. Did you see the way she walked? I'll bet there was natural swank underneath that uniform. Go – follow her and look closer for yourself."

"I'm not going to go follow her! What would I do, go ask her to show me her ID? Excuse me madam, my friend thinks there's a swanky old bat underneath that uniform. How about a little look-see and then your driver's license? Get off it Jake; I thought all the hallucinogens were out of your system."

"The drugs are out of my system and I'm paying attention."

"Yea, you're paying attention alright, eyeballing the backside of a woman twice your age. We gotta get you out of here. And by the way, your mother is sleeping right over there," Frank finished and pointed at Jake's mother.

"No. You're not paying attention," insisted Jake. "How'd you get in the FBI anyway?"

"Getting a little testy aren't you?"

"No, it's just your lack of attention to detail."

"Those are the kind of words that will cost you friends. You need to just settle down. Is everything alright, Jake?"

Jake clinched his fist with the caplets. "No, it's not! The hands ain't right; she ain't right. You need to open your Goddamn eyes," snapped Jake and woke his Mother. Jake tugged at the blanket over him, flung the TV remote to the side, swinging on its cable to the ground. "What is all this crap anyway?" he continued at an accelerating pace. "What the hell do you know anyway? I'm getting out of here."

"Not in my presence you won't. I will not tolerate that vulgar language!" scolded his mother as she came out of her slumber. "Remember the bar of soap. I'm not beyond it."

"Awe. Soap you," he said as he jumped out of bed. "And screw everybody else that thinks I'm a druggie."

"What are you doing? Get back into bed," ordered Frank.

"You get in. I've had enough," yelled Jake as he hurled the sticky and dissolving capsules at Frank. "I'm leaving."

"Jacob, honey, please settle down. What's going on?" beckoned his mother.

Harshness gave way to hallucination as the sensations infiltrated his body. The feeling was familiar; a fleeting moment of Jake's sanity recognized it and tried to subdue and control the flush expanding throughout his body. He commended it to stop and willed its reversal with all his might. Mind over madness, control; "No!" his inner mind cried. Euphoria attacked the fragile flit of rationality and again his mind cried: "No!" Warmth reached his toes and they tingled with pleasure as shreds of realization lost the battle and an uncontrollable excitation moved in.

"Damn you got a big head, Frank. Get a haircut baby." said Jake as he did a backstroke dance towards the door, inadvertently back handing his Mother's breasts.

She shrieked, "I can't believe this," and slapped him hard across the face. "Your father was right and I was so wrong. How can this be?" she cried as the sobbing began.

"Wo, wo, the old bat's got a punch. Ye ha. How bout another mumsee."

She didn't reply, her sobbing just intensified. Jake danced out the door singing his own tune of gibberish to bounce off Kora who had come to investigate the commotion. Frank followed him out the door; two of the shift change nurses had also come to assist. Kora and one of the other nurses tried to subdue him, each grabbing an arm, but he easily flung them aside, and knocked Frank to the ground with a football block and elbow to the abdomen.

The stairwell was just down the hall and clearly marked with an exit sign that even Jake could still recognize. In the charge down the hall, he knocked over a medical cart and flew past another nurse before entering the stair well. When he reached the ground floor, he burst through the door in search of an exit. He had to go, but where. Ah there he knew, the front door. Hospital gown open and flapping to the rear, he charged the main entrance running over a small child and her mother; he didn't notice. All he knew was that freedom lie outside. Two hospital security guards blocked his path and meet the same consequence as the mother and child.

He was free; onward and outward. As he entered the parking lot, he ran passed an elderly woman that smiled at him with familiarity, but it didn't register. On he ran at full speed, across Fairborn Street, down a side street, turned left down an alley and then right on another side street. The further he ran, the better he felt.

His bare feet carried him long and far where buildings were no longer pristine and tourist kept. Bars guarded store fronts and the sidewalks were littered with broken bottles and trash. Deteriorating hotels and dilapidated apartment buildings passed him on the right and left as he ran. His mind refused to focus on what he wanted but the energy was uncontrollable and he exploded onward. In the early hour, he tripped over a cardboard box with two residents sleeping. They

    Brian David Simmons

yowled and barked at him as he continued his insane quest. He turned right down an alley and, with a final burst of energy, charged down the alley. Jake crashed head first into stacks of rotting produce at the rear of a small market. The euphoria had disappeared and he felt every accelerated violent heartbeat. Every muscle screamed in agony, but paralyzing forces rejected every attempt for even the slightest movement. Pain and terror exploded and his mind screamed, but no words came forth.

Chapter Sixteen

PREPARATIONS

IT WAS OVER; COLE HAD BEEN DUMPED. CALLS TO DOMInique had gone unanswered, which was a clear message. She could have at least sent him a text telling him to it was over. But how could it be? Everything had seemed just fine the last time they talked. Maybe she just didn't want to associate with a destitute appearing desert dweller. But then, he couldn't have told her the truth. It would have certainly driven her away. So maybe it was better this way.

The weather had turned warm and it was time to move on. Cole missed the mountains of Idaho, although he would never return to Coeur d'Alene. But fifty miles on a dirt road down river from North Fork was the confluence of the Salmon River. And a few miles further, at the end of the road, was the Sodder bar and campground. He could spend the days fishing and the nights at the remote bar.

The camp trailer needed new tires and that was first on the agenda for tomorrow. Then the fridge and heater needed repair. He'd drop the trailer at the RV dealer after tires. Maybe just spend a few nights in the back of the truck.

THE ARGENTINES HAD BEEN BUSY. THE POGOS HAD been reloaded with high energy HTPX-20 and mated with their nozzles. Space Sciences had provided the design, nozzles, and electronic components for the two-stage version of the POGOs. The movable, high-performance nozzles along with electronic guidance controls had been received and assembly operations were running at a feverish pace. Beech was on hand to supervise stacking and final assembly operations. He was also there to collect his final payment. His long endeavor was almost over. With his final payment, he could retire to the French Riviera, or for that matter, anywhere in the world. But his plans were for the Riviera. He was particularly fond of the French high-society lifestyle, their wine, and their women.

With Beech's help, the Argentinians had a full-up two-stage system capable of striking any of their neighbors. Beech's activities were all illegal but easily rationalized, at least by him. His integrity was only minimally scarred because he only broke inane commerce restrictions, not because he had really done anything wrong.

Beech had only provided the Argentinians with fifty-year-old ballistic missile technology that somebody else would have provided if he hadn't. And he had provided it to a nation at peace with no current enemies. Since the dispute with the British over the Falkland Islands, the Argentinians had been at peace with the world. The weapons were only deterrents against possible unknown future confrontations with their neighbors. They would probably sit in a silo somewhere for years until the propellant grains cracked and crumbled away.

Even if the Argentinians did use them, who would they use them against and what payload would they deliver? The missiles were ballistic in design and capable of delivering large payloads, but they had limited range and utility as a ballistic missile. Unlike the U.S. Minuteman, Peacekeeper, or SICBM, the two-stage POGO wasn't capable of intercontinental attacks. For close range against Chile, Brazil, or Bolivia, the POGO would provide a lethal, fly-to-the-target type of fast burn ballistic missile. With its new nozzle and guidance system, it could easily put a conventional warhead on the presidential palace in Santiago, Chile. But what purpose would that serve? No, the weapons were only for defensive purposes. Beech was sure of it, and had assurances from the Argentinians to support his assessment.

Even with the turmoil in Russia, nuclear warheads were still a guarded item. It was improbable that the Argentinians could acquire any. Even if they did, when it became known, the wrath of the world would come down on the Argentinians and they would be punished like Iraq, Iran and Kosovo.

With the limited range of the POGOs, a strike against the United States or any distant target was not possible. The maximum range of the POGO was calculated by Beech to be about twenty-seven hundred miles and that assumed minimum inert weight and minimum payload. The closest a POGO could come to the United States was Mexico City, and it would arrive with all its propellant exhausted and only a small warhead to explode. It would be like a giant plastic Coca-Cola bottle falling from the sky with no harm to anyone, unless they were standing directly under it. Beech was absolutely positive the POGO could never be used against the United States.

His conscience was satisfied and all he needed now was his final payment. He was to receive two million traveling cash and wire transfer deposits in his French, Swiss, and U.S. bank accounts. The Argentinians had, for reasons unknown to Chris Beech, chosen to launder their payments through Bank Islam. It really didn't matter why as long as he got his money. To him though, it was a frustration because payment was far too slow and he was still owed eight million for each of the fifty-two POGOs. Every dime of it was profit. He had paid all of his expenses along the way with millions he had milked out of Argentinians. This final payment was for him and him alone.

Beech held back on delivery of the final component. To separate the lower stage from the upper stage rocket after it had expended all its fuel, a chevron-shaped charge of plastic explosive encircled the inter-stage. Each interstage was to have a small electronic logic circuit to ignite the shape charge. It was a simple component that became active with first stage motor pressure and acceleration, and then triggered with first stage motor pressure decay. Beech had specified the design of the interstage so that the logic circuit could be installed following final assembly through an access panel. This logic circuit was the final component for the missiles and the leverage for Beech's final payment.

Assembly operations were in a large warehouse on the docks of Avellaneda just south of Buenos Aires. From outside, the warehouse looked like any other, with deteriorating planking and tin roof, but its appearance was deceptive. Inside, the walls had been sheathed, concrete floor sealed, cranes installed, and lighting installed to illuminate every corner of the interior. It was as modern as any stateside production facility.

Beech walked the floor, monitoring work at each assembly station. It was like an assembly line: lower stage nozzle installation, upper stage nozzle installation, igniter installation, interstage preparation, stacking, final assembly, inspection, and shipping container packaging. Beech was impressed with the attention to detail that went into the shipping containers. They were barrel-like wood containers that were several feet in diameter larger than the missiles. The missiles, once assembled, would be installed in the containers and held suspended at the center of the container with retractable clamps that locked the missile in place. The containers had an external, enclosed metal frame structure to allow for both vertical or horizontal handling and storage of the missiles. Even the dimensions on the external structure were precise. It was far more elaborate than was required and didn't make sense, but Beech really didn't care. After he got his money, the missiles were theirs and they could Christmas wrap them anyway they wanted.

Chris Beech got his final payment, or at least part of it. He had actually figured that they would cheat him in the end. The Argentinians arranged for half of the four hundred million still owed him to be released from the local bank. The other half was promised in thirty days. Beech knew they would never pay unless they needed his services again, but this was the kind of thing he expected and it was actually better than he had hoped for. He accepted their promise at face value and provided them with the interstage separation circuitry. Within a few hours, each of the POGOs had a logic circuit installed. Beech departed a happy man and returned to his hotel.

Chapter Seventeen

TERMINAL ALLEY—JACOB

THE TORMENT ENGULFING HIS BODY WAS NOW ALMOST tolerable. He lay in the fetal position to counteract the cold shivering in his mind. He was wide awake and yet he saw nothing. He had semiconscious dreams of frantic flight through space and time that quickly changed to obscure images of home and fantasies of Wyoming wild fires. The first tangible realizations were of the sunlight peering down from between the buildings and a warming piece of cardboard that covered him. His head pounded beyond reason and thirst, yes, water or anything else liquid consumed his first thoughts. His legs and torso ached with a stiffness he had never known. As he lay motionless, his mind gradually began to grasp reality and, with a squint, opened his eyes. The brilliance of the sunlight brought them back closed and only with repeated attempts did he manage to capture his surroundings. Ooh, something stank, he thought. The alley was narrow and trash filled. The wall across from him had small blackened windows and a padlocked door that looked like it hadn't been opened in years. He closed his eyes and dozed momentarily. Nausea was overwhelming and he wretched but nothing came out. He dropped his chin, moved his hand lethargically to his chest and realized the front of his gown was covered in dried vomit. Gown, oh yea, the hospital. Where am I? Why am I shivering when I'm not?

Jake fought against the lethargy and gradually straightened his right leg and then his left. What is this, he thought as he slid the section of a cardboard box off to the side. The sun was now warming and the thought of shivering subsided. He could hear traffic and voices from the entrance to alley; if he could just get up, help was near. He tried to call out but a dry hoarseness prevented it. He rolled slightly forward and pulled both knees up underneath him and then rose up. The nausea returned with light headedness and he dropped back to the pavement. Breathing deeply helped clear the nausea and fog from his mind. He struggled to a kneeling position facing the back of the alley. Eventually, with more deep breathing and the wall to steady him, Jake managed a shaky stance. He looked down at his gown; it was a mess from his own bodily fluids and those of the alley.

He hoarsely beckoned an elderly black man for help. The man sped up his pace and quickly vanished from Jake's blurred vision. Three men heard his plea. Jake flayed a limp wave at them; no intelligible word would come from his mouth.

"Hey look at this one," cackled one of the men.

"Holy shit this white boy fucked up," chided another.

As they circled Jake, the harassment escalated, "Bare-assed nitey must make him somebody's bitch."

"Nobody would touch em. He stinks to high heaven."

"How bout it white boy? You somebody's special thing?"

"You putting out for drugs? You got 'em hid some-where? Huh?"

One of them picked up an empty whiskey pint and prodded Jake. Jake batted feebly at the probing bottle and fell back against the wall.

In a sweeping kick, one of the three knocked Jake's feeble legs out from underneath him and he fell backwards smacking his head hard against the asphalt. A kick hammered his unprotected ribs and rolled him to his stomach. He rolled to his side with a kick to the side of his head and managed a fetal position to try and protect himself. The blows didn't seem to hurt as bad as they should; his tortured body was already overwhelmed with enough pain that this was just minor. A blow directly to his face sent him sprawling backward; then came another kick, another, and then another. All the while the taunting continued. Jake again managed a fetal position and rolled with each successive blow to lessen the impact. His thoughts were now alive and he resolved to endure. Jake recalled the Pinedale Rodeo where he'd managed to ride a bull the required eight seconds, spurring all the way and receiving a near perfect score. But at the end of the ride his hand failed to release from the knotted bucking strap and he flayed and flopped endlessly across the back and over the head of a raging Brahma. A rodeo clown eventually freed his hand and the pounding stopped. He remembered the pain he'd endured both from the ride and afterward with multiple compound fractures to his right arm, five broken ribs, broken collarbone and a mild concussion. This beating couldn't be worse than that; they weren't inflicting nearly enough pain to be doing that much damage. This is minor he thought; at least by bull riding standards. The beating continued and it seemed like hours.

"Is that a special dress just for you, sweet thing?" said one of the gang bangers as Jake received a hard blow to the rib cage and rolled to his stomach splayed out with his elbows along his sides and his hands alongside his face.

"Oh, he's a thing of beauty."

Another kick to his ribs and Jake's body rolled. They all laughed as one of them shoved him over to his back and then unzipped his fly; he began urinating on Jake and the other two joined in and they laughed even harder. Jake's mind was fully engaged but his body failed to react to any commands. He screamed inside to block the thoughts; bitter anger, hatred, racism, and a willingness to do things he'd never considered before, were now embraced. His mind shrieked in pain when his motionless body took a hit to his genitals.

"Awe man, look at the shit on my shoe," commented one of the three.

"Looks like blood to me, Gorman my man."

"He's had enough," added another.

"You white piece of shit," shouted the third as Jake received a final kick.

Jake opened his eyes wide enough to capture the image of their faces and tattoos before they strutted off. Thirteen was the prevalent tattoo symbol; he would remember it.

Chapter Eighteen

ISTABAH

THE SMALL SETTLEMENT OF ISTABAH ON THE EASTern shores of the Mediterranean was blessed with a gentle rain. Its population of less than a hundred residents had migrated from different Middle Eastern nations to this insignificant piece of Syrian coast to support shipping operations of the Coalition of Arabic Nations. Some had come under duress. Others had come with the expectation that the community would grow and they would benefit financially. But it wasn't so; shipping operations were limited to the occasional arrival of the *Ankara* and *Servant of Allah*. Istabah had docks, cranes, and warehouse facilities, but was isolated without railroad or adequate highways for distribution of goods. Other than the shipping, Istabah had no trade or commerce of any kind, yet was maintained as a settlement by the Coalition of Arabic Nations.

Over the years, only three ships had ever docked at Istabah: *Ankara*, *Servant of Allah*, and the *Shir Ali Kahn*. The *Ankara* had originally been built by the Soviet Union in the 1940s and named the Novosibirsk, but it had been sold to Turkey and then title had been transferred to Syria. But its title was changing again to a new Jordanian company.

Although official title of registry for the *Ankara* was still Syria, it sailed under a Turkish flag and bore Turkish markings on its stack. It was a small ship, as far as modern ships go, weighing only one hundred fifty-one tons. It had been upgraded with its own derricks and deck cranes to accommodate loading from poorly equipped ports.

The aging oil-fired, steam-driven vessel normally ferried grain from the United States to Turkey and the rest of the Middle East. To avoid empty return journeys, it had been modified to serve as a crude oil tanker with tanks deep in its hold. Each return trip from the Middle East delivered a small load of crude to the offshore docking station near New Orleans. Thus, its dual cargo capability made it a profitable ship, frequently seen in the shipping lanes and in the Gulf, just off New Orleans.

The *Servant of Allah* was a small diesel-powered Egyptian vessel that normally restricted its operations to Europe and the Mediterranean Sea. It was an inefficient vessel built by Germany in the 1940s and abandoned off the Egyptian coast after World War II. The Egyptians had laid claim to it, resurrected it, gotten it operational, and put it into service transporting bulk goods and other supplies. It ferried anything and everything, from cars and machinery to packaged food goods to clothing, in order to satisfy a culture starving for western commodities.

The *Shir Ali Kahn* had had continual problems with its propeller drive train and had been dry docked for a complete rebuild. It was a similar vessel to the others, also of Egyptian registry. It had been purchased by Turkey from Japan as an obsolete fishing vessel and then sold to Syria and then again sold to Egypt. A new Chinese registry and name change to *Al Kaing* was currently in work. But it still sailed under its Turkish name and flew Syrian flags. It, like the other vessels, had such a convoluted history that ascertaining its actual ownership at any one given time was almost impossible.

Hafez sheltered his head from the rain with his coat as he hurried past the dock's warehouse facilities. He entered a small brick building with Saud ibn-Wahhab's name on a placard over the entrance. Inside, he was greeted by the office manager who promptly provided him with the ships' logs for his perusal. Hafez sat at the manager's desk and quickly scanned through the books.

"Good," he replied to the office manager. "But the *Ankara* and *Servant of Allah* are done for the year. I have a special cargo for each of the ships. When can they be ready to set sail with empty holds?"

"They cannot. I have contracts in place that put both ships on a very tight schedule."

"How dare you! You imbecile! I said the ships are done for the year. Why must I say more?"

"My apologies, Sahib," the manager meekly replied. "The *Ankara* is one day out with a load of grain from the United States and the *Servant of Allah* is in port at

Bengasi. They are unloading as we speak. Both ships can be ready to serve your purposes within a week's time, Sahib."

"Good, then send a communiqué to the captain of the *Servant of Allah*. Have her remain at port in Bengasi for one week and then put in here eight days from today."

"Should I have the ship remain idle? I do not see the reason. The captain will want to know."

"Since when do I need a reason? Just do it!"

The manager nodded reluctantly and replied, "Very good, then."

"When the *Ankara* arrives, get it unloaded and have it refueled and ready to set sail in two weeks' time."

"And the cargo?"

"Make ready for transportation of the crews to their homes and prepare a severance in the amount of five hundred American dollars for each. One thousand dollars for the captains."

"A severance? Are you dissatisfied with their service?"

"They are done! Why must I always repeat myself? Maybe you should prepare a severance for yourself as well."

"No, Sahib. I will make the necessary arrangements. But, why are they being dismissed? I mean, what should I tell them?"

"I do not care. Tell them what you like."

"Yes, Sahib. And when the *Servant of Allah* arrives, what will its cargo be?"

"I am making the arrangements. In a two weeks' time, you will prepare severances for the crew of the *Servant* as well, but do not tell them before they get here. Is that clear?"

"Yes, Sahib."

"Good, then make them in the same amounts and give yourself a bonus as well. Two thousand American dollars."

"Thank you. Thank you. It will be done as you command."

Chapter Nineteen

CALLS

TRAILER REPAIR IN QUARTZSITE SEEMED TO MOVE AT snail's pace and Cole had just gotten it back from the RV dealer. He towed the camp trailer back out to his now really isolated spot in the desert. Distant neighbors had headed back to wherever they had come from to escape the ever increasing daily temperatures. Cole seemed to have the desert to himself. He sat on the steps of the trailer and popped the top on a beer. He was preparing to dial Kevin to tell him about heading for Idaho and the Salmon River when his phone rang. Cole stared at the incoming number, made a fist and blew through it. "Shit," he said.

The phone rang six times before he finally answered, "Hello, Dominique."

"Hey Cole."

Cole didn't respond.

Dominique broke the silence, "Mad at me? I can tell."

"Not mad. Just uncertain."

"Listen, I know it's no excuse for not returning your calls, but I've had a hell of a lot work lately. So much you can't imagine. It's been my focus night and day. I know it doesn't justify my behavior, but I really am sorry."

"Okay."

"You are mad at me. I can tell."

"Dominique, you have issues. I have issues. And I don't know where the two of us go from here."

"What does it matter? Everyone has issues. I really do like you, you know. I have some time off and I want to spend it with you. Would that be alright?"

Cole's internal defenses were breaking down and yearnings of the heart were gaining ground. With his background and circumstance, logic and reason said "No" to this relationship. It wouldn't be fair to any woman, especially this very exceptional one. But, the very thought of her touch, the subtle fragrance of her skin, the intrinsic connection with her soul, the all-immersing joy of her presence, and everything else about her were winning out. Cole's mind said "No" but his heart spoke, "Yes."

"I'll get a flight," Dominique quickly responded. "Can we go dancing? Can we go to some of those mines and places you told me about?"

Cole smiled, "Sure."

"I'll get a flight and then call you tonight and let you know what my plans are. I'm excited. I can't wait to see you. I lo. . . miss you, you know."

"I miss you too."

"Okay. I'm going to run now: finish up one work item, get a flight, get a rental car and then I'll call you later tonight. Bye now. Love ya."

Confusion and emotion consumed Cole. Maybe he just didn't understand women, at least not this one.

And that was all compounded by his circumstance. He should end it. But what if he could return to life as normal? She was definitely worth the gamble. But would he put her in danger? He had no answers. The call to Kevin became more important than ever.

Kevin answered on the second ring, "What."

"That's not a very nice way to answer the phone."

"I'm busy working."

"Doing some of that cyber sneak stuff?"

"Yes ass hole. Do you remember the name Beech from the money laundering racket?"

"No."

"Well, it's strange but your name is included in a CIA report I got off Blaine Higgins's computer. Higgins is the director of the CIA's Strategic Resource department. The focus of the report is a Chris Beech."

"That doesn't make any sense."

"It didn't say much; it just listed your name along with a dozen or so others. It was written by some clandestine CIA analyst. A Jacob McCarry."

"So what is my name doing in a CIA report?"

"Bingo, that's the question. It really doesn't say much. The good thing is that it lists you as deceased."

"Kevin, what am I to make of all that. Does it mean I'm off the hook because I'm officially dead? Or is there something more I should worry about?"

"I don't know."

"I was going to hide out in Idaho and do some fishing. But I met someone and I want to rejoin the normal world."

"My God. Thinking with your little penis head again. It's just one of your cha-cha-cha one-nighters. Let it go."

"No Kevin. She is a very beautiful, very smart, travel agent and I like her a lot."

"Travel agent – what kind? Did she take you on a tour? I'll bet you already traveled around the world; that's a lot of cha-cha."

"Kevin! Knock it off! Help me figure out how to get back into the real world."

Kevin paused and then responded, "Without completely new DNA, fingerprints, and face, you will always be at risk. I already tried to get you out of the FBI's FACE database; it didn't work. It almost got me ID-ed. So the best we could do is something significant to your face, which isn't easy. Growing a beard and wearing sun glasses doesn't work anymore. You have to feed the recognition algorithms erroneous data. It's a matter of complex, interrelated Eigen features rather than simple occlusion. I'll work on it. By the way, what's her name?"

"Dominique."

"That's pretty. What's her last name?"

Cole recognized the ploy to gather enough data so that Kevin could do his cyber research on her. The truth was he didn't even know her last name and the best response he could come up with was: "Dominique is enough for now. Let's just leave it at that."

Chapter Twenty

TERMINAL ALLEY—FRANK?

JACOB MCCARRY WAS LYING SPRAWLED ON HIS BACK with his eyes opened to the bright sunlight. Remarkably clear skies lie overhead with small white wispy clouds floating near the reaches of space. An airplane miles overhead slowly moved past, leaving a signature contrail. He could hear traffic noise from the street nearby and a horn honked. He was alive, but with an exhaustion like he'd never known. A searing pain bit him in the side at his first attempt to move and he relaxed to relieve the pain. He heard voices off in the distance, but they did not come; he was alone in the alley. Several pieces of cardboard covered him and felt like a hundred pounds on his chest. He pulled his arm closer to his body and was again met with intense pain, but overcame it to pull his other arm to his side, as well.

Then he heard a ruffling sound and rolled his head slightly to the right; a woman dressed in a long coat with a scarf over her head was pulling a garbage bag out of the now overflowing dumpster. "Over here," Jake tried to speak, but only a barely recognizable croak came forth.

Another night came and passed into morning; Jake's eyes opened. He immediately recognized the comfort of the cardboard that covered him. The memory of the beating was still clear in Jake's mind, even through a mind crushing headache. But the bodily effects of whatever coma he had been in were gone. Jake wiped dried blood from his nose and felt around on his ribs: maybe one or two broken ribs, hopefully no internal damage, and lots of bruises. Just breathing and every slight movement seared with pain and tried to persuade him to just remain motionless. With time and the realization that death was near, he overcame the stagnatory force that held him in place and rolled out from underneath the cardboard. He inched forward on his stomach towards the garbage pile and entrance to the alley beyond. Grasping the asphalt with finger tips and shifting leg by leg, Jake inched forward. He desperately needed help and water, but the entrance to the alley was not an option. Jake searched the alley with his eyes and came up with an appalling option. Self-talk helped overcome the reluctance to do the disgusting. This is survival. Don't have to smell it or look at it, just eat it. Do it or die. If you don't, you're dead. If you do, you might live. Jake crawled to the bag of rotting produce, hesitated for a moment and then and ripped into the bag spilling its contents onto the asphalt. The odor was disgusting but he sorted through and came up with apples of mush and browned leaf lettuce that were, by normal standards, inedible. Mush of the apples soothed his throat and he consumed the best three. As he sorted for more edible items, he heard a noise behind.

The elderly black woman in the full length coat had returned. She was carrying a small duffle bag and approached to ask, "Find anything good?"

"Depends on your point of view," hoarsely replied Jake.

"Well, let me take a look? Would you?"

"Okay."

"We need to hurry. The garbage truck will be along soon and all this will be gone," she said as she began pawing through and sorting bad from vile. She used the remnants of the plastic bag to capture bad bordering on vile. As she worked, she said, "You know I've seen you here for a quite a while."

"How long?" interrupted Jake.

"Oh I don't know, several maybe; more like a week probably, but could be more. You were sleeping and having some kind of nightmare: peaceful for a moment and then striking out at the world. I felt sorry for you and didn't know what to do. I just fed you water when I came. You sipped it down just like a baby; eyes closed and everything, even made a little sucky sound. You are pretty much naked you know, but I didn't look." she quickly added. "Oh, here is a good one. Try this onion."

"Thank you," said Jake as he savored a crunchy bite of the onion.

The rear of the garbage truck nudged into the entrance of the alley and the old woman cried, "Oh no, we have to hide. They yell at me, call me names and throw things at me." She frantically gathered up the sorted findings and her duffle bag, and then scampered deeper into the alley.

Jake's body pained with his commands to hurry and he could do little more than crawl as he followed her to the end of the alley. The truck was backing in and Jake was sure he had been seen in the truck mirrors. Two large men jumped out of the truck. After picking up loose trash, the driver of the truck climbed back into the truck and began backing farther into alley to position its dumpster forks. Jake forced his body to stand and staggered forward.

"Get away from me," the burly man shouted as Jake approached.

"One phone call, please, just thirty seconds," pleaded Jake as the driver jumped out of the truck to join the conversation.

The burly man stared at Jake and then surprising said, "Sure." The driver looked at the burly man and they exchanged some kind of unspoken communication: just nods and smiles. The burly man said, "You ain't touchin my phone."

"Nope, you make the call. I'll give you the number. Just say 'Jacob McCarry needs you' and give him the address. That's all. His name is Frank."

The man smiled at Jake as he removed his gloves and then pulled a phone from his pocket. "Let's have it, the number," demanded the man.

Jake gave him the phone number, one number at a time, and watched with ever hopeful anticipation.

The man thumbed his phone and the call was placed as soon as Jake had completed reciting the numbers.

The burly man looked back at the driver for more unspoken communication. The man listened, waited, and then spoke, "This Theodore Kwanser. Did you get that? Theodore Kwanser." Theodore paused, smiled at the driver and then looked back at Jake.

Jake pleaded, "Please."

Theodore then continued, "Me and my buddy here, Jeffro Newsom, are here in the alley next to Swisher's Market on Addison wit a Jacob McCarry. He says to tell you that he needs you."

Theodore then listened and replied, "Yah, yah. The alley beside Swisher's Market." He paused and listened before replying, "Sure thing," then paused and listened again, "No that's Kwanser: K-W-A-N-S-E-R. And Newsom: N-E-W-S-O-M. Got that?" He paused and listened again. "Okay, sounds good," and listened again, "Will do," before tapping the screen to disconnect.

The man looked at Jake, and said, "Hope you're happy. He said to wait right here. Now get the hell away from me."

"Thank you. My God thank you," Jake said as he stepped backwards, deeper into the alley.

Hydraulics of the truck squealed as the truck completed dumping the dumpster and then slowly moved down the alley. Jake and the elderly black woman watched together.

She said, "You shouldn't have talked to them," as the truck exited the alley and turned right on Addison.

The woman gave Jake a plastic water bottle. Frank would be there soon and he would escape from hell. He finished the water and returned the bottle to her.

"I have to go now," the woman meekly said. "You should come with me." She was in a strange hurry and said her good-bye to go about her wanderings. He would have gone with her, but Frank would soon be here.

It seemed like an eternity. Maybe the man had just faked the phone call. Maybe he had given the wrong address. Maybe there was more than one Addison street. What if it wasn't even Frank that had answered the call? Maybe the man just called the FBI and left a message. Jake watched the foot and vehicle traffic passing the entrance to the alley. What doesn't kill you, will make you stronger, he reminded himself. But this was hell. Time passed and the sun settled into late afternoon and despair settled into Jake's heart.

Then a slim figure appeared at the entrance to the alley. Jake's heart raced and reveled.

"Jacob McCarry," came a call.

Jake struggled to his feet as the figure came closer. The figure reached around to the small of his back, under a suit jacket. When the hand re-emerged, Jake knew it was for a gun. The figure studied the alley, left and right, and kept advancing. The figure challenged the dumpster and every other obstacle with his eyes and gun. Jake couldn't see his face in the dim alley light but it had to be Frank.

"Thank God," Jake sighed.

"Don't move," the figure commanded and pointed the weapon directly at Jake. "Is there anybody else in this alley?"

"Nope, only me, Frank."

"Just stay where you are," came a command.

"You have no idea how glad I am to see you."

But the man turned and started back towards the alley entrance with hastened pace.

"Frank - wait. Where are you going?" called out Jake.

"Just stay where you are," came the repeated command.

Alone again in the alley, Jake watched the passersbys at the alley's entrance. His mind now starting to clear, he couldn't understand why Frank left. He just couldn't rationalize it. Cars in the now crowded street worked their way slowly past. Jake stretched his body; first just squatting, then standing with aid of the wall, and finally to stand without support and managed a teetered walk.

Day past and the alley darkened. Traffic at the alley entrance diminished and Jake continued to yearn for Frank to return. Chill began to set in. The truck had taken Jake's cardboard and he was now strangely furious with them. Where the hell was Frank? It occurred to him that when Frank told him to stay in the alley, the words were delivered with an accent. Maybe it was time to leave the alley.

     Brian David Simmons

Jake crept towards the alley entrance; every muscle of his legs ached and he winched with every step. As he neared the alley entrance, he heard a familiar voice tease, "I told you whitey would still be here."

Jake recognized Gorman, the prick that had jabbed him with the bottle, and the other two. But they were accompanied with a new companion; this time there were four of them. He figured they were maybe eighteen, or twenty, years old, and reasonably well muscled. Could he take them, he pondered? Not a chance, not even on his best day. Jake stumbled back, deeper into the alley. They pushed him. Think boy, think, he challenged himself as they pushed deeper and deeper into alley.

"You weren't kidding about him being dressed for BF-ing," commented the new comer.

"God he's pathetic. We goin pop em?"

"Woth ten big ones. And damn right we goin pop em," said Gorman as he swept Jake's feet out from underneath him.

Jake went down hard, but didn't let out peep as he crawled deeper into alley. Gorman kicked him in the butt and then the new comer took a shot at Jake's ribs. Jake rolled clean over and kept crawling.

"We ain't going to get caught are we?"

"No way. Nobody miss this piece of shit. We chuck him in the dumpster and cover em up. Who'd ever find him? And this place stinks so bad, nobody ever smell him. Dorsey says this is where he dumped that squealing little bitch that talked to the cops. They never found her."

"I had a piece of that before Dorsey put one in her eye," added the youngest looking of the four.

"So did everybody else, stupid."

"Hey, lightened up. How you wana do it?"

"Like Dorsey did it: in the eye."

"Okay, Xavier this is your chance. Initiation time for you and ten big ones for us," said Dorsey and handed Xavier the pistol. "You gotta use this piece – that's the rule."

Xavier took the pistol, pointed it at Jake in sideways fashion. In the past weeks, Jake had escaped death twice and his Wyoming bravado blossomed. Just get on your feet he told himself. Jake struggled to his feet with feebleness of the knees and began swaying back and forth in an unbalanced stagger as he faced the pistol.

"Hold still you bastard," commanded Gorman.

Jake saw Xavier close his eyes and then the pistol boomed. The bullet struck him square in the right shoulder and he instinctively turned his head away from the point of impact. Jake's mind registered a second, almost instantaneous shot. Sound echoed, reverberated, and exploded within the confines of his head. Jake's body fell backward into the wall and slid down to a sitting position with his head cocked. Blood quickly covered the side of Jake's head, flowed across his face, filled his right eye, and onto his hospital gown.

     Brian David Simmons

Chapter Twenty-One

TRAINING

IN THE LIBYAN DESERT, THE SAND RADIATED ITS warmth into the sky as Hafez and his trusted body-guard thundered through the night on horseback. Their destination was only eleven kilometers away, but on horseback it was a challenge to make the entire round trip under cover of darkness. Hafez hated horses; every onward thrust jarred his bones and sent froth, from the animal's neck, streaming back to soak his pants. Hafez leaned forward and compensated for his hatred by spurring the animal's ribcage and lashing its rump with his quirt.

As they sped across the Libyan Desert, he pulled a GPS unit from his pocket, triggered it for a reading and then veered to the left. The horse underneath him pounded on and then stumbled as it crossed a set of deep tire tracks in the sand. "Fools, all of them fools," yelled Hafez as he spurred the horse even harder. In his anger, he continued to demand more of the horse and the blistering pace quickened. His companion began to fall behind and Hafez encouraged him on, "Faster, we have no time."

The kilometers flew past and Hafez triggered his GPS unit again. Then, with a hundred more paces, he pulled up sharply on the reins and brought the animal to an abrupt stop. The desert was still and the only sound was that of the two horses wheezing. Hafez studied the sand dune in front of him and pointed. "There," he declared and spurred the horse; it jumped forward toward a pinpoint of red light emitted from the base of the dune. As they neared, a camouflage door big enough for a large vehicle slowly opened. Hafez and his bodyguard entered.

They were met by the Egyptian delegate, Aysut. Hafez began his tongue lashing of the Egyptian before he had even dismounted, "You fool! There are tire tracks in the desert. You know they have eyes above and watch our every move. How can you have left them? Send someone out at once to desecrate them."

"Hafez, I assure you we take every precaution."

"Yes, and so do the Americans with their spy satellites. They look for everything. Even the smallest trace of our existence will give us away. That is why we must do more than take every precaution. Now, send someone out at once!"

Aysut waved his hand and commanded three of his guards into the desert. The camouflage door closed and the lights came on to reveal a concrete corridor. While the horses were being tended to, the three men marched quickly down the hall to a side room.

"I'm glad you decided to visit," stated Aysut with falseness in his voice. "This is where we do our briefings. Each morning, the crews rotate through here and start their day with a video drill, just as if they are aboard their ships. This keeps them fresh and seaworthy. Would you like to meet them?"

"No!" snapped Hafez. "I want to see the training articles."

"Follow me."

"Wait here," commanded Hafez to his bodyguard.

Farther down the corridor, Hafez and Aysut entered a locked room. The large room had a high ceiling with a beam-mounted crane. A circular platform elevated to chest height was in the center of the room. It was surrounded with narrow scaffolding allowing only limited footing for access. Off to the side, two six-foot half clamshells with a paraboloid shape stood facing each other.

Hafez pointed at the corner. "Is that it?"

"That's it."

"It isn't very big, is it? Are we sure that's enough? It's not exactly what I expected," said Hafez as he walked over to the conical shaped device. "It's amazing something so small could contain so much destruction." Hafez stroked it with his hand.

"Except for the plutonium, that's exactly like the ones in storage at Batum," commented Aysut.

"Quiet!" blasted Hafez and then continued in a whisper. "Do not speak of such things. There may even be ears here. You do not know. Everything must be of its own, separate from the whole. This is how we survive."

"Yes, Hafez. I will only speak of those things that are known to this place. I am sorry."

"Very good then. How does it assemble?"

"Rather simply. It's lifted with the crane, set on the payload platform in the center of the room, and then manually positioned in place. After it's bolted down, it's armed through that little door. Right there," said Aysut as he pointed. "Then the payload fairing shells over there are mated together; the fairing assembly is lifted with the crane and placed on the missile over the warhead," continued Aysut while pointing out the overhead path of the payload fairing.

"I'm impressed. I assume that is the other article," asked Hafez, pointing at a device with polished stainless steel cylinders, miniature gages, valves and tubing.

"That's a mock-up. The real one is a little bit different and has a parachute. We practice handling, mounting, assembling, and arming both units in the light and in the dark. The crews do it in teams, with each team performing a single operation, followed by the next in lockstep. Our time is becoming faster and faster and soon we will be proficient, even in the darkest night. We will be ready when the time comes."

"I believe you will. Very good, Aysut."

"Soon we will be able to discard our Russian instructors and continue drills on our own."

"I suppose it must be. I must leave now if I am going to return to Siwa before sun up. Let's see if my animals have recovered."

Hafez and Aysut returned to the corridor and were joined by Hafez's bodyguard en route to the entrance.

The horses had been given a small quantity of water and their breathing had returned to normal, but they were noticeably subdued. Hafez's horse hung its head and stubbornly resisted when Hafez tried to lead it toward the door, but with a snap of the reins, the horse complied.

"If you ride that horse very hard, he will surely die," stated Aysut.

"Then so be it," barked Hafez as he mounted. The door opened and Hafez dug his heals deep into the animal's sides. The horse lunged out of the entrance and Hafez snapped it with his quirt to accelerate its charge. They disappeared into the night and the camouflage door closed.

Chapter Twenty-Two

Adventures of the Heart

Cole sat on the steps of the trailer waiting for Mister Slow to appear – and for Dominique's call. She had promised one day, then two, which had then turned into a week. At least she was now airborne and would be at Sky Harbor in Phoenix in a few hours. She wanted to explore the Arizona desert but Cole didn't think she realized daily temperatures were now breaking ninety. None-the-less, Cole had offered her a tour of Patton's WWII training grounds, Beer Hill, Apache Cabin, Spanish Cabin, Dripping Springs, and the Hog's Back.

Mister Slow showed himself and began his advance. Cole thought the snake had grown at least six inches in length and swelled to a bombastic girth since he'd started feeding him; Mister Slow was just plain fat. Mister Slow probably knew it too because he now only showed himself every couple days as if on a self-imposed diet.

After the feeding event, Cole went to work on the trailer. The inside was clean but, when Dominique got here, it would be immaculate. The inside of the truck got the same treatment. Cole prepped the fire pit with Mesquite firewood and positioned new zero-gravity camp chairs in anticipation of a romantic evening. As the day crawled onward, Cole's heart soared. She was beautiful, but she was so much more than that. She filled a huge void in his soul and, even through the cell phone airways, the mere sound of her voice made him feel like the happiest man in the world. He was unmistakably hers, if she only knew.

Cole's cell phone rang and his entire being rejoiced. Dominique's flight had just touched down and she would be in Quartzsite before six. She didn't know if she could find the camp, so their evening would start where they first met, Crazy's Pizza.

Cole was there at five and secured a corner table within sight of the bar. He ordered a single beer and just let it sit on the table. As he watched the white ring of foam at glass's edge dissolve back into amber liquid, his mind traveled down paths of future possibilities: exploring everything from the Aztec ruins of the Andes, to the castles of Europe, to the coral reefs of Australia, to the back acres of his farm in Hungary, and maybe even the beaches of Tobago.

Then she was there, right in front of him. He had no words; she was breathtaking. She took his hand and gently pulled him from his chair; electrifying excitation and calming sedation simultaneously surged through his body with the magic of her touch. He held her close and she kissed him long and hard. With only her heavenly image in his eyes, she led him to the door and out into the parking lot.

They got into Dominique's rental car and drove straight to a motel room she had reserved. Love making was fantastic. As the midnight hour approached, they fell asleep in each other's arms. Cole woke first and pulled Dominique close. And it started all over, again. And again.

As the world of love transitioned back to the present, Dominique asked about the plan for the day. Cole gave her options and they settled on Patton's WWII training ground, but only after coffee and breakfast at the diner across the street. Cole admired her beauty and relished every spoken word as she dressed in a white top, pink shorts and short hiking boots.

They traded Dominique's rental car for Cole's truck and headed northeast out through the desert. The first area they came to had rocks laid out in ten foot numbers to identify the 428th Infantry. Roads, parking areas, tent areas, walking paths, and common areas all had rock boarders. Cole and Dominique walked the entire area, speculating on locations of the commander's tent and the mess hall. It was like a trip to the past, bringing up mental images only really known to past generations. Cole had a surge of patriotism. Dominique had similar feelings. Temperature was on the rise and they consumed several waters from the cool chest in the back of the truck. Dominique ventured out into the desert adjacent to the historical Army encampment and found a quartz crystal. It was nearly an inch in diameter. She was so excited. Cole rejoiced in her excitement. He explained that it had been formed over a million years ago. She wanted to have it polished and made into a special keepsake necklace.

The next stop was a similar area identified by a ten foot "4" laid out in rock. Cole searched it on his phone and they speculated it was Patton's Fourth Armored Division. Dominique imagined she could see where tanks had left their tracks in the desert ground. They explored further and found more signs of testimonial to one of the world's most incredible armies.

Day flew by and they found themselves back at the motel. The shower was amazing. Dominique was completely uninhibited and the love making was incredible. Cole had never known such feelings as he felt for Dominique.

The second day's adventures took them to cabin remnants. Apache Cabin was nestled in low lying hills adjacent to mining areas. It was hard to imagine how someone could survive the harsh desert environment in days gone by. There were certainly no amenities; water and all else had to have been hauled in by horse back – amazing. Generations of the past were nothing but tough. Spanish Cabin was similar but much closer to I-10 and Quartzsite.

They ended up back at Crazy's Pizza and again enjoyed a Woo-Zoo pizza. Cole fed the Touch Tunes machine and country western music filled the pizza place. They danced and danced. Dominique was persistent in her desire to learn the pretzel. But Dominique couldn't seem to get the swing of the seven sequential moves. "You need alcohol," commanded Cole and the drinking began: Montana Mules and Vodka Tonics. Eventually Dominique got the moves. Dancing became spin, pretzel, pretzel, pretzel, spin, cuddle, spin, and more; they looked like pros on the dance floor. Cole made a trip to the restroom and, on his return; Dominique was studying something from her little handbag. She nervously replaced it as he returned.

Dancing continued until closing time. It had been a long time, if ever, that Cole had had so much fun, especially in the company of the most beautiful woman in the world. The world was normal again and he was over-indulging in every moment. The day ended as it had before, falling asleep in each other's arms.

Cole hadn't had a change of clothes in three days so today's adventure would end up back at the camp trailer. Dominique packed her bag and placed it in the back of the pickup and then they were off. Today, it was the Hog's Back. They stopped at Dripping Springs and made the hike back into the canyon. Petroglyphs told a story of Native American history. Dominique used her imagination to interpret for Cole. It was about "Chief Having Too Many Wives." He kept them all in separate shallow caverns in the canyon. But they were all too much for him and eventually he thrust a spear through his mid-section as depicted in the last element of the petroglyph. They laughed. She was so much fun.

The pickup was in four-low as it crawled upward towards the Hog Back. All four tires spun and the frame dragged as it clawed its way over a large rock. Dominique slid over on the bench seat, ever closer to Cole, and put on the center seat belt. Cole loved every moment of it and knew she had never been four-wheeling before. As they reached the top, Cole pulled the truck to the side of the trail. They shared a beer from the cool chest and studied the challenge ahead. The Hog's Back was little more than a goat trail running down the ridge-line of a step series of mountain crests and saddles, eventually leading to the valley below. Dominique was noticeably worried. Cole informed her it was too late to turn back now. In some ways, it was like the relationship he was now building with Dominique; there was no turning back; he was hers.

Dominique got another beer out of the cool chest and then climbed in next to Cole. She fastened the seat belt. Cole carefully maneuvered the truck down the ridge-line; a mistake left or right would send the truck tumbling more than a thousand feet to the canyon below. At one point, the trail dropped away on the right; Dominique shrieked as the truck tilted sharply; she dropped her beer and grasped Cole's arm. Cole increased pressure on the throttle and turned the steering wheel to the left; the truck tilted some more but the front tires caught and the truck leveled itself as it crawled back onto the ridge line. When they descended to easier parts of the trail, Dominique pleaded "No more Hog's Backs, please."

Back at the camp trailer, they spent the evening hours watching the camp fire, barbecuing hot dogs, and just plain enjoying each other's company. It was amazing how much Cole was attracted to this woman. She was so unique. But it was more than that. Cole feared what would happen if she found out what he really was and pushed the thought from his mind to just enjoy her company. When the fire dwindled to a smolder, he took her hand and they entered the trailer. Tonight's love making took on a new tenderness of gentle, touching, communication of feelings. Eventually, they fell asleep in each other's arms.

Dominique woke first, or so she thought, and went about making percolator coffee. Cole again secretly watched her through his near closed eyes. It reminded him of the first time she had made coffee. Cole watched as she checked the pot, waiting for it to boil. Then when percolation started, she turned to check the time on the wall clock. Just as before, she readied two cups. When the coffee had perked long enough, she carefully filled both cups. He watched the steam gently rise upward.

Then, she glanced in his direction; Cole didn't move. She is so beautiful, he again thought. Dominique turned from the stove top to the kitchen table and retrieved something from her little handbag.

    Brian David Simmons

When she glanced back in his direction, her eyes and face spoke of something strange - something eerie.

Then he watched as she opened a little vial and held it over the SDRMC cup. She again glanced in his direction. Now her face and eyes spoke of something more than eerie – it was pure evil.

Chapter Twenty-Three

BEECHED

CHRIS BEECH FELT TERRIBLE. HIS ENTIRE BODY ACHED and each breath was becoming more and more of a challenge. It had progressively gotten worse over the last several days and had now reached a point where he needed help – professional help.

Chris hacked and gasped for air as he attempted to slip his trousers on. With one leg in, he stumbled and fell to the floor of his hotel room. Mustering his strength, he managed to slide his other leg into his trousers and then used the corner of the bed to raise himself. Panting persisted from the effort and an intense sense of fatigue settled in. Checking for the car fob in his pants pocket, Chris managed to stumble from his room. The elevator was just down the hall and in sight. Momentary delay waiting for the elevator, gave Chris a chance to catch his breath and assemble some sense of composure. He entered the elevator and pressed "P" for the parking garage beneath the hotel.

His rental car was a short walk and he actually felt a little better after completing the hike. The car started, he activated the on-board GPS system and then commanded, "Virginia Hospital Center." His voice was raspy, but the system screen came to life, flashed "VHC – serving Arlington and surrounding neighborhoods," before displaying the map. The system commanded, "Proceed to route" and Chris put the car in reverse. The screen changed to the backup camera, but it didn't help. The car bumped into another as Chris's eyes momentarily closed. Chris put the car in drive and was able to exit the parking structure. Miraculously, the car made lefts and rights just as commanded by the female GPS voice. Chris recognized the Emergency sign and maneuvered the car off of George Mason Drive, cutting off two on-coming cars in the process. The blaring of horns and screech of tires woke Chris from his stupefied mental confusion and he managed to bring the car to a stop at the emergency entrance. He opened the car door and struggled out to stand alongside. One foot in front of the other, he thought, as he plodded towards the entrance door. The automatic door slid open, but the fatigue was overwhelming and Chris Beech fell face forward.

Nursing staff charged towards the door and the downed man. He was hefted onto a gurney and hustled in to the trauma center. Doctor McCain was in charge for the morning shift and took command, barking orders and beginning triage. Two of the nursing staff captured vital signs and Dr. McCain commanded, "Category One, Urgent!" Ventilation, saline solution IV, heart monitors, blood sample, and Covid swab were first priority. Blood and saliva samples were whisked off to the lab for analysis as McCain continued to interrogate the symptoms of his patient.

Hospital security staff arrived and were given the patients wallet and personal belongings. They identified the patient's name and insurance information. A property record was created and ring, watch, cell phone and cash amount were recorded. The patient's property was placed in a labeled and sealed bag and then carried off for safe keeping.

Lab results came back quickly. McCain studied the results and then ordered, "Two CCs Dexamethasone-H1, stat. Check CT availability and prep for ship." The patient was immediately given an injection and then the gurney was hustled down the hall by two of the nursing staff with McCain following. The CT machine buzzed and hummed as it scanned the patient's entire body. McCain didn't wait for the machine to complete the entire process before inspecting results. As soon as regional pixel data became available, McCain began his interrogation.

Both of the nursing staff that had accompanied McCain and the CT operation staff were surprised when McCain blurted out, "What the hell?" He continued to study the screen of pixels and then the next. "Shit! Congestion expected, but not this. At least not this extensive. We are dealing with Covid, right?" McCain stated as he looked at his two nursing assistants. "Call Dr. Deschler and get him down here. He needs to see this." McCain continued studying the CT results and then went back to the blood test results.

     Brian David Simmons

Deschler arrived and slipped his wire-framed cheaters on, "What have you got?"

McCain pointed at the screen, "You've seen this before." Going to the next screen, he repeated, "And you've seen this before." Going through screen after screen after screen, McCain's words were the same until he came to the end. "Have you ever seen a living soul with the sum total combination of severely congested lungs, inflamed liver, failing kidneys, intestinal blockage, enlarged heart, blood vessel restrictions, and what's that in the ear canal? I've never seen anything like this?"

"This is Covid?"

"Yes. And if it's a new variant, we need to alert the CDC."

"Is your prognosis the same as mine?"

"In that he doesn't have one?"

At that moment, the heart monitor alarm sounded. Deschler looked at McCain and just shook his head.

Chapter Twenty-Four

LOADING

IT WAS A MOONLESS NIGHT, BLACK AS BLACK, AND THE caravan of four trucks crawled along the dirt road. Only dimmed lights operating through slit covers on the first truck illuminated their way. Dust stirred by the tires of the trucks swirled upward and engulfed the caravan, making it invisible. The journey across Turkey from Batum had taken four days, stopping at pre-selected hiding places during daylight hours and creeping along at a snail's pace at night. As they crested the gentle hill, the lights of Istabah could be seen below and the trucks picked up speed.

Hafez was in the first truck and commanded the driver, "Slow down. No mistakes."

The front tire bounced over a rock and Hafez bit his lip. He thought to himself, almost there. Soon, very soon, I can rest. He closed his eyes and thought of his wife, but he had been gone so long that he couldn't picture her face. It matters not, he thought. That is all that matters. Brakes on the truck squealed and his senses jumped back into focus.

Quietly," demanded Hafez. "Why must I tell you everything? Have you no sense?"

A gentle breeze from the sea blew the dust rearward and the night sky became crystal clear; Hafez and the driver breathed easier as the dust cleared from the cab of the truck. They entered the settlement and drove past the warehouse buildings directly to the dock; the *Shir Ali Kahn* was waiting. Hafez directed the driver out onto the dock and the truck stopped under a waiting crane. The caravan was exactly on schedule and Hafez got out.

He was met by Aysut and immediately questioned him, "Where's the crew?"

"Right behind you. The truck is pulling in behind your convoy."

"They should have been here two hours ago. What took them so long?"

"They came all the way from Siwa and are only two hours late. I think that is pretty incredible to only be two hours late."

"I do not. We cannot afford to be late, even a single minute. Quickly now, go and direct the loading. The ship must be gone before the sun rises."

"Yes, Hafez."

"Quickly," said Hafez as the *Shir Ali Kahn* crew came jogging to the forward truck. He watched as the loading operation began. All but three of the crew boarded the ship, some readied it to get underway, and others remained on deck to receive the conical-shaped devices while the three on the dock operated the crane and made the necessary hook-ups. They were extremely efficient in their movements and the loading progressed quickly.

Hafez touched Aysut on the shoulder and said, "This is very good, Aysut. I am satisfied. Now, I must check on the status of the *Ankara*. Its arrival in Annevella is imperative. Continue your operation."

Hafez departed for the Saud ibn-Wahhab building as the *Shir Ali Kahn* crew worked in a flurry of activity, loading and stowing each of the warheads in the hold. Hafez glanced at the outline of the *Servant of Allah* resting peacefully in the darkness; tomorrow night it would be her turn.

     Brian David Simmons

Chapter Twenty-Five

Dominique Jaclyn Portemay

Tears formed in her eyes as she stared at the vile positioned over the SDRMC coffee cup. Her body, mind, and heart said no. She was the best in the world at what she did and had made a fortune doing it. Yet Dominique Jaclyn Portemay was frozen with conflict exploding within herself. She had failed with McCarry. Another failure would certainly result in her own death warrant.

Graduated high school at fifteen, earned a BS in Criminal Science from UCLA at eighteen and then topped it off with a Law Degree from Stanford at twenty-one. It had never seemed enough to her; always wanting more and being driven by dissatisfaction. She had been accepted by the FBI academy and sailed through all the training with honors, only to reject an offer in the Office of Legal Affairs. She joined the prestigious New York law firm of Stanley and Stanley specializing in the legalities and manipulations necessary to export U.S. manufactured goods to foreign nations, some reputable, some not. She had traveled extensively to Europe and the Far East; clients quietly spoke of her remarkable beauty yet respected her brilliance. Stanley and Stanley quickly rewarded her accomplishments and client following with a $530,000 salary plus bonus in an attempt to keep her employed by, and focused on, the firm. But her employment was short.

Dominique had made her first kill almost by accident. She had been sent to Buenos Aires by Stanley and Stanley to establish conditions and fee for exporting mine explosives provided by Chris Beech's Space Sciences Corporation. Her contact was a high level minister within the Argentine Ministry of Defense. The meeting had been arranged in a luxury hotel room overlooking the Rio de la Plata bay. She had expected to meet with the minister and his legal team, but when she arrived, it was just him.

The expansive, fourteenth floor, hotel room was more than just a hotel room. It included a sleeping room, sitting room with adjacent balcony area, and conference room. The handshake greeting was brief and she was led into the conference room where there was a bottle of wine and two glasses on the table. Dominique sat her brief case on the table, opened it and began laying out documents on the table. The minister insisted they have a glass of wine before conducting business and she reluctantly agreed. Her glass of wine turned out to be a roofie. Her head swirled and the dizziness almost took her off her feet. She was thrust back onto the conference table and felt his hand reach underneath her skirt and up between her legs to grab the crotch of her panties. With a single violent move, he ripped them from her body.

It wasn't going to happen. Dominique transformed the dizziness into aggression and repelled him backward with such force that when his head hit the floor he became unconscious. A small bottle spurted from his jacket pocket and spun on the floor. Confused, drowsy and struggling with memory, she picked up the bottle, opened the lid and poured the entire contents in his mouth. The fluid in his mouth brought him back to consciousness. He struggled to his knees as Dominique scurried to put the documents back in her brief case. A stray thought said 'wine glass' and she put that in her brief case as well. She closed her case, picked up her panties and pushed past the minister, who was now on his feet. She headed back into the main seating area and he followed, catching her shoulder and spinning her around. She ran towards the door, but in her confusion, it was the wrong door; she stepped through the open door leading out onto the balcony. The minister followed in an enraged charge; Dominique saw him coming and stepped to her left just as he passed. She didn't even look over the railing. She just exited the hotel suite and made her way back to her own hotel room.

The following morning, she was awoken by a knock at the door. When she opened the door, a courier of Arabic decent handed her an envelope and simply said, "My employer wishes to thank you for a job well done last night. The minister has been stealing from us for some time and recently presented us with ransom demands. Thank you and good day."

Dominique opened the envelope and found a bank account statement with her name on it and a balance of one hundred thousand dollars. The account had since grown two-hundred-fold with some jobs worth a hundred thousand and others worth a million. Now it didn't matter. In the end, both she and the one man in the world she loved would die at the hand of the Saudis.

The deep male voice broke her trance and she quickly tried to conceal the vile.

"Are you crying? Is everything okay?" Cole added with concern, "What's that in your hand?"

Dominique struggled for words as she turned to face Cole. She started to speak but an onslaught of tears gushed forth and all she could do was step forward and cling to Cole for dear life. Crying and sobbing continued. Cole held her tight, yet gentle, and let the tears flow.

Dominique finally managed a few words, "Who are you really?"

"Hamilton Cole Davis."

"Is that your real name?"

"It is."

"Is there any reason someone would want you dead?"

Cole released his hug, held her at arms distance, and stared into her eyes. She didn't see anger or fear. All she saw was a questioning love. Formulation of his response was slow but now he knew. Maybe I shouldn't have asked the question, she scolded herself.

    Brian David Simmons

"Yes. There are many people that would like me dead. That's why you're here, isn't it? Why did you change your mind?"

Dominique stepped back and with open hands showed Cole the vile. "Oh God. I don't know. I can't. Who are you really?"

"What's in the vile?"

"I'm going to scream. I am so confused. I have had the best time of my life with you. I want you in my life so bad. But I can't have you. They're going to kill me now too. Maybe I should drink the Covid," she said as she moved the vile towards her lips.

Cole grabbed it from her hand re-tightened the lid and threw it in the sink. She followed as he gently took her hand, led her to the bed and gently laid her down. He slid in alongside her and cuddled her with all-consuming warmth. They laid there for an eternity and Dominique's heart swelled. She felt loved, even though she'd only known this Hamilton Cole Davis for a short while. How could it be? But it was and it was wonderful.

Emotion gradually yielded to logic and she spoke softly in Cole's ear, "They're going to come after you, you know."

"I love the way you add 'you know' to the end of your sentences. I think it's just your way of confirming receipt of the message you're trying to get across."

Dominique pushed away. "I'm serious," she stated forcefully.

"You forgot 'you know,' you know."

"You're avoiding my question!" she said.

"I'm thinking about the word 'serious.' But first I need to feed Mister Slow."

"What?"

"My friend Mister Slow hasn't eaten lately. Come on. Let's go feed him," Cole said as he rose and pulled her from the bed.

Dominique slipped on shorts and a top as Cole dressed and pulled something from the refrigerator. They stepped out of the camper into the blazing sun and Dominique immediately missed her sun glasses. They sat on the camper steps and Cole tossed what was now obviously a chicken breast out onto the sizzling desert sand.

"Watch," he said.

She grabbed his arm when she saw it begin to slither out from under a bush and cried, "Oh my God."

Cole stated matter-of-factly, "I could kill it if I wanted to, just like the Arabic looking characters I saw when we first met."

Dominique was shocked by his casualness. Who was this man, she continued to question?

"How much?" Cole inquired.

"What?"

"How much were your Arab friends paying you to kill me?"

"I don't want to talk about it?"

"We need to."

"One hundred thousand."

"Not much. If you need the money, let me know."

"No. No," she replied and paused as she watched the snake coming closer. "This shit-hole trailer and that ancient pickup are just a facade, aren't they? Isn't that snake getting a little close?"

"I find solace in the desert and it's a good place to hide. But it's boring as hell."

"Who are you hiding from?"

"Don't know for sure. Apparently I made the list for your Arabic friends."

"So have I – now. The Saudis will come for both of us." Dominique paused and starred at the snake. "Why are we sitting out here watching some reptile slither towards us? Shouldn't you do something? It's getting scary close."

"He's just hungry. So this is a no-bull-shit, come-to-Jesus conversation we're about to have. I like you more than you know but how can I trust you? Why do your Arab friends want me dead?"

"You, I'm not sure. Others I get some sense of the why, but not always. All I knew about you was that my contacts started watching you after you triggered border facial recognition. The Saudis have access to U.S. Border Patrol still and video. They've been keeping an eye on you with drone and visual surveillance waiting for me to finish other business."

The snake arrived at the chicken breast and began its feast as Dominique continued, "This is weird, I've never confessed to anyone before. But I do want you to trust me. What do you think I was doing in Arlington Virginia? I had a contract worth five hundred for one of my ex-clients. I loaded his soup bowl with the same concentrated Covid I was going to give you."

"How many contracts?"

"That's not fair. It's ugly," pleaded Dominique.

"So is Mister Slow. Now, come-to-Jesus. How many?" insisted Cole.

"Twenty-two, including the first one, which really doesn't count."

Cole leaned over and kissed her on the cheek. "The thought of feeding you to Mr. Slow had crossed my mind."

"I figured that much out. I wasn't born yesterday."

Cole momentarily glanced at the sun and then made a fist and slowly blew through it. "It's getting hot. I have an idea of what's next; I've been formulating a plan. You may not like it. But couple of things before we go. First, do you mind if I take your picture with a very, very secure satellite phone?"

"Final test or will there be more?"

"No, there's more." Cole retrieved his satellite phone, "No smile now," and clicked. With a few touches of the screen, Dominique watched as her picture was whisked away somewhere.

"They'll be watching, you know," said Dominique. "The Saudis, you know."

"I'm counting on it."

     Brian David Simmons

Cole sat back down beside her. It was repulsive as the damn snake finished its meal. She was relieved when it slowly began its retreat back to whatever rock it had crawled out from underneath. Questions twisted in confusion. Dominique wasn't sure of anything anymore. She had always been in charge of her own destiny and association with this man was so strange. She had divulged things to him no one knew and now it felt like she was at his mercy. On top of the confusion, emotions were exploding within her, ten-fold, increasing her desire to be with him.

All of which clashed with rational thought. I want this man in my life. Why would he want someone that was hired to kill him? What could I say? What should I say? Why would the Saudis want some desert dweller terminated? Who is this man? What if I'd completed my contract? Then everything would be normal; that is, if my life could be called normal. And God knows it's not. Why didn't he just feed me one piece at time to that hideous snake? Who names a snake, anyway? Maybe it won't matter; the Saudis will kill us both. That's a laugh; find true love and get to share the same six foot hole. I need a long shower, toothbrush, clean clothes and time to sort it all out.

The silence was broken by a whirl of blades from a drone overhead. "Don't look up," she said.

"Just one more come-to Jesus test," Cole said. "Tell me about your first."

"What about the drone?"

"They need to watch. Now about your first?"

Dominique thought about it for a moment. She didn't understand but decided it really didn't matter at this point. "It was an accident. I was working international trade agreements for Chris Beech of -"

"Beech," interrupted Cole. "As in exports to Argentina?"

"How did you know?"

Cole struck like a coiled rattlesnake, grasping her with both hands around her neck and jerking her to her feet. His hands re-positioned themselves around her throat as she grasped his arms. She thrust her knee upwards towards his groin but was blocked by his leg. God, he was strong. His grasp around her throat was firm and unbreakable, yet somehow gentle. But his thumb was digging deeper and deeper into the tissue next to the left side of her throat. The pain was excruciating. She reached to claw his eyes out but he pushed her backward to hold her at arm's length and lift her off her feet. She felt his thumb pressing harder and harder and working its way back and forth as he shook her like a rag doll. She began battering back, striking him repeatedly with her fists, but the rag doll shaking just intensified. His thumb pressed in deeper, harder and accelerated its stroking back and forth. She was fading. She was going to die. Damn his thumb hurt. She kicked him and then again. She grasped his wrists again and tried to pull his grip from her neck but there was no relief.

     Brian David Simmons

She began punching at his mid-section – nothing. She managed wide swings that battered his head – nothing. Pain from his thumb pressing deeper and harder was excruciating. She was fading further. Her mind screamed but nothing passed through her vocal cords. She registered the thought: "so this is how death is." Strength was all but gone as she managed one final blow to his mid-section before blackness came.

Aakifah and Zayan intensely watched the video feed from the drone. He was strangling her. The American eahira qatil was fighting back with a vengeance. Her arms and legs flayed furiously striking many blows. But then it was over. He laid her on the ground with her face pointed at the heavens. But both Aakifah and Zayan knew she had departed for Jahannam. The Davis man took her by both hands and drug her to the pickup and forced her lifeless body into the passenger side. He went to the trailer, gathered some things from inside, and then exited to pull a shovel from the ground. He threw it along with a small bag into the back of the pickup before climbing into the cab.

Aakifah expedited recovery of the drone and Zayan began dialing his phone. The answer was immediate.

"What?"

"Hafez, we have problem. The American eahira qatil did not succeed."

"Don't," shouted an infuriated Hafez, then paused, and collected his composure before continuing. "Tell me more."

"The Davis man has strangled her. We have video. He took a shovel and now, as we speak, is driving away with her body farther out into the desert."

"May Allah banish and torment the very essence of the incompetent whore assassin. Send me the video of her demise. I wish to relish her last breath." Hafez paused again and then continued, "You must succeed where she has failed. The Davis man must not rise another day. Do not disappoint. Go now."

"Yes Hafez. It will be done."

Aakifah and Zayan jumped into the car. The instant the car started, Zayan floored it, leaving a swirling cloud of dust. They flew past the Davis man's trailer, which was now ablaze. Aakifah readied an Uzi and waited in anticipation. The truck was out of sight but Zayan could see the dust cloud ahead and pressed on the accelerator even harder. The car was on the edge of controllability, swaying left and right, shaking violently as it bounced over graveled rocks. Zayan slammed on the brakes as a wash appeared in his path. The car smashed into the wash as the front bottomed out with a horrible noise. As the car emerged from the wash, Zayan again smashed the accelerator back to its fully depressed position. They made their way across three more washes and down a myriad of dirt roads before the pickup truck itself became

     Brian David Simmons

visible. It had come to a stop at the crest a small hill. Aakifah shouted, "tammata" as he pointed to the hill top. Zayan momentarily took his eyes off the path ahead and didn't react soon enough as the car entered yet another wash. Entering the narrow wash was not an issue, but the road leading up the bank on the other side was too much; Zayan had both feet on the brake pedal as the car smashed into the steep incline. The front of the car crumpled and began releasing a cloud of steam, spewing oil and expelling other fluids. Airbags exploded first catching Aakifah's Uzi and swinging it in Zayan's direction and then thrusting Aakifah and Zayan back into their seats. When the air bag exploded, Aakifah had inadvertently pulled the trigger on the Uzi.

As the airbags deflated, Zayan cried out. His legs were trapped beneath the dash and his mid-section was bleeding profusely. Aakifah looked down at his Uzi and pleaded, "Allah have mercy." Moments later, Zayan closed his eyes. Aakifah closed his own eyes and reminded himself of the penalty for failure. His fate would be the same as that of Zayan. He opened his eyes just in time to see the pickup pull away.

Chapter Twenty-Six

SECRET OF ALL SECRETS

IN DAMASCUS, THE SPIRITUAL AND POLITICAL CENTER of the Muslim world, preparations were underway for observance of Eid-al-Adha. Teachings of the Koran were reminders to all in this period of sacrifice. The Five Pillars of Faith - profession of Muhammad, prayer, alms giving, fasting, and pilgrimage - were in the forefront of people's thoughts. Prayer was methodically performed five times a day as required. Streets were crowded as the noon hour approached and the Muezzin chanted for the noontime prayer from the Minuet at the Umayyad Mosque. Muslims crowded to gain entry to the Mosque and begin the ritualistic washing of hands, face and feet. As the Mosque filled, six men discreetly slipped away for a prayer of their own.

One by one, they moved away from the crowds and ventured to the subterranean tombs beneath the Mosque. Each one entered from a different access and made their way through the maze of tunnels to a secret location. As they arrived, each used a special key to gain access to a newly constructed chamber. Inside the chamber, a small room, protected from electronic surveillance, had been constructed.

As they arrived, nothing was said. They stood outside the small room staring at one another with a somberness befitting the most serious of events. When the sixth man arrived, they entered the Faraday cage-protected room. It was barely large enough for the six men to crowd in.

The meeting began with greetings and then a prayer. Hafez, still distrusting the Faraday cage, whispered to further guard his conversation from electronic ears, and the others followed his lead. This was their final meeting and Hafez feared that if their conversation, or any part of it, was captured, their countries would suffer irreparable rebuke and punishment from the West. The secret of all secrets had to be guarded with every means possible, especially at this moment.

"This is the final decision, my friends," whispered Hafez. "After this, there is no turning back."

"Is all ready?" questioned Aysut, the Egyptian.

"Only if Hafez has completed his duties," stated the Iranian.

"Do not fear. I have fulfilled my obligations."

"Bah. The ships? The missiles? All of it?"

"Yes, my friend. All of it. And each of you has done equally as well. We are ready and the world's attention is not upon us. Our brothers in Iraq endured the stranglehold of the West, suffering great loss of life and liberty. They invited pain and more pain so as to draw attention away from us. The foolish UN went down the path we paved for them, providing us a great service in the end. In their blindness, our preparations are nearing completion. Aysut's superior crews are at sea readying for their mission. They nurture the weapons you have prepared and make them ready for the greatest of all accomplishments. My brothers of the Quaraysh Unity, I am satisfied with each of you."

"Ah, Hafez. We have all done well, but you still must complete the final preparation," slighted the Iranian.

"And that is why we must make the final decision. Once I leave here, you will not hear from me again until it is done. I will go to Argentina and personally ensure the *Ankara* sails. It is up to you, my brothers. We must be united."

"Maybe this is not the time; maybe we should wait," reluctantly offered the Jordanian. "What if they discover our ships at sea? Surely then they will starve us in our own homes. The Koran teaches patience. Should we not wait?"

"No. We must strike now to punish and destroy the Great Infidel once and for all," lambasted the Iranian.

"No," argued another delegate. "It is perfect. The United Nations and the emissaries of repression have disillusioned themselves with repression of Russia, China, Iraq, Palestine, Somalia, Serbia, Korea, India, Pakistan, and the entire world. They are occupied with their own false self-worth, placating themselves as the saviors of the world. They are false to themselves and blind to our accomplishments. They will never see the hand that strikes them."

     Brian David Simmons

"It is our destiny to do this great thing," added Aysut. "The Koran also teaches courage and honor. We will accomplish this deed and, even if we are discovered and suffer in our homes, it will be the greatest of sacrifices and we will be celebrated. There is no loss; in the end, all things are recorded in the record of Allah. We will either attain martyrdom or be hailed for our great feat. This is our path to greatness and all should join in celebration."

"This is boldness beyond belief," resisted the Jordanian dissenter. "I can not join you in heart, but I will carry the message that we are proceeding back to my king. We will prepare for the coming of Armageddon. Allah be with us."

"Then it is settled; all are in favor. Return to your homes and make as if nothing is to happen."

The delegates departed one by one, each returning to the gathering above by the path they had come.

Chapter Twenty-Seven

Looking for Love

Country western music was playing somewhere.

> …I was alone
> Searching eyes of strangers for a sign
> Then a glimmer of light filled my heart

Dominique opened her eyes and stared at the ceiling. Something smelled strange and she grabbed her neck. It was bandaged and was emitting an odor reminiscent of a vapor rub. Slowly she turned her head towards the sound of the country western; it was the radio on the nightstand. Then her hand slipped down her neck to her chest and the questions started. What the hell am I wearing? Where is this? Why are my feet up? That bastard killed me. Why am I alive?

She retracted her legs and kicked at the pillows that were supporting her feet. The pillows went off the bottom of the bed and she jerked herself upright to a sitting position only to be driven back down by dizziness. She fell over on her side and stared at the radio.

> Eyes of stranger spoke the words
> At last, I'd discovered you, oh you

"You bastard. The day I discovered you, my life went to hell." A pair of denim pants and a white button-up top were across the back of a chair. A pair of shoes was beneath them on the floor, something between tennis shoes and boots; God they were ugly. She looked back at the top; it might do, but the denim pants could go in the trash with the shoes. "You bastard," she shouted.

She tried again to sit, only this time more slowly. She succeeded and the dizziness slowly faded. Hair brush, curling iron, toiletries and other things were all laid out on the table in front of the chair. There was also a bra, hateful thing; it should be tossed with the shoes. She realized this was a hotel room, and a pretty nice one. She was wearing pajamas, absolutely unnecessary things that just take up space in a suitcase.

There was a birthday card of some kind standing up on the table. "You bastard," she again shouted. Dominique managed to get to her feet and steadied herself with the night stand. The radio was now playing another song.

> As long as the stars shine above
> Cause you're the star in my heart
> Forever is forever

"If only. You bastard." Dominique lifted her hand from the nightstand, stood up straight and took a step towards the table. The dizziness was almost gone and she ripped the vapor rub smelling thing from her neck. Each step increased her stability as she approached the table. The table had a variety of lipstick, hair spray, combs, brushes, scissors, makeup pads, powders, highlighters and artificial eyelashes all laid out. She used very little makeup and most of it was crap, anyway. The toothpaste wasn't even her brand. The hair spray might as well have been glue. And the deodorant was meant for sweaty Mississippi women. The lipstick was no better than an open-for-business sign for hookers. One of the perfumes was a possibility, but the other was hog spray. Dominique picked up the card and read:

> I'm sorry. I hope I didn't hurt you too bad. It was necessary to deceive your Arab friends. Please forgive me. If you choose, your new identity will arrive soon and you can simply depart. I hope you won't. I'm in room 206 next door.
>
> Your friend and more,
> Cole
>
> PS—there is a sandwich and water in the refrigerator

Her fury intensified, "You bastard," she screamed but the sandwich was delightful. Dominique looked down at the white top and denim pants as she ate. "You and your damn country western." A new song played on the radio.

I like my women in Daisy Dukes
Tight buns and boosoms
Makes me spin out of control
Extra lipstick and rouge
Gets me hot and going confused
An, the whiff of perfume
Makes me high on fumes
Yeah, I like my women in Daisy Dukes

"Okay you bastard, I'll show you. Wait until you get a load of this," she said out loud. She felt clean but showered anyway and brushed her teeth. She looked in the mirror, smiled and then laughed. She blow dried her hair, applied mousse, twisted four sections into a chigon, and then pinned it in place for several minutes while she inspected the denim pants. With scissors meant for hair, she jaggedly cut the legs off the pants right at crotch level. She went back to her hair and worked with two inch sections: curling and applying voluminous hair spray, eventually working all the way around. It was great; could only have been better if it was blond. She giggled and bounced back into the bedroom and the short shorts. They fit and just barely covered the edges of her panties. "Perfect," she exclaimed. She selected red lipstick, blush, rouge, and eye highlighter and went back to the bathroom mirror. When she'd finished laying it on, she laughed out loud at what she saw in the mirror. She liberally applied the hog spray perfume as a finishing touch.

Back in the bedroom, she put on the boots and button up white top. But only the one button between her breasts was required. She rolled the bottom of the top up underneath revealing more than just her belly button and tied the tails tightly under her breasts to provide additional lift. Dominique stood in front of the full length mirror on the bathroom door, pinched her nipples to make them hard and stand out, and said, "Daisy Duke, I make you look like Mary Ann Bevan."

She left her hotel room and walked right past 206. The hotel had a bar and restaurant; she went straight to the bar. She ordered water, a vodka tonic with a splash of cranberry, and a crackers and smoked salmon dip appetizer. She was still starving.

The bartender took her order and she said, "Make sure you charge it to room 206. The bastard's up there watching TV. And put a five-hundred dollar tip on the bill for yourself."

The bartender looked in the direction of her chest, smiled and said, "Okay lady." He then went straight to the house phone.

Dominique looked at the clock and began counting. He would be down in a minimum of two-hundred-thirty seconds. At precisely the right moment, she slid off her bar stool and began a swanky walk towards the door. Cole came through the door before she got there. She walked right past him and then turned around to look at him. With a perfect southern drawl, she said, "Oh hi, sugar. Scoozz me while I visit the lady's room. Jump up there to the bar and order me up some fried green tomatoes and turnip greens. Will ya, darlin?" She turned and headed off. She knew Cole's, as well as the bar tender's, eyes were focused on nothing but her ass.

In the bathroom, she pinched her nipples with extra vigilance. She slapped her cheeks to bring out even more blush. When she returned, the bar tender's mouth was partially open and his eyes told her that her nipples were having the desired effect. Cole turned and she slid onto the bar stool next to him. "Miss me, darlin?" she said.

Cole leaned in close and asked, "Are you alright?"

"I'm fine, darlin. You be'in such a sweet thing and all. I mean you show a girl such a fine time."

"I apologize."

"You should. Bastard! But naw that's all just nasty talk. I mean trying to kill me and all. Bastard!"

"What's the matter with you? And where did you get those clothes?"

"I'm just fine, sugar. And these clothes are just the little ole things you bought me. You wanted a trashy little Daisy Duke, didn't you?"

"I give. I have no clue what's going on."

"An sweetie, you shouldn't. Where's my fried green tomatoes and turnip greens, anyways."

"They don't have any."

The appetizer arrived and she ate crackers and dip. She was so hungry and it was so good. "Oops," she said.

"Did you see where that cracker went?" She smiled and then added, "It went right down there," as she pointed at her cleavage. "Mister Bartender, is there anything you could do about that?" The bartender blushed. He was speechless and couldn't stop staring.

"Dominique, what the hell is going on? And I didn't buy you those clothes."

"Why sure you did. How do like the perfume? I put on extra just for you. It attracts hogs," and then with emphasis added, "Ya know!"

"I give. I know you're pissed. I get that. Is that what you're trying to tell me?"

"Why sugar, ya have no idea, do ya? How do ya like the perfume? Attracted?"

"Sure."

"How bout my hooker red lipstick? Trashy enough for you?"

"It, ah, is fine."

With that, Dominique slid off her stool and took his hand. "This way," she said and led him towards the door. They went past 206 to her room and she slipped the key card into the lock. She stepped inside and turned to face him while blocking the doorway. She said, "Yo loss sugar. See y'all later," and slammed the door.

Cole had no clue. Are all women this nuts? What the hell is the matter with her, he pondered as he stared at the closed door? The door had been closed for only a couple seconds when it swung back open.

     Brian David Simmons

"Get in here," she said and grabbed the front his shirt to pull him in her direction. She wrapped her arms around him and began a forceful, sustained kiss. She grabbed her breath, did it again and he responded, pulling her ever closer in embrace. She kicked off her boots before the door closed and the Daisy Dukes hit the floor soon after. Cole's clothes weren't far behind.

Passion and emotion continued late into the night until both Cole and Dominique were exhausted. They lay there holding each other, rejoicing in each other's company.

Dominique whispered, "Where are we, by the way?"

"Albuquerque."

"Wow. How long has it been? I don't even know what day it is."

"Two days. I was getting worried."

"What did you give me?"

"I didn't give you anything. I just massaged the soft tissue surrounding the Vagus nerve in your neck, causing it to swell and constrict around the nerve. The Vagus nerve measures blood pressure. With just the right amount of pressure and soft tissue damage, it can be massaged into a state of registering extremely high blood pressure. The brain receives the high pressure signal and responds to lower the body's blood pressure, resulting in fainting and extended unconsciousness. When swelling of the soft tissue around the nerve decreases, even slightly, the Vagus nerve returns to its normal function; it's like turning the lights back on with no residual effects."

"And the Saudis believed you strangled me. Why didn't you let me know ahead of time?"

"Through the eye of the drone, it had to look realistic. You wouldn't have fought back like that if you'd known it was play acting."

"It was real enough, all right. I'm not over my mad at you, you know."

"I apologize."

"I know. What about the Saudis?"

"The last I saw them, their car was disabled out on the Kofa National Refuge where no vehicle traffic is allowed. They're about fifty miles from I-10 and fifty miles from Quartzsite. Going to be a long walk."

"They're still going to come after you, you know."

"Yep." said Cole and then continued, "By the way, you're quite impressive: Dominique Jaclyn Portemay, age thirty-one, parents unknown, foster child, child prodigy, BA from UCLA at eighteen, Stanford law degree at twenty-one, FBI, Stanley and Stanley, and a nineteen million dollar Turkish bank account."

Dominique pushed away from Cole, "What agency are you with? Who the hell are you? And how did you get my life's history?"

"I got the info from Kevin. Let's make a call. Maybe it'll help you understand. That is, if it's possible to understand Kevin. You're about to learn that I can put up with a lot more than Daisy Duke." Cole retrieved the satellite phone and rejoined Dominique in the bed. He dialed the numbers to route the signal from earth to satellite to El Segundo to satellite and then to Tobago.

"It's kind of late, isn't it?" commented Dominique. "Doesn't matter."

Kevin answered after only two rings, "You should call more often. You choose to call now when everybody's asleep. Sylvia won't chew your ass, so I will. . ."

Cole covered the mouth piece and said, "Give him a minute." Cole tipped the phone so Dominique could hear.

"...Are you listening? You can't just go for weeks without calling. And when are you coming for a visit. But then again, maybe we don't want you to visit. You'll bring your psychotic psychosis with you. Killed any little black babies lately? If you came to the island, you'd probably wear your white hoodie and go hunting, wouldn't you?"

"Kevin," interrupted Cole.

"I'm not done yet! Then, you'd go off letting that little penis head do all the thinking. Oh, how's Miss Dominera? I'll bet you've been dominated more than once. Haven't you? But that's all you care about anyway. Or have you cast her aside yet? I'll bet..."

"Kevin!" shouted Cole. "Saudi Arabs put a contract on me, tried to kill me, and are now hunting me. I need your help."

"Oh, well. Anyway, call more often. How could they know?"

"No idea. But it has to be related to some of our past acquaintances. Look for specific links to the Saudis. Chase any leads coming out of that CIA report you downloaded off Higgins's PC. I have one of the locals that the Saudis recruited all bound up in sheets here in this hotel room. I'll work this one over, learn all I can, and then let's meet."

"That's the word, only as in 'steak.' 'Steak' is location. Number of letters in my pride and joy minus three days is when."

"Kevin, this is an encrypted line. You don't need to code it."

"I know. Bye," said Kevin and hung up.

"Tied up in the sheets and going to work me over. I think that might be fun," said Dominique. "Or should I become Dominera? What was that about black babies?"

"How bad do you want to know?

"If it's about you, I want to know it all."

"What do you want to know?"

"Everything!" demanded Dominique.

"It's a long story."

"Then start at the beginning."

Cole reluctantly began, "You said your first kill was an accident."

Dominique looked directly in his eyes and replied, "It was."

"Mine wasn't."

"Go on."

"Google Kootenai County Sheriff."

"Why?"

"He was responsible for my mother's death and he personally killed my father."

Dominique studied her phone as results came up. She'd never heard anything about this. "What's the Patriot Rebirth Society?" she asked.

"A white supremacist organization."

"Unbelievable." She tapped the next article and read again in near disbelief. "How old are you?"

"Twenty-eight."

"So you were, like, junior high."

"Thirteen."

"The article says it was one of the most gruesome."

"Gutted like a hog and fed his entrails."

She continued reading but couldn't help from occasionally looking up at Cole. When she'd finished reading, she said meekly, "I don't know what to say."

Cole read her thoughts, "You demanded to know. Now you're wondering why I don't deserve the Covid vile." He paused and then continued, "I brought it with us. It's out in the truck."

Chapter Twenty-Eight

REALIZATION

JEFF MONSON HAD A PLATE FULL OF PRIORITIES, DRIVEN by continued unrest in the Middle East, more difficulties with Iraq, Russian interactions with Europe, Chinese threats against Taiwan and the ever persistent North Korean missile launches. The Treasury Department was demanding the CIA's help quelling an influx of counterfeit hundred-dollar bills from the Middle East; Iraq was the suspected source. New taunts were coming from Iraq that they would never comply with U.S.-driven UN resolutions. Isis had resurfaced and U.S. aircraft over Iraq continued to be tagged by anti-aircraft radar and had even been targeted by several small missiles. An alarming number of small arms, aircraft replacement parts, and surface-to-air missiles were also finding their way into Iran and Iraq from a variety of sources. The Ukraine conflict was driving oil-starved European nations to trade "humanitarian" supplies to Russia for oil.

As five o'clock approached, Dell stuck her head in Jeff Monson's office and informed him, "He's still here."

"Any idea what he wants?"

"Nope, he just says he's not leaving until he sees you. I'm not even sure how he got past security and the badge readers. Do you want me to call security and have him escorted out?"

"You said he identified himself as FBI?"

"Yes, Frank Wallace of the FBI. And he's got a FBI badge but no CIA badge, not even an escort required badge."

"So he got past security and all the way to my office; interesting. Have the FBI send over a picture. If he's a match, show him in. If he's not, have security arrest him for illegal entry into a secure facility and get him out of here."

In minutes, Dell had Frank's photo and invited him to follow her into her office area. She pointed at him and laid down the rules, "Deputy Monson is a very busy man and you need to keep this short, very short." She led Frank through the conference room adjacent to Monson's office and then into his office.

Jeff Monson barely gave Frank Wallace a chance to get through the door, "What is so important you would throw away a career and risk jail time for sneaking into a highly secure and sensitive facility? And after you tell me what is so important, you're going to tell me how you did it!"

"Yes sir."

"Let's have it!"

"Jacob McCarry."

"History," interrupted Monson.

"No sir. Did you get my report?"

"Why would you send me a report?"

"Because I couldn't get it elevated through my chain of command."

"You have thirty seconds!"

Frank started and it took more than his thirty seconds, "It was the drugs that Jake took; they weren't what they seemed. I kept the capsules Jake threw at me in the hospital and had more than just the standard tests run. The standard tests found hallucinogenics and amphetamine and that's it. I had the lab do photomicrosscopy, FTIR, and GC mass-spec to dissect and fingerprint the substances inside the capsule. All the common street stuff was just a guise for the real killer drugs. Inside the capsule were tiny thermoplastic caplets the size of a grain of salt, and they were loaded. Inside the caplets was either a combination of tilemine hydrochloride and zolazepam hydrochloride along with helium or dextroamphetamine with helium. What's more; in exact ratios, the caplets dissolved at different rates depending on temperature and acidity level. My friend in the lab thinks the caplets are designed to dissolve low in the digestive tract making them even more potent and absorbed almost directly into blood stream. At first the helium made no sense whatsoever, but then I figured it out. The helium was added so that the net specific gravity of the filed miniature caplet was exactly that of water. It made the caplets so that they would float and be nearly invisible in water, which is what I saw a nurse give Jake. Jake picked up on it; I didn't. She had the face of a fifty year old but the hands of a twenty year old." Frank was now getting vocal. "Do you know what that means?"

     Brian David Simmons

"I'm afraid I don't."

"What would happen if all the muscles in your body were paralyzed and you drank caffeine from ten thousand cups of coffee? That's what it means Mister Monson!"

"Is that what Jake went through?"

"Frank was becoming animated as he continued, "Worse - a lot worse. This stuff was an engineered drug that goes undetected by standard test methods, but is designed to be lethal; in fact it has no purpose other than to kill! The tilemine and zolazepam hydrochlorides are dissociative anesthetic agents that tranquilize muscles but leave thoughts and other functions alive. Dextroamphetamine is a super speed concentrate that can kill all by its self when taken into the bloodstream. The dissociative agents, when taken in combination with the super speed, makes all the muscles go to sleep while the heart and mind - which are already confused and excited by the hallucinogens - go bizerk trying to absorb the amplified effect of the speed. What's worse is that, long after the street hallucinogens wear off, the time release of the caplets continues, it doesn't quit; it just keeps hammering and hammering the brain and heart until they die from exhaustion. I have no idea how Jake could have survived just one dose. He got two!"

"Survive," meekly mumbled Monson. An unusual emotion swelled within Monson and tears formed at the edges of his eyes.

Frank replied, "Maybe. At the hospital, he only got the mini-caplets in the liquid potion. And not the big caplets with the full dose. It's possible. We need to find him! He's one of yours and somebody tried to kill him. Doesn't that get your attention? Doesn't that get your ire up? Doesn't that make you want to hunt somebody down and string them up by their balls? That's why I violated the sanctity of the CIA. And yes, it's worth career and everything else."

Dell stuck her head through the door and inquired, "Jeff?"

Monson knew he'd missed the boat somewhere somehow. He glanced back at Frank and then barked at Dell," Get Roger Sims up here post haste. Get Mr. Frank Wallace here an unescort CIA badge. Find a report that was sent to me by Mr. Wallace here. And then get Evert Hooster on the phone."

"Badging has already gone home for the night."

Jeff raised his voice, "Dell, now!"

And then he turned back to Frank, "Where would Jake be now if he was alive?"

"In hiding."

"Where?"

"Where would you go, if you could, when the world was against you? Home that's where. But I've made multiple inquiries: credit cards, cell phone, airline, bus, his parents. And nothing."

"You have no idea, then, if he survived the second cocktail."

"None."

The office phone buzzed and Jeff looked at the display before answering, "Hi Ev. I've got one of your agents sitting here in my office. His name is Frank Wallace." Jeff stared at Frank as he continued, "I want him put on special assignment to me as a liaison between myself and a tiger team I'd like you to set up. I want him given top level priority in your shop. Give him all the resources he needs. Can you do that?"

Evert Hooster, Director of the FBI, questioned, "You going to give me some idea of what's going on?"

"Domestic assassination attempt, at a minimum, and probably the murder of one of my analysts. First and foremost, I want to find my analyst; he's either in hiding or, worst case, dead. Either way, I want a full court press to find him. There's a report in your system written by Mr. Wallace here. That's going to be my starting point. We'll see where it goes from there. But in the end, as Mr. Wallace so eloquently put it, I want to find who's behind it and string them up by their balls."

Chapter Twenty-Nine

STEAK, AS IN NEW YORK

DOMINIQUE AND COLE FLEW BY PRIVATE CARRIER from Albuquerque to the private air terminal at JFK, which avoided TSA security and the threat of facial recognition software. Jack Cross from Friendship Aviation had insured Dominique's and Cole's departure and arrival were surreptitious. The ten seat Gulfstream GIII also provided a mile-high-club experience that was beyond belief for both Cole and Dominique; flight time passed quickly and they hurried to get their clothing on as the plane pulled up to the terminal. Jack and his GIII had been used before and proven to be discrete, at least with the right tip amount.

From the private terminal, they took a cab to Stuyvesant Town. Kevin and Cole owned an upscale condo on the fourth floor of an elite apartment building. Cole seldom used it but kept it as a last resort safe house. No one had ever been brought there before. Now Dominique and Cole stood at the entrance. Cole had a tinge of uneasiness. He was about to let Dominique truly invade his safety zone. He said, "Duck as we pass the security cam," as Cole touched the key pad and they entered the building. The elevator required more entry on a key pad tand the swipe of a key card. They were quickly on their way to the fourth floor.

Uneasiness returned as they reached the condo door.

Cole swiped the key card and they entered. Kevin was sitting in a secret room at a computer terminal. The room was normally concealed by trim that hid the edges of a door and sliding access panel cover that was nearly flush, making it all look very innocuous. Kevin was oblivious to their entry as he rattled a keyboard against a backdrop of tiny LED lights and the faint hum of electronics equipment.

Cole watched as Dominique studied the condo and then returned her focus to Kevin sitting at the computer terminal. In a raised voice, Cole said, "Kevin," and got no response. He repeated the inquiry and still got no response. Finally, with almost a yell, Cole got Kevin's attention.

When Kevin turned, he bolted from his chair and shockingly exploded, "Who's she?"

"Dominique."

"I don't care who she is! She shouldn't be here. You know better."

"Unusual circumstances makes her part of the family now."

"Bull shit. I don't like her."

"I do and you'll eventually get over it. And the sooner the better."

"I will not get over it. Just do your psycho thing right now and get rid of her."

Dominique intervened, "Cole brought me in because I might be able to help with information on the Saudis and why they want Cole dead. I'm just here to help. Just give me a chance."

"No. I don't like you," replied Kevin.

Dominique coerced, "Is that a rack of servers on the back wall in there. I bet you have a teragig of computing power."

"It's more than that. And stop looking at my stuff."

"I bet you have your own cloud of servers somewhere too."

"Maybe. What do you know about that?"

"Not much, but I'd like to learn more."

"Not from me you won't!"

Cole cut Dominique short, "Kevin, I don't have the patience for this. Can we have a private conversation in the bedroom, please? Now!"

"No. I'll say what I have to say right here. It's not her. It's you. You can't control yourself. She probably lifted her skirt an inch and you went all goo-goo. And then you invited her here. Why? Probably because you got tired of motel beds and wanted to try this one out. That's why. And then, after you've had your fun, you'll go find another. Get rid of her! All you can do is think with your penis. It led you to Mexico for your cha-cha-cha with the senoritas, you got ID-ed, and that's why you're in the shit now. You're such a dumb-ass."

"Maybe you're right, but not about her."

"And why not?"

"Because," Cole hesitated and looked at Dominique before continuing, "I love her."

Kevin exploded, "Oh my God! You're unbelievable."

Cole looked deep into Dominique's eyes. She took his hand and squeezed in reciprocation to his words. They just stared at each other letting time pass.

Kevin continued, "Does she know what you are? Does she know you are the psycho of all psychos? Does she know the things you've done?"

"She knows."

"Did she puke when you told her? Damn white supremacist anyway." lambasted Kevin and then spun around to return to his computer.

Cole and Dominique found the couch to let Kevin cool off. Cole knew he would eventually come around. Cole explained his upbringing in the compound. The environment in the compound was so alien to Dominique; it wasn't like anything she'd ever known. She confessed though, in some ways, it had parallels with her own background. Never knowing her parents, Dominique had been passed from one foster home to the next, each with its own set of horrors: boarded in filth, hungry, beaten, molested twice, and ran away seven times. She talked about her escape from childhood through study. She found solace in books and excelled at school, eventually leading to a prestigious law degree from Stanford.

The conversation shifted to the present. Dominique offered, "I really don't know why the Saudis want you dead," and then paused momentarily. "I can only speculate."

"You need to tell me everything. Maybe we can figure it out."

"I'm scared of what you might think of me. I feel sick when I think of telling you some of the things I've done."

"If you know something, now is the time," coerced Cole.

"You may not like me anymore when I do. And that's what scares me. I don't want to lose you," pleaded Dominique.

"Well, trying to give me the vile of Covid from Hell didn't drive me away; there isn't much you can say that would."

Dominique thought for a long moment. Cole watched her eyes as she searched for the right words. He already knew she was a paid assassin. What possibly could be worse than that?

She started slowly, "I'm never given much information, you know. I usually just get a name, some pictures: maybe an address, phone number, or photocopy of a driver's license. And I usually get told the circumstances, you know: very public with an obvious message to others or very discrete without a hint of suspicion. I'm never given any background. I build a file on my own from public records, social media, video surveillance, receipts from the contract's trash, either paired or parabolic listened to phone conversations, et cetera. When I'm done gathering information, I know most the details about the contract's life before I ever develop a plan."

"Did you build a file on me?"

"As best I could. You were a little bit of a challenge. I knew about Boston, MIT, and your time at SDRMC. But not much else. Lately, the Saudis have been keeping me busy. Your contract was for discrete without suspicion. And you were near the last in a series of related contracts. The Saudis don't realize that when you string all the individual pieces of information from multiple contracts together, you get a pretty good picture of what they're doing, at least in a general sense. So I know more than they think I do. I also knew that my contracts with them were nearing an end when I met you. Right now they are cleaning up loose ends for some highly guarded secret. And I wasn't long from becoming a loose end, myself." Dominique paused before continuing, "After you, my plan was to slip away, never to work for the Saudis again. I have a really big contract offer for a political figure from another client that was going to be next on my list. You actually did me a really big favor with your strangulation show. But I'm still not quite sure I'm over my mad at you for not letting me in on the charade, you know."

"So how exactly how am I a loose end?"

"I'm sorry. I know Brent Somersbe was a friend of yours."

"I knew him from work at SDRMC, that's all. I think he worked avionics."

"Then he wasn't a friend?"

"Not really."

"I'm so relieved. I was so worried what you'd think when I told you he was a contract."

"So you still haven't told me how I fit."

"The Brent Somersbe contract was execution style in public after the Saudis got what they wanted. The Saudis knew you and Somersbe worked together at SDRMC. After his death, you burned your rental house to the ground and then disappeared. As a loose end, they assumed you knew what Somersbe gave them and went into hiding out of fear."

"I hardly knew Somersbe; some fine people from Atlanta burned my house down; and Kevin and I disappeared because we relieved fifty, or so, of the Nation's slimiest individuals of their stock market investments."

"The Saudis couldn't have known."

"No. The only other connection might be from some activity in the Utah desert. But that was as if I was never there."

Dinner was delivered by Uber-Eats and the conversations continued. Kevin made a dramatic point about sleeping in the bedroom and leaving Cole and Dominique to sleep on the couch. And they did, sleeping as one, holding each other in embrace until the sun peeked through the window.

Kevin's ire had softened, especially when Uber-Eats delivered his morning pancakes with bacon - crispy. They all sat at the kitchen table and ate breakfast. It was a start to Kevin's gradual acceptance of Dominique.

Kevin started the conversation, "The data has lots of pieces but the central figure seems to be Chris Beech. We need to get close to him and learn who he reports to. We need . ."

Dominique interrupted, "You probably won't want to get too close to him. He's dead. Died of Covid."

Kevin looked at Dominique strangely and continued, I got a start on a number of leads out of a CIA report off Higgins's home computer. The report was focused specifically on Beech and his export activities. His company, Space Sciences, is an aerospace firm. Yet, he exported ocean going ship parts to the Middle East, industrial size bread dough mixers, and all kinds of industrial equipment to Argentina. By now the CIA will have figured out that Beech was being paid in a complex escrow scheme through a real estate firm in Arkansas. We might be able learn more if we could follow the money in and out of the escrow accounts.

Dominique again interrupted, "The owner of the real estate firm is dead and the FBI confiscated all the company's records and computers."

Kevin again looked strangely at Dominique.

Cole asked, "How did he die?"

"Botulism and liver failure, which ultimately causes swelling of the brain and then death."

Kevin hesitated before continuing, "The source of the money was re-routed through several corporate accounts, but it could have originated in the Middle East. CIA may or may not have figured that out and more. It would be nice to know what the CIA has learned, but I've checked Higgins's home computer several times; it's been wiped clean of all files except for limited personal stuff. I have the email address of the CIA person that wrote the original report and I've tried to get him to open an email with an embedded routine. But his computer has gone completely silent; it's like his IP address no longer exists."

Dominique interrupted again, "Jacob McCarry is dead. Overdosed on drugs twice before the Saudis finally took care of him. Needless to say, they were furious with me."

"What?" said Kevin with a puzzled look. "There's something here I'm not getting. How do you know? And why would the Saudis be mad at you?"

Cole knew, "Let's not go there right now. Let's focus on what we can do. Where are people's lives? We should concentrate on social media, internet, home computer, cell phone, family, friends, and government data bases. What can we do with that?

"Cell phone," said Kevin. "I can do a lot with that."

"Okay then. Which one?"

"Beech is the focal point. His."

"Okay then. How do we get access to his cell phone without having the actual phone?"

Kevin struggled with the answer, "Some of it is possible, but we'd really be better off with his phone."

"I can get it," said Dominique.

"How?" asked Kevin.

"When somebody dies, their personal items are held for release to the family. Beech has no family, except perhaps for a new half-sister – me," said Dominique and then paused. "Kevin, can I use your computer? I need to access my files, photo-shop some pictures and create some documents." She quickly added, "I'd like your help, too."

Dominique slid one of the kitchen chairs into Kevin's alcove and the two of them went to work. Kevin accessed hospital records in the Arlington Area. Beech had died at the Virginia Hospital Center and there was no record of his body being released. Dominique verified with a phone call to the hospital morgue. She then called an Arlington funeral home and made arrangements to have her poor deceased brother cremated followed by a ceremony with only a small audience, perhaps twenty-five. Kevin, then turned the computer over to her so she could remotely access her files and computer server. Cole watched as the two worked and chit-chatted along the way. It was several hours before they completed and hit the print button.

Dominique inspected the photo-shopped pictures of her and her half-brother as children and adults, their parents, Beeches birth certificate, her birth certificate, and various other receipts helping to establish her identity. The short timeline meant she had to use her Washington Regional nurse Sandra Roberts' pictures for the photo-shop exercise and rely on previously created Sandra Roberts' identification, which was a risk she confessed to Kevin.

She checked the time on her phone as she exited the alcove and faced Cole, "Cole, I've got a seven o'clock train to Arlington this evening. Kevin can fill you in on the details of the plan. I've got to get going. I've got a cab picking me up two blocks down. I'll be back tomorrow night."

"I'm going with you."

"Don't get all macho on me. This is a walk in the park. And you'd just get in the way."

She gave Cole a kiss on the lips and whispered, "I love you." And then they embraced. "I have an apartment in Arlington and Kevin has the access codes to my computer system and video surveillance. I'll send you kisses before I go to bed tonight."

Kevin was there with her suitcase, handbag, and briefcase freshly loaded with the paperwork they had created. Dominique gave him a little peck on the cheek and he blushed.

And then she was gone. Cole felt the void as soon as the door closed. He should have gone with her. But then maybe she was right; she was a very capable woman and probably didn't need his macho protection.

Kevin interrupted Cole's thoughts, "I guess maybe she's okay."

Chapter Thirty

TERMINAL ALLEY— DOMINIQUE

DOMINIQUE ARRIVED IN ARLINGTON AND TOOK A late night cab to a safe corner near her apartment. She waited and watched in the shadows. Traffic was at a minimum and there was no pedestrian traffic. When she felt sure she hadn't been followed, she made her way to her second floor apartment. She punched eight numbers into the key pad and the door lock release mechanism granted her entrance. She turned on the light and studied the apartment; it was just as she had left it.

In the bedroom, the Nurse Robertson wig, facial pieces and makeup were all in place. Tomorrow Chris Beech's grief stricken half-sister would visit the mortuary and arrange for her brother's hastened cremation and service. For an accelerated cremation and service she would pay a premium and pay it up front. Of course, all she really wanted was for the mortuary to begin making inquiries and apply pressure as to when they could pick up the body. Giving the mortuary some time, she would visit Chris Beech's last known hotel and see what personal effects could be recovered.Then, it would be a visit to the hospital morgue and capture Beech's cell phone. She hoped it would be enough for Kevin.

Dominique was exhausted. Cole had kept her going both during the day and then late into the night with extracurricular activities. She smiled at the thought. Dominique went back into the living room and looked up at her video surveillance camera; she waved and then blew a kiss before returning to the bedroom. It was only moments before she fell into a deep state of well needed sleep.

Kevin and Cole watched her on the computer monitor. Cole smiled and his thoughts wondered. Kevin looked intently at the monitor and then commented, "She's too good looking to be so smart."

"How so?"

"Oh, well. I did a little checking with the info she gave me."

"Not surprised."

"It's like everything is really well thought out. Her surveillance cameras, for instance, are really secure. I'm not even sure I could access one of them without the codes. The video feed is encrypted at the camera, itself, and then routed to her own server. With pass codes, she can access it with her cell or from anywhere she can get on a computer. And right now, she and I are the only ones that can access the feed."

Cole's thoughts went down several tangents as Kevin continued, "It's the same kind of thing with her cell phone, laptop and servers. And when I went looking," Kevin paused, "it really wasn't spying. It wasn't. She has all kinds of specialty codes. I found one that uses a convolutional neural inclusion, rather than occlusion, as a way of deceiving facial recognition software. It tells her exactly what she needs to add or detract from her face to give the facial recognition software erroneous geometric data. It's brilliant. Her cell phone is a custom Purism Librem that has superior encryption and precludes pairing or access, even with Stingray or Hailstorm. It also has another feature; it automatically triangulates cell phone towers and tells you where an incoming or outgoing call is located. And, even better, it defeats any recipient's location diversion apps so there is no doubt about location. Cole, are you listening!"

"What?"

"You didn't hear a thing I said, did you? I said, she is one brilliant woman."

"Get some rest, then check her video surveillance for anything unusual. Go back at least a month."

"It does it automatically with motion detectors. No reason to."

"Just humor me. Code something that does a rapid scan. Find a subtle breeze at the window curtain. Find a bird flying past the window. Find the slightest movement of anything. Can you do that?"

"Sure."

"Good, I'm done for the night. I'll see you in the morning. And yes, you can still have the bed. I'm good with the couch."

Cole stripped to his skivvies, stretched out on the couch, pulled the blanket over him, and laid there for a moment before his thoughts went to Dominique. How could he feel for this woman the way he did? Perhaps it was because she was a kindred spirit. In the recesses of her very being, she was probably as messed up as he was. Her childhood was different from his, but just as disturbing. He had opened up and told her things he'd never told anyone before. And she had done the same. With her, all the evil seemed far in the past and the burden was gone. She made him feel renewed and wonderful. She made him feel like life was blossoming and he did love her. She must feel the same way, he hoped. Cole stared at the open alcove door. Kevin was still in there. He watched. There was only silence coming from the hidden alcove. It actually seemed unusually quiet, even the city sounds seemed to fade and Cole was soon fast asleep.

Cole slept late into the morning when Kevin woke him, "Get up. Something's just not right."

Cole mumbled and rolled to a sitting position on the couch. "Coffee. First things first," he said.

"Coffee's made. Get your head out of your ass and then come see what I got."

Cole got his cup of coffee and joined Kevin in the alcove. Cole knew Kevin had been up all night. It's just the way he was. Kevin was staring at the computer monitor studying lines of alphanumeric gibberish mixed in with symbols and numbers.

     Brian David Simmons

Kevin pointed at the screen and said, "See that. Right there. That's where I accessed Dominique's video feed this morning and watched her leave. See that?"

"No Kevin. I don't see it. All I see is a bunch of unintelligible computer speak."

"You don't see the transition. For hell's sake. Right here," said Kevin as he pointed again. "That's where the video feed continues saving to the server but also begins live feed."

"I'll just take your word for it."

"But this is a secondary feed. I almost missed it. See that <!101110%*&(dt011) string right there. That means I'm number two." said Kevin and he brought up another screen. "I went back months to find this: <!101110%*&(dt001). Do you see that?"

"Uh, one number is different?"

"Exactly, that's where the first live feed started. Somebody has been capturing and probably recording the video from Dominique's apartment for months!"

"I thought you said it was unhackable."

"It is. Unless you're good, really good."

"Who? FBI? Do you think they're on to her?"

"No way to know. I wrote some code to tag the feed and it led me to a cloud based server with a whole host of security protocols, all of its own. There's no way of telling and I'm just fumbling around blind, and in the dark. I can't figure it out and it pisses me off."

"Dominique should know. Call her."

"I've tried but her phone is powered down. Before

she left her apartment this morning, she showed me as she powered it down."

"She was going to the mortuary and to the hospital. See if you can track her down. Fastest way to Arlington is the train. Get me a ticket."

Eight hours later, the train was nearing Arlington. Kevin's cell phone triggered a relay transmitter hidden in the wall of a hotel room in El Segundo and Cole's phone rang.

"I got her," started Kevin. "She didn't turn her phone back on until she got back to her apartment and started stripping off the Nurse Robertson disguise. I told her in a coded kind of way about the compromise to her video surveillance system. She didn't take it so well. She said she had a package to ship and then would meet you there."

"Package? Did she say what it was? And meet me where?"

"She was real cryptic. I don't know what she's doing, Cole. She was only specific when she told me to remember the code."

"What the hell? Package? Remember the code? What does that mean? I don't like any of this. Give me the address. How did she even know I was headed for Arlington? Did you tell her?" quizzed Cole."

"She already knew. You didn't talk to her?"

"No!"

"The location she gave me is strange; it's actually in a raunchy area of Buckingham."

"Text it to me."

"I don't understand."

Cole blew threw his fist as the thoughts came together: "We're getting played. Figure out what the hell is going on, Kevin." finished Cole and hung up.

The train pulled into the station. Cole stepped off the train. He studied the platform. The train would be returning to New York and perhaps he and Dominique would be here before it left. Cole found a good observation spot and studied all the faces coming and going. He surveyed the crowds and studied the faces harder. No one was following. He dialed Dominique: no answer. Each time he tried, her phone went straight to voice mail. He called Kevin and still no word from his end either.

Cole took a cab and let it deliver him directly to the address Kevin had given him. He stood in front of a small market. Vehicle traffic on the street was light and few pedestrians were out. A four story apartment building across the street was blocking out the days last few remaining rays of sunshine. Cole studied each pedestrian: no threats. He too was being studied; with pale skin, he was out of place and could feel the questioning eyes.

Cole stepped into the market and studied the shelves. The market was getting ready to close and the woman inside hastened his decision to buy a bottle of water. Back on the sidewalk, Cole strolled north studying every passing vehicle, pedestrian face, and building. He finished his water and tossed the bottle into a small pile of trash. Where was Dominique and why would she even come here in the first place? Cole started back to the south. The apartment building across the street was disconcerting; it had too many windows with too many potential eyes. Perhaps Dominique was behind one of them. Cole passed the market and came to an alley.

Cole studied the alley. It was blind with no escape route. Light had all but disappeared but he could make out a garbage dumpster and miscellaneous trash strewn throughout. Other than the dumpster, there was no hiding place. It was probably safe, except for the lack of an escape. Cole blew through his fist as he made the decision to enter.

He inched his way towards the dumpster and unknowns that might lie behind. He approached the front corner of the dumpster, using all his senses to interrogate the unknown. A glimmer of light reflected off something on the ground. Then he spotted several more; they were shell casings, probably 9mm from the size. His alertness intensified even further. His eyes cut through the increasing darkness. And, with imagination and part vision, he saw it and then his mind filled in the unseen. A foot was sticking out from underneath a piece of cardboard and underneath the cardboard was a body. He'd seen the foot before and agonizing emotion exploded within him.

     Brian David Simmons

Khalil watched through the rifle scope. The safety was off and he was ready to fire his specially prepared 9mm bullets protected by a sabot. The bullets had originally been fired through a 9mm Glock, recovered, encased in sabots, and reloaded for the .50 caliber rifle. It detracted from accuracy and the powder load was light, but he could easily reach the target at a hundred meters.

Ibrahim stood watch with light enhanced binoculars. His cell phone buzzed.

"Update," commanded Hafez the instant Ibrahim answered.

"As planned," calmly stated Ibrahim. "The assassin whore used her cell phone capabilities and came as you had suggested. The American gangsters, though, are incompetents. She would have defeated them all had Khalil not finished her. Now, as you forecast, we are watching the Davis man. He is alone in the alley with her. If the American gangsters do not arrive soon, Khalil will have to - "

"No," Hafez interrupted. "They are essential to our anonymity! Wait. Wait. Patience will be rewarded. I am confident."

"Yes Sahib. We will wait."

"Excellent. You and Khalil please me. Call when it is finished."

Ibrahim looked down the alley through his binoculars. The Davis man was sitting against the back wall holding the whore assassin, rocking back and forth. The Davis man's mouth moved as he screamed something. It looked as if the Davis man was wailing like he himself done many times at evening prayer. There were probably tears coming from the infidel's eyes, he thought.

"Are you seeing this?" Ibrahim asked of Khalil.

"Weak Americans. This one mourns for an eahira qatil. How pathetic. I excrete on him."

Ibrahim laughed, "Soon it will be Eblis excreting on him in Jahannam.

The Davis man continued holding the eahira qatil, rocking back and forth, as final rays of sunlight disappeared. Khalil changed his scope to infra-red. Ibrahim set the binoculars aside and put on a thermal sensing monocular. It was almost too much. Street lights and vehicle headlights were a continual distraction.

Finally, the American gangsters arrived at the alley entrance and stared into the darkness. They entered slowly. Khalil and Ibrahim watched as the American gangster's eyes adjusted to the alley light and their pace increased. They stopped as they neared the end of the Alley, blocking his view of the Davis man and the whore assassin.

Hamilton Cole Davis stared up at the intruders in his lament. He was sick. The loss of Dominique was crushing his very existence. She was all he wanted in life. Even the deaths of his Mother and Father paled in comparison to the crushing pain he was now feeling.

    Brian David Simmons

"She all fucked up, huh, white boy," commented one of the intruders.

Cole's senses began shifting to the present. "Did you do this?" quietly asked Cole.

"Damn right we did. Too bad she so fucked up; we didn't get a chance to poke that bitch. Should'a done that first," said another one.

Cole gently sat Dominique against the alley wall and closed her eyes. He wiped the tears from his. Dominique's cell phone was lying within reach. He picked it up, looked at the screen and then slipped it into his pocket.

"Oh look, he's crying," said one of the five.

"Why?" pleaded Cole.

"Just cause - and we do the same to you," said the apparent leader.

The smallest of the group pulled what looked like Glock-19 from his waist band and pointed it at Cole. Cole slowly slid up the wall to a standing position. Loss and heartache were transitioning to rage. His focus was shifting to the challenge in front of him. The Glock was held sideways in some kind of a look-cool gang style. There were five of them. They were all reasonable in size, but maybe ten years his junior. They had apparent recent injuries: blackened eyes, busted lips, and developing bruises. One of them appeared to be favoring one leg. The tattoo with number 13 was prevalent. They were all ten feet, or so, away, which was within his fight or flight limit for a single armed adversary. But for Cole, rational thought was gone.

"Your mother should have flushed you down the toilet at birth," calmly stated Cole. "And when I'm done with you, I'm going to hunt her down and kill her too."

"Fucking shoot him, Xavier," screamed the leader.

Rage increased ten-fold and was now pure hatred. With an explosion of uncontrolled energy, Cole flew from the wall directly at the leader, instantly eliminating the distance between them. The Glock fired but the bullet went elsewhere. Cole drove his knuckled right deep into the leader's throat, crushing esophagus, trachea, glottis, and subglottis. In a whirling rebound from his punch, Cole planted a full fisted, full force, left directly to the side of Xavier's head. The third gang banger was approaching, as if to grab Cole. The fourth and fifth were pulling pistols from their waist bands. With continued rotation through Xavier's head, Cole unleashed a rearward kick to the inside of the advancing man's knee. Cole snapped through his rotation to face the two remaining gang bangers. He instantly charged forward at the remaining two. Along the way, Cole drove his heel, and the kneeless man's nasal bone, deep into his skull. Cole came face to face with the fourth gang banger with a pistol that had just cleared its waist band. Cole helped him replace the pistol, front and center, in the waist band and pull its trigger five times in rapid succession. He shoved the still standing, but soon to be dead, banger directly at the fifth man, who got off a shot that went wide with

 Brian David Simmons

the impact. Nonetheless, Cole felt a strange sensation in the mass of scar tissue on his left side. He grabbed the pistol-ed left hand of the fifth man, spun him, and wrenched his hand up behind his back. Cole's right arm swung up under the banger's chin as they rotated towards the alley entrance. Cole forced the banger's pistol-ed hand up higher behind his back as he prepared to snap the man's neck. Then, without a sound, Cole felt the man's inner body balloon from the impact of a bullet just under Cole's elbow.

How could a bullet have just entered the man's center of mass? And from where? Cole instantly recognized the sensation in his side. He was a target. Cole let go of the now dying banger and darted for cover of the dumpster. Another bullet close enough to feel its wake whizzed past his head. Then, a sharp ping rang out just as he reached the dumpster. The bullets were coming from the building across the street, third or fourth floor for maximum vantage point, concluded Cole. Fight or flight, Cole questioned? Screw it! Fight and fight now.

Cole pushed on the dumpster; it started moving. He pushed harder and it accelerated towards the alley entrance. As it neared the alley entrance, two wheels hit sacks of garbage bringing it to a stop. Cole didn't stop; he kept going, charging across the street, darting left and right. He burst through the main building entrance and raced up the stairs to the third floor. He charged down the hall, stopping where he felt an apartment window had direct view of the alley.

Cole listened at the door. He could hear a TV and passed it up for the next door. He heard a man's voice and burst through the door ready to strike. A man and a woman were sitting at a kitchen table eating. Cole charged back down the hall and up the stairs to the fourth floor. Again, he stopped at an apartment that had a view of the alley. He didn't hesitate and burst through the door. No one seemed to be home. He quickly scanned the interior and checked the window. It had a perfect view of the alley. Cole didn't stop at the final possibility on the fourth floor and burst in. Kids screamed and a woman jumped in front of them to protect them from Cole. He quickly exited the apartment.

Cole was out of control and had gone too far. But the shots had to have come from this building. He made his way to the second floor. Down the hall, he could see that a door was standing open. He approached cautiously and then peered inside. It was empty and unoccupied. Cole checked the front window. It had a view of the alley, but the elevation wasn't even close to optimum. Then it came to him. The bullets weren't supposed to have a downward trajectory. Cole stood at the window and blew through his fist. There was always a reason. The question was "why." It was then that he remembered his side. A small trickle of blood had been absorbed by his shirt, but the mass of scar tissue had effectively been unaffected, even though it now hurt like hell. Shell casings strewn on the alley

     Brian David Simmons

floor and level trajectory were part of a ruse. But what for? A siren was approaching off in the distance. It was time to go.

The train ride back to New York was long and lonely. Dominique filled his thoughts and soul. His yearning for her love was overwhelming; tears streamed from his eyes as the train worked its way north.

Chapter Thirty-One

Gifts from Dominique

Kevin and Cole sat at the kitchen table and blankly stared at emptiness. Breakfast, not even morning coffee, seemed to matter. Morning dragged on towards noon. Neither had dressed; both just sat there in t-shirts and underwear. Eventually Kevin retreated to his computer alcove and Cole turned on the TV. A resolution was slowly building in Cole's subconscious. After the Kootenai County sheriff killed his father in a jail cell, it had taken Cole nearly a year to plan and prepare for the sheriff's execution. This time it wouldn't matter how long it took or how many casualties fell along the way, because whoever was responsible for Dominique's death would die by his hand.

Something was blabbering from the TV. Cole got up and went to his pants lying on the floor. He hesitated; it was hers; it was a part of her. He just stared at his pants; her blood was on them. Sorrow swelled within him. But it was a starting point; Cole picked up his pants and removed the cell phone that had fallen from Dominique's lifeless hand. Dominique's phone was at less than five percent charge, but the screen was still illuminated. Cole studied it and then sought out Kevin.

Kevin quickly found the correct charge adapter and plugged it in. He studied the illuminated screen. Ordinarily, the Purism Librem would have locked out access of any kind, but it was now locked open.

"Oh my God," mumbled Kevin. "She had to have done this knowing. She did it for us." Kevin continued to study the screen and then continued, "She could have just left her phone unlocked, but instead she made sure this screen was displayed. It's a message or data she wanted us to know."

"What message?"

"This screen may explain why she went to the alley. The Purism Librem displays as much information as is possible on the caller or the one being called, including location. We could . . . no, that's not right. The signal strength is too strong. It had to have been boosted. It's as if . . . You know how we use the cell phone relay in El Segundo; this is the same. The boosted signal means they knew the cell tower triangulation would take her right to the alley and, with the relay, they weren't even there. It was a damn trap." Kevin tapped the screen to bring up the call log before continuing, "This number has never been called before. Odd. Time is brief."

"The caller must have been somebody she thought she could trust?"

"Probably. I'm going to download her phone and see what else I can learn. This call actually went to voicemail."

"Kevin, I want these son-of-a-bitches, every last one of them."

"Ordinarily I'd give you shit. But this time I agree."

Kevin went to work on Dominique's phone, downloading address book, call log, email, activity logs, settings, and every app. Everything was subject to interrogation. Cole watched for a while and then just paced.

"Cole," cried out Kevin.

He tapped the phone screen to replay the voicemail again: "Dominique, this is Cole. Meet me in the alley next to Swisher's Market on Addison in Buckingham. Don't tell anyone, I mean anyone, where you're going. It's important."

"What the hell. I never made that call," said Cole and then blew through his fist. "Play it again. Listen real careful at the words Swisher, Addison, and Buckingham."

The voicemail played again and then Kevin played it over and over, before commenting, "It's hardly discernible; but Swisher is ss-wish-her. Addison is add-e-son. Buckingham is buck-ing-i-am."

Cole blew through his fist and then recounted, "First time I met Dominique was in a pizza place. We were there for a good eight hours. I said every word in that voicemail more than once, except for Swisher, Addison, and Buckingham. When we left, I noticed two Arabic looking characters at a distant table. Those son-of-a-bitches recorded everything that was said, dissected it and constructed that message."

"It's artificial intelligence voice cloning," stated Kevin.

"What?"

"It's not that hard. But you have to have the technology. Whoever these Arabs are, they are good – real good," meekly added Kevin.

Cole again blew through his fist as his thoughts converged, "They knew she could track the location of the incoming call from a relayed signal; plus she thought I gave her the location and instruction to be there. They knew she would go to the alley."

Kevin continued to work with the phone. Hunger was now outweighing sorrow and food seemed like a good idea. Cole ordered Italian with Meal-Dash delivery. It seemed like an unusually long time before the intercom finally buzzed. Cole pressed the intercom and confirmed the delivery. Cole exited the condo, took the elevator, and stepped out the main entrance. He handed the Deal-Dash driver a cash tip and watched as the driver went back to his double parked Tesla. Cole ducked his head for the overhead surveillance camera and was about to re-enter the building when he caught a glimpse of another man approaching.

Cole's senses went on high alert. The man was wearing a ball cap, covid mask, and sunglasses, even though the sun had already set. Cole turned to face the man; the man kept coming. The man carried a hard-sided suitcase of some kind. Cole clinched his left fist and loosened his right hand grip on the Italian food bag. Dinner was about to hit the ground.

"Good evening," said the man. "Do you have something for me?"

"You have no idea," replied Cole as the man stepped forward and began studying Cole.

"Okay, input it right here," said the man and pointed at a touch screen on the hard-sided case.

Cole was confused, "Input what?"

"Fourth floor, six foot, brown hair, blue eyes, muscular build, gorilla hands, I think so. One of two descriptions I was given. If that all fits, I just need you to input your code right here," replied the man as he again pointed to the key pad.

"Code?"

"Yes, a code," said the man who was now becoming irritated.

"I don't know what the hell you're talking about."

"All right then. I'll just return the item to her."

"Her. Who is 'her'?"

"I don't work to names, just description, location, and code. Have a good evening sir."

The man turned to walk away; Cole dropped dinner, grabbed the man and spun him around, "I'm sorry. You just caught me by surprise, that's all."

"Hands off," said the man. "Right now there's a flat shooting 7mm round, two hundred yards out about to come your way."

Cole released the man. Code pondered. Could it be? No way. But . . . The man was walking off. Cole called after him, "Wait! Her description is the most

    Brian David Simmons

beautiful woman in the world: five-eight, muscular fit, green eyes, brown hair, hundred ten pounds, B-cup bra size."

The man stopped, turned and slowly walked back to Cole, "I still need a code. No code, no delivery. Guaranteed secure is how I stay in business. So if you have a code, we'll do business. If not, the delivery gets returned. Now I do have a second description. Same location. Five-eight, wild black hair, one-forty weight, glasses. Maybe he has the code."

Cole racked his brain for code. Perhaps it was some form of personal code Kevin and he used. His mind went backward to their first call to Kevin and it came to him. "Steak, as in New York," he blurted out.

"You're new to the process so I'll cut you some slack. You're not supposed to tell me the code. You're just supposed to input it right here," said the man, again pointing to the key pad.

Cole tapped the key pad and the metallic case's lock mechanism retracted. The man opened the case; Cole retrieved a bag containing a wallet, cell phone and other miscellaneous items, along with a laptop computer. The man snapped the case shut and walked away without another word.

Cole returned to the fourth floor and presented the laptop to Kevin. Kevin's eyes grew as the machine powered up.

"Present from Dominique," stated Cole. "This is Beech's wallet and cell phone, too."

Kevin was too captivated by the laptop to respond. He USB-ed Beech's laptop to one of his servers and went to work writing code. Dinner was cold by the time Kevin emerged from the alcove. Over midnight dinner, Kevin explained that getting passed Beech's laptop password was pretty simple, but there was very little on it other than purchase orders, shipping invoices and other innocuous appearing records. He would sort it out in the morning.

A week passed, Kevin had been working continuously with Beech's Cell. He couldn't get past the biometric security. He had no pass code, no finger print and certainly not facial recognition information to feed the I-Phone. And every circumvention routine he tried proved futile. The phone had enhanced security. And it was only a few more login attempts to wiping out all data and locking up forever. He felt like pulling his hair out.

Cole was becoming an irritant. Kevin had given him the task of sorting through the invoices on Beech's laptop, but he had already scanned the files and knew they contained no revelations. It was the interruptions that irritated him the most. First Cole wanted to know if there was any way to check this against that; then it was lunch; then it was some news story on TV; then it was let's go for a run; and on and on. He wanted to return to Tobago and his Fugaku clone, and he didn't want Cole there.

Cole stepped up behind him. Kevin answered before Cole could ask, "No. No. And go away."

"I think you're working too hard again."

"I'm doing everything I can. I can't get around this damn I-Phone security."

"That's what I mean. Instead of trying to go around it, why don't you just go with it? Get a finger print off Beech's wallet, laptop or cell phone and then make up a dummy finger. Get a picture of Beech and hold it in front of the screen."

"That's a stupid idea."

"Why?"

"Simple, the phone knows the difference between a two dimensional picture and the real thing. That's why. The I-phone wants three dimensional convolutional neural inclusion that's . . ." Kevin paused as realization was developing: Could it? No. Maybe. Kevin stopped breathing and went motionless as his mind dived into the unknowns of an inclusional spacial array. Numerical construction and computation would be a huge challenge with multiple functions derived by integration defining shape as modified by interaction of each of the other functions. And then would the phone even recognize it as a substitute? The answer hit him like a sledge hammer – another gift from Dominique.

"Out," Kevin yelled at Cole.

Dominique had a routine to help her create disguises defeating facial recognition software. It used convolutional neural inclusion and that would be his starting point. He went to work. Kevin had the two dimensional images of Beech that she had used to photo shop family pictures. It would work, he thought as he began rattling at the keyboard. Three hours later, he had it. Ported through the data/charging port, Kevin turned his numerical code loose on the phone. It came to life. He stared at the screen as the app icons appeared. He pressed the phone symbol at the bottom of the screen. "Recents" appeared and at the bottom he had two voice messages. Kevin slid back in his chair and laced his fingers behind his head. He had it.

But now what, contemplated Kevin? Whoever these Arabs were, they were good, really good. Maybe even better than him. They could capture private conversations, deceive cell phone locations, manufacture voice messages, access border security video, run facial recognition and who knows what else. They probably had Hailstorm type capability to listen in on cell phone conversations, the ability to hack computer systems and devices to track a person anywhere; the sum total of capability was frightening. And they were ever clever, oh my God they were. They were probably even cleverer than Cole and himself. "Shit," sighed Kevin.

Chapter Thirty-Two

THE ENEMY

ON THE SIXTH FLOOR AT LANGLEY, FRANK WALLACE had an eleven-thirty time slot with Jeff Monson and was early. He waited in the anteroom and studied his phone. He read each text and email as it came in. He had a scenario and the incoming data continued to confirm it. Dell invited him in and he took a seat in front of Monson's over-sized desk.

"I have answers and they're not good," started Frank. "Buckingham PD got a shots fired call nine nights ago for a location off Addison. Five MS-13 gang members apparently tried to assault a Miss Dominique Jaclyn Portemay. Interesting that Miss Portemay had been through the FBI academy, but turned down a job offer in Legal Affairs. She also had since been enrolled in martial arts training. It appears Miss Portemay was more than they bargained for. Four of the five died with wounds inflicted by Miss Portemay: collapsed esophagus, blow to the head, nasal bone driven into the brain, and extensive gunshot damage in the pelvic area with a MS-13's own gun. The fifth died of a stray round from a Glock-19. Unfortunately, Miss Potemay took two rounds. . ."

Monson interrupted, "What does this have to do with McCarry?"

"I'm getting there. Miss Potemay's body was found sitting against the back wall of this alley. Some sharp Buckingham cop noticed that there was dried blood splattered on the wall, at head height, directly above Potemay. Yet Potemay was not shot in the head and she wasn't even that tall. As part of their investigation, they took a DNA sample, sent it in for testing, and that's when I got the call. It was Jake's."

Frank paused assuming he'd get a question from Monson. Monson just stared at him. Frank reminded himself to bury emotion and mater-of-factually continued, "I've had a team in there working twenty hours straight. We have accounted for every round that was fired in that alley. Nine bullets and nine shell casings were from a 9mm Glock-19, which was recovered in the alley. Two bullets and two shell casings were from a S&W .30, also recovered. Five bullets and five shell casings from a 1911, also recovered." Frank paused and pushed the emotion down, "Horrible news is that one of the 9mm bullets was recovered from the center of what appears to be Jake's blood. We found more of Jake's blood in a garbage dumpster that had been dumped. We're searching the waste transfer site now." Frank again paused to manage his professional delivery, "In summary, some weeks earlier, Jacob McCarry was shot and killed by the same Glock-19 that killed Miss Potemay. The perpetrators were MS-13, who are now deceased. "

In a somber voice, Jeff Monson relented, "Put it in writing, all of it: the drugs, the hospital, and the MS-13. And let me know when you find Jake. On your way out, have Dell step in. I'll start arrangements for a fallen agent."

"Just five points of confusion I haven't figured out." added Frank and then continued his analytical delivery. "First, the Glock-19 was found with fifteen rounds in the magazine; it has a capacity of eighteen. Yet nine rounds were fired. Did they reload in the middle of battle? Second, the coroner couldn't decide if Potemay died while sitting or lying. Did she sit up after death? Third, Potemay's liver temperature was three degrees cooler than any of the MS-13s, which ordinarily would put her time of death a couple of hours earlier than that of the MS-13s'. Fourth, we have touch and blood DNA at the scene that is not in our database. There may have been someone else at the scene. And finally, Jake's truck is missing. It's a fifty year-old, very out-of-place, vehicle. We've searched hundreds of hours of traffic and other video. It has just vanished."

"Put it in the report, Frank. All of it," stated a somber Monson.

IN NEW YORK, KEVIN WAS MAKING DISCOVERIES. Beech's phone was a wealth of information. Kevin had names, phone numbers, notes, calendar and everything else that comes on an I-Phone. Cole and Kevin decided it was time for a test. Kevin would route all attempts through encrypted satellite links routed back to earth and through two cell phone booster-relays. They tried a dozen calls from Beech's most "Recents" list that all went unanswered. They went to Beech's contacts list and tried three more before one out of country numbers was answered.

"Lagos," came a reply.

"Uh, how's it going?" is all Kevin could come up with.

"Who is this?"

"Beech said I should give you a call. How's it going?"

"Fine. What do you want?"

"I want to know about the Arabs," said Kevin truthfully.

"The Saudis are happy. And by the way, Beech is dead."

"Yes, I know. I'll check back later on the Arabs. That's all for now," finished Kevin and hung up.

He didn't like any of this and lambasted Cole, "Why am I doing all the calling? I'm no good at the interpersonal shit. You know that. You call next time."

"No, not yet. For now, it's you. My turn will come. What's Logos' location, even if we can't trust it?"

Kevin rattled the key board and then replied, "Buenos Aires. Actually it's Avellaneda, just south of Buenos Aires. Triangulation of Argentine cell towers is kind of a guess but looks like it's right close to the harbor."

"Could be false, but okay. It's actually two hits now for Buenos Aires. The McCarry report had Beech shipping all kinds of equipment to Argentina." Cole blew through his fist and then continued, "Time to go play tourist. Time to get even for Dominique. Time hell paid Mister Lagos a visit."

"I want to try something first," said Kevin. "I've been looking at this. See the file labeled "Select" in the "Notes" app, said Kevin as he pointed. "The most peculiar entry is one labeled HSIW with a single twenty-seven-digit number. It's code for something or a satellite phone number, I'll bet."

"Dial it."

Kevin began dialing the twenty-seven-digit number. After the first eleven numbers, a phone rang and then a woman from Wisconsin answered. Kevin studied the number. Why twenty seven numbers? The Notes App also contained a single twelve digit number with no reference. Cole pointed at that number and it was next. The call processing was lengthy, passing through two delays and several clicks, which ultimately resulted in a low level hum over the phone line. Kevin listened for a while and then hung up.

Perhaps it was like a calling card. Kevin went through the dialing process again on his satellite phone to reach the low level hum and then punched in the additional twenty-seven numbers for a total of thirty-nine numbers, start to finish. A phone rang, rang again, and then came an answer: "Hafez."

Kevin put the phone on speaker and looked at Cole. Cole just pointed back at Kevin.

"Hafez. Who is this?" demanded the man on the other end of the call.

"Half-Ass?" mumbled Kevin. "Uh, wrong number."

"How did you get this number?" Came the furious, but inquisitive reply with each word forcefully articulated.

Cole signaled with his hand to keep it going. Kevin, fearful, but realizing his complete anonymity, simply stated the truth, "I got it from Beech."

"Then he spoke it to you from the grave."

Kevin wanted to hang up but Cole motioned again to keep it going. He replied, "I guess he kind of did at that." With distance, anonymity, and a moment of bravado, Kevin added, "Hey, you lost anything lately? Maybe some Arabs in the desert?"

"No, that's been taken care of," Hafez replied cautiously. "So just exactly how did you get this number?"

"Like I said, Beech gave it to me," replied Kevin, increasing in cockiness.

"Fool!" Came Hafez's furious but controlled response. Hafez paused and his tone then became seductive, "Then, tell me, what is your number? I mean, I wish to call you back."

"Nah, I don't think so. This is a private line; I don't give it out to strangers."

"Yes, but it is not exactly fair. You know my name and satellite and I do not know who you are. Maybe just a first name? Then at least I know what to call you. That can not hurt, can it?"

    Brian David Simmons

"Bill, Bill Gates."

"Ha, you are a clever one. Then tell me, Beal, what do you know of lost Arabs, as you put it?"

"I could tell you a lot of things about Arabs, but I think we both know they didn't work for Beech."

"Yes, this may be true."

"Maybe. I don't think there's any maybe about it. And I know what you did to Dominique."

"Haw, the whore assassin. Her demise is of no consequence."

"You think so. You're going to pay for it!" said Kevin blossoming in bravado.

"I think not. I think you will not be making very many more phone calls either."

"Oh, why not?"

"You see, there are many Arabs. I think maybe you will not live very long. Good day to you, Beal. Do not call again."

The line went dead; Kevin swallowed and looked at Cole. Kevin was shaking and felt the depression coming; interpersonal conflict was not in his DNA.

Cole said, "Progress. A lot was inferred, but two statements were precise: 'You know my name and satellite.' Figure that one out. And the second statement, 'the whore assassin. Her demise is of no consequence', means he's the son-of-bitch responsible for Dominique's death."

Kevin's way to fight against the depression was to immerse himself in solution of a technical problem, and Half-Ass had just given him another challenge. Kevin speculated Half-Ass was actually Hafez ibn-Wahhab from his internet search, some kind of Saudi elite. Kevin began mentally wrestling with the phone call possibilities, but nothing was obvious. It wasn't a cell phone. Was it just a satellite phone? Or was it something else? Could it really be his personal satellite? Could it be a Starlink kind of system? No way. So what is it? Maybe he's using somebody's communication satellite? Whose? Sky Bridge? Who? Thirty-nine numbers? Code! That's it! But code for what?

Kevin set the numbers up for speed-dial and dialed the first twelve numbers again. He listened intensely and then punched in twenty seven arbitrary numbers—nothing. He tried it again, and again nothing. Trial and error was not meant for humans and, with a little coding, put the server bank to work. It was a simple task and the computer bank hit almost instantly. He got a string of jumbled numbers and letters.

Kevin squirmed in his chair and studied the monitor. He studied it harder and then turned to Cole, who was looking over his shoulder at the monitor; "GPS," blurted out Kevin. But with the realization, came new questions: Why GPS? GPS and communications together? How?

GPS is provided by the Air Force's Navistar system consisting of twenty-four satellites that provide precise worldwide global positioning. Most modern GPS equipment, including handheld units, use the Navistar system to determine position by triangulation of satellites and the source. Computer calculation of the source's position is done only at the source itself. This was different; the system supported both position via satellite and voice communications via satellite. That's when Kevin realized that the jumble of numbers defining GPS was actually defining their location, which was now an urgent reason to escape the condo. Cole started making travel arrangements and Kevin went back to work.

Kevin tapped into the web and searched on satellite communications. Navistar had replaced the Navy's aging TRANSIT satellite system. It consists of seven satellites providing global positioning and limited telephone communications to ships. Coding to calculate position was archaic and iteratively resolved locations between vessel, satellite, and a fixed point. It had to be. It was actually a brilliant idea to tap into the dying TRANSIT system for untraceable satellite phone use. Kevin was impressed.

Kevin started creating code that would couple the two independent TRANSIT functions of location and voice. Kevin verified his hypothesis with additional random checks and then went to work on a new program, "transtap." Half-Ass was now his subject. We'll see how clever you are, he thought to himself and immediately went to work creating a program that would enable eavesdropping through Half-Ass's own system.

In Phoenix Arizona, Jack Cross from Friendship Aviation was just getting started on a really good
drunk and there was a gorgeous woman in his sights.
She sat three stools down from him at the bar and
every now and again he'd get a little more view of leg
as she squirmed on the bar stool. The white dress she
had on showed plenty of cleavage and he was sure he
was going to see more. He anticipated planting his
nose right between those big perky things and she was
going to get the ride of her life.

His cell phone buzzed and distracted his thoughts.
"Shit," he said before answering.

His first words were, "No. I'm not doing it."

Chad Melloncamp, CEO of Friendship Aviation,
replied, "Oh yes you are. It's Microware again and it's
you or nobody. They only want you to pilot."

"It's my day off and I'll blow at least a one-0. You
have to be nuts to ask me to drive."

"Look. I hit them with rising fuel costs, short notice
fee, extended pickup fee and some other BS. We're getting ten times the going rate. And you're going to fly.
Get a cab and get your ass to the airport. I'm having
the G-III fueled as we speak."

"Do I get a second seat?"

"Sure. Put one of them in the cockpit with you and
give them a captain's hat."

"Great. What's the run?"

"Pick them in New York and deliver them to New
Orleans."

     Brian David Simmons

"Right, I know what that really means and so do you. Plus, getting out of Safe Harbor is a nightmare and JFK is hell. I'm liable to rear end somebody."

"Just get some coffee at the airport. Get your ass moving!" finished Melloncamp and disconnected.

Booze and women had gotten Jack kicked out of the Navy for stupid stunts while on leave, but at least the Navy never asked him to fly drunk. "Jesus Christ," he mumbled. This right now shit was going to cost him his license to fly - if he got caught. Jack called for a cab.

In New York, the time margin of safety was running out. They needed to be gone. Kevin was confident his code to couple location and voice of the TRANSIT would work. But eavesdropping through encrypted communications was a complete failure. He listened to another call of unintelligible sounds and decided he would just have to accept the .500 batting average. Cole watched the clock and paced. It was a five hour flight from Phoenix to JFK plus some time for fueling, loading, and taxiing.

Kevin set and checked the security video, motion detectors, and listening devices of the condo. Data from the devices went encrypted directly to his servers, similar to Dominique's system. He missed her. He hoped the sophistication of his system would prevail when whatever technology infiltrated her system came after his.

Chapter Thirty-Three

It Begins

Cole and Kevin watched as the Gulfstream III taxied to the private terminal at JFK. It was an aging aircraft but it had twin Rolls Royce engines and easily moved at 550 mph. More importantly, Cole had flown undetected in and out of the country with Jack Cross before and knew his capabilities. Dominique was on Cole's mind as the Gulfstream rolled to a stop on the tarmac and boarding stairs flopped into place. Cole and Kevin met Jack half way to the plane. Cole and Jack shook hands and then Kevin followed with an extended hand.

"Where's your lady friend?" inquired Jack.

"Cole stared at him a moment and then provided a deflected response, "It's a sad subject. I'll tell you some-time after we're airborne if you really want to know."

"Good enough. I'm going to hit the head and get something to eat while they're gassing it up. Make yourselves comfortable. There's coffee on, water, pop, beer, and cookies in the galley. Help yourselves."

Kevin and Cole boarded the plane and found the coffee. It was black and nasty and had been cooked for hours. Cole looked out one of the side windows. The plane was being fueled, but there was no sign of Jack. Cole checked the cockpit; it smelled of warm electronics and a very faint hint of bourbon.

Jack returned and they were soon airborne. Cole joined Jack in the cockpit while Kevin studied his laptop. Kevin had extracted all information from Beech's and Dominique's computers and phones, which were left at the condo.

Jack started the conversation, "Where we really going?"

"Tobago first."

"Figures. Then where?"

"Later, after we make Tobago."

Jack looked at Cole and responded, "Just the wild blue yonder, then."

"For now."

Jack was an expert at jumping out of the flight lanes. He had lots of practice flying for all types of questionable clients. Cole counted on it. Jack cleared Houston radar by skipping out across the Gulf at near sea level and then climbing to forty thousand feet, which was above commercial traffic. He disabled GPS and black box transmission and all recording functions. He pushed the plane to an air speed of five hundred seventy miles per hour and navigated a flight path that skirted Cuban airspace. He dodged air traffic control and radar fields in the Dominican Republic and Jamaica and then descended to Tobago. It was late afternoon when Jack contacted the airport at Crown Point and gained clearance to land. Once on the ground, Jack ordered fuel and, at Cole's request, a taxi.

Kevin and Cole arrived at the bungalow and the reunion with Joe and Sylvia was a tearful one. Sylvia wouldn't let go of Cole's arm. They talked about her crafts, the Tobago wildlife, and the sunset walks her and Joe made every evening. Accordingly to Sylvia, Cole hadn't been getting enough to eat and she needed to fatten him up a little. Joe offered to take Cole fishing and talked about the abundance of sea life. But the reunion lasted less than an hour.

Cole retrieved a large hard-sided gun case and Kevin provided Cole with a backpack. If Hafez ibn-Wahhab was some kind Saudi royalty, he no doubt had an entourage and the kill would have to be at a distance. And there was no doubt that Hafez ibn-Wahhab was going to die. The gun case housed a fifty caliber Browning Model 1500 Special Application, which easily had a range of a thousand yards. Should be enough, surmised Cole. The backpack contained a multitude of Kevin's creations, all conceived for electronic surveillance. Cole surmised he was going to need all the help he could get.

Joe wouldn't let go of Cole's hand as he prepared to leave. They locked eyes. Joe always knew more than was ever said. As they parted, Joe simply said, "Come back."

Cole had the waiting cabbie take him straight to Scotiabank, where a pre-arranged withdraw was waiting.

Cole returned to the airport with gun case, duffle bag and backpack. Jack was doing some kind of pre-

     Brian David Simmons

flight check as Cole boarded the plane. Cole joined Jack in the cockpit and when the GIII was given tower clearance, it charged down the runway and was soon airborne.

Jack asked, "Okay. Where to?"

"South. Buenos Aires."

"What?"

"Buenos Aires, non-stop."

"Hell no. We don't even have enough fuel."

"Get this thing aloft, go easy on the throttle, use your reserve, and we'll make it."

"On fumes, maybe."

"How's a twenty-five thousand dollar bonus for getting me there sound?" offered Cole.

"You ass-hole."

"And another twenty-five for getting me home."

As they turned south, Jack pulled his maps I-pad up off the floor and attached the Velcro straps around his leg. He tapped the screen a few times and replied, "Not as far as I thought. Buenos Aires then in six, maybe seven, hours."

After dinner, Kevin left the company of Joe and Sylvia and retreated to the basement. He hoped he could have some answers for Cole by the time he landed. He sat in front of his monitor waiting for the Fugaku clone to come to life.

The FINCEN offices were quiet. Unbeknownst to those who normally fill the offices, the telephone rang and an electronic umbilical was established through the phone system to the heart of the system. Tonight was similar to his previous assault, except he modified his log on approach. He let the Fugaku sequentially search for a name and password with Top Secret access. He found none and went back to Confidential access. Kevin became Debra Livingston with the password "VIRGINISLANDS." Again, he ventured into the FINCEN computer world exploring its databases, programs, and capabilities. This time he found an access to IRS-related files and personal databases on U.S. citizens.

They had electronic information on every working person in the U.S. with a social security number: tax returns, bank account records, automatic teller transactions, credit card activity, property tax, vehicle ownership records, stock market transactions, and more. They were spying on the general population. Then, was it really any different from what Kevin was about to do? Kevin had almost forgotten the reason he had violated the FINCEN computer.

Kevin was becoming comfortable with his ability to gain Confidential access and he'd visited Secret once. But what did Top Secret have to offer? Kevin explored beyond this shackled security limitations. He implemented a plan with alternate strategies. Once entering the computer with a designated security classification, he was tagged, shackled, and restricted from access to Secret or Top Secret databases and files. He

     Brian David Simmons

had to live with the shackles, but devised a software cloak to conceal his shackles. He called his program "incognito." If that didn't work, he would try a more brute force approach and crash the security program to momentarily bring it down; then he could slip through a piece of data to establish a link that made him look like a Top Secret user. He named his second program "topcrash."

Kevin brought up "incognito," but the security system instantly recognized the attempt to disguise the shackles. An internal siren sounded and the alert went out. The security system reached out and branded Debra Livingston as a security violator. Kevin hammered the keyboard in an attempt to stop it and snatch her name from the grasp of the security system, but it resided in the secret world beyond his reach. She would probably be questioned by her supervisor and then investigated by the FBI, or somebody, on Monday, maybe even sooner. Kevin knew he didn't have much time and brought up "topcrash."

"Topcrash" created a momentary short circuit within the security system as Kevin hit "enter." The security system blinked and Kevin passed through the security wall only to find himself in an electronic void, a moat through which nothing passed. His data was severed from its umbilical back to the Fugaku and left him to float in the black emptiness of the moat. The umbilical snapped back through the password interface, terminal server and voice mail. Kevin was abruptly and violently rejected. Mentally, he was thrust to reality in front of his keyboard. *What damage have I done? Is my path compromised? Did it recognize the covert intrusion? Can I fix it?*

Kevin quickly re-entered the system. Luckily, the Gatemaster was still keeping time. He tried to log back on, but Debra Livingston had been locked out. He retracted the "enslaver," reset the Gatemaster and closed his communication link to give him time to think.

The problem was system architecture. Top Secret access apparently opened up a different realm, separate from the rest of the system, possibly with a hard-wired entrance beginning at the password interface. The interface wasn't about to accommodate hundreds of thousands of iterations it would take to hack in. Kevin went for a shot in the dark.

He modified "topcrash" to blindly implant a new user and password combination. The electronic void he had encountered had to allow access from the other side. He would try instantaneous deception when the security system momentarily blinked by establishing an artificial command coming from the other side. With microsecond timing, the artificial command would receive rather than direct.

He was blind to what lay beyond the secret wall and only had guesses as to what the software-augmented architecture looked like. With limited time for his shot in the dark, Kevin wrote fourteen variations

     Brian David Simmons

of his name and password implant. He would try to sneak all of them through at the same time.

Kevin re-entered the system, enslaved the Gatemaster and accessed the confidential level as Henry Woo with the password 12WITCHYWIFE. Halfway in, he downloaded the updated version of "topcrash" and as he hit "enter," the system blinked, and his access was abruptly terminated. Again, Kevin was slammed back to reality at his keyboard, but this time "topcrash" had left remnants of name and password code in the password interface.

Again he re-entered the system, pausing momentarily to check on the Gatemaster. Kevin stopped at the password interface and gave his new name and password: "Presidential Access" and "1BIGDUDE!". Kevin thought the connotations might prevent somebody from questioning its presence in the user database. He added the Top Secret classification, hit enter, and then, with only a millisecond of hesitation, he was in.

The first thing he tried to do was to help Debra and Henry, but it was too late. Even the Top Secret clearance didn't allow him to eradicate attempted security violations. They would have to fend for themselves.

Kevin explored the advantages that the Top Secret clearance had given him. The databases and files he could access now included high-level criminal activities: suspected, known, and, in some cases, condoned. That wasn't all; with a simple handshake and without password obstructions, Huey could communicate directly with the FBI, CIA, Secret Service, and other government agency computers. Access was completely unrestricted. It was all through direct, encrypted communications lines. Eventually, he thought, the encryption codes might open up even more doors.

Kevin set his focus on Half-Ass; after all, that was why he was here. He built several batch runs for the Cray to crunch looking for files related to the Islamic World, Hafez, Beech and Argentina.

Kevin's alarm went off and he realized it was time to escape. He downloaded what he had and quickly retreated to the safety of Tobago.

Chapter Thirty-Four

Arrival in Argentina

Kevin speed-dialed the numbers on his satellite phone: twenty-seven of them.

"Morning," came Cole's reply. "We'll be in Argentina before the sun comes up. Did you get me a location on Half-Ass?"

"No, I haven't made another call, yet. I really don't want to talk to that guy, you know."

"Just do it, Kevin. He has no idea who you are and there's no way he can ever get to you. Let me know when you get something."

"Okay."

"See you. Bye."

Kevin readied Fugaku and set his satellite phone aside. This time he used his cell phone; if he could track Half-Ass via the satellite system, then Kevin could just as easily be tracked if he used his satellite up-link. He dialed the numbers, all thirty-nine of them. The connection bounced through the call service, relayed through El Segundo and Houston, transmitted to a TRANSIT satellite, and then it rang. It rang four times before being answered.

"Hafez," came a curt response. "I am busy. I do not wish to be disturbed. Imbecile."

"Hello, Half-Ass. Do you remember me?"

"Who is this?"

"This is Bill."

"Beal?" came the reply and then a short silence. "Yes, Beal, I remember you. What can I do for you this morning?"

"I was looking for Allah and thought maybe you could help me out."

"No, I don't think so. So Beal, obviously my friends have not found you."

"I doubt if you have any friends."

"Sure, I have lots of friends. You will see."

"I see just fine."

"Then I will instruct my friends to start by carving your eyes out when they find you."

"You can't find me, jerk," concluded Kevin and hung up.

Kevin read the numbers on Fugaku screen and then quickly looked up the location: Avellaneda docks, southeast of Buenos Aires. Good, thought Kevin. He's still in Argentina. Cole shouldn't have any trouble finding him. I'll tell Cole to carve his eyes out, thought Kevin. I hope he makes Half-Ass suffer a horrid death, especially for Dominique's sake.

JACK WAS DEAD-BEAT TIRED AND WOULD SLEEP FOR hours after arriving in Buenos Aires. Cole explained there was over a hundred thousand in the duffle bag. Fifty of it was already Jack's: twenty-five for getting him there and twenty-five for getting him home. The rest was a matter of trust. But if Cole didn't return in five days, the cash was all his. Cole took several bundles of hundreds, shouldered the backpack, picked up the rifle case and grabbed his gym bag. He set off for Avellaneda, just south of Buenos Aires. It was nearly four a.m. and he had to hurry; the sun would be up soon.

A taxi driver was sleeping on the front seat of his car, planning to be the first in line when flights started arriving; but the first flight had already arrived. Cole shattered his slumber with several open-handed, bellowing blows to the passenger side door. And with a little hand waving, it didn't take much Spanish to convey the urgency of the fare. As the taxi driver sped away from the airport, Cole dialed his satellite phone. "I'm here. You got me? Where are we going?"

"I got you," said Kevin as he locked in Cole's GPS signal and got ready to begin giving directions. "Destination is southeast to Avellaneda. Call me back when you get there."

Cole relayed the instructions to the cabbie. There was no traffic on the expressway and the little taxi sounded like it was going to come apart as it governed out with its gas pedal flat on the floor.

As they entered Avellaneda, Cole dialed Kevin.

"Got you. Go about a half-mile south southeast."

Cole studied the city as they neared a half-mile and reported his observations to Kevin, "Looks like we're heading for the docks; warehouses and side streets congested with parked trucks."

Kevin continued to update the status of Cole's moving location and Cole barked out left and right directions to the cabbie. As they neared the dock, Cole slowed the pace.

Cole had the driver stop five hundred yards from the dock. A hundred-dollar bill and promise of two more if the cabbie would wait left the cabbie smiling. Cole carried the backpack, gun case and gym bag as he slipped into the darkness. He stopped alongside a dock warehouse and exchanged his traveling clothes for body armor and combat fatigues. He strapped his sheathed knife to his leg on the outside of his pants and cinched the straps on his backpack. If circumstances presented themselves, he would return for the rifle hidden in the shadows. But reconnaissance came first.

He dialed Kevin again for final directions as he worked his way along the dock in the dark. Kevin's directions and voices in the distance led him to his destination. Cole made note of the ship at the dock and relayed the name to Kevin before signing off. It was the *Ankara*. There was a surprising amount of activity for the early hours of the morning. Lights lit up the ship's deck, dock, and an adjacent warehouse. Longshoremen shouted back and forth as they worked. Two armed guards were stationed at the front of the warehouse. Cole sneaked closer until he stood at the front corner of the warehouse. If the guards had been paying attention, they would have seen Cole; he was in plain sight. A large roll-up door on the front of the warehouse started to close. It made enough noise to allow Cole to scale the chain link fence and drop out of sight in the darkness of the alley alongside the building.

He made his way along the building, looking for a window or some other point of entry. He circled around behind and then up along the south side, but there was none. He retreated to the rear of the warehouse where he would try out one of Kevin's creations. The building had tin siding, but surprisingly deadened all sound from the racket out front. Cole removed a small, slow-turning and extremely quiet, battery-powered drill from his backpack and used it to quietly pierce the tin siding. The forward motion of the drill stopped as it penetrated the siding. With a penlight, Cole investigated the scene through the tiny hole. The building was more than appearances yielded; it was of concrete construction and the tin was just camouflage leaving the back side of the building impenetrable.

Cole surveyed the backside of the building and spotted a rain gutter downspout. Long past memories of Atlanta and of being hunted flashed through his mind as he hurried along the back of the warehouse to the downspout. Cole grasped it and tested its structural worthiness. It was a four-inch solid pipe firmly attached to the building, nothing like the flimsy downspout he had climbed in Atlanta. "Easy," he mumbled as he started up the pipe.

Going hand over hand, his muscles strained. The building was taller than he realized and he strained for help from his adrenaline to clamp the pipe with each progressive grasp of his hands. His feet were little help and the backpack was now noticeably heavy. He got momentary relief when he reached the top where the pipe jetted out to the gutter. The eave was larger than it looked from the ground, extending out from the building several feet.

Cole contemplated the challenge of making the transition to the roof. The wall was too far away for him to push off with his feet and get the momentum necessary for a gymnastics move to put his body above the edge of the roof, especially with a backpack. He was also further up than he had anticipated; the building was at least four stories high and a mistake would be fatal. But he had come too far to back out now.

Hanging from the pipe underneath the eave, Cole inspected the gutter and corner of the roof. There was a way. Wedged with one arm over the pipe and his feet against the wall, Cole struggled out of the backpack. He cut the waist strap and one of the shoulder straps from the pack, extended them fully and then connected them in series with the remaining shoulder strap, making a large loop. Cole turned and flipped the loop over the corner of the roof. The strap slipped down and caught the edge of the gutter. Cole carefully worked the strap to get it between the roof and the gutter and then worked it back toward him. It wedged

     Brian David Simmons

itself tightly around the gutter about six inches from the end where the gutter was spiked to the roof. Cole let the backpack swing freely.

He worked himself into position under the eave on the drainpipe and then stretched out with one hand to grasp the gutter. Cautiously, Cole stepped out onto the backpack, turned, and then extended his leg to lift his upper body above the edge of the roof. The gutter creaked as he transferred his weight to the backpack, but it held tight. With both hands grasping the gutter, Cole extended his arms and let his upper body fall forward onto the roof. With his cheek against the tin roof, he brought his knee up over the edge of the gutter and then inched himself forward. He was up.

Cole quickly retrieved the backpack and made his way to the center of the roof. He had a great view of a ship named *Ankara*. The ends of twelve rectangular containers jetted strangely from the midsection of her cargo hold. Thirteen more forty-foot containers were stacked horizontally on her forward deck and another thirteen on her aft. The crew was at work securing the containers and preparing to protect them with tarps. All very interesting, but all Cole was really interested in was a look at, and hopefully pictures of, Half-Ass and his entourage. Cole studied the surrounding buildings and general layout of dock structures. To pick off Half-Ass with the rifle and still have an escape route, would be a real challenge. Cole concluded he would have to get him coming out of a hotel or restaurant. But if his entourage was small enough, it might open up other options. It was time for a look.

Cole backed off from the peak of the roof and once again got out Kevin's slow-turning drill. Moments later, he punctured a hole in the tin roof. A beam of light pierced the darkness as he withdrew the drill. Cole nervously covered it with his finger. Still covering the hole, Cole dug through his backpack and retrieved a remote viewing periscope that Kevin had modified with zoom and rotation capabilities. He assembled it to a miniature video camera and extended the apparatus through the tiny hole.

"What the . . ." Cole increased the zoom. The interior of the building was brightly lit and buzzing with activity. Cole swallowed hard; it was a final assembly operation for multi-stage rockets. He counted twelve missiles in work at differing phases of completion. Gauging from the size of a man, each stage was approximately six feet in diameter and twenty feet long. He zoomed in on a single stage to study its construction. Its rough, black exterior said that it was a high-pressure graphenol epoxy case. Its nozzle was partially submerged in the aft end of the motor, indicating a high-performance thrust vector control system optimized for package-ability. Actuators extending from the aft motor boss to the nozzle exit cone meant that the system was controllable and, with a guidance system, could be programmed to hit a target regardless of launch origin. The only apparent difference between the stages in work was the exit cone length. Half of the motors had an exit cone markedly longer and larger in diameter distinguishing the upper stage from the lower.

Cole did some quick mental calculations: approximately two hundred cubic feet of propellant per stage burning at a thousand pounds per square inch for fifty seconds and then staging to expend its spent lower stage, ultimately to accelerate to more than twenty-five hundred feet per second—maybe enough to escape the earth's pull of gravity, achieve a few minutes in orbit, and then re-enter. These were far more than simple short-range ballistic missiles, like the Iraqi SCUDS.

Cole rotated the aperture, searching for something they might be assembling to a payload platform. His fear was that he would find conical-shaped warheads shielded by a forward shroud. Cole zoomed in on staging platforms and the assembly operations in-work, but there was no payload. The missiles were being assembled without a payload. But why?

Cole then focused on the final operation and realized that thirty-eight of the missiles were onboard the *Ankara*. There was a beehive of activity around the packaging of a missile in its rectangular container. Cole maximized the zoom on the aperture and studied the suspension of a missile in its container. The missile was suspended in its container by odd shaped rigid links to a cylindrical tube inside the rectangular container. After zooming in and panning to get the full picture, it occurred to Cole that the containers could double as portable launch silos, and thirty-eight of them were about to disappear on the high seas. Once they got wherever they were going, the missiles in their containers could be off-loaded onto trucks, making them mobile. They could be hidden in underground silos, or even made launch ready in a multi-story building. It was possible that they could even be fired from the *Ankara*, but the rocket exhaust gases would undoubtedly burn through the ship's hull. And, of course, there were no payloads and it would be almost impossible to complete any assembly operations at sea. But then…?

Cole withdrew the periscope and checked available storage on the camera's microdisc. He inched up to the peak of the roof. He hid his outline by hiding behind a roof vent. They were obviously preparing to get underway. He videoed every aspect of the ship and cargo for Kevin's benefit. With the sun about to come up, he wasn't going to get much more video looking east into the sun. But windows on the *Ankara* bridge were wide open and he decided to try another of Kevin's custom creations.

The modified paintball gun didn't exactly fire paint balls. Kevin called it a "talking gumball gun." Cole assembled and loaded the gun. The open window on the *Ankara* was out range for the carbon dioxide-propelled projectile, but it was worth a try. Cole estimated the trajectory, calmed his breathing, timed the beats of his heart, and then gently squeezed the trigger. "Tho-oup," responded the gun as its semi-plastic projectile exited the barrel. Seconds later, it splattered just below the open window. Cole reloaded, compensated with a little more elevation and fired again. This time the gumball splattered on the wall inside the bridge and stuck like a glob of chewing gum. Inside the glob were a tiny microphone and transmitter.

Cole set up his receiver and listened to see if it had survived. Tests run by Kevin only yielded about a fifty percent survival rate for the mini-transmitters.

Cole listened intensely; it survived. The language was strange and foreign to him. He had no clue what was being said but there was no excitement to indicate they had detected the gumball. The words were a choppy mix of confusion to Cole and he switched on the recorder to capture them for deciphering later. The crew worked feverishly to cover the deck and missiles with camouflage tarps, and then the on-deck activities subsided as the sun cleared the horizon. He dozed, only to rouse momentarily as he heard the word "America" come through his earpiece, but mixed amongst all the confabulation, it didn't mentally register.

The sun beating down on the tin roof was becoming intensely hot, but Cole was determined to stick it out. He had the perfect vantage point and he wasn't going to miss the departure of the *Ankara*. He continued to record and capture every spoken word.

Cole hadn't seen Half-Ass, but he had to be here somewhere. He blew through his fist and the realization came to him. It was all about this, every bit of it: Dominique's assassinations, her death, Chris Beech, Jacob McCarry, the Arabs – all of it. Half-Ass might have to wait.

The *Ankara* pulled away from the dock with the help of a single tug in mid-morning. Cole watched as the ship was maneuvered out into the main thoroughfare and then was released from the tug to find its own way to the open sea. It struck Cole odd that the *Ankara* carried a large skiff mounted cross-wise on its rear deck. The transmitter signal faded before the *Ankara* disappeared from sight. Its range was limited to less than a mile. Cole was tired and sunbaked to a toasty crisp when the *Ankara* finally vanished from view. He had had enough and packed up.

Cole looped the backpack strap around his shoulder and slithered over the edge of the gutter and then down the pipe. The two guards weren't anywhere in sight and he scampered over the fence and down the dock. The rifle and his gym bag were where he had left them. Back in street clothes, he was soon headed back to where he left the cab.

The cab was there and again he jolted the napping driver alert with a few slaps to the door. His instructions to the driver were simple and understood: hotel, Grand, and two hundred dollars. Cole was exhausted and ready for a cool shower and rest.

He checked into the hotel as Christopher Beech, with instructions not to be disturbed. It was a high-dollar tourist hotel and most of the hotel personnel spoke English. Kevin had already arranged for the room adjacent to the one he'd just rented, under the name of Cody Calhoon. Tomorrow the Beech room would get a full installation of hidden surveillance cameras and listening devices. Cole dozed off to get some long overdue sleep.

In Tobago, Kevin had garnered the nerve to make another call. He was ready with his location and communication software and started the dialing process. His cell phone signal was routed through El Segundo and Dallas and then to the TRANSIT satellite. He got an answer on the second ring.

"Hafez."

"How are you this fine evening?" asked Kevin in a cheery tone.

"Good evening yourself, Beal. You know I am going to kill you," came a cold, creepy reply.

"That doesn't sound very nice."

"Tell me, Beal. Why do you do this harassment to me? I will kill you surely as I talk to you today. There will be nowhere in the United States you can hide and I will celebrate the coming of your death."

"Maybe that's why I'm harassing you. You couldn't find me even if you tried."

"Finding you won't be necessary. All things will be taken care of in due time."

"How's that, Half-Ass?"

"You are only a miserable abortion of the Infidel. I have already arranged for your death and will snuff out your miserable life like I would smash a roach."

"Roach, am I? You know, I'm really starting to dislike you."

"You are the semblance of all that I hate. You are the filth that breeds to pollute the world with greed, corruption, and oppression. You deserve nothing but the most miserable of deaths and this, I assure you, you shall have. My only regret is that I cannot witness the imminent hostility you will suffer."

The words sent a shiver through Kevin's body and he replied in a broken voice, "I think I have a friend who needs to pay you a visit." Then Kevin added a feckless threat, "He'll make you suffer!"

Hafez's cold, calm, monotone reply exacerbated Kevin's fear, "Then send him. I will enjoy his company as I would enjoy yours."

Kevin swallowed and then asked, "Where should I send him?"

A moment of silence passed before Hafez responded, "I think now this call is over. Do not try to call again; there will be no answer."

Kevin's hand was shaking so badly he could hardly push "end" on the phone after the line went dead.

Chapter Thirty-Five

ARGENTINEAN POLICE

WHEN COLE AWOKE, ROOM SERVICE DELIVERED dinner and the concierge personally delivered Cody Calhoon's new clothes. Each delayed departure until Cole anteed up with a moderate tip.

Cole started the evening listening, analyzing word by word, rewinding the recorder and listening again to the verbiage from the bridge of the *Ankara*, but it all meant absolutely nothing to him. He set it aside and began planning his evening. The missiles were something frightening and entirely different from what he expected. His objective was Half-Ass but this was a distraction that couldn't be ignored. Alberto Lagos was the key link to Argentine activities. Cole knew that he needed to have a conversation with Alberto tonight.

He packed and checked his backpack and then called Kevin, "How's the warm country?"

"I had a real frightening conversation with Half-Ass. He threatened to kill me and he scared the gibeebers out of me."

"What'd you expect? Phone sex?"

"Yeah, but he was absolutely certain I was dead. He put it to me in words so cold and cruel that I'm still shaking. He thinks I'm in the States and said he could find me real easy. We need to do something about it. He's in Buenos Aires, too."

"Let me worry about it," comforted Cole.

"I suppose."

"Just don't let it bother you. His time is coming."

"Hey, remember I told Half-Ass that my name was Bill Gates. Pretty good, huh?" offered Kevin.

"Yes, Kevin. That was good. Now we need to get on to some more important stuff. Did you see the missile pictures I sent last night?"

"What do you want me to do with them?"

"You to help me figure this all out. I got more than just the stills. I got video and sound of some first-class stuff. Thirty-eight ballistic missiles shipped out on a ship named *Ankara* and another twelve are still in work."

"What are they going to do with them?"

"What'd you think? Somebody's going to have a real shooting war. I didn't spot any warheads, but those missiles are capable of delivering almost any kind of warhead from thousands of miles away. You understand?"

"Nuclear?"

"Hard to say. Could be."

"Shit," said Kevin and then swallowed. "That fits with something Half-Ass said. He said it didn't matter if he found me. I would still suffer an 'imminent hostility.' What are we going to do?"

"That CIA guy, McCarry, was looking into Beech; the CIA has to know something."

"I went in. You know way in, past security levels that no one should have been able to bypass. The CIA has a little more on Beech. But not much. Pretty much just what was in McCarry's report. They have an assessment of Argentina's POGO missile capability, but it's only for the battlefield with short range, no guidance, and conventional war heads."

"I think somebody ought to tell them. Sounds stupid, but could you just send them an email?"

"Yeah, sure."

"Then send them this: 'Relative to your Beech investigation, thirty-eight ballistic missiles capable of delivering nuclear warheads shipped out from Avellaneda aboard the *Ankara*. Their destination is unknown but their purpose is undoubtedly hostile.'"

"Is that enough?"

"That's all we know for sure. I may know more in the morning; I'm going after Lagos tonight. Find me a location for him."

"Okay. I'll have to do some searching and call you back."

"Do it. While you're checking, see what you can find out about the *Ankara*."

"Okay. Hey a couple of other things. Half-Ass's last location was the Coalition of Arabic Nations building. He's some kind of finance minister or something. He's not a prince but he's pretty important in Saudi Arabia."

"Good, I'll call you back in a little bit."

Cole paced back and forth; even if it was only half an hour, it was too long, but then it was also too early to venture out into the night in search of Lagos. Cole opened the shouldered bag Kevin had packed for him and removed a cell phone booster-relay. He inspected the hotel room looking for just the right place. The phone line was plugged into a wall jack adjacent to an electrical outlet behind the nightstand. Cole retrieved his knife and planned his cuts. He sawed through the drywall to expose the electrical and phone lines and create a hole just large enough for the relay. He was very careful to wire an additional hot line for the relay. Similarly, he tapped into the phone line. With a sixty-cycle converter and a snap of the phone jack, the relay had power along with cell and landline access. Cole slid the relay into the hole in the wall and then replaced the drywall piece he had removed. With a little tape and spackle, the wall almost looked undefaced.

He called Kevin, "What'd you find out about the *Ankara*?"

"I can't find anything on it, even through the net. I'm not sure it's a real name. But I'm still looking."

"Any updates on Lago's location?"

"Nope, can't find him anywhere. The Argentinians haven't joined the modern age. They don't have all their phones or addresses in electronic databases. The best I can do is check credit card usage."

"Later. I want Lagos tonight. I'll see what I can scrounge up on Lagos on my own. See ya, bye."

     Brian David Simmons

Cole opened the phone book on the nightstand. There it was plain as day: Lagos, Alberto. "So much for surfing," mumbled Cole. He scribbled down the address and stuffed the note in his pocket.

Cole couldn't resist calling Kevin back. "Hey, computer geek, I found Lagos."

"Where?"

"Where most people look: the phone book."

"Well, I could have found it eventually."

"Yeah, well, so much for all that cyber shit."

Cole checked his backpack one more time and exited the room. A cab was waiting at the entrance to the hotel and Cole was shortly en route. He directed the cabbie to a location, missing Alberto's address by what he estimated was two blocks. The cabbie delivered Cole to the specified location. Cole got out and left the cabbie with a crisp hundred-dollar bill.

Cole found the address after first walking in the wrong direction and then backtracking to ensure he wasn't watched by the cabbie. It was a modest apartment building by American standards, but with a security entrance. For Argentina, it was probably upper middle class. The building was dark and most of the residents were asleep. Cole pulled a baseball cap and glasses out of his bag and approached the entrance.

He found the name Lagos on the intercom panel, pushed it, and waited for a response. After a few moments, he pushed again. A sleepy voice answered, "Hallo."

Cole responded, "Got something for you from Beech."

"Qué usted dijo?"

"I said I've got something for you from Beech," insisted Cole. "Let me in before I'm seen."

"My work with Beech is done. Go away."

"It's a substantial payment with a simple request. Let me in."

"Gringo estúpido," mumbled Lagos as he buzzed the latch on the security door.

Cole entered and scanned the poorly lit stairs above. He went up. A door on the third floor was open a few inches. Cole strained to see through the crack into the darkness for signs of a figure or movement; there were none. He paused momentarily at the door to speculate on his adversary's reaction to the late night interruption. He probably has a gun, probably trying to get the drop on me, and in hiding - but where?

Cole pulled his knife from his boot and held it in his right hand along with his gym bag. In the dim light, the shape of the gym bag concealed the outline of the knife. The hunt now went both ways. He pushed the door, letting it swing fully open before entering.

"Alberto Lagos," he whispered, hoping for a response. "I've got a request and compensation for you right here," he said, swinging the bag forward. With three more steps to the center of the room, the lights came on. Alberto was standing directly in front of him at the entrance to a hallway. In his right hand was a .45 semiautomatic pistol. His left hand was on the light switch and his eyes were just transitioning from their nocturnal focus.

Cole had only a fraction of second to react, an instant in time to gain the advantage. He lunged forward and swung the gym bag forward, letting loose with his fingers. The bag struck Alberto in the chest. With the same motion, he wheeled his knife across Alberto's arm, slicing it to the bone and severing arteries. The slash of the knife dislodged the gun from Alberto's hand but not soon enough to prevent it from firing. A bullet struck Cole in the left center of his chest shredding Kevlar fabric and exploding the steel energy dissipation plate of his bulletproof vest. Cole was repelled by the impact and stepped back to maintain his balance. He reached around behind and slammed the door shut before sprinting forward to intercept Alberto's lunge at the gun.

As Alberto's hand neared the gun, Cole thrust the knife downward through Alberto's hand, pinning it to the floor. Alberto screamed in agony only to be met with a sharp backhanded blow to the face. The momentum of the blow knocked Alberto to his back and a fraction of a second later he had a stranger sitting abreast his chest with a hand grasped around his throat.

Cole leaned forward and whispered the requirement not to scream, "Make one more sound without me asking and I'll cut off your hand and use it as a gag. Do you understand?"

Alberto, unable to speak, nodded his head.

"Now let me explain the meaning of life, or death, to you. I've come here for a little information exchange. If I get your full, uninhibited cooperation, you live. If I don't, you die," said Cole as he eased his grip. "Do you understand?"

Alberto gagged and coughed and responded, "Sí."

Cole reached to the knife still pinning Alberto's hand and brushed the handle, causing a pain-induced jolt, and then shouted, "Lesson one: no more Spanish. Now, let's try something simple. Can you spell missile?"

Alberto, accustomed to a hard life of pain, replied, "I didn't have anything to do with any missiles."

Cole withdrew the knife from Alberto's hand and, with a rounding motion, swung it around behind and drove it to the bone in Alberto's leg. "Lesson two: don't lie," shouted Cole. "Now, what's forty feet long, six feet in diameter with two stages, and comes with its own portable launch silo?" asked Cole.

"A missile," conceded Alberto.

"Good. Now, what ship did they sail on?"

"There's no ship," Alberto responded hesitantly.

Cole reached back and twisted the knife, digging at the muscles and scratching the bone. Alberto squirmed in pain and grabbed Cole's arm, but Cole had him firmly pinned and his neck firmly in his grasp.

"You just don't get it, do you? I'm going to cut and carve on you every time I get a wrong answer. Too many wrong answers and there won't be enough left of you to put back together. Now, let's try again. When I say ship, what name comes to mind?"

"*Ankara*," mumbled Alberto.

"That's better. And see? No more pain. Now let's try some accounting. How many missiles were on-board the *Ankara*?"

Alberto hesitated, but yielded a mumbled answer, "Twelve."

Cole pulled the knife out of Alberto's leg and thrust it into the floor next to Alberto's head, slicing his ear. "I don't believe you're that stupid. Next lie, you start losing parts. I'll start with your hand! Now, how many?" demanded Cole.

"Thirty-eight."

"Tell me about them."

"Twelve stored vertical in the hold. Twenty-six on deck."

"To whom?" said Cole as he slid his hand across the handle of the knife to give it a little twang.

"To a man, Hafez ibn Wahhab. It's him that bought fifty-two missiles."

"Tell me about him."

"I don't know that much, but he frequents the Coalition of Arabic Nations."

"More," demanded Cole.

"We sold him fifty-two missiles for forty metric tons of gold. My country will have its economic recovery. No more hungry children. Care for the elderly.

Welfare for the indigent. Everything America has. And all for a few missiles."

"What is their target?"

"Don't know and don't care."

"You better care," he said as he reached for the knife.

Alberto stopped him with a pleaded response, "I really don't know. Nobody ever said."

"And the missile payload?" inquired Cole.

"We just sold missiles with a weapons platform, no warheads. They are going to mount their own warheads. We just built to requirements."

Alberto's dark skin was showing signs of going pale and his speech was beginning to slur, but Cole wanted more. "What's the range of the missiles?"

"Don't know. We didn't do the design work."

"Who did?"

"Chris Beech."

"And that's why I'm here. By the way, Beech is dead. So let's talk about Hafez ibn Wahhab. I want him."

"I don't know, but he works out of the Coalition building in La Baca."

"Why did the Saudis pay so much for the missiles?"

"For them, it changes the world. How much is that worth?"

"How is the world going to change?"

"You figure it out. You're the Great Satan."

Cole was alerted by voices outside the front door. He quickly went to the edge of the front window and

     Brian David Simmons

glared down at an Argentinean police car. Somebody must have heard the gunshot and Alberto's cries of pain. The police had responded faster than any stateside police and he was caught, trapped in the man's apartment.

A series of sharp raps to the door came with a demand for entry. Cole had nowhere to go. He sheathed his knife, picked up his bag, and headed down the hall. Knocks at the door and demands for entry became louder. Cole sensed it was only seconds before they forced their way in. He had to get out.

Cole exited the master bedroom onto a balcony. It was three stories up and flight wasn't an option. He heard the front door crash in and closed the sliding door behind him. With no other choice, he slipped over the railing of the balcony and lowered himself to hang from the balcony floor. The sliding door opened just as the tip of his toes touched the railing on the balcony below. He let go of the floor above and lowered himself, quietly stepping off the railing and assuming a motionless stance against the wall. In the darkness, he watched the shadow from above step to the edge of the balcony and study the night.

The shadow above retreated with the shuffling of feet. Cole quickly slid over the railing, again lowered himself to floor level, and then dropped to the ground. He slipped into the night as a figure on the balcony reappeared, but the darkness was his cloak.

The hotel offered temporary safety but it was too far to make the hike. Cole ran for a while in the direction of the hotel, stopping for a few minutes to change his blood-soaked pants and discard the destroyed bulletproof vest. The only pants he had in his gym bag were his combat fatigues, but Americans probably all looked strange to the Argentinians anyway. It was better than nothing. He wadded up his bloodstained pants and put them along with the vest in a dumpster. Risky, but he had no choice. If he got caught with them, he'd have no chance for escape. He knew that a thorough police search would find them, maybe ascertain that the pants were newly purchased and track them to the store where the concierge had bought them, then perhaps couple them with a description from Lagos and ultimately track them to him. But hopefully, their investigation wouldn't get that focused for several days. However, he was quickly wearing out his welcome in Argentina.

Cole hiked through the back streets in slum areas, always traveling in the general direction of the hotel. Every breath he took was a painful reminder of the bullet that had hit his bulletproof vest. Cole entered a back street bar. Its customers were subdued from long hours of drinking and the thought of even longer hours at work the following day. He came in almost unnoticed. Cole ordered a beer with some finger pointing to cross the language barrier and then communicated the need for a cab. He was out of place but the

     Brian David Simmons

bartender didn't pay it much attention; he too had been drinking.

Cole had the cab driver drop him four blocks from the hotel and then quickly made the hike to safety. He strolled past the female night clerk who was flirting with the doorman. They hardly noticed him, if at all. Cole estimated he had one more day before things became really uncomfortable. He needed to visit the Coalition of Arabic Nations building. He would leave the hotel tomorrow for the last time. But now it was time for sleep.

Chapter Thirty-Six

BURGLAR

As morning dragged on at the CIA's Information Resources, Rachael retrieved a cup of coffee from the coffee pool before returning to her desk. A strange email arrived and her computer beeped. It had no sender in the "From" field. The message read:

> Fifty-two ballistic missiles have been purchased from Argentina by Hafez ibn Wahhab and thirty-eight of them have been shipped out of the country aboard the *Ankara*. The missiles can carry nuclear warheads and will be launched at the United States.

Rachael scowled. With no sender in the "From" field and an outlandish threat, it was obviously a hoax. She immediately forwarded it to IT. Submitting false information to the CIA was punishable by a $10,000 fine and six months imprisonment. It was IT's problem now.

In Buenos Aires, Cole slept until mid-morning when he was awakened by maid service. He shooed her away and ordered breakfast. Before breakfast arrived, Kevin called.

"I sent our e-mail. I sent it to the main Langley CIA office. When the cavalry comes charging in, you'd better not be around."

"One more day. I want to check on your last Half-Ass location tonight. In the meantime, I got a little challenge for you. The recordings from the bridge of the Ankara have got to have some good stuff on them. Anyway I can get them translated?"

"I don't know. You have to send them to me first."

"It's all on microchips. How do I do that?"

"You need to get a laptop, encrypt them and upload them to the cloud. I could send you shopping. Certainly that kind of technology exists in Buenos Aires."

"We don't have time. What if I just played the tapes over the phone to you?"

"It'll deteriorate the quality of the recording."

"So? You've got to translate it anyway."

"Give me fifteen minutes to get set up and I'll call you back."

"Done."

Breakfast arrived and Cole hurriedly ate. He plugged in the recorder, loaded the first microchip, and listened to the strange verbiage. He reset at the beginning as the satellite phone rang. After a short coordination discussion with Kevin, he started the playback. After the first microchip completed, he loaded and played the next, and then the next. When the old-fashioned transfer was complete, Cole signed off and Kevin went to work.

Time passed and led on into evening. It was almost time to go out again. Cole called the private terminal at the airport and confirmed that the Gulfstream was still there. He left a message for Jack to ready the plane and let him know they'd be leaving soon. He called Kevin.

"Hello."

"Get anything off the microchips?"

"I got something. I started with a speech-recognition program and then had it write to an HTML document. Then I used a translator to go from Arabic to English. Then I spent the next five hours trying to decipher what I got. It's pretty garbled."

"So what'd you learn?"

"The best I can interpret it is that the captain of the *Ankara* is telling a story about his housekeeper. He imported some impoverished thirteen-year-old housekeeper from Iran and his wife was insanely jealous. He had to beat her more and more every time he came into port. He had paid the Iranian family two hundred fifty American dollars for the girl and she was well worth it, according to the captain. He had taught her numerous ways to satisfy a man and then went on to describe them. The captain only wished his wife was half as good; that way he wouldn't have to beat her so much. Juicy stuff, but absolutely worthless."

"That's it?"

"Just about. I scanned on through. There are periods of silence, stories about women, talk about Allah

     Brian David Simmons

and some crap about the greatness of martyrdom. Then somebody wants a Coke and it gets delivered."

Cole swore. "I was hoping for more. The hotel room next door is still booked for another week. I've got a rental car in Beech's name. I had the concierge withdraw some cash from the Beech bank account you set up. Everywhere I go I have let it be known that Beech is here. I was sure Hafez would pay me a visit, but he didn't bite. So where am I going tonight?"

"The La Baca section of Buenos Aires was where I talked to Half-Ass last. When you get there, give me a call and I'll do the directing again."

"Talk to you in a few."

Cole, posing as Chris Beech, requested that the concierge have the rental car delivered to the main entrance. He had had enough of taxis. Without checking out, Cole had the bellhop retrieve and load his luggage. The bellhop had to make two trips; Cole watched as he struggled with the very large and heavy rifle case.

Before leaving the hotel, Cole asked the concierge for next week's weather report from France and confirmed his stay in Buenos Aires for another six days. The concierge smiled ear-to-ear when Beech, a.k.a. Cole, presented him five hundred-dollar bills.

The rental was waiting curbside and Cole left the hotel for the last time. He navigated through the city to the La Baca section of Buenos Aires. It was an older part of the city with narrow criss-crossing streets providing access to an amalgam of small shops, businesses, and residential areas. Cole easily found the Coalition building. It was a historic-looking building near the harbor that had been converted into an office. Small print on the door was distinctively Arabic. As he drove by, he called Kevin and confirmed the location.

Parking spaces were a premium. Traffic was almost non-existent on the narrow streets, making Cole feel conspicuous as he looked for a parking space. He searched up and back and then left and right, but couldn't find a legal or even semi-legal parking space. Eventually, he decided to park in a blind alley. He backed in, anticipating a quick escape if things went wrong. Tall buildings on both sides of the alley shielded it from the lights of the city and the street out front. It reminded him of the alley where Domi-nique had died. Despair struck his heart and crushed his soul. He had to force it aside; it couldn't bear on tonight's activity.

Cole changed into his fatigues and checked his equipment. He glanced back into darkness as he exited the alley. There was nothing more than an indistinct glimmer of light off the windshield. Cole advanced on his objective anticipating every forward move, stopping in the shadows to study ahead, and then advancing again.

When he arrived at his objective, he found shelter from light in a doorway across the street from the Arabic office building. He waited, watched and studied. The two-story building strangely had French, or maybe

Italian, architecture with an arched front entrance. It had a number of ornate features distinguishing it from neighboring, much taller structures. Cole speculated that it might have been a residence at one time, complete with a back door.

He crossed the street and disappeared into the darkness alongside the building. As he moved along the building, the unmistakable foil tape signifying a perimeter entry security system was visible, even in the darkness, at each tall arched window. Standing at the corner, he studied the rear of the building. It had a rear entrance, but a security camera covered it. He might approach from either side of the camera without being captured, but it was a risk.

He mumbled, "Aw, crap," as he glanced upward alongside the building. He stepped back and studied the wall. The ornate features of the corner offered foot holds to get him even with the window. From there, it would be fingertips to raise him to the level of the second story window where he would have to reach and step across to the window. Not probable; he needed a ladder.

He moved back to the front corner of the building, stepping back momentarily to avoid being detected by the headlights of a passing car. The front archway was scalable and provided direct access to an upper story window, but it was in plain sight of the street. It was risky. He studied the street and the neighboring buildings. The neighborhood was quiet and its windows were dark. Probably not a real threat, but the traffic was. A car passed every couple of minutes, providing illumination for the poorly lit street. He would have to move fast.

Cole waited for his moment and scampered up the arch to stand in front of the second story window. He searched for foil or other security features. There were none. He pulled his knife as he saw a car approaching. He jabbed the knife between the sliding window frames and, with a horizontal smack of his hand, rotated the latch. The window screeched as he raised it to the full open position. The car was upon him. Cole froze, motionless; his dark shape against the red-brown brick was his only cover. He was invisible to the unobservant as long as he provided no movement to attract the passerby's eye.

As the car passed, he jumped through the window. Cole watched the car as it proceeded on its way; it hadn't seen him. He closed the window behind him and began taking mental inventory of the building. His penlight revealed a bedroom. Its interior was barren with only a bed centered in the small room. The mattresses were bare and the closet was empty. The bed was probably a leftover from some previous occupant. Cole carefully worked his way through the other rooms finding them equally as devoid of furniture or signs of occupation.

He ventured down a narrow staircase to the main floor to what was once a living room that had been

		Brian David Simmons

transformed into an office. Before stepping off the last stair, he studied the office with his penlight. He traded his penlight for night vision from his backpack. The penlight might be observed from outside and there was no reason to take chances. He spotted a control box for the alarm system. It was key operated and looked to be aging twentieth-century vintage; no real threat since he'd already entered.

Cole began his search by going through desks and file cabinets; returning to his penlight to try and decipher the strange, confounding Arabic text. After searching for several hours and finding nothing that had meaning, Cole re-focused his attention to the structure of each desk, the floor, ornate interior features of the room, and wall hangings. Anything of value wouldn't be readily accessible. It would be hidden - but where?

With his night vision, he searched the room: looking behind paintings, pulling at crown and baseboard moldings, thumping the floor, inspecting desks, and finally returning to the staircase. Scrape marks on the floor led him to the bottom stair. It didn't meet the floor and, with further inspection, he found that the first four stairs were suspended by a vertical hinge hidden by trim moldings. On the other side of the stairs, adjacent to the wall, he found a release button. His finger stroked the button, but he hesitated and retracted his hand.

He quickly dialed Kevin on his satellite phone and spoke softly, "I'm inside. Need to disable an alarm. Got any ideas?"

"Sit tight for a second. Let me see what I can find."

Kevin went to work clicking his mouse and hammering the keys as he began quizzing Cole, "Describe it."

"Foil tape on all first floor windows. Key locked box located just inside the front door. The box is about four by six. 'Faufman' is imprinted in the metal door."

"I'm looking," said Kevin as he searched the expanses of the internet. "Maybe. Let's see, could be—how about a model 1706, providing perimeter protection for home or office. Looks like it's obsolete; it was sold in the 2000s. If you open the control box, just turn it off."

"Got it."

Cole snapped open the alarm box and switched it off. He hesitated at the front window watching for anything unusual—nothing. Deactivating the alarm was simple.

The button on the stairs released the bottom four stairs and they swung out to reveal a safe. Again he called Kevin, "Let's go again. A safe. Brand name: 'Homssafe.' Model thirty-two. Tumbler type. Any ideas?"

"Looking," replied Kevin. "If it was electronic, I could try to crack it. If it's tumbler type, it must be an antique," continued Kevin as he queried the Internet. "Got it. Probably manufactured in 1972. Search for a serial number. I'll pay Homssafe a visit and see what I can find."

"Looks like serial number 0124387643."

"I'll call back in fifteen if I can come up with any-thing," concluded Kevin

Kevin went exploring. Homssafe had been bought out by Securesafe, Incorporated. Kevin's Fugaku dialed up Securesafe, quickly hitting extensions until it found what Kevin was looking for. The Fugaku screeched in electronic lingo and made contact with their computer. Kevin rolled up his sleeves and mentally crawled inside. The CPU was friendly and unguarded; but its tower of drives prevented access to anything of value. The only available databases were employee phone numbers, corporate newsletter, and corporate earnings statements. Everything else was restricted to password-authorized users.

Kevin probed the password shield. He found an access hole behind the search-and-verify interface that limited the number of failed attempts to enter a password. With a few lines of coding, he disabled it. He then reached back to the Fugaku and copied "iterate" to its internal memory. From the phone list of employees, Kevin selected three with low employee numbers, assuming they had been with the company the longest and more likely to have access to all databases.

He set the computer to work with each of the three names iterating on seven-letter passwords. It took almost fifteen minutes until one of them hit and seconds later he was in. With a little searching, he found what he was looking for. A serialized listing of combinations had been scanned in for safes dating back to the 1940s. He found the Homssafe serial number 0124387643 and copied its coded combination. While still deep inside the computer, Kevin called Cole, "Got it."

"Took you long enough. You take a scheduled break or what?"

"Yeah. I had breakfast, took a stroll, and then watched Bugs Bunny. Jerk."

"What have you got?"

"A combination. It may have been changed by the owner or some distributor along the way but let's give this a try. Try two spins to the right to six, left to twenty-eight, right to fifty-three, and then back to eighteen."

Cole repeated the numbers back to Kevin as he spun the tumbler. When he reached the final number, Cole mumbled, "I don't believe it!"

The handle on the safe released the door and it swung open. Cole conceded, "Someday you're going to have to teach me how you do that. Bye."

THE SAFE HAD SOME CASH, MAYBE TEN OR TWENTY thousand in U.S. hundreds and a handful of file folders. He quickly leafed through the paperwork, stopping when the text changed. It was still unintelligible, but recognizably Russian. He scanned down through the text searching for something perceptible. He found enough: "SS18" and "U235." Day was rapidly approaching and he'd have to study the paperwork later. Cole emptied the contents of the safe into his backpack, and then returned safe, stairs, and alarm system to their original condition.

He was on his way up the stairs when a BMW pulled into the driveway. From the bottom step, he glared out the front window to see two Arabic men get out of the car. The lapel on the passenger's suit jacket flopped open to reveal a shouldered semi-automatic. Cole had waited too long. As the two men approached the front door, Cole evaluated his options.

He quickly retreated to the back door and stood ready. He was in plain sight of the front door, but maybe with the right timing he could get out undetected. Cole watched and listened for the dead bolt on the front door to receive its key. It clicked and thumped as the bolt retracted from the door jam. Cole rotated the knob on the back door dead bolt, opened the door just enough to pass, and escaped only fractions of a second before the two men entered. The first man inside concentrated on deactivating the alarm system before its time delay expired. That gave Cole the moment of inattention necessary to close the back door unobserved.

Cole scurried along the building ducking down as he passed each window. As he approached the front of the building, he could see light and slow moving traffic on the narrow street. He stopped momentarily at the front of the building, and then dashed for the street, only to be spotted by one of the Arabic men returning to the BMW for some forgotten item. He yelled something unintelligible but didn't give chase.

It was no time to be shy. Cole bounced across the hood of a slow-moving car and brought another in the oncoming lane to a screeching halt as he forced his way across the street. Still the man didn't follow; Cole was relieved.

He was out of place and the focus of attention, charging down the street in combat fatigues, complete with pack. By now, he'd been seen by dozens of drivers and he felt naked. It would only be a matter of minutes before the Arabic gentlemen realized they had been burglarized. After rounding the corner, Cole poured on the speed, attracting the attention of the morning crowd. It was only a couple more blocks to the alley.

He reached the alley and glanced over his shoulder before entering. He saw the BMW turning the corner, two blocks behind him. If he had seen them, they had probably seen him.

Cole's heart skipped a beat when he saw a garbage truck blocking his exit from the blind alley. He squeezed passed the truck on the passenger side to reach his car. He unlocked his car and threw his backpack inside. Cole ran to the driver's door of the truck and flung it open. It was empty, but luck was with him and the keys were in the ignition. Cole jumped in the driver's seat and cranked it over. First no gas, then a little gas, then he repeatedly pounded the accelerator pedal. Finally it started. Cole put it in what should have been reverse, but the truck lunged forward. He calmed himself and focused on the task at hand. Cole pulled the large red knob on the dash and crammed the shift lever into second.

He saw the BMW in the rearview mirror and simultaneously mashed the accelerator to the floor and released the clutch. The truck jumped rearward with a squeak from the rear tires and accelerated toward the street. The truck bounced off the wall as speed increased; Cole corrected and kept it accelerating down the alley. The driver of the BMW honked as if to signal the garbage truck to stop. Cole had no intention of stopping. The garbage truck crunched into the BMW, shoving it out of the alley, across the street and up the curb, pinning it against a building, squashing the car, showering garbage, and shattering building windows.

Shaking off the impact, Cole jumped from the truck and made the forty-yard dash to the rental car. It started without hesitation and he accelerated down the alley. As he approached the alley exit, he was met with a flurry of 9mm rounds. Cole ducked behind the dash, raising up just long enough to veer the car into his assailant. The car crushed the Arab as it ricocheted off the garbage truck and bounced into a traffic lane. Cole floored it. He glanced in his mirror to see the second man take aim and fire a handgun. Two bullets struck the rear of the car and then a third exploded the rear window. The fourth passed Cole's head by inches, blasting through the windshield and leaving a gaping hole.

A quick left and it was temporarily over. Cole worked his battered car through the ever-increasing traffic, finally reaching the parkway and then the airport. The information he now had was more important than cutting Hafez's throat. Hafez would have to wait. Cole drove past several small aircraft hangars on the fringes of the airport until he found a hiding place for the battered car. It fit right in amongst damaged and stripped airplane fuselages and other discarded collectibles in a wide corridor between two hangars.

Cole inspected the bullet holes when he reached the back of the car. Two bullets had impacted the trunk lid and made large entry holes. That wasn't right. They should have been small, half inch or so, holes in the light sheet metal. Whatever they were firing weren't off-shelf-rounds; they were explosive.

He opened the deck lid and was alerted by the sound of screeching tires. Glancing at the contents of the trunk, he selected the only item that afforded him a chance for survival, the rifle. He grabbed the case and took off. As he ran farther back between the two hangars, Cole pulled the rifle, and its six rounds of ammunition, from the hard-sided case before discarding it. He hopped a chain link fence just as two cars came into sight. The first pulled in between the hangars and the second slowed but then sped by. He had seen them and they had certainly seen him.

Cole scampered to the top of a large crate leaning against the back of the hangar and peered around the corner; they were coming. Two were advancing down the corridor between the hangars and the other two were inspecting the contents of his car's trunk. The other car had sped off and was probably trying to flank him; he had no time. Cole quickly loaded a round and slammed the rifle into its one hundred meter position. Two cars, four men per car, that's eight and only six shots. "Not good," muttered Cole. He whirled around the corner of the hangar to take aim. The elevation of the crate wasn't much and his footing was shaky, but it was just enough of an advantage. He had clear view of all four men. A shot rang out and ripped a gaping hole in the hangar just above his head. Cole's breathing slowed, he felt the pulsation of his heart in his eyes and between beats. He fired. In the moment before Cole pulled the rifle back around the corner, he saw the man closest look down at his chest in disbelief.

Cole loaded another round and jumped from the crate as a barrage of gunfire chewed away at the hangar. He jumped through the window at the rear of the hangar and rolled to a sitting position, gun poised at the hangar wall. The morning sun was just peaking over the horizon and he could feel warmth from the metal siding radiating inward. Cole waited, listened. His senses intensified to interrogate movements on the other side. His ears strained to capture the sounds of cloth brushing against steel and whispered words.

His mind visualized the image as it crept along, and then he fired. The shot boomed and echoed inside the hangar as he took off for the front of the hangar. It had two doors: one large for aircraft and the other small for people. Loading another round in mid-stride, he raced for the small door.

He reached it in seconds, unlocked it and then cautiously emerged at the front of the building; no one was in sight. Cole crept to the building corner and, quickly gaining control of his breathing, stepped into full view of his assailants. Neither detected his presence and they continued to advance towards the rear of the hangar. Cole steadied his aim at the back of one of the men's head and then, as if by controlled accident, the rifle again fired. The man's neck snapped forward and he did a head dive into the dirt. Cole was back around the corner when a shot from the corridor exploded in the corner of the hangar. He felt the impact of the explosion and took a half-step forward to keep his balance.

He loaded another round and mentally prepared himself to again step from the edge of the hangar when a bullet burned past his cheek. He whirled to take aim at two men advancing across the front of the building. He fired—no result. They both steadied their handguns and, in the moment of perfecting their aim, Cole dodged back through the hangar doorway as two simultaneous shots rang out.

Cole jumped away from the front of the hangar door and quickly dived behind a large mechanic's

     Brian David Simmons

toolbox. He loaded his second-to-last round and, as he rolled into firing position, he felt the pain in his back. A wetness crept around his torso and began pooling under his chest. A flickering of light, perceptible only at ground level, dancing under the edge of the large aircraft door caught his attention. It was two sets of feet; one there and another right behind. Cole smiled. He visualized the figures as they lurked along and then, choosing the one to the rear, he fired. Up in an instant, he was back at the doorway almost before the boom and echo inside the hangar subsided. He heard the figure in the rear drop to the ground and then the pounding of footsteps, away from presumed danger, away from his dead friend to the rear, and toward Cole. Cole surprised the man at the doorway and thrust his hunting knife deep into his abdomen and then upward past his sternum.

Cole sheathed his knife, ejected the shell from the rifle, loaded the last round, and again stood ready to step from the corner of the hangar. Concentrating on his breathing, he readied himself and then quickly stepped from the corner only to come face to face with his adversary. Cole fired the loosely held rifle immediately. It recoiled and stabbed deep into his shoulder spinning him around to see a car charging in his direction. He dropped the rifle, jumped over the dead man in front of him and charged down the corridor toward the chain link fence as fast as he could run, but it wasn't fast enough. He heard the car bounce over the man he'd just shot and then, only moments later, it slammed into him, hurling him into the chain link fence, which reacted to his impact like a trampoline and rebounded him onto the hood of the car.

The sky flashed by in a corkscrew, his mind shrieked in pain and then a black cloud with brilliant streaks of light encroached on his vision. He fought back at the trespassing darkness and, with ethereal strength, rolled from the hood of the car to meet the driver; the door was open and the driver had already stepped out. Cole grasped the driver's extended gun-wielding hand, pulled it forward, twisted it in an upward direction and then thrust the arm downward across the top of the door's window frame and back through the window opening, snapping the elbow, tearing ligaments and ripping skin. The man cried out in agony as Cole grasped the man's debilitated hand and helped him pull the trigger. Sound reverberated between the hangars as the explosive round excavated a major portion of the man's leg and he flopped to the ground, screaming in terror. Cole whipped the gun upward and trained it on the passenger in the front seat. Cole's finger increased the pressure on the trig-ger as the doomed man screamed at him, "Who are you? I command you to tell me now." The tone was somehow familiar and Cole hesitated; he relaxed the pressure on the trigger. There was something else too; he was dressed distinctly different from the others in an immaculate three-piece suit.

     Brian David Simmons

Cole forcefully responded, "I don't think you command very much of anything." He again focused his aim and increased the pressure on the trigger.

"You are a fool. So little do you know," came the man's coldly spoken words. Cole relaxed the trigger pressure and replied equally as cold, "We'll see. Now get out."

The man hesitated and Cole insisted, "Use that hand to open the door and get out or I'm going use the explosive round in this gun to remove it."

"I will not! You miserable product of the Infidel."

Without hesitation, Cole concentrated his aim and fired; the man's hand disappeared and blood-laden mush splattered throughout the car. The man didn't scream; he didn't even let out a whimper. He just stared at Cole in defiance.

"Now get out of the car! Now!" screamed Cole.

The man shivered to restrain the outcry of his pain and clutched what was left of his mangled wrist, but this time he complied. With the several flicks of the barrel, Cole signaled him to move to the back of the car. Cole threw the handgun to the ground and withdrew his hunting knife.

"Who are you?" Cole questioned with incredible calmness.

"I am Hafez ibn-Wahhab," proudly boasted the man. "Who are you?"

"Half-Ass, I'll be damned," said Cole, smiling. "I'm really glad you came to the party."

"Who are you? I demand that you tell me."

"I'm Bill's friend. You know, Bill Gates."

"Beal? No, Beal is a nothing. It cannot be."

"Oh, yes, it can," said Cole as he jabbed him in the chest with the point of his knife. "Bill tells me you've been making threats. Why don't you tell me about those threats?"

"I tell you nothing. I spit on you as I spit on all those that rape, steal, and oppress. You will undoubtedly kill me to prove your false strength, but my spirit will rejoice. For in the end, I shall torment your twisted soul and stomp out your miserable life, even from my grave. You and all that are like you are dead."

"I'm tired and I don't have time to screw around with this! Tell me about everything: missiles, nukes, the *Ankara* - all of it."

"You are a fool. I will tell you nothing."

"You know," paused Cole as he glared into Hafez's eyes. "I believe you're right."

Cole pressed his knife against Hafez's throat, forcing him back onto the trunk of the car. Cole's glare transformed into a soul-piercing demonic dagger and he felt the reaction of Hafez's swallow against the blade.

"I have a gift for you on your way to meet your forty virgins. Die with the knowledge that the entire house of ibn-Wahhab shall perish. This is your sentence for killing Dominique Jaclyn Portemay," stated Cole before he slid the blade across Hafez's throat.

Chapter Thirty-Seven

Escape from Argentina

Jack sat in the cockpit peering in the direction of all the noise; he watched as a figure in the distance came ever closer. The figure was dressed in combat fatigues and looked like he'd just walked out of hell's battlefield. He walked with a limp and carried a backpack in his hand. As he walked past the terminal building and picked up his pace, Jack realized that part of the camouflage montage was red—blood red— and he was coming directly at the plane. Jack reached down under his pilot's seat and touched the handle of his stub nose .38. As the man's appearance became more discernable and frightening, he put his hand on the pistol grip and anticipated pulling it from its holster. Blood covered the right side of the man's face and he had a broad black-red streak across his other cheek. In a hurried pace, the man's limp became more noticeable and Jack saw the sheathed knife strapped to his leg. Jack pulled the .38 from its holster when the figure reached the front of the aircraft. The figure waved and only then Jack recognized him; it was Cody.

He heard banging on the door and quickly dropped it open. Pointing the .38 at Cody, he firmly spoke, "You're the cause of all that shooting. I told you I don't get involved in your guy's business, especially not disputes. Now, you can just lie down right there on the tarmac until the authorities get here or you die. Either way, you are not getting on this plane!"

"Jesus, Jack, you don't understand."

"Then enlighten me."

"I don't have the time, Jack, or I would," said Cody calmly before his voice turned angry. "Now if I don't get on that airplane right now, I will implicate you in theft, rape, murder, and anything else they want me to confess to. They will execute you right alongside of me. Do you understand?"

"Not if I shoot you first."

"Then do it! Because I'm getting on that plane."

"I'm going to shoot you."

"Get out of the fucking way," said Cody as he forced his way into the plane.

It was a mistake and Jack knew it, but he stepped aside, "By the looks of you, it probably wouldn't make any difference. You're a dead man walking."

"Not in Argentina. Crank it up and put it in gear."

Jack figured he'd just stall until somebody came and took this Cody ass-hole off his plane. For him, he wondered what Argentine prisons looked like. Maybe Chad Melloncamp could get him off. "I got preflight checks and I need to submit a flight plan. Be at least a half hour."

Jack retreated to the cockpit and Cody followed.

"Fire it up and roll. We don't have time," said Cody as he climbed into the copilot's seat next to Jack. "For now, assume Miami is our destination. Let's go."

"I don't have enough gas."

"Refuel in Caracas. Let's go."

"You son-of-a-bitch," replied Jack. He began going down his preflight checklist and making preparations for flight.

Cody was relentless and asserted, "Start the engines. We're leaving."

Jack hesitated but then put his clipboard aside and commanded the engines to life.

"Start taxiing and get us out of here."

Jack reached for his headset, positioned it on his head, and Cody followed suit putting on the copilot's headset. "FPJ604 requesting ground instructions."

"Copy. FPJ604 proceed runway C1," came the reply in English. Jack navigated the Gulfstream to the end of the runway and received his clearance, "FPJ604 clear."

Jack let the engines turn at slow RPM at the end of the runway as time clicked by. Fine new mess you've gotten yourself into: aiding and abetting a known criminal escape a foreign country, he thought. "Shit," he finally said and replied with an abrupt throttle-up of the engines and a burst of acceleration. The Gulfstream roared down the runway quickly reaching 150 knots. Jack's hands tightened on the control column preparing to gently pull back. And then, at the moment of lift-off, a frantic voice came through the headset, "FPJ604 takeoff is not authorized! Shut down immediately and return to the terminal."

"Negative control, not enough runway," replied Jack as they went airborne.

"FPJ604 shut down immediately," shouted the voice from the tower.

"I repeat, control. Negative. We are airborne."

"Roger FPJ604. Climb to one thousand feet, circle and return to runway C1. I'm clearing traffic now. Repeat: Climb to one thousand feet, circle airport and return to runway C1."

"FPJ604 copy," Jack calmly replied. "Returning to airport."

"No, we aren't!" yelled Cody, who then pulled his knife, still dripping with Hafez's blood.

Jack just stared at the other man in the silence of the cockpit. Jack was uncertain and his nervousness now manifested itself in beads of sweat on his brow. But he was the pilot and nobody was going to intimidate him while he was in command of his plane. "If you think that little knife's a threat, just try and stick me. With my dying breath, I'll go flaps up, full throttle, stick to the dash and ram this bird into the asphalt."

Cody winced and then backed off. "You're right, Jack, I'm sorry. But you have to understand that if you land, they'll kill me on the spot."

"What makes you think I care?"

"All right, let's find something you do care about. How about the continental United States? How about a few hundred million people? Got any friends or family? What if I told you the Argentinians manufactured ballistic missiles and sold them to an Arabic cartel? I don't know how yet, but those missiles are going to be used against the U.S. of A., and if you care, you won't land this airplane."

The control tower interrupted, "Altitude five by five, FPJ604."

"Roger, beginning turn now," replied Jack.

"For Christ's sake! You're not listening to me," screamed Cody.

"Shut up. I know what I'm doing. And quit bleeding all over my airplane; that stuff doesn't come out."

"Jack, please. There's a ship out there called the *Ankara* and she's got thirty-eight dual stage missiles on board. When they get where they're going, they're going to be mated with nuclear warheads off old Russian SS18s. I got video of the assembly facility, audio from the bridge of the *Ankara*, and Russian documents from the Arabs. I got it all and I don't want to give it back."

"Tower, this is FPJ604 coming around to get in the lane. Request final approach instructions," said Jack.

"FPJ604 traffic is clear. Land runway C1."

"Roger that, tower."

"Jesus Christ, what have I got to say? Please help," pleaded Cody.

"How about: 'I'll be quiet and let the pilot do his thing,'" Jack coolly replied as he continued to line up with the runway, gently jockeying the slow moving aircraft back and forth. He was also jockeying options.

"All right. All right. Dump me off on the runway, anything, but then you've got to take the backpack to the CIA," pleaded Cody.

"Is Cody your real name?"

"No. What does it matter? Please Jack. You have to help me!"

"Like I said, I know what I'm doing. Now shut up and let the pilot do his thing!"

"Jack," screamed Cody.

"Tower, this is FPJ604. Mechanical problem. Engine out. Aircraft non-responsive. Going down," stated Jack as he went full throttle, backed off on the flaps, rolled left, and pushed the nose down.

"FPJ604, we have you on radar and visual. Land your aircraft immediately. We are scrambling fighter aircraft. Insist you land. If you do not land immediately, they will shoot you down. Return to airport and land, immediately. Reply!"

The Gulfstream accelerated as it headed for the ground. Cody frantically found the buckle ends and fastened his seat belt and let out an "Oh God."

Jack coolly responded to the tower, "Negative, tower. FPJ604 out." He wiped the headset from his head and pulled Gulfstream's nose up to level off. It continued to accelerate, straight east at one hundred feet, out over the Rio de la Plata.

"I hope you ain't lying, whoever you are," Jack said as he turned to Cody. "This thing's no match for the Argentine Air Force. If they want us, they'll get us. Our chances are slim to none."

"Thanks for trying," offered his humbled passenger.

"Well, we'll make the best of it," said Jack as he snuggled the Gulfstream down to within fifty feet from the water. "At least we'll give them a run for their money. Keep your eye out for ships. We don't want to take out somebody's smoke stack."

Jack steered south as the north shoreline of the bay came into sight. The Gulfstream broke five hundred seventy miles per hour. Jack asked for more. The plane vibrated and shuddered, but gradually yielded more.

"Ship on the right."

"Got it," replied Jack, coolly. "Watch for aircraft coming from above and behind. If they scrambled their air force, it shouldn't be long now." He picked up the headset and positioned it, waiting for an expected last chance call. His passenger followed suit.

"You got a plan?" shouted Cody over the vibrating and shuddering of the plane.

"Of sorts: guess work, timing, a few mistakes on their part, and a whole lot of luck. We need more distance. I need them over the Atlantic."

"Then what?"

"At this altitude, they can't see us with their radar. They'll have to spot us visually. That shouldn't be too difficult, but it should buy us a little time. And then it depends on them. If they just sneak up from behind in their Mirages with a short blast of 30mm, we'll splash and it'll be over. Of course, if they like the spectacular, they'll fire an Exocet and we'll be burnt toast before we hit the water. Either way, we're dead. The only chance we have is if they give us a little warning. We'll need luck. But, just maybe, we have a chance."

Jack got his warning, "FPJ604, do you copy?"

Cody swiveled his head and pressed his face against the side window searching for the voice, "I can't see them!" He looked up, leaned forward, and looked left and right. But there were no aircraft in sight.

"Both high; one directly behind us and another slightly behind the leader, below and to the left," stated Jack. "At least, I'll guess left today."

Jack waited before replying to the request, "This is FPJ604. I copy."

"This is Lieutenant Gengrego of the Argentine Confederation. I have you with missiles locked and demand you return to Buenos Aires Airport. Do you copy?"

Again, Jack waited before he replied, "Roger. Gaining altitude before returning to Buenos Aires." Jack pulled the nose up gently and squinted as the glare of the sun engulfed the cockpit. The shuddering and rumbling of the aircraft subsided as it began its climb and lost speed.

The Gulfstream climbed to one thousand and then two thousand feet before the trailing Mirage made contact again, "FPJ604, suggest you begin turn now."

"Negative, Lieutenant. Need more altitude. Will climb five thousand feet before making turn."

"FPJ604, I have missiles locked and suggest you begin turn now."

Again, Jack waited before he replied, "Negative, Lieutenant. Rudder operation is erratic. Turn must be made using ailerons. Request you allow altitude of five thousand feet."

The radio was silent. Morning sun was blinding and Jack kept the Gulfstream climbing directly at it. He gradually backed off the throttle, quarter inch at a time, as the aircraft continued its climb. Four thousand and then five thousand feet clicked past the altimeter with no response from the trailing aircraft. Then, as they approached fifty-three hundred feet, a demanding voice came over the headset, "FPJ604, begin turn now!"

"Roger." Jack was only guessing, but his instincts and combat fighter training were now fully engaged. He clicked the flaps back one notch and pulled the throttle back to compensate for altitude gain. The airplane abruptly slowed without gaining altitude. An alarm went off in the cockpit. Jack's harness dug deep into his shoulders and waist. The Mirage behind, with a face full of Gulfstream now blocking the rays of the sun, slammed on the brakes and pointed its nose skyward, missing only by feet. Thundering turbulence from the Mirage shook the Gulfstream and condensation from its exhaust clouded the windshield. Back to full throttle, Jack went flaps up and stick back to launch the airplane upward.

Jack was forced deep into his seat and his harness went slack. The wings on the Gulfstream creaked and popped. Its tail moaned at the bending stresses and the airframe vibrated. He heard his passenger mumble another, "Oh God." Another alarm began; Jack focused on the glaring red light on the instrument panel. It read "STALL." With the nose pointed to the heavens and, with the last of the Gulfstream's forward speed, Jack stood on the left rudder and cartwheeled the airplane to the left. He was right; there was a second Mirage.

The pilot, after watching his comrade's near miss, had throttled back and climbed. But he was now faced with his own dilemma. He was on a collision course with the cartwheeling Gulfstream.

The Mirage pilot jerked the stick back and to the right. The Mirage dodged upward and to the right, only to find itself on an intercept course with its comrade who was leveling off from his skyward jolt. Surprise led to panic and adrenaline amplified strength, the pilot of the second Mirage again pulled the stick back. The Mirage pitched upward but then, without command, its nose pitched downward. The pilot throttled up, but it was too late: he had scrubbed off too much speed and air flow over control surfaces of the supersonic wings failed to return a response. The pilot frantically tried every control, including flaps. But the Mirage began to yaw and its forward pitch transitioned to roll. The panic-stricken pilot jerked

     Brian David Simmons

and tugged at the unresponsive stick until he was left with only one option. He reached over his shoulders with both hands and pulled the ejection handles. The canopy blew and the rocket-propelled seat blasted him free of his Mirage.

The Gulfstream's nose had rolled over and the plane was now pointed straight down at the sea and accelerating at full throttle. Jack rolled the plane slightly to get a visual of the Mirages. The first Mirage was descending and banking right, away from them. The second Mirage was in a contorted tumble and headed for the sea.

The Gulfstream quickly picked up speed: Three, four, five and then six hundred miles per hour. The Gulfstream shook violently as speed approached supersonic. Jack could hardly hold on to the steering yoke as it hammered back and forth. God help us, he mentally pleaded. Jack took one last glance out the side window; the Mirage was breaking up and shedding pieces of fuselage that glittered in the sunlight.

"Scratch one. I was hoping for two," he yelled as he worked the ailerons to roll the belly of the Gulfstream toward the events behind. Sound of the air frame's violent shuttering was now becoming defining.

"You going to do anything about that?" squeaked Cody.

"About what?" yelled Jack.

Cody pointed at the rapidly approaching sea and said, "That!"

"Oh, that. Let's hope luck and the tail stay with us," he said and pulled back on the yoke.

Jack felt the pressure on his seat begin to increase and he heard his passenger manage yet another, "Oh God," as the pressure increased even further. Jack looked over at Cody and recognized the signs of fleeing consciousness. Jack shook his head to stay alert and overcome the rush of blood from his head to his feet. The Gulfstream's wings and fuselage strained under the ever-increasing pressure to engulf the cockpit with the roar of the violent fluttering and vibration. Jack imagined he could hear the sound of rivets popping before the airplane finally leveled off, just above the ocean swells.

Jack fine-tuned the controls to get every ounce of power from the engines and keep speed as close to supersonic as possible. He leaned over to take a quick look at the face of his passenger and confirmed his suspicion; Cody, or whoever he was, was out cold.

Consciousness came to Cole as a pinhole of light that gradually expanded to full peripheral vision and, with a fog filled mind, he managed to speak, "The ocean - where's the ocean? We didn't crash?"

Over the continual noise of air frame vibration and fluttering, Jack replied, "Yes, it's an ocean. It's right below us, and no, we didn't crash."

"Good."

"Is that all you have to say after that incredible piece of flying?"

"Where'd they go?"

"They're gone for now," said Jack as he began filling Cole in on the future. "It'll take the Argentine Air Force a few minutes to regroup. When they do, we won't get another chance. They'll shoot us on sight. But hopefully, by the time they figure it out, we'll be over Uruguay skimming treetops. If we make it that far, it'll be on to Brazil. The Argentines will look east, further out to sea, or maybe they'll think we splashed. If they do, we might even make it home. But we got a couple of problems. First, FPJ604 is now a wanted bird. The word will go out to everybody, including stateside airports. I shut the TRACON and ARTCC transponder down but I'll have to turn it back on before we get stateside. Then we'll get more attention than we can stand. Second, we just wrenched the air frame on this million dollar bird and I'm continuing to destroy it at this speed. No telling how long or how well this thing is going to fly. We may have the opportunity for a close-up inspection of a rain-forest somewhere and nobody will ever find us, especially with the plug pulled on all the black boxes. Third, we ain't got enough fuel to go very far. This high-speed low altitude flight plan is going to suck the gas right out of the tanks. We'll need some JP-1 somewhere over Brazil. Fourth, I turned off the VOR, DME, and INS navigation aids just in case somebody's got a clever tracking device. We're flying by compass and I-Pad, which means we're guessing. And fifth, I don't know how bad you're hurt and how long I'll have the pleasure of your company. All of which leaves me up the creek without a paddle."

"I'll be fine. I'll see if I can get us some help," said Cole, unbuckling his harness. Cole squeezed through to the rear to find his satellite phone.

"Kevin, I need help."

"You have that right. You need lots of help," Kevin said sarcastically.

"Just find us a place to land in Brazil. Some place discreet where we can fuel up with JP-1 without being seen."

"Sounds like you need to fuel up with the drug dealers. You aren't expecting to have your windshield washed, are you?"

"Knock it off. I'm not in the mood for your shit! Just find us a place to land. I also need new registration for this Gulfstream. We are a wanted plane. The Argentinians will have an APB out on us and we can't land stateside with these call-out numbers. I'll fill you in on the Argentinians, Arabs, and the other crap later."

"In other words, you killed them."

"Yeah. You don't have to worry about Hafez anymore."

"Good, I'm glad. From your GPS location, it looks like you're about to hit the Uruguay coast."

"And the Argentine Air Force is right behind us."

"You must have really made somebody mad."

"They were upset when we took off, but now they're really pissed; Jack put one of their fighter planes in the Atlantic."

"You are not a good person to be around. Did you kill the pilot?"

"No, he had a parachute. I'll fill you in later. Call me back with a thumbs up on JP-1."

Cole felt the airplane jerk upward as they passed the Uruguay coastline and Cole was reminded of the pain in his back. He took off what was left of his shirt and got a look at it in the mirror in the bathroom; it was worse than he thought. It had a hundred chewed gashes, some of them large and some of them with embedded sheet metal. He reached around behind and pulled the largest of the pieces from his back. Blood rushed from the gash and a queasy feeling came over him. Jack was right and Cole knew he needed help. Cole pulled another large piece of hangar shrapnel from near his spinal cord and thought, "Christ, I'm lucky."

Kevin called back before Cole pulled a third piece. "Dealer's fuel stop is in Barra do Cardo. You should fit right in. Maybe have a snort while you're there."

"Screw you," snapped Cole.

"You just get to Barra do Cardo and I'll have a fuel truck waiting."

"What about the plane ID?"

"You're no longer FPJ604. You're now BBJ604 en route from Miami to Atlanta. Your flight plan is about sixty seconds from being uploaded."

"What about the electronic signal – the transponder?"

"I think it's two systems: one flight, the other control tower. I'm going to try and upload code that substitutes BBJ604 for FPJ604. But that will take some time."

"Do they have a hospital in Barra do Cardo?"

"Why?"

"I'm going to need somebody to remove a couple of pieces of shrapnel from my back and stitch up some cuts."

"I'll check."

"Just do what you can."

"Cole, are you all right?"

"I'm fine. Just help me get back to the states, buddy."

"I will, Cole. Count on it," assured Kevin and signed off.

Cole returned to the cockpit, but he didn't sit back down in the copilot's seat; instead he just hovered in the doorway. "Think you can find Barra do Cardo? We'll have a fuel truck standing by."

Jack turned around and surveyed the drying blood and massive bruise on Cole's chest and then replied, "Sure, I'll find it. Hand me that I-Pad over there."

"My partner says you're now BBJ604 and you'll get a flight plan from Miami to Atlanta. Kevin's going to electronically substitute BBJ604 for FPJ604 for the transponder. We'll still need to change the markings on this thing in Barra do Cardo."

"Here it is, Barra do Cardo - right here," pointed Jack. "That's coded as a primitive runway. It's nothing but a dirt field."

"Yeah, so are you a pilot or what?"

"This thing is not made to land on dirt fields."

"Better than a rain-forest somewhere."

"Right. Who's your help?"

"You met him. Geeky little shit we dropped off in Tobago. He's first rate. I'm going to rest back there in the first chair for a while."

Cole put a towel over the first seat in the rear and then timidly and painfully sat down. Through the open door, Cole watched as Jack precisely veered around a small city and increased his altitude slightly. Then back to two hundred feet and onward, further north. Jack studied the map and set his course north/northwest three hundred fifty-three degrees, his best guess for a direct flight path to Barra do Cardo.

Chapter Thirty-Eight

RENDEZVOUS

TO THE EAST, UNBEKNOWNST TO THE REST OF THE world, the *Ankara, Servant of Allah,* and *Shir Ali Kahn* had rendezvoused. The ships were lashed together, side by side, riding the swells of the Atlantic in unison. The *Ankara* was the only ship under power, her twin screws providing just enough revolutions to maintain directional control. She was in the middle of the three-some. Her forward and aft deck cranes were in operation transferring loads to and from all three ships. The ship decks were alive with activity as crew members scrambled to receive and send loads.

The *Ankara* off loaded eight missiles onto the *Servant of Allah* and eighteen onto *Shir Ali Kahn.* The missiles were loaded onto the *Servant of Allah* vertically and onto the *Shir Ali Kahn* horizontally. Forward payload fairings were removed from the vertical missiles on the *Ankara* and the *Servant of Allah* to expose the warhead platforms.

Twelve conical-shaped warheads with the distinctive markings "CCCP" in red were unloaded from the *Shir Ali Kahn* onto the *Ankara.* The conical-shaped warheads were thirty-eight inches tall. An onboard crane delicately lifted each warhead one by one and set them in place aboard their missile. Each warhead was greeted by a small crew to position it precisely on its missile payload platform. With positioning complete, they moved to the next missile to receive and position the next warhead. A second crew followed the first from missile to missile, securing the warheads in place. A third crew coded and armed each warhead. The final step was the mating of the payload fairing.

Twenty-eight cylindrical pressurized canisters were unloaded from the *Servant of Allah* onto the *Shir Ali Kahn*. Another forty-nine were installed in clusters of seven on seven of the eight vertical missiles onboard the *Servant of Allah*. The canisters were installed one at a time and handled with extreme care. A single canister was first secured to the center of the warhead platform and then six more were secured in a group around the first. Each of the canisters contained anthrax: an innocuous-looking white powder that resembled flour but more deadly than the plague. A safety valve was removed from each canister exposing the first of two spring-loaded burst diaphragms. The first one was designed to rupture when the external pressure decreased on missile ascent at twenty thousand feet, the second one would rupture on platform descent at five thousand feet and begin releasing the contents of the canister. The final steps for each of the eight platforms were installation of an altimeter-controlled parachute pack, complete with drogue chute, and the mating of the fairing.

The eighth missile onboard the *Servant of Allah* was reserved for a nuclear warhead. Assembly crews from the *Ankara* boarded the *Servant of Allah* and installed the last warhead. Use of the cranes onboard the *Ankara* would have been an implausible task with the difference in pitch and roll of the two ships. The warhead had to be manhandled into position. It was an awkward and difficult process, but they managed. It was secured in place; then armed and the fairing mated.

Assembly crews and many of the ships' personnel left their ships to board the *Shir Ali Kahn*, leaving only minimal crews aboard the other two ships. The *Shir Ali Kahn* was first to be unlashed from the *Ankara* and immediately powered away. The *Servant of Allah* was then unlashed from the *Ankara* and veered off northeast as it headed for its final destination. The *Ankara* maintained its northerly course and was soon back at full speed.

Chapter Thirty-Nine

STOICISM

COLE HAD DOZED OFF AND WAS AWAKENED BY JACK'S beckoning, "We're close, but how close I don't know. I'm going to have to turn on some navigation."

"No, don't," said Cole in a cranky voice. "I got it covered." He turned on his satellite phone and dialed Kevin, "Guess where we are."

"No guessing to it. You're sixteen miles too far east and flying right by."

"Just give me directions."

"Roger that. Turn left and I'll give you dead on bearing."

Cole relayed the instructions to Jack. He pulled back on the stick to gain a little elevation and rolled left. With a little fine-tuning from Kevin, the Gulfstream was on a direct flight path to the secluded runway west of Barra do Cardo.

"By the way, did I tell you how much jet fuel was going to cost you?"

"No."

"You bought the tanker. They said they would throw in some red paint for free."

"How much?"

"A bargain. Only seventy-five grand. I hope you've been frugal. I think you better pay, but be careful. They may want more. They sounded a little on the shady side when I made the deal. I also got you a doctor. His price is only five grand."

"Will do. I think I see it coming up. We'll talk later. See you in Atlanta."

Jack throttled back and went to partial flaps as he passed over the runway. The tanker was there, manned by a fat fellow and two kids. An aging white Mercedes was parked next to the tanker and Cole feared the worst.

"See anybody in the car?" called out Cole as they flew by.

"Nope, but we have to land. The fuel warning light has been on for ten minutes."

Jack circled around and dropped the Gulfstream on the short runway, applying the reverse thrusters and brakes as soon as he hit. He taxied the plane over to the tanker and spun the Gulfstream around with the door facing the vehicles. Jack emerged from the cockpit carrying his .38. Cole backed away from the exit to study the Mercedes. An older gentleman in a three-piece suit emerged from the car and Cole concluded that he looked pretty harmless. Cole pulled Alberto's .45 from his backpack and then handed Jack eight bundles of hundred-dollar bills and asked him to make the transaction. After some quick strategizing, Jack opened the door and stepped out to meet the owner of the tanker.

Cole watched out the window as the transaction was made and Jack directed the older man toward the door of the plane. He entered the plane carrying a small bag and addressed Cole in broken English, "You are in need of doctor?"

"Yeah," said Cole and he turned around to reveal his back.

"Uh," grunted the doctor. "I need take to hospital. This is more than I can do here."

"Where?"

"Chinsmo, which is about an hour drive."

"No good. Do what you can here," commanded Cole.

With fueling operations underway, Jack stepped through the door and, having seen Cole's back for the first time, exclaimed, "Sweet mother of God!"

The doctor continued as he probed Cole's back, "I must irrigate with sterile solution, remove fragments, irrigate some more, suture the wounds and then apply sterile bandage. I do not have supplies for this."

Cole commanded, "There's water in the galley, plenty of antiseptic booze in the cabinet, and towels in the bathroom. Do what you can."

"Señor, I have no anesthesia."

"So be it."

"It is your pain, Señor. It will not be pleasant."

"Let's just get on with it."

"A matter of American dollars must be settled first."

"Right, here you are," said Cole handing the man five thousand in hundred dollar bills. He tossed his duffle bag to Jack.

"Very good. Now, where do we do this operation?"

Cole looked rearward at the small fixed table. "There," he said, pointing.

"Sí, Señor. Lie across the table."

As the doctor began scrubbing and probing the wounds, Cole clenched his fists, closed his eyes and tried to imagine Sylvia's gentle touch. Jack mumbled something and left to check on the refueling operation. The pain was horrific, and Cole fought to contain his agony and maintain consciousness. Blood red water rained off the edge of the table and soaked the carpet. Then came the pulling and digging at his flesh; he heard the repeated sound of fragments dropping in a metallic ashtray. The pain became unbearable but Cole recalled Hafez's restraint and fortitude to the end. *Am I a lesser man than Hafez?* The tinkling sounds from the ashtray quit and the cleansing returned, this time with the smell of alcohol and with a deep burning sensation to accompany the brisk pulling, probing, and scrubbing. Cole's fists clenched ever tighter and he could control it no longer; he screamed in a great release of agony.

Jack jumped through the open door, and at the sight of Cole's torment exclaimed, "Oh, my God!" He paused and then continued. "Is he going to be alright?"

Cole screamed again. As the doctor continued his work, he replied, "Indeed. This looks much worse than it is. It is not life-threatening; it is just a lot of work. He will need a week or two to recover and then he will be fine. But he must seek further medical attention to ensure infection does not set in."

Cole screamed again and Jack said, "I think I'll just wait outside."

The torment subsided as the doctor retrieved and prepared his sutures; momentarily, Cole regained composure. Then the suffering intensified again, but now with the distinctive prick of the needle followed by an intensely intolerable itch as the thread pulled through and cinched flesh together. He anticipated the end to his hell and mentally followed the doctor's progress across his back. Finally, it ended and the doctor bandaged him, using all of his sterile pads, towels from the bathroom and duct tape.

THE AIRSTRIP WAS COMPLETELY DESERTED. JACK inspected the wings and fuselage of the Gulfstream, expecting to find stress cracks or some other damage from the recent overload events. It looked fine, at least externally. Jack repainted the letters on the tail and FPJ604 became BBJ604. The sun was setting and it brought peace to the close of a long day. Cody's screaming had subsided. Jack wandered around the airplane giving it one last inspection in the diminishing light.

Jack strolled around the fringes of the airstrip. It was a warm evening full of sounds from the nearby forest and flying insects. The walk gave Jack time to think and plan out tomorrow's events. As soon as they hit ground stateside, he would find the CIA or FBI and help Cody tell his story. Then he would call Melloncamp and tell him to come get his airplane. No more flying for that greedy bastard. It didn't matter if he had to wash dishes. He was done.

Several hours had passed since he last stepped into the plane and he ventured a peek inside. Cody was sitting in a seat with his mid-section bandaged. He had a noticeably weary face. The doctor was applying some ointment to his cheek and was almost done. The plane was a mess and smelled of blood, alcohol and sweat. The doctor finished, collected his things and Jack handed him another thousand dollars from the duffle bag before ushering him out the door.

Engines on the Gulfstream started one at a time, drowning out the sounds of wildlife in the dense forest. Jack taxied the Gulfstream to the far end of the runway, gave it full throttle and roared down the short, dark strip to pull up just short of the trees towering at runway's end.

Jack climbed to forty thousand feet, above any commercial traffic, and headed for Miami. Soon after reaching altitude, Cody was asleep. The flight seemed to take forever for Jack and his mind kept racing through the excitement of the day's events that were in remarkable contrast to the peacefulness of the night sky. Eventually, as he neared four hundred miles off the coast, he dove under the radar to roar in at just over a hundred feet. Then, just like he'd sneaked out the traffic lanes at Dallas, he sneaked back in at Miami and then flew on to Atlanta in accordance with his flight plan. Cody slept and was only awakened by the sound of tires chirping as Jack gently set the aircraft down. BBJ604 requested a taxicab to meet them at the private aircraft terminal.

Chapter Forty

SELF-SERVING INCOMPETENCE

COLE WAS STIFF AND STILL TIRED, BUT HE WAS ON HIS feet. Why Kevin had sent them to Atlanta he didn't know. Cole called Kevin and gave him status and also let him know he wouldn't be checking in immediately. First they were going to make a drop-off at the FBI.

Jack was overly anxious and just wanted to go; Cole had to restrain his enthusiasm. Jack was even reluctant to go along with his plan to make sure they covered their trail from the airport, but in the end he agreed.

The taxi showed up shortly and they departed the hangar area. The cab swung around onto the main thoroughfare and then dropped Cole off at the main airport terminal. Jack stayed with the taxi and departed the airport. Carrying only a backpack, Cole rented a car under his alias, Cody Calhoon, and then also departed the airport. The taxi dropped off Jack at the Fremont Hotel, a rundown leftover from Atlanta's downtown glory days. A few minutes later, Cole retrieved him and the rest of the luggage in front of the hotel. They had breakfast and, as soon as Walmart opened, bought a lap top and high capacity USB sticks.

Using the Cody Calhoon alias, Cole checked into the Magnolia Inn, an aging motel along the interstate.

They made copies of Cole's microchips. If Jack had any doubts, review of the video dispelled them. He became more anxious to share the information with the FBI and could hardly contain himself; he was like a little kid with the world's greatest secret to tell. He became fervent with the frustration of waiting. He couldn't decide whether to sit or stand and he wouldn't shut up. He was about to drive Cole nuts when they finally finished the third copy of the final microchip.

"All right, all right," conceded Cole. "We're going to do this my way. First, we call them and tell them all about it. We offer them USB drives and watch to see if they come get them. And we do it anonymously. If they don't come get the drives, you can talk to them, but you'll be wired. I'll sit tight close by and listen in. You have a chat with them. Tell them all about it. Give them video and voice USBs. They can go do their thing and we'll go our own separate ways. But remember, trust no one!"

They left the motel and drove to the Federal Building in downtown Atlanta. Cole drove around the block twice to scope out the area and then dropped Jack off at the downtown mall to purchase a cheap cell phone.

Cole dialed the number for the Atlanta office of the FBI. "I need to talk to an agent Wilcox please, at least I think it was Wilcox. Maybe it was Williamson."

A sweet southern female voice came charmingly back through the phone, "Well, it probably wasn't Wilcox. Could it have been Washburn?"

"Maybe. What is his first name?"

"Neal. Would you like me to connect you?"

"Certainly."

"Y'all have a nice day now."

"We'll see," said Cole as the phone line clicked and transferred.

"Federal Bureau of Investigation, Washburn."

"Oh, I must have the wrong number. Sorry." Cole hung up; he had what he needed.

They left the downtown area and stopped just past a used car lot. Cole gave Jack two "talking gumballs" from his backpack. Jack put one in his shirt pocket and reluctantly smashed the second one under his armpit. Its outer coating softened and made for a discomforting sensation when Jack moved his arm and the gumball tugged at his underarm hair. Now he was wired and Cole could listen in on the conversation to come.

Cole was careful to keep the rental car out of sight and left the curb immediately. Jack, with a little coaching, went in to purchase a car. He bought an ugly little Geo with the title in the name of Neal Washburn. Jack used the address of the Federal Building as a place of residence. The used car salesman recognized it but didn't care; he only cared that he got cash.

Jack drove directly to the Federal Building, stopped in the no-parking zone out front and ran inside with the USBs for the receptionist. He ran back out to the Geo and merged back into traffic and then made the call. Cole worked his way up behind him in traffic.

He stayed back, but never out of range of the tiny transmitter.

"Neal Washburn, please," asked Jack.

"Yes, sir," the receptionist said as she transferred the call.

"Federal Bureau of Investigation, Washburn."

"I have information that the Arabs have nuclear missiles. The missiles are on board a -"

"Do you realize it's against the law to make prank telephone calls?" Washburn interrupted. "I suggest you hang up and don't try this again."

"This is no prank telephone call. This is for real. I have -"

Again he was interrupted, "You can't say I didn't warn you. I'm starting a trace on this call. If you hang up now, it'll be no harm, no foul. If you stay on the line, you'll be arrested."

"Better yet, why don't you listen to what I've got to say and then go downstairs and pick up the USBs. The Argentinians built fifty missiles with nuclear capability and sold them to the Arabs." The phone line went dead.

Jack redialed and got the receptionist. Before she got a word out Jack asserted his demand, "I need to talk to the branch office chief, now!"

"Yes, sir." The phone clicked and transferred.

"Deputy Hollings' office," came the voice of a secretary.

"I need to talk to him and it's urgent."

"I'll take a message and he'll return your call, sir."

"No, you don't understand. I need to talk to him right now!"

"I'm sorry, sir. He's not available. Can I direct your call to someone else? Perhaps Agent Washburn?"

Jack paused, "Okay."

The phone clicked and Jack waited. Several minutes elapsed before Washburn came on the line, "Yes."

"Look, this is serious. Just hear me out."

"Why don't you give me your name first?"

"I'd rather not."

"How can I believe you, if you don't give me your name?"

"Jack Cross."

Cole smacked the steering wheel in a burst of frustration. He knew life for Jack was about to get real uncomfortable.

"Good, let me turn you over to an expert in these matters. He'll be able to help you much better than I. Just hang on the line." The line went silent for twenty or thirty seconds before another voice came on. "Jack, my name is Roger Dickerson. I need some information from you before we can get down to business. Let's start with your name. It's Jack Cross. Is that right?"

Cole continued to follow Jack around the block, monitoring the conversation. Dickerson didn't care what Jack had to say; he was just keeping him on the line: where do you live, where are you at, where can I contact you, is there anybody with you, do you fly airplanes? Cole was beside himself that Jack could be so naive.

     Brian David Simmons

When they circled the block for a second time, a sedan with three antennas merged in behind Jack. Cole was several cars behind and watched as an Atlanta police car, with all the markings, momentarily pulled alongside Jack and then accelerated to pull in front of him. A few seconds later, blue and red flashing lights from the unmarked car's back window began flashing. The light bar on the cop car lit up with red flashing and rapid blue strobe lights. All three cars pulled over in unison. As Cole passed, two men in suits had already gotten out of the vehicle in the rear and were taking guarded positions behind open doors. The passenger had a shotgun aimed at Jack.

Cole made a right turn into a parking garage and squealed the tires as he made his way to the third level. He parked on the street side and jumped out of the car, receiver and binoculars in hand. The events on the street below were almost out of range for the tiny gumball transmitter, but he managed to get enough of the conversation below to get an idea of what was going on.

Jack was handcuffed, face down on the Geo. One of the plainclothes men was reading Jack his rights. Jack began to plead for them to hear him out. The reply was delivered along with a subtle jab to Jack's abdomen, "We already heard you out. It's on tape. If you're Jack Cross, the way you tell it ain't the way we heard it. Just eight murders in Argentina. And you're going back."

Jack was grabbed by the arm and thrust toward the curb. He stumbled over the curb, but managed to stay upright, which angered the plainclothes cop. The cop asked, "Are you resisting arrest?" He kicked Jack in the back of the leg, bringing Jack down. Cole heard Jack hit the concrete through his receiver and the signal went dead.

Cole switched frequencies to receive the transmission from the second transmitter. He was too far and it was too shielded by Jack's arm for its signal to be received. Cole watched as they hefted Jack off the concrete and rammed him into the back seat of the Atlanta police car. The police cruiser pulled into traffic with the white unmarked car directly behind. Cole wasn't far behind, exiting the parking garage and quickly making his way through traffic.

He caught up with them just as they turned into the Atlanta police station. He parked in the first available space and filled the parking meter with quarters. They weren't getting the message and time was wasting.

Cole entered the police station as if he knew where he was going. He wiped his nose with his sleeve and then looked down to obscure his face from the security camera as he walked past the officer hiding behind bulletproof glass. When he bypassed the metal detector, he flashed his FBI identification.

Cole explored the police station without being challenged. The obvious mark on his cheek was a concern and whenever possible he looked left to keep it from sight when passing someone in the corridors of the station. He should have displayed his badge like the other cops, but as long as he looked like he knew where he was going, nobody questioned him. If they had, he would use his FBI identification. His search ended in the hallway outside the detective offices. At a vending machine in the hallway, he spotted the FBI agent that had pushed Jack. Cole reached in his pocket and retrieved his glasses and put them on as he approached.

Cole stepped up to the machine alongside the agent and started a conversation. "How's it going?"

Elated with capturing the Argentine's most wanted criminal and the thought of what it might do for his record, he was in a talkative mood. "Pretty darn good. If I could only get this thing to take my dollar, it would be great. Seems like these things are too particular about what you feed them. How 'bout yourself? How you doing?"

Cole looked at the badge hanging out his pocket and then down the hallway. The badge read, "Special Agent Washburn, Federal Bureau of Investigation." Cole took a second look down the hallway and then, like a striking rattlesnake, struck out and grasped Washburn's throat with his powerful right hand. Washburn grabbed Cole's arm with one hand and reached for his gun with the other, but Cole was ahead of him and seized Washburn's transitioning hand, pinning it against his chest, before it reached the holstered pistol.

"Just pay attention and you won't die, right here, right now," whispered Cole as his eyes lit with burning fire. "You listen to my friend Jack. You hear what he has to say - every word! And then you apologize for being such a prick. The man came to you with a message. He came to you in good faith and you won't even give him the time of day. A lot of 'somebodies' somewhere in the world are going to die as the result of a ballistic missile attack. Even your miserable life, along with a whole bunch of others, could very possibly be saved because of him. I want you to listen to him. I want you to become his friend. I want you to watch his video. Don't let anybody near him that might do him harm. The Argentinians want him deported to anywhere so they can kill him. Don't let it happen."

A cop entering the hallway glanced in their direction, but turned to walk away and then entered a bathroom. Cole had his back to him and the events transpiring at the vending machine didn't register. Washburn's face was turning blue from lack of oxygen and blood. Cole sensed Washburn's strength diminishing. Cole only had a few more words for Washburn, "One other thing: I hold you responsible. If Jack gets hurt, even a little, I'll come back and pay you another visit. I'm very good at this kind of visit. I'll find you when you're sleeping, going to the store, or just watching Sunday football. You won't be safe anywhere. And when I come back, I won't be so sweet."

     Brian David Simmons

Washburn's face was now bright blue. His bulging eyes rolled back in his head and then his legs failed him, leaving his full weight supported by Cole's iron grip. Cole maintained his grip to suspend Washburn's weight and push him, feet sliding backward, to the side of the vending machine where Cole gently set him down.

Cole took out a gumball and picked away most of the gum. He stuck the tiny transmitter under the collar of Washburn's suit jacket. Washburn slumped into a fetal position and fell over sideways. Washburn's oxygen-starved lungs gasped for air and Cole quickly departed down the hallway. Washburn would regain consciousness in minutes and then all hell would break loose. Cole needed to be clear of the station. Cole made it to the front entrance and exited being careful not to look in the direction of surveillance cameras.

Washburn's eyes opened but his mind was still off in a clouded state of unconsciousness. He coughed and gasped as he rolled out from behind the vending machine. The pounding of his heart pulsed oxygen to every part of his body, resuscitating it back to life. He rolled over and struggled to his hands and knees. His body, still recovering, twitched erratically. His mind began to recover, recounting the events that had just transpired. Using the vending machine as an aid, Washburn struggled to his feet and beckoned for help with an empty yell. He managed little more than a painful wheeze.

The cop that had glanced at Cole and Washburn minutes earlier re-entered the hallway. Washburn stretched out his arm in a plea for help. In a few minutes Washburn had lots of help, including paramedics. His throat was severely bruised and blood rushed to fill damaged tissue. He could speak, but only in a whispering wheeze. It was five minutes before the general alert went out for a violator of police station sanctum and by that time, Cole was gone.

It was almost two o'clock when Cole, using his Jason West alias, checked into the Siloxi Motel. It was a two-story motel frequented by call girls with their clients from the neighboring white-collar businesses. It was clean and free of gang and drug activities, but it was a far cry from the Ritz. Kevin had selected it because of its central location and lack of police attention.

     Brian David Simmons

Chapter Forty-One

THE GREAT INFIDEL

THE PHONE RANG JUST AS COLE STEPPED THROUGH the door of his motel room. It was Kevin.

"We need to talk," were Kevin's urgent first words. "Come over right now."

"I'm tired, Kevin. I need a half-hour rest."

"Rest later. This is important."

"All right, Kevin," said Cole and he proceeded to Kevin's room where the conversation continued.

"What's so important that I can't have half an hour?"

"Did Jack get to the feds?"

"Yeah, he got to them all right and they got him. They threw him straight in jail and lined him up for extradition into the Argentinians' loving arms."

"That's not good."

"What's the matter, Kevin?"

"It's the translation from the bridge of the *Ankara*. I got some pieces of the translation that are real scary. Sit down here," said Kevin as he pointed at the laptop. "Just read the translation."

Cole sat down and began scrolling through the garbled text. "You want me to make something out of this?"

"Just keep going."

As Cole scrolled down, he realized just how formidable a task the translation was. It contained a mix of translated, untranslated, symbolized, and mistranslated verbiage. Kevin had overlaid his interpretations and extrapolations on much of it. Most of it was the same: periods of silence, commands to the crew, gossip, and the exchange of short stories by the captain and his first officer. But as the ship's departure neared, the text took on a more somber demeanor. Cole read all the more closely. What he read brought a lump to his throat:

> …When do we &*$% XTELA the crew LDGHK our mission?
> Nine days ^&*(&H now. We will XCVC to reflect %^ receive solace.
> The martyrdom that awaits $%& is beyond any worldly greatness *&#$% monument built in our honor. ASGNOT^&*%, they will be willing to strike down the great infidel. PKL%^& carve out its heart with a horrifying terror known only to Hiroshima and Nagasaki. ZXJUHD United States of America will ihfgP894 and exist no more. This they will gladly accept;…

Cole paused and then asked meekly, "Does that say what I think it says?"

"So you read it the same way I do?" quivered Kevin. "But it's okay because the feds will do something, right?"

What did nine days mean? Was Armageddon here and now? For Cole, the days and nights all ran together: one, *Ankara* set sail; two; three, Lagos; four, the Coalition of Arabic Nations; five, escape from Argentina; six, flight to Atlanta; tomorrow would be seven. Time was running out. Jack had failed. A more direct approach was required.

Cole responded to Kevin's question while searching for a course of action. "No. It's all messed up. The FBI doesn't believe a word Jack says. I stopped by and tried to leave a message that may help, but I'm not sure." He paused before continuing as a plan began to take shape. "Find me somebody to talk to: a CIA weenie with some clout, a director or deputy in Washington. Get me as high as you can find and get me a home address."

"I'll see what I can do. Why?"

"Just do it. We don't have the time to screw around. This time I won't give them a chance not to listen."

Cole got a seven-thirty-five flight to Dulles and standby for an early morning flight back to Atlanta. Kevin went to work on the computer. Cole's last words before leaving Kevin's room were curt, "Get me an address before I get there."

"Like I said, I'll see what I can do."

Cole paused and blew through his fist before asking, "How do I get a single bullet through TSA?"

"Easy, wrap it in foil and check your bag."

Traffic was miserably slow which further fueled his panic. No accidents, just too many people. Why couldn't they use mass transit or car pool? Cole pushed hard, dodging in and out of lanes, taking every advancing inch with a vengeance. He drew hand gestures and honks as he bullied his way through traffic and eventually squealed his way into the airport.

Short-term parking was nearly full. He found a space at the fringes, abandoned the rental car and ran for the terminal.

Cole picked up his ticket, verified his early morning standby status and checked his bag. He found a convenient bar and tried to call Kevin. The satellite phone was unique in appearance; far different from that of a compact cell phone and Cole was fearful he might draw attention to himself. Maybe they would just assume it was an antique cell phone and Cole was a parsimonious redneck. With the anxiety of their own travel rush, maybe they wouldn't even notice. Nonetheless, it made him nervous to use it in public. Kevin answered and Cole didn't give him a chance to speak. "Did you get it?"

"No, I'm still working on it. Be a little patient, will you? "

"Okay, bye."

     Brian David Simmons

Chapter Forty-Two

MESSENGER BOY

COLE'S FLIGHT ARRIVED LATE AT DULLES INTERNAtional. It was almost midnight before he got his rental car. Cole Davis and Jason West didn't need to leave a trail in Virginia; this was Cody Calhoon's trip. Cody had just about worn out his welcome everywhere. Cody rented a car for a week and paid cash.

Cole headed east with directions from Kevin. Kevin had obtained Jeff Monson's address through a roundabout computerized discussion. Monson's number was unlisted and not generally available through electronic directories, but computers at phone companies lack sophistication, and communication occurs between them on a continual basis. From inside the Salt Lake cell phone billing record computer, Kevin linked the local service carrier and got what he needed: Monson lived in Cabin John, across the Potomac and east from Langley. He verified that Jeff Monson was home with a simple "sorry wrong number" phone call long before Cole ever arrived at Dulles.

Searching electronic title records, Kevin found the name of the contractor that built Monson's house and then correlated the title data to plan number 602 on the builder's Internet site. The home was simple enough in design: two stories, large master bedroom with adjoining bathroom, den, living room, et cetera. It also included something Cole hadn't considered: the plans showed the layout for an alarm and camera system.

After Cole's adventure as a burglar in Argentina, Kevin had already gone through the mental exercise of how to bypass a computer-controlled alarm system; he hoped it would work this morning. For Kevin, the more complex the system was, the more avenues for access there were. Working on the assumption that Monson would have a security system that included monitoring by a security company, he identified the one and only security company on contract to the CIA in that area. Kevin accessed the billing records with a little password manipulation. He found Jeff Monson's account, payable by the CIA.

From there, Kevin nurtured and romanced the computer until it opened its control center heart to him. Monson's system had perimeter sensors that alerted a programmable main controller. The controller provided timed delay to allow for coded disarming after entry and delayed rearming after exiting. An activated alarm alerted occupants with an irritating buzz emanating from several sources within the house. It also autodialed the security company to register the alarm's activation. Primary notification was through the landline phone system with secondary notification through a cell phone. The computer received both inputs and responded through both systems to confirm the alarm. Occupants had a limited response time to reset the system and stop an impending call to the police. With Monson's system there was an addition parameter, the CIA operations center would also be notified.

Kevin mesmerized and seduced the computer, caressing its microchip circuitry and blowing gentle kisses at its machine language memory. It yielded to Kevin's seduction like so many others had. He was now its master and it was his slave. He pit the cell against the landline system so that any alarm trigger was instantaneously reset, thereby precluding alarm activation. It also set the camera feeds into format mode, thereby erasing footage. There would be only one test to determine the success of his efforts, but Kevin was confident.

Cole was in Cabin John shortly after two a.m. With final instructions from Kevin, he drove past Monson's house once. It was readily approachable from all sides in an elite tract of houses. Division between houses was provided by spacious yards, now covered with a late frost. Cole chose a driveway belonging to Monson's neighbor to the rear.

He didn't expect to be gone long and left the car conspicuously parked in the driveway. Sometimes the obtrusive is the most hidden. On foot, he crunched through the thin layer of frost, which seemed to broadcast his every footstep throughout the chasm of the housing tract. Cole's senses were on high alert. From the rear, the Monson house was dark and he wasted no time circling around to the front. The porch light flickered on as he stepped into range of its camera motion sensor. He jiggled a locksmith's latchkey in the deadbolt lock and was inside within seconds. An LED on a small box on the wall led him directly to the alarm controller. He waited, staring at the LED. If the alarm activated, he would leave the contents of his backpack on the stairs and flee. His fate was not to be the same as Jack's. He checked his watch, monitoring the seconds as they slowly ticked past. Three minutes passed and nothing happened. Kevin was a magician.

Cole quickly surveyed the downstairs using his night vision and then proceeded to the stairs. As he moved slowly up the stairs, he paused to study the framed photographs on the wall. A boy and girl populated the photographs. Near the bottom of the stairs, the children were young: playground photos, a school play, a soccer game. As he moved up the stairs, the age of the children increased. The final photos were of a young Marine officer and a young woman in cap and gown. These were the children of this man he was about to visit. A lump formed in Cole's throat and he asserted an affirmation that no harm would come to this man, even if he were discovered and the ensuing clash meant his life. He would not raise a hand against this man.

Cole entered the master bedroom. His night vision revealed a couple sleeping like spoons. Cole began his

search of the room. He feared a loaded gun and concentrated on potential hiding spots. With the man's
back to him, Cole credulously searched the nightstand
and even lifted the edge of the man's pillow, but saw no
gun. Cole slid his hand along the edge of the mattress
and the tip of his finger brushed against something
out of place. Cole retrieved a 1911 semiautomatic pistol.
Fearful of the noise it might make, he stepped out of
the room to unload it and then returned to slip it back
into its hiding place.

Cole delicately unsnapped the telephone line from
its jack and then set out his offering on the nightstand:
original voice and video microchips, USBs, a file folder,
and a .45 caliber round from Alberto's gun.

It was time to make his point. Cole positioned a
chair between the bathroom and the bed, removed
his night vision, re-packed his backpack, and then
turned on the bathroom light behind him. From his
back-lighted position in the chair, Cole transgressed
the silence, "Jeff Monson, sir." And then a little louder,
"Mister Monson, sir. Mister Monson."

Jeff stirred and then rolled away from his
wife to be bludgeoned by the brilliance of the bathroom light. He mumbled something about Ida's night-
light and then without thinking squirmed toward the
edge of the bed, pulled back the covers, slipped his leg
toward the floor, and was halfway up in his rock forward before he saw the man. He froze, contemplating

his options and challenging his mind to decipher the figure in the chair.

Jeff Monson's mind scrambled for answers and a plan. He's here. He broke in. He's going to be armed. Only an armed man would take such a chance. What's his motive? Burglary? Murder? Both? Is this a messenger from my past? If I reach for the .45, would I find it in time? His eyes filtered the glare from the bathroom to reveal the figure. The figure was perfectly still, hands in his lap, and no visible weapon. Street clothes with a light jacket showing no bumps or bulges to indicate a shouldered pistol. The only place for a weapon was the backpack sitting alongside the chair. It could easily contain a pistol. If it did, I'd need to be faster on the draw. Fair odds, but I'd have to be in position first. As he came to an upright position and his feet slid to the floor, the figure spoke.

"Sir, I'm not here to hurt you," started the figure in a calm soothing tone. "I only have some information I want to share with you. If I'd wanted to hurt you, I could have easily done it while you were sleeping. I only need a few minutes of your time and then I'll be gone. Just hear me out. That's all I ask."

Ida rolled to her back and opened her eyes. She started to speak but then, in an unspoken plea, beckoned comfort from her lifelong love. Ida's movements gave Jeff the excuse to slip back onto the bed and position his hand nearer the .45. He might listen to what this man had to say but the opportunity to gain the upper hand was paramount.

     Brian David Simmons

"I'm sorry, ma'am," offered the figure. "Believe me, if I had any other choice or more time, I would have done this another way."

"You would have done what in another way?" quizzed a cool Jeff Monson.

Equally as cool, came the reply, "I would have told you that an Arab named Hafez ibn-Wahhab purchased fifty-two dual-stage, energetic propellant, high-pressure guided missiles from the Republic of Argentine. I believe they are here, within range, parked on our doorstep, and the United States is about to be rained on by nuclear warheads. These are fly-to-the-target, fast-burn type of ICBMs that have on-board guidance easily capable of hitting a baseball diamond from a thousand miles away. You get, maybe, ten or twenty minutes before it's all over. If they're fired from short range, you get no warning, no time to react, no time to run; they just show up as a bleep up on your radar screen and then we're gone. There's digital video of their final assembly operation on the nightstand next to you. You'll find the audio equally as entertaining. Put some of your smart guys on it and they'll confirm my assessment."

Ida clung to Jeff harder and harder. Jeff's thoughts left the gun and concentrated on the horrific image being painted. He interrupted, "Who are you?"

"That's not important. Let's just say I'm an agent from Hell who stumbled onto some information. Listen to me carefully. Technology, design expertise, and high-tech components were provided by an American named Chris Beech."

At the mention of Beech, Jeff's eyebrows flinched in a sign of recognition. The man sitting in the chair continued, "Beech is dead. McCarry is dead. Portemay is dead. And many others. All loose ends assassinated."

Jeff started to interrupt but then chose to hold his tongue.

"I am here with you and I'll stay here, stateside, until it's over. My fate is in your hands."

"The second item on your nightstand is a file folder taken from the Coalition of Arabic Nations. It contains Arabic and Russian documents. Pay particular attention to the Russian documents; they include the reference 'SS-18' throughout and the figures are very revealing. I think it's what amounts to a bill of sale for nuclear warheads."

"Nobody just stumbles onto that kind of information. You have to go after it."

The comment was ignored and the figure continued. "You know the who, what, and how. From where, I don't know. That's up to you. You'll find footage of a ship named the *Ankara* on the video. The *Ankara* is an ugly old cargo ship that carries thirty-eight missiles; twelve of which are locked and loaded in vertical firing position. For the when, translate the audio. On the last one you'll find that the great infidel is going to be struck down in nine days. I recorded that seven days ago. You don't have much time; find that ship and deal with it."

     Brian David Simmons

"Why did you wait so long?"

"That's another story. The fourth item on your nightstand is a .45 round. The tip has a sealed explosive grain that destroys whatever it hits. I took that one from an Argentine and then I was at a party with a group of Saudis that had those things. If you go looking to question anyone involved, a bulletproof vest is little help. If you're lucky and the round hits the blast plate, you may be able to crawl away. Otherwise, it'll put a ten-inch diameter hole right through you. Now, if you don't believe me, you can let me know right now. Pull your .45 out from under the edge of your mattress, load that round, and remove my head. I prefer to die that way rather than face the death that awaits tomorrow or the next."

Jeff got his option for the upper hand and he didn't hesitate. He slipped his hand under the edge of the mattress, withdrew the .45, and momentarily pointed it at the intruder. Then very quickly he pulled the slide halfway back and peered into the chamber; it was empty. He grabbed the single round from the nightstand and in seconds loaded the round and snapped the slide back to ready the pistol. The figure sat motionlessly and just calmly watched. Then as Jeff raised the pistol and pointed it at the man, he spoke, "That's too bad. I thought I could count on you."

"You can count on this: I'll check out your story, hold you for questioning, and if things are as you say, I'll take the necessary action."

There was something strange about the backlit figure; he couldn't see the intruder's eyes, yet even against the back-lighting Jeff could sense the glare of conviction. The two men locked in a battle of conviction with unseen eyes and then the figure broke the silence, "Good, except you won't hold me for questioning. I have places to go and people to see. You'll have to kill me to keep me."

Ida shrieked. Jeff sensed the conviction and read it in the man's voice. Jeff was also now in control and the decisions were his. He could still have everything: video, recordings, information and a witness. He could shoot to wound rather than kill. But what if the bullet was as deadly as the figure described? Jeff chose to back down. "I don't think that'll be necessary."

"Good. In that case, I need three favors. First, I need a man named Jack Cross protected, guarded, and treated like a hero. He's the reason you have the video and information. He's the reason I'm alive. He got me out of Argentina in a private jet with two fighters in pursuit. He outsmarted them. He out-flew them. He even splashed one of them into the Atlantic. Then he eluded their radar to deliver this same information to an agent of the United States of America. He did these things because he chose to, not for pay or other personal motivation. He just did them with courage from the heart. Jack Cross is a hero and he's currently in the Atlanta city jail. He is being treated like a common criminal. I need you to get him out of jail, feed him breakfast and treat him like the hero he is."

     Brian David Simmons

"I think I can manage breakfast."

"Second thing you can do for me is to fire an FBI agent named Washburn. He's the reason you didn't have this information sooner. He ignored the information and chose a path of his own, even with my persuasion. When you fire him, tell him that someday I will look him up and pay him another visit. He'll know what it means."

"Third, the house of ibn-Wahhab in Saudi Arabia needs to be eliminated – all residents. It's the heart of the serpent. It produced Hafez ibn-Wahhab and will continue to promote his ideology. Cruise missile is appropriate. Sorry for the interruption, ma'am," said the man as he smiled and then reached to flip off the light switch.

The intruder was already heading down the stairs when Jeff found the lamp on the night table. Jeff started to pursue, but the man was already gone.

Chapter Forty-Three

ACTION

JEFF MONSON, BEING CAREFUL NOT TO DISTURB ANY existing fingerprints, slid a USB drive into his home computer and waited as it warmed up. He clicked and the screen brightened and he immediately picked up the phone. Images of a missile assembly facility were unmistakable. He dialed Dell, his secretary, as the video panned across the facility.

The phone went unanswered for six rings and then finally a response came. "Hello," responded a groggy female voice.

"Dell, this is Jeff. I need your help. Get a pencil."

"Do you know how early it is?"

"Yes, Dell. I know what time it is. Get a pencil."

"Wait. I have something. Okay. What?"

"I need you to help me with some calls. First, I want my direct reports in the office at 4:30 a.m. Don't take no for an answer. Give them code 'Dog Red Alpha.' Got that? 'Dog Red Alpha.'"

"Yeah, I got it. What's going on?"

"I want you in the office as well. You'll find out when you get there.

"Okay."

"Get that kid, too. Um, Frank Wallace. Yeah, that's it. In fact, he's first on your list of people to call. Also get Undersecretary Woods. You got it?"

"Sure," came an irritated response.

"Second thing I need is a crash team at my house. Get them rolling after you make your other calls."

"Crash team. Are you okay? What happened?"

"At the office, Dell. I want you in on this. Oh, one other thing. Call my boss. Invite him, too. See you at four-thirty," finished Jeff.

The video zoomed in on a payload fairing and then moved to focus on a weapons platform. Jeff retrieved his satellite phone from his briefcase. It was his twenty-five-thousand-dollar handset that provided secure communications anywhere in the world via the one-billion-dollar Mil-Star satellite system.

Jeff dialed and got an immediate answer, "Operations Center."

"Who am I talking to?"

"Lieutenant Mindencoff."

"Do you know what 'Dog Red Alpha' means?"

"Yes, sir."

"Good, this is Deputy Director Jeff Monson. I want the chiefs of staff and the vice-president on standby at 9:30 a.m."

"Are you calling 'Dog Red Alpha,' sir?"

"Not yet. Just alert them."

"Yes, sir. What about the plane, sir?"

"Just standby. Don't put the president on it yet. Just don't leave your post. I will call you back at 9:30 a.m. I expect you to answer."

"Yes, sir."

The video zoomed and then retracted, moving from component to component. It zoomed in on a nearly completed missile awaiting mating of the payload platform. From the camera's aerial vantage point, electronic control and guidance boxes could readily be seen. Jeff fast-forwarded and yelled to Ida to bring down his clothes. The fast-forwarding video shifted to an outside view. Jeff slowed the play and his heart sunk. There they were, just as his visitor had described: twelve missiles locked and loaded in individual launch tubes and another twenty-six on deck.

He punched the buttons on his satellite phone and made another wake-up call. "Good morning, Admiral. This is CIA Deputy Director Jeff Monson. I don't have time for pleasantries; so here it is. We have a potential coastal threat. I wanted to put you on alert. It's a ship called the *Ankara*. We don't have her location yet, but as soon as we do, I recommend you be in position to shadow it. It'll be East Coast or Gulf. I'll fill you in as things develop."

Jeff dialed again: this time to his friend Evert Hooster, the FBI director. "Good morning, Evert. This is Monson. I have a crisis I'm working this morning and I need a favor. I don't have time to explain, but I expect to have some answers on this thing by six-thirty. Come by my office at six-thirty and you'll learn more than you want to know. What I need from you is your agent Washburn and a prisoner named Jack Cross.

     Brian David Simmons

Washburn works out of your Atlanta office and Cross is being held in the Atlanta City Police lockup. I need them in Washington, in my office, before sunup. Ev, this is serious, no shit, get them on a company jet."

The satellite phone only left his ear for a few seconds at a time as he dialed more wake-up calls. Jeff worked as he talked. He carefully placed the microchips, USB drives, file folder and .45 round in a plastic bag and then left the house. He drove toward Langley continuing to dial and talk until he reached his office. He was met in the lobby by a small, sleepy-eyed crowd of CIA specialists awaiting his command. And command he did. The army was dispatched, each with a clear assignment and deadline.

By 5:30 a.m., half of Washington was scurrying for information. The other half was asking, "What's going on?" Jeff had just put his career on the line. If this turned out to be a hoax, he would be accused of crying wolf, not going through channels, poor decision-making, incompetence, usurping presidential authority, and probably a few other things. He would be the subject of numerous office jokes and find himself in retirement before winter. But this course of action was right; he knew it. Inaction was not an option.

Chapter Forty-Four

DECISION

COLE BOARDED THE EARLY MORNING FLIGHT TO Atlanta as the six-thirty status meeting in Jeff Monson's conference started. The best Cole could get was a center seat in cattle class. He sat between two business types who started working immediately upon finding their seats: one with a laptop, the other reading and highlighting sections of a financial report. As far as they were concerned, Cole wasn't even there. That suited him just fine.

MONSON'S CONFERENCE ROOM WAS PACKED. THOSE of stature sat at the table. Those who had spent the last two hours scrambling for answers took positions standing along the walls. Some of them overflowed out the door into Dell's reception area. Evert Hooster, the FBI director, sat on Jeff's right and Frank Wallace took the invited position on the left. Frank's presence at the table, the sought-after left-wing position, drew silent ire from his directorate chief and several others at the table. But it was Monson's way of remembering and giving credit to Jacob McCarry.

Jeff Monson's boss, Director Justin Alforn, showed up late and ejected one of his underlings from the table with a haughty command, "Out." Before sitting he lambasted Jeff, "What the hell's going on, Jeff? I've had six phone calls this morning, one from the president, all wanting answers."

"We're about to find out, Justin. Take your seat," coolly replied Jeff.

The first presenter was Bob Summers, expert in ICBM construction and technology. As Bob called up his first chart, Evert Hooster leaned over and whispered to Jeff at the head of table, "Shouldn't the NSA be here?"

Jeff's response was abrupt and overheard by all, "Forget the NSA. By the time they find their head and get it out of their ass, this thing will be over." Just as abrupt, Jeff signaled Bob and instructed him, "Let's go!"

Bob started, "I've got two charts that summarize the ICBM's capabilities and then pictures. Before I go into that I'd like to comment on the quality of the intel. This intel is almost too good to be true. I've never seen field intel come in with this kind of quality or comprehensiveness. It's usually blurred, distorted single-shot photos of the wrong thing from a half-concealed miniature camera fifty yards out. This video is really good. It covers every inch of a rocket, facility and a ship. It's great. I don't know where you got it, Jeff, but you might consider it too good to be real."

"I'll consider it. Let's go."

Bob simultaneously started his presentation and the video on an overhead projector. "The missiles are two-stage, high-performance, computer-guided rockets capable of delivering a small warhead up to an estimated 2,100 miles."

"What kind of warhead?"

"You mean, does it have nuclear capability? Yes. It could deliver any number of different warheads: ours, Soviet, Indian, conventional, nuclear, any of them. I calculate it'll lift just about anything out there. Range is the issue."

"Next chart."

"My second chart summarizes stage construction. Each stage is identical except for nozzle expansion ratio. The first stage—"

"Thanks, Bob," interrupted Jeff. "Let's move on to the documentation. What have you got, Alvin?"

Alvin Crespool, Soviet weapons expert, moved to the front of the room and called up a chart. The overhead projector continued playing footage of the Argentine assembly facility. "I'd like to echo Bob's assessment of the intel. We usually don't get things this good. These documents are the originals. We're still working to complete the translation but I excerpted a couple of sections. The first, highlighted here, is from a design document," said Alvin as he pointed at the slide. "It describes dynamic loads that the SS-20 imparts to its MRV. I'm speculating, but whatever the delivery vehicle is, too much acceleration or acoustic vibration might affect the MRV."

"What's next, Alvin," interrupted Jeff. "Just summarize."

     Brian David Simmons

"Well, there's handling, installation, and other assembly-related documentation for several old Soviet MRVs. We haven't completed translating everything, but there is nothing concrete to say Argentina received any nuclear warheads. Within a day or so, I should be able to give you a complete picture."

"Thanks, Alvin. Gerald, what have you got," said Jeff, waving at his Arabic language expert to take center stage.

Gerald slid a viewgraph on to an old fashioned machine, but covered it with a sheet of paper to hold the audience at bay until he got ready to make his point. He inserted a USB stick into a small player and then started his presentation, "Audio quality is mediocre, at best. It was recorded by a bug at the fringes of its range. My guess is that the bug used is similar to our old KJA-402, at least similar in capability. The signal received was not only weak but also subject to local interference, indicating utilization of a common frequency. This, in turn, assures it was not one of ours."

He started the recording. "This is my literal translation of the pertinent verbiage on the USB." Audio from the ship's bridge could be heard along with Gerald's interjected interpretation. Gerald removed the paper covering his single viewgraph. The audience got the benefit of both the written and audible translations:

Voice one: When do we tell the crew about our mission?

Voice two: Nine days from now. We will give them some time to reflect and receive solace.

Voice one: Will they accept our destiny?

Voice two: The martyrdom that awaits them is beyond any worldly greatness they could ever achieve. Our families will worship the monument built in our honor. Their names will become known to Arabs throughout the world. To achieve this, yes, they will be willing to strike down the great infidel. They will carve out its heart with a horrifying terror known only to Hiroshima and Nagasaki. The United States of America will crumble to its knees and exist no more. This they will gladly accept; I am sure of it.

Gerald stopped the audio. The audience was dumbfounded. Jeff broke the silence, "Thanks, Gerald. When will you have the complete translation?"

"This afternoon by three."

"Okay, folks. This audio was recorded seven or eight days ago." Jeff paused to let the message sink in and then continued, "Satellite. What have we got on satellite surveillance?"

"Before we go on," interjected a directorate chief, "does nine days mean these missiles will be launched tomorrow?"

"It means that as early as the day after tomorrow somebody is going to be praying that the great infidel is struck down. Launch location is still unknown at this time."

A large man exceeding three hundred pounds began to work his way to the front of conference room. His size made the task a challenge. Among his co-workers, he was lovingly referred to as "Hanky." Those at the table scooted their chairs forward; those standing shifted and flattened against the wall as he passed. Hanky's forte was interpretation of satellite images. Years of dedication and extraordinary decryption abilities earned him recognition as the world's foremost expert on satellite imagining. His conclusions were never wrong and seldom challenged.

He waved to the back of the room to stop the Argentine video and cleared his throat. With slow, monotone delivery, he started, "The first shot coming up on the screen is of the Avellaneda docks. The ship, presumably the *Ankara*, is circled. This sun-synchronous satellite shot was taken in the afternoon. Note that the deck is clear and there is little activity."

"Excuse me, Hanky," interrupted Higgins. "What do you mean sun-synchronous shot?"

"Well, sir, it's not very technical. It just means that we have a satellite that orbits the earth over the poles. Understand that with this satellite we only get one pass of the satellite over Avellaneda in a given day and it's only over Avellaneda in the afternoon. The next shot of the dock was taken on day two. There is quite a bit of activity. They are erecting some type of camouflage. Of course, it could just be a sunscreen of some type. On day three, the sunscreen or camouflage shields the dock area and the deck of the *Ankara*. The camouflage is there on day four and five. Then on day six, I get another opportunity to see the Avellaneda dock. The camouflage is gone and so is the *Ankara*. Assuming a mid-morning departure, I followed the off-angle shots of two high inclination retrograde satellites out into the Atlantic and located what I believe to be the Ankara on a northeasterly course. We don't shoot very many shots out over the water so this one doesn't have the magnification or resolution of my previous photos."

Higgins again interrupted, "Inclined retrograde. What's that?"

"We don't have time for orbital mechanics," halted Jeff. "Keep going, Hanky."

"Yes, sir. The notable feature about the ship, and it's somewhat speculation, is that the decks of the *Ankara* are quite full, but I can't make out the cargo. Note this fuzziness here on the deck, he said as he pointed to the screen. "With a little imagination, I think it might be large cargo containers with an enormous tarp type cover. The containers could be as long as long as sixy feet."

"Can you get any better resolution of the deck?" came a question from the table.

"I blew up this photo but the resolution is so poor, it's not worth presenting. We are doing some manual and computerized digital enhancements that I should have for you in about an hour.”

“What about the mid-section of the ship? Any speculation?” asked Jeff.

“It’s real tough to tell. Something is obscuring our view, but I believe that with my off-angle view, eventually I will be able to show that whatever it is sits rather high above the deck.”

Another question started to come from the table, but Jeff Monson interrupted, “Thanks, Hanky. Package it up and get it to Dell—hardcopy and electronic.”

Hanky again worked his way past chairs and crowded walls. Jeff Monson commanded that the video be restarted and fast-forwarded to ship’s departure. He then summoned the next presenter.

“I don’t have any charts, Jeff, because I don’t have anything to report. Our field operations haven’t picked up anything other than the publicized reload of POGO single-stage missiles.”

At that point, it was decision time. Jeff had already made his decision and he wanted concurrence by those at the table, especially that of his boss, Justin Alforn. Ultimately, he would be the one who would explain it to the president.

The *Ankara* was slowly moving out to sea on the video as Jeff brought the meeting to a climax. “Okay. We have a lot of other data to cover: location of a Mr. Hafez, Eschelund report, Middle East activities, *Ankara* registry, et certera. But at this point we need to make a decision. Let me state it simply. We have a confirmed missile threat, nuclear or other. It is substantiated with video, audio, and satellite reconnaissance. This by itself is enough to go to a state of alert. Any objections?"

Justin Alforn was the only one at the table willing to challenge Jeff. The others knew better. Besides, if this turned out to be a poor decision, Jeff was really the only one stuck to the tar baby.

"I'm not sure I have an appreciation for the validity of some of your data," said Justin. "If the data didn't come from our field office, then where did it come from?"

"That's still a little bit of a mystery," conceded Jeff. "I had an early morning visitor that delivered it to my house. He was very persuasive."

"An anonymous source? Come on Jeff, you know better. Not without secondary confirmation, and I sure didn't see any. You have essentially nothing from satellite, you have nothing from the field, and all that leaves you is speculation. I don't think you have enough here to convince anyone of anything!"

"The data backed up by Hanky's satellite photos are enough for me. And we either have, or will soon have, my visitor's accomplice."

"I'm not sold, Jeff. I think you'd better go do some more homework," said Justin and followed it with an armor-piercing glare.

Jeff's eyes locked onto Justin's and he committed himself, "I have enough and I am sold, and unless there's a serious objection, I am going to call it in."

"Your decision. I won't stop you, Jeff, but under-stand my position. You don't have enough of anything to put this country at alert status. Nobody has done that since the Kennedy days. And I don't think the president will see things the same way you do. With-out more data, this is political suicide and no one will be able to help you. Do yourself a favor and do the homework."

"We don't have the time. Today's the day and now's the time."

In an act of confident defiance, in front of his staff, and in violation of security procedures, Jeff picked up his satellite phone and dialed the top-secret number. The answer was immediate, "Operations Center."

"Who am I talking to?"

"Lieutenant Mindencoff."

"This is Deputy Director Jefferson Monson. Authority three. Personal Code one-six-four-two-seven. Confirm."

"Confirmed."

"Dog Red Alpha. Confirm."

"Confirmed. Dog Red Alpha," responded Lieu-tenant Mindencoff and then added an unauthorized conclusion to the phone call. "God help us all, sir."

Justin Alforn stood up and spoke. "I'll take my leave now. In a few minutes I'll get my summons to the catacombs of the Pentagon. You put your story together, Jeff, and be there by noon."

Chapter Forty-Five

EMANCIPATION

THE DATA REVIEW CONTINUED. THE TOPIC WAS THE *Ankara's* registry and country of origin. Dell interrupted. She got Jeff's attention from the back of the conference room and announced, "They're here."

Jeff stood and delegated control of the meeting, "Higgins, you take over. I'd like you to work with Dell to pull together a briefing package summarizing this morning's data review." Then he faced the audience and directed them, "I expect all of you to support Dell and Higgins. Give them whatever they ask for."

As he moved toward the door with silent admiration from his team, he put his hand on Evert Hooster's shoulder and quietly said, "Come with me."

Jack Cross, Agent Washburn, and four other FBI agents were waiting in the large conference room across the hall. Jeff and Evert entered. Monson clenched his fists when he saw Jack. He was unshaven with uncombed hair. He was in a prison jumpsuit, shackled at the feet and handcuffed. Washburn proudly stood next to his prisoner with his hand clasped around Jack's arm.

"I assume you're Washburn," coldly questioned Jeff.

An excited Washburn eagerly replied, "Yes, sir."

Jeff dismissed the four other agents and then directed Washburn, "Lose the cuffs."

"Sir?"

"You heard me. Lose the cuffs!"

Washburn got the message. He hurriedly keyed and removed Jack's shackles and cuffs. Washburn stood alongside his prisoner and forced broken words from his swollen throat, "This man is being held for extradition to Argentina."

"Is he?" replied Jeff, who then addressed Jack. "Mr. Cross, are you hungry?"

"Yes sir. I'm starved."

"I thought so."

"Agent Washburn, I'd like you to run down to the cafeteria and fetch Mr. Cross some breakfast. I'd say pancakes and sausage - no, make it pancakes, sausage, bacon, two eggs over easy, toast, and hash browns. Oh, juice and coffee also. And don't forget syrup. That's the least we can do for our guest. Go now."

A puzzled Washburn questioned, "Sir?"

"Go now. Get," replied Jeff and waved his hand to shoo Washburn along.

Washburn, still with a puzzled look on his face, left as directed. Jeff invited Jack to take a seat at the table. Jeff and Evert also took a seat.

"Mr. Cross, I understand we owe you a debt of gratitude. I understand we are the beneficiaries of your flying skill."

"I just fly when and wherever I'm paid to, as long as it's legal."

"Is it legal to fly in and out of the country without

a flight plan, passport, or custom's check?"

"Not exactly."

"Does it also include shooting down an Argentine fighter?"

"I didn't shoot anybody down. I fly a Gulfstream."

"That's not the way I hear it."

"You got it wrong. Who'd you hear it from?"

"I had a visitor this morning. He told me about your heroic escapades in Argentina."

"Then you got the video. Thank God. What are you doing about it?"

"That's what the commotion across the hall is about. What do you expect us to do about the video?"

"Sink the ship with the missiles."

"What's the ship's name?"

"Well, I'm not sure. But it's on the USB."

"When did you see the USB?"

"When we copied the camcorder micro discs onto USB drives."

"We being who?"

"Cody and I."

"So you and he are partners?"

"No, sir," replied Jack meekly. "I just flew the plane. He got the video."

"So tell me about this Cody. What's his last name?"

"Calhoon."

"Is that his real name?"

"Probably not."

"Tell me about him."

   Brian David Simmons

"Real nice guy unless you tell him no. He's some kind of super spook. No offense, sir. I flew him to Buenos Aires and waited for him while he was off doing his thing. I really don't know how he got the micro discs or anything about the other stuff."

"What other stuff?"

"Just stuff. You have to know about all the gunfire at the airport. They said I was going to be extradited for eight murders. It was a battlefield - I wasn't there - it was all him. He took fire and wrote it off like a scratch. I've never seen shrapnel wounds before; but they're ugly. That plus cuts, bruises, scars, old and new. It's not the first time he's taken fire."

"Who is he working for?"

"I don't know."

Jack continued to tell all he knew until Washburn returned with a full tray of breakfast. Jeff took the tray and slid it in front Jack with a smile and nod of recognition.

As Jack nibbled at a sausage link, Washburn got his instructions. "Agent Washburn. Mr. Cross is to remain as our guest for the near future. No handcuffs. No shackles. You and the four agents in the hall are to defend and protect him. He is to be treated like a hero. His wish is your command. If he wants a change of clothes, you run out and buy it for him. If he wants a cigar, you light it for him. If he wants a hooker, you get him two. Do you understand?"

Washburn forced out a reluctant and gruff, "Yes, sir."

"Set Jack up with a computer artist to get a composite of this Cody Calhoon. Find out everything you can. Review Dulles video. Find him. Find his arrival and departure. Locate his whereabouts. For now, I don't want him brought into custody. I just want him found."

Jeff turned to Evert, "Anything else?"

Evert shook his head no, and then added, "Let's keep Mister Cross nearby until it's over."

"Something else, Agent Washburn," said Jeff, contemplating his next action. "I was asked to make sure you got fired over this incident but I don't think I'm going to ask Evert to act on it. I will, however, pass on a comment from my visitor. I don't know what he meant, but he said you would understand. He asked me to tell you that he would pay you another visit."

Washburn's face went white. Jeff and Evert were both alarmed by the instant terror they saw in his eyes.

     Brian David Simmons

Chapter Forty-Six

NO COFFEE

JEFF MONSON HAD ONLY HAD A COUPLE HOURS OF sleep slumped over at his desk. His age was showing this morning. The few hours of sleep weren't enough for the long day that lay ahead.

First, teams were to report on the investigation of the break-in at his home. Then he would review updates on Argentina, Istabah, Escelund, Soviet warhead thefts and/or sales, history of Christopher Beech, field reports from around the world, satellite reconnaissance, Coastal Air Force and Navy deployment, and the location of the *Ankara*. It all needed to be reviewed, committed to memory, and packaged in presentation format by noon.

Jeff was scheduled for two o'clock with the Joint Chiefs of Staff and other key decision-makers who had been locked in a secure subterranean stronghold of the Pentagon for nearly twenty hours. They were like a vacuum, sucking information from every element of the government. Between presentations, the elite team planned and simulated scenarios predicting the outcome of every possible decision. They were waiting for the right recommendation and that recommendation would be forwarded to the president. The president, along with a few select others somewhere high above the clouds in Air Force One, eagerly awaited this recommendation. Time was running out. This was to be the day of action.

Dell, who hadn't left her station all night, woke Jeff with the announcement, "They're here." Jeff instructed her to find Frank Wallace and invite them in.

The first order of business for Jeff was to demand coffee. When nobody responded, he barked again at the small team, "Get on with it. Make it to the point."

This time he got a response, "Yes, sir. The intruder walked to your house from the block behind. He entered your house through the front door without forced entry. Proceeded to your alarm system, disabled it and then disabled your security cameras. He terrified you in your bedroom, as your wife described it, sir. And then left without leaving a single clue inside your house. No video. No identifiable prints. No unaccounted-for hairs or clothing fibers. Absolutely nothing. The only evidence we have is size ten tennis shoe prints in the grass. The shoes are commonplace, sold in hundreds of stores. The model and type are distributed to Walmart and other stores in Georgia and Alabama. The tracks show a distinct limp and weight estimates from prints in the grass put him at approximately 195 pounds. That's it. That's all we got."

"Thanks, boys." said Jeff and then barked out the door to Dell. "Next. And where's my coffee!"

Jeff didn't get his coffee. The next group was ready. They only had a few minutes before meetings in the conference room started. Jeff hurried them along, "Let's have it. Keep it simple."

"A Cody Calhoon arrived at Dulles from Atlanta only an hour before the break-in at your house. He rented a car at the airport and paid cash for a week's rental. The woman at the rental counter remembers him well. She identified him from the composite developed by Cross and Washburn. He had an unusual burn or bruise mark on his cheek and he paid for the rental with hundred-dollar bills, which was why she remembered him. She remembers the unusual way he handled the bills; each one was carefully extracted from his wallet using the fingernail of his forefinger and thumb. We recovered the bills, but based on her description of the way he handled the bills I doubt if we will find any of his prints. We're also checking to see if the bills are counterfeits out of the Middle East."

"I'm assuming Cody Calhoon is an alias?" questioned Jeff as he studied the composite.

"Yes, sir. Mississippi driver's license but that's as far as it goes."

Analyzing the composite, Jeff added his observations. "He didn't wear glasses when he visited me. He was backlit and I couldn't make out his facial features, but what I did see was the start of a beard, but no glasses. Work up a second composite with no glasses and a beard."

"Yes, sir."

"Is the composite drawing out on Mr. Calhoon?"

"Yes, sir. Every law enforcement agency in the country has it."

"Any clue that he's still in Washington?"

"He rented the car for a week but that doesn't mean much. We have an APB out on the car but it could be anywhere. He could even have abandoned it and left the area by some other means of transportation."

"Concentrate on international flights. I think he might be tempted to leave the continental United States."

"Yes, sir."

"The FBI has a team going over the Friendship Aviation Gulfstream. Early reports suggest we will get a lot from the plane; they say there's a lot of blood. We'll for sure get DNA. Pretty sure we can also get prints."

"I want this guy. Find him!" concluded Jeff as he stood and gathered the previous day's notes from his desk. "That'll be all, boys. Just find him."

Jeff joined the meeting already in progress in the conference room. The meeting paused momentarily when they entered. Higgins was enjoying every opportunity to command in Jeff's absence. Jeff took his place at the head of the table and the meeting continued.

From Atlanta, it was time for another call. Cole now had an acquaintance at the CIA. He used the TRANSIT satellite link to call the CIA in Langley, "Deputy Director Jeff Monson, please."

     Brian David Simmons

"That extension is 7843. I'll transfer you now," said an operator.

"CIA, Deputy Director Monson's office. How may I help you?" came a feminine voice.

"Can you deliver a message to the deputy director?"

"I could. Who may I say is calling?"

"Cody Calhoon. I am sure Mr. Monson will want to talk to me. He knows me personally and I know something about missiles. You know what I mean by missiles, don't you?"

"I think so. There are rumors."

"Good, then I don't need to say any more about them. What's your name?"

"Joann."

"Okay, Joann, what I do need is for you to personally put a note in his hand. Do you think you can do that?"

"Yes, sir."

"Good, write this down: Cody Calhoon will call you at six o'clock this evening at this number and this extension. Got it?"

"Yes, sir. Would you like me to check with his secretary to confirm his availability?"

"No, that won't be necessary, Joann. He will make time to talk to me. It is a matter of national security. And Joann, it is absolutely critical that you personally put that message directly in his hand."

"I will."

Cole hung up.

Monson concluded the morning meeting with a review of the action items. The entire CIA staff was working long hours but the list continued to grow instead of shrink; Jeff Monson demanded the most of his organization.

The meeting ended and then Higgins, Jeff and Dell huddled at the end of the table. Jeff outlined the charts needed for the afternoon meeting. Dell and Higgins went to work.

Jeff finally got his cup of coffee and escaped to his office for a few moments of peace. He had over a hundred unreturned phone messages, not to mention an overflowing e-mail in-box. He leafed through the phone messages and was about to select one when he was interrupted by one of the executive secretaries. He sipped his coffee as she handed him the message. When he read the message, he half swallowed and half inhaled followed by coughing, hacking, and spilled coffee.

      Brian David Simmons

Chapter Forty-Seven

LATE

Jeff Monson arrived at the Pentagon at one-thirty. He worked his way around the Pentagon, seeking the fastest route to the inner wing; upstairs, downstairs, through a tunnel, and then up again. The Pentagon is a maze of corridors and, once inside, all sense of direction disappears. Five pentagonal rings connected by corridor spokes sprawl over seventeen acres to confuse even those who work there every day.

Jeff knew exactly where he was going and hurried in almost a jog, but he arrived late nonetheless. He was granted entrance to the third level basement by the Defense Protective Service. It was 2:15 p.m.

His feet barely hit the steps as he shot down the three levels of stairs. Two Marine guards stood at attention at the first of three sealed doors. With a check of his ID, facial recognition verification and a call to the inner sanctum, Jeff was admitted through the first door. He was met by two more Marine guards who guided him through a metal detector, patted him down and searched his briefcase. With another ID check, he was admitted through the second door and it was sealed behind him. He was alone and used the moment to gather his composure. Jeff inserted his ID into the reader and entered his personal code. The door release mechanism triggered and, with a whoosh of escaping air, slowly opened. Jeff entered the inner sanctum.

He was greeted by an Army Bird Colonel who escorted him down a corridor to the Operations Center conference room. He stood just inside the doorway while the colonel discreetly announced his arrival to the man at the head of the table.

"You're late," pointed out Justin Alforn. Jeff didn't reply. He handed his access code chip to the colonel and began his presentation. He started with satellite photos of the *Ankara*. They clearly showed the ship's deck-mounted cranes, covered rectangular objects protruding from the hold and an empty deck. Cargo on the fore and aft decks that had been clearly visible in early satellite images were now gone. How could the cargo disappear at sea? Jeff only had speculation on the two other ships and took a severe verbal beating. The gentlemen at the table turned hostile and took turns emasculating Jeff. He struggled through his presentation to the last chart, managing to fend off the feeding sharks with the loss of only a few extremities.

His final chart was a recommendation. They didn't let him discuss it; they didn't let him say a single word about it. It was the recommendation they had been waiting for; it was the only recommendation. Jeff was excused without thanks or recognition of the work his agency had performed; he was simply shown the door.

     Brian David Simmons

Jeff was exhausted and wanted nothing more than to go home and sleep, but he had an incoming phone call. The north Pentagon parking lot was at best a traffic jam. Civil servants eager to escape for the weekend bottlenecked the exits. He wasn't going to make it back to the office by six. The phone call would have to be relayed to his cell phone. Jeff called Dell to set it up.

Cole dialed the twenty-seven numbers and the call was routed to Dallas, Dallas to the hotel in Buenos Aires, Buenos Aires to satellite, and finally to Langley. But Kevin had modified the TRANSIT satellite feed to report the location as the house of ibn-Wahhab.

Moments later, he had the CIA telephone operator and started the ploy, "Extension 7843, please."

"I'll transfer you now," said the operator. She responded quickly and had obviously been alerted to the importance of the call.

"CIA, Deputy Director Monson's office," came a feminine voice.

"This is Cody Calhoon. I am calling for Monson."

"Yes, sir. Can you hold a moment?"

"What for?" replied Cole knowing full well that the call was being traced.

"Deputy Director Monson is hung up in traffic. We are transferring this call to his cell phone. Please wait one moment."

Monson came on the line. "This is Jeff Monson," he said slowly and then continued. "You're almost an hour late."

"That's the way it goes. Let's hope you're not too late in bringing an end to this thing. I have another piece of data I wanted you to have."

"What's that?"

"The *Ankara* is not the only ship involved. There are three ships that use the Istabah docks: the *Ankara*, *Servant of Allah* and the *Shir Ali Kahn*. All three have similar histories. All three are at sea. All three are not on their scheduled course."

A cool and in command Monson replied, "We know."

"So what are you doing about it?"

"Read the morning paper. Do I call you Cody or Hamilton?"

"Call me whatever you like. No Armageddon, then?"

"Not today."

"In that case, watch for an overnight Fed-X envelope addressed to you. It contains a list of Islamic names: Iranian, Taliban, Iraqi, Sudanese, Jordanian, and others. They came from Hafez ibn-Wahhab's satellite phone and Dominique Portemay's cell. They were a part of this and now they're yours to deal with."

"I appreciate that. You're quite a resourceful individual. Why don't you and your friend, a Mister Kevin McKuel, come work for me?"

"That's an interesting offer," said Cole and then paused. "Maybe you start by purging all FBI, CIA and police data on Kevin and I. Then maybe we'll consider it," finished Cole and disconnected.

CREW OF THE *SERVANT OF ALLAH* SCALED DOWN rope ladders to lifeboats waiting below. The seas were unusually calm and the only sound was that of water lapping between the hull of the *Servant of Allah* and the small lifeboats. With the glow of the morning sun just beyond the horizon, the crew could still see the lights of Tangier off in the distance to the south. This was their destination.

As the last boat rowed away from the *Servant of Allah*, the captain unlocked and opened a small suitcase, exposing its illuminated interior. Two rows of eight switches, each with stenciled lettering in English, had a clear purpose. The first row of switches was illuminated in red with the words ARM under each. The word FIRE was beneath each switch in the second row. He extended a short antenna and then paused as he studied the serenity of the *Servant of Allah*. He licked his lips as if preparing to say something, but then kept silent.

He swallowed and flipped the first switch. The illumination changed to the second row. He paused again, studying the *Servant of Allah* once more. He closed his eyes in a moment of prayer and then let his finger toggle the switch.

The serenity of the *Servant of Allah* erupted into blinding brilliance and pulsating thunder as the first missile ignited. Flames shot through a water-filled rearward duct to scald the ocean. The missile emerged from its canister, first moving slowly upward and then quickly accelerating. As speed increased, it gradually began its transition to an easterly trajectory.

Residual smoke engulfed the *Servant of Allah*, obscuring it from view. The captain placed his hand on the second ARM switch and looked upward at the brilliance of the missile exhaust.

In the catacombs of the Pentagon, the presidents most trusted staff were in communication with captains of two Trident submarines: one coming from the west and heading directly towards the *Servant of Allah* and the other approaching from the east.

The U.S.S. Michigan, a Trident submarine, was emerging from the Straits of Gibraltar and had the *Servant of Allah* targeted. Range and the position of her class lead, the U.S.S. Ohio, were a serious concern. The *Servant of Allah* was beyond maximum range and a miss meant the torpedo might acquire the Ohio as a new target. The captain of the Michigan had the Ohio on the squawk box and discussed the options intermittently as he directed the helmsman to fine-tune the submarine's course. Jointly the captains of the two submarines made the tough decision. The captain of the Michigan fired his four loaded torpedoes with only seconds between each. As they raced for their intended target, the captain of Ohio followed suit and also fired four torpedoes. Sitting in the lifeboat with the suitcase in his lap, another captain also made a decision: he armed the second missile.

Strategically, the objective was to destroy the ship's hull below the waterline and sink the ship as quickly as possible before missiles could be fired. The destructive power of eight torpedoes penetrating the *Servant of Allah's* hull would sink her in seconds, hopefully taking the missiles and warheads to the ocean floor with her. If the missiles ignited without the guidance systems being activated, their flight would be erratic and lateral acceleration loads would destroy them in flight, leaving the warheads for later recovery. A similar plan was in progress miles away in the Gulf of Mexico.

In the darkness of night over the Gulf, two Lockheed P-2H Neptunes, approaching from opposite directions, dropped sixteen thousand pounds of torpedoes before passing over the *Ankara* at smokestack level. The crew of *Ankara* had departed aboard the large skiff it had carried on its aft deck. The captain was alerted to the urgency of his mission by the planes overhead and quickly opened his case. He didn't hesitate; he went to ARM and then immediately to FIRE with the first missile. He followed with each of the remaining eleven sets of switches on his console in succession. Two F-35s, synchronized with the slower moving P-2Hs, each released targeted smart bombs. The smart bombs aligned their trajectory with the fore and aft decks of the ship to avoid a direct hit with a missile warhead.

The first missile onboard the *Ankara* lifted its nose from its silo as the first of the P-2H torpedos hit. The second and third missiles were on their way up when smart bombs penetrated fore and aft decks. The entire ship filled with a single explosion, rupturing rocket cases, deflagrating rocket propellant, and disintegrating the ship's hull. Four missiles exploded from their shipping containers, leaving an erratic trail in the night sky.

The entire ship disappeared into the sea in seconds, taking all but four of the warheads with it. The four now unguided missiles that escaped chose a path of their own. The first one corkscrewed as it traversed a course in the direction of the coastline. The second missile went up and then looped back down into the ocean at full speed. The lower stage on the remaining two ruptured, stealing the missiles' propulsive power and dropping them back into the ocean. The spiraling missile headed for the coast was the last one to go down. It scarred and blackened the white sand on the beach as it augered in and its propulsive missile stages exploded; the warhead remained intact.

The scene at the Straits of Gibraltar was similar; the port side of the hull of the *Servant of Allah* had violently exploded, allowing the sea to rush in and steal its buoyancy. It rolled over, exposing its hull bottom to the torpedoes of the Ohio. When the torpedoes struck, starboard and port sections of the hull split and the ship sank, but not soon enough. Two of the missiles had been liberated and were headed skyward.

The missiles accelerated away, leaving a trail of exhaust to cloud the morning sky. With ever-increasing speed they continued to gain altitude and gradually transitioned their course further east. They flew over the Straits of Gibraltar and then on to the Mediterranean. They dropped their first stage motors over Islas Baleares. With second stages ignited, the missiles accelerated to 3,200 feet per second and passed over Tunis. Second stages burned out over the Mediterranean and were jettisoned, tumbling toward the ocean fifteen miles below. The payload platforms continued on their preplanned trajectories and, as gravity overcame vertical velocity, they began to descend. Still moving east, their speed slowed in unpowered flight and eventually, triggered by elevation sensors, parachutes deployed.

Sirens sounded throughout the streets of Jerusalem. People were awakened in their beds, cars stopped in intersections, people on the streets ran for shelters, the air force scrambled fighters - all to no avail. At five thousand feet, pressurized canister burst discs ruptured, ejecting dry anthrax-laden dust. The payload platforms began to spin, further distributing the virulent powder. The dust dispersed, each particle drifting on a path of its own.

At one thousand feet, the canisters finished expelling their blanket of death. The platform parachutes and their empty canisters gently drifted to earth, leaving the dust to float down upon Jerusalem.

 Brian David Simmons

Chapter Forty-Eight

Anti-climax

The front-page story in Sunday's paper had the details of the missile attack on Jerusalem. Two missiles, each carrying canisters with deadly anthrax, had discharged their contents over the city. The United States was leading a United Nations effort to airlift vaccines and provide medical supplies. The first of four fully loaded C-130s had already departed. A sect of the Hesimite terrorist organization had publicly taken responsibility for the attack. International furor was at an all-time high. Intelligence organizations around the world were vowing to participate in a united search for the terrorists. CIA spokesman Herbert Higgins was quoted as promising that the CIA would not rest until the terrorists had been located and brought to justice.

The story of two maritime accidents appeared on page twelve. The *Servant of Allah* had sunk off the coast of Morocco. The cause of the maritime disaster was under investigation by maritime authorities. The crew had been rescued and was being held as part of the investigation. The United States Navy was assisting with the investigation and salvage operations. In a similar mishap, the *Ankara* sank off the coast of Mississippi while en route for New Orleans. The ship was apparently off course but there was no cause for its sinking. Since the disaster occurred in U.S. waters, the Coast Guard and the U.S. Navy were cooperating in salvage operations and leading the investigation. The crew was being detained by Immigration until questioning could be completed and return passage to Istabah could be arranged.

Also on page twelve was the story of a small airplane crash on the beach near Destin, Mississippi. It was a drug smuggler's aircraft and the cargo had been strewn over a large section of the beach area. The beach was closed until all of the heroin and marijuana could be cleaned up and properly disposed of. Authorities were estimating at least a week before the beach could be reopened to the public.

The third Istabu ship wasn't there. Jeff Monson was true to his word and had taken care of two of the ships. It was logical that the third ship had been dealt with as well. Monson, after all, had stated that he knew about the three ships.

Jack Cross sat in a little-used cell in the basement of the main administration building. It wasn't much of a cell and it really wasn't jail at all. He had TV, movies, music, magazines, newspapers, anything he wanted for entertainment, and hourly room service to ensure his every need was satisfied. A courier delivered a special delivery envelope; it wasn't censored or even opened by his jailers; it was delivered

    Brian David Simmons

directly to him. He opened the package to find an account statement and a printer-generated note. The unsigned note read: "Congratulations on your recent success in the stock market. Buy yourself an airplane or two. We may need your services again sometime in the future. Thanks for everything."

KIM JONG-UN WAS ELATED WHEN HE FINALLY GOT the call from Port Donghae. The *AlKaing*, of Chinese registry, had just docked. His trusted envoy reported that the cargo was intact and all accounted for, just as promised. Kim Jong-un closed his eyes and began uncontrollably laughing and clapping his hands.

KEVIN CRANKED HARD ON THE REEL AS JOE CHEERED him on. It was going to be the first fish Kevin had ever caught. The Snapper got a new burst of determination and the fishing reel sang as its tension yielded more line. Kevin lifted the pole pulling the fish a few feet closer and then frantically cranked on the reel. With Joe's instruction, Kevin repeated the process over and over. Joe was ready with the net when Kevin finally landed his monster.

BOB GODDARD, OR AT LEAST THAT IS WHAT HE called himself recently, sat on the steps with two beers missing from the six-pack at his feet. He had almost forgotten who he really was in his yearning for this thing called normalcy. His heart ached for the love of his life. Sometimes he felt her ethereal presence and that made his sorrow even more intense. Dominique would have been his companion in this pursuit of normalcy. But now, he was again all alone. Peace and living within society's perception of right and wrong were his goals: live and let live, harm no one, eyes down, soft words, politeness, meekness, and above all - no hostility. But it wasn't to be.

Brian David Simmons

Acknowledgement

The toil of pre-publication readers that endured an unpolished manuscript is so appreciated. They found typos, missing words, grammatical errors, confusing text and more. With their help, the Imminent Hostility story is so much better. Thank you so much— Maureen, Connie, Rex, Joni, Patty, and Mike.

Coming Soon From Bright Crescent Sky

Invited Hostility:
The Kevin and Cole saga continues.

Leadership – Plain and Simple:
Compilation of stories from the workplace
and the way to get more done with less.

Bloody Mary Tours:
Life's adventures in search of the
ultimate Bloody Mary.

www.ingramcontent.com/pod-product-compliance
Lightning Source LLC
Chambersburg PA
CBHW030057310726

48970CB00004B/1041